THE EMERALD GUARDIANS

Hougan Manor

By

Josiah Cornell

The Emerald Guardians
The Vale of Hougun • Coniston Country • The Ancient Lands of Cumbria

THE EMERALD GUARDIANS
CONISTON COUNTRY, THE CUMBRIAN FELLS
WHERE LEY LINES BREATHE
DRAWN BY ORDER OF HOUGUN MANOR · IN THE AGE OF THE DRAGON BOND

GREY FELL
Wind-carved and ancient.

GREAT CARRS
Cold stone remembers.

SWIRL HOW
Storms gather without warning.

WETHERLAM
Silent watcher of the vale.

BRIM FELL
Paths vanish in the mist.

SUNSTONE VALE
The Nexus Hearth.
A day's journey north of Hougun.
Where light is channeled,
but always known to the North.

High winds. Older than any prayer.

Beyond the fells, the storms have no name.

2 DAYS RIDE

HAWKSHEAD
Grammar School & Market

EMERALD CRAGS
Domain of Myrcanthor.
The Dragon's Lair.

THE LABYRINTH
Tiberthwaite Ruin.
Shifting paths.
Forgotten purpose.

CASTLERIGG
The Whispering Stones.
Ancient Node of the Ley Network.
Where prophecies were carved in bone.

3 DAYS RIDE DANGEROUS IN WINTER

SEDYWAITE TARN
Still waters.
Deepest secrets.

DOW CRAG
Tarn - Silver Eastern Face

CONISTON VILLAGE
The Copper-mines.
Where darkness was first disturbed.

Nothing returns unchanged.

HOUGUN MANOR
Seat of the Emerald Guardian
Where the land breathes strongest.

LOW WATER
Dark currents pull deep.

ASHEN WASTES
Waina Scar Wastes
Where Ashenfang was forged.
The dead things never truly leave.

PEEL ISLAND
Wild cat isle.
Old magic sleeps.

1 DAY RIDE ROUGH TERRAIN

GRIZEDALE FOREST
Whispering Glade
The trees remember what men forget.

Voices heard. No source found.

CONISTON WATER

NIBTHWAITE SHORE
Southern watch.
Quiet does not mean safe.

RIVER CRAKE
South to Staveley
and the Coppermines.

MAP KEY
Ley Lines (Ancient Power)
Ancient Roads & Paths
Emerald Crags (Dragon Lair)
Hougun Manor
Stone Circle (Power Node)
Lakes, Tarns & Meres

N NE E SE S SW W NW

0 5 10 15 20 MILES

The land has a heartbeat.
Press your palm to the cold soil of Cumbria's
wildest reach and you'll feel it.
Talon Valskar, Lord of Hougun Manor

The Emerald Guardians - Hougun Manor

Copyright © 2025 Josiah Cornell

ISBN:979-8-89965-379-7

Formatted using Lacuna

Dedicated to Talon Briers

TABLE OF CONTENTS

Author's Note

On Mental Health, Monsters, And Magic

When I started writing The Emerald Guardians, my intention was to craft an adventure filled with dragons, warlocks, and ancient deities. However, as the story unfolded and the characters began to express themselves, I discovered something deeper within their journeys:

This narrative transcends mere fantasy.

It delves into themes of grief, abandonment, and the way we grapple with pain that lingers, even when we wish it would fade.

Talon wields his sword valiantly, but beneath that bravery lies a battle with survivor's guilt, feelings of helplessness, and an ever-present fear of failure. His struggles are not just his, but ours too.

Lira's existence is defined by her creation, which leads her into a profound struggle for identity, self-worth, and the quest to define her own purpose.

Myrcanthor carries the weight of ages, a primordial guardian who has witnessed countless losses, burdened by a responsibility that often feels too heavy to bear in silence.

These characters are not just fictional arcs; they are pieces of my own heart, each reflecting a struggle that many of us carry but often feel unable to voice.

Fantasy offers a unique refuge, presenting us with monsters we can name and battles we can fight, while illuminating darkness with flickering flames.

Yet, beneath the vibrant layers of The Emerald Guardians, there is also a mirror held up to reflect our most profound questions:

Am I enough?

Why did they leave?

What do I do with all this pain?

Can I still be whole after everything that's been taken from me?

This book doesn't promise perfect solutions or easy paths to healing. Instead, it acknowledges the war within us, the screams we hold in silence, and the glimmers of hope that persist, even in the darkest times. It understands your pain.

If you've ever felt lost, broken, or forgotten, know that this story was penned with you in mind. It's a reminder that you are not alone in your struggles; your voice and your presence matter.

Thank you for joining me on this journey through a world that acknowledges both the pain and resilience we all share.

Warmly,

Josiah Cornell

Author of The Emerald Guardians.

CHAPTER ONE – THE RISE OF TALON VALSKAR

The legend came later. What came first was a boy who was never really a boy at all.

I grew up in the wild, misty hills of Cumbria, in the kind of country that had no patience for softness. Mornings here were not gentle things. Dawn arrived like a blade, driving cold into your bones, before the eyes had fully opened, and the ground beneath my boots was always either frozen solid or thick with mud that pulled at every step as though the earth itself was trying to keep me in one place. I had learned early not to fight it and that the land had its own ideas about most things, and that arguing with it cost more than it gave back.

I had never tended livestock. Not the ordinary kind. The creatures that moved through the margins of my childhood carried something behind the eyes that ordinary animals did not, a weight, a knowing quality, as though they had not forgotten what they were before men arrived and started naming everything. I had learned to read the difference between the way something moved when it was simply afraid and the way it moved when it was deciding. It was not a skill anyone had taught me. It was something I had absorbed, the way I had absorbed most of the things that mattered, through proximity and attention and the particular education of surviving what I probably should not have.

Beyond the crumbling walls of the only home I had ever known, Grizedale Forest rose on the outskirts. It did not invite it. It simply existed, vast and dark and layered with a silence that was not empty but withheld, thick with the kind of rot, stagnant water and cold that lived in places the sun could not reach. Most people stayed at its edges. I had never understood most people, they were an enigma of my mind.

I moved through the pre-dawn dark without a torch. I had not needed one in years. The forest had become a language I read without thinking, a grammar of shadow and sound and the specific quality of air moving through the gaps between old trees. Each step landed with the deliberate care of someone who had been taught by experience rather than instruction that the ground would betray him if his attention slipped, and mine never slipped. Not in here. Not where it counted.

Twenty-five winters, I had been on this earth. In some company, in some light, that would have sounded young. I had never been in that company, nor did I want to be surrounded by people that would drain me mentally. I carried the twenty-five in the precise economy of how I moved, in the scars hidden by my sleeves, in the way my eyes catalogued every space I entered before I had finished crossing the threshold. They were not gentle years.

They had worn at me the way water wore at stone, stripping everything unnecessary until what remained was something harder and less forgiving than what I had started as. I was not lean from hunger. I was lean from having been distilled.

I could still taste the cold iron of blood of the boar I had gutted two hours ago lingering at the back of my throat. Rain from the night before clung to my hair, and I pushed it back with two fingers without breaking stride. A reflex. A motion worn smooth by so much repetition it had stopped requiring conscious instruction.

The creatures of Grizedale knew me. Not the way prey knew a predator, though that was part of it. It was something older. Something that operated in the register below instinct, closer to the place where recognition lived. They slipped back into the dark when I passed, and I had long since stopped reading it as fear. They were not afraid of me. They were acknowledging something in me that I had not yet found a name for, and they were doing it the same way every time, with a consistency that would have been unnerving if I had allowed myself to think about it too carefully.

My body came to a halt, not a decision, I would of made. My body stopped before the instruction arrived, weight settling back, hands loose at my sides. The forest had changed quality around me. Not a specific sound but the arrangement of sound, the particular density of silence that fell when things that had been moving had decided to wait.

My hand did not go to my blade. The reflex was instant and reliable, worn smooth by years of repetition, but I kept it still. Whatever had made the forest hold its breath, steel was not going to be what answered it. I had been in enough wrong-shaped situations to know that particular truth.

The air shifted next. Rain and pine and cold copper, that was what the last hours had given me. Now something underneath all of that. Metallic. Warm. Too much of it. The kind of scent that bypassed the nose and settled into the back of the throat and simply stayed there.

I followed it, to the old oak tree, a majestic, spawling giant. A deep fissure of grey and brown trunk and a wide canopy and gnarled branches blocking out the sky above.

The oak was one of Grizedale's oldest, enormous and laden with a gravity that had nothing to do with years and everything to do with what had happened in its presence over the course of them. The druid had come to rest against its roots as though the tree had reached out and caught him. Perhaps it had. I had seen stranger things in this forest and stopped keeping a tally.

The emerald of his robes survived only at the shoulders and cuffs. Everywhere else the red had claimed it, spreading from the wound at his ribs with the slow, methodical patience of something that could not be argued with. The smell of blood was everywhere now, crowding out rain and rot and pine, sharp and animal and carrying the particular warmth that blood held in cold air for only a short time before it surrendered.

The druids eyes were wide open. Not glassy. Not absent. Open and awake and pale as river ice in January, and they found my face from across the clearing with a precision that had no business existing in a man losing blood at that rate. They did not search for me. They had already known where I was going to be.

Something contracted in my chest. Hard. Once. Then my body did what it had trained itself to do in the presence of threats whose shape I could not yet determine. It went still. Not frozen. The coiled kind of still. The kind that could break in any direction without warning.

I crossed the clearing and crouched at his level, because standing would have been the wrong register entirely, and I looked into those ice-pale eyes and waited.

"You are not what you seem, boy."

The voice was a ruin. Scraped raw, dragged over something that sounded like broken stone, and yet it carried across the clearing with the weight of something that had been waiting a very long time to be delivered. It did not ask. It did not suggest. It arrived in the centre of my chest like a verdict rendered by a court that had been sitting in judgement before my birth and had only now gotten around to announcing its findings.

I had stood at the edge of enough last breaths to know the difference between a man unburdening himself and a man completing something. This was the second thing. The blood soaking through his robes was incidental. He was here to finish a task, and the task was me.

The pulse arrived without asking.

One moment I had only my own heartbeat, familiar and steady and entirely mine, the one constant I had carried through everything. The next there was something running beneath it. Below the frequency of my own body. Deeper than my boots. Deeper than the cold soil pressing up through the leather. A thrum, vast and patient and completely indifferent to whether I understood it or not, moving through stone and clay and the root systems of every tree in this clearing and up through the bones of my feet and my ankles and my shins with a patience that was more unsettling than any speed would have been.

My gaze went to my forearms before I told it to. The veins glowed.

Faint, yes. Green-gold, tracing the paths beneath my skin in a rhythm that matched the thrum in the earth and did not match my own pulse. I stared at them for exactly one second. Then something that lived below my conscious mind closed my jaw on whatever sound had been forming and brought my eyes back to the dying man in front of me.

The druid was watching me with the expression of someone who had been waiting years for a specific thing to happen and had just watched it happen exactly as anticipated.

"You feel it, don't you?"

Not a question. He already knew.

My jaw tightened. My knuckles had gone pale against my knee. The world had pulled very close around this oak and this clearing and this man who was completing a task with the last of what he had, and the pulse in the earth was not stopping, was not going to stop, was already starting to feel less like an intrusion and more like something I had simply failed to notice before now.

Which was worse. Considerably worse.

"Yes." Nothing else. The word came out stripped of everything except the bare truth of it.

Something shifted in his face. The particular exhaustion of a man who has been holding something heavy for too long and has finally been given permission to set it down.

Eryndor. The name arrived from somewhere in the back of my memory the way things arrived when the forest had a hand in it, not from any introduction, not from anything I could account for, surfacing through still water when something disturbed the surface from below.

He exhaled. Long. Careful. Rationing what he had left.

"The earth energies." Each word placed with the deliberate precision of someone who knew they had a limited number remaining. "Not myth. Not something a man picks up because he wants it badly enough and has the right bloodline for it. It does not function like a blade. It does not respond to prayer." His fingers pressed into the soil beside him, trembling with something that was not weakness but urgency, as though he was searching for something that kept slipping past his reach. "They are veins. They run beneath everything. Beneath this forest, beneath stone and clay and the bones of everyone buried in this earth before either of us was born. They carry what the land has absorbed." He paused, and the silence that filled it was not empty. It was thick with centuries of blood soaked into soil that had never offered a single word of absolution. "They have been watching you for longer than you know."

The cold that moved through me then had nothing to do with the temperature of the morning.

"Hougun Manor sits at the convergence." His voice had dropped, not from fading but from the gravity of certain truths that required careful handling. "The ley lines beneath it are not sleeping. They have not been sleeping for some time." His pale gaze did not leave my face. Not once. "They do not serve kings. They do not acknowledge the authority men grant each other. They belong to no one who has simply had the presumption to stand on top of them." Another pause, and the pulse in the earth shifted its pressure slightly, the way things shifted when their name was spoken aloud by someone who understood what they were naming. "Those who try to take what is not offered pay in blood and the dissolution of everything they believed themselves to be. Those who refuse the call," he stopped, and what filled the silence was worse than anything he might have said to complete it.

"What does that mean?" Not a question. A refusal to let the weight of that statement stand without being forced into specifics.

He looked at me for a long moment. Long enough that I began to wonder whether what he had left was running out before the answer could get here. "There is something gathering at the edges of this land. It does not want territory. It does not want a crown. It wants the lines themselves. It wants the pulse." The pause that followed had edges. "And it has been patient."

Patient. The word settled in the wrong place in my chest.

Everything about this conversation was settling in the wrong place. In the specific, unmistakable way of things that were true.

I looked at my forearms again, at the faint glow still tracing beneath my skin, and I thought about the life I had built on the principle that nothing owned me. Nothing had ever owned me. I had walked through every attempt the world made to claim me and come out the other side still recognisably myself, which was everything, which had always been the only thing I was certain of.

The land pulsed beneath me, steady and patient and entirely indifferent to my deliberations.

Eryndor's fingers found the soil one more time. His eyes drifted toward the eastern treeline, toward a gap in the trees that had not been there when I arrived, a narrow opening into deeper dark that offered nothing except the certainty that it was meant for me.

I understood without words.

I rose up off the ground.

We moved together, or I moved and Eryndor followed on whatever the forest had lent him to get this far, and the trees closed behind us and the pulse in the earth climbed with every step, not louder but more specific, orienting toward me the way a compass needle oriented toward north, with the calm certainty of something that had always known.

The glade arrived without warning.

One step the forest was dense and layered and close, and the next step the world opened without announcing itself and the air changed its fundamental character and my body stopped walking before I had finished deciding to stop. The same involuntary arrest from the clearing with Eryndor but larger. More total. The specific feeling of being submerged in something that had no temperature.

The stones stood at the glade's centre.

I tried to count them. Lost it. Tried again. Lost it again. I stopped trying, because whatever they were, they had no interest in being quantified, and I was beginning to understand that forcing ordinary frameworks onto this space was not a useful approach. They were covered in moss so densely green it read as black in this light, and they were old in a way that made every old thing I had ever stood beside seem recent. And they were not dormant. A phosphorescence moved through them in a slow rhythmic pulse that rose and retreated like the breathing of something enormous and unhurried, and with a jolt of vertigo I recognised the rhythm.

The glow in the stones. The pulse in the earth. The thing that had traced my veins in the clearing.

The same frequency. The same beat.

My breath had stopped. I discovered this when my lungs made a sound like something being dragged over stone and insisted on continuing.

The scent here had nothing in my experience to match it. Wet earth and decomposing leaves and beneath both of those something that registered not as a smell but as a pressure behind my eyes, a sudden acute awareness of the specific smallness of my lifetime against what these stones had witnessed. I was standing in a place that had been old before the first man put a name to any part of this land. Before the Romans built their roads and left and became indistinguishable from the soil they had marched across. Before any of it. These stones had been here through all of it, glowing their slow and patient glow, waiting for someone who could hear them.

"The Whispering Stones." Eryndor's voice arrived close and quiet. "They speak only to those who listen with more than their ears."

He reached out and touched the nearest stone with the delicacy of someone approaching a thing that could unmake them if startled. His fingers found the moss. The glow beneath his hand brightened, just slightly, just for a moment, and something moved through his face that stripped years from it before the exhaustion settled back in.

I knelt down by the stones. Not a decision. My knees found the cold damp earth before my mind had finished deliberating, and my hand reached out, and my fingers touched the stone's surface. Cool. Solid. And beneath the moss, faintly, unmistakably warm, in the way that warmth felt when it was not temperature but something else entirely, something that had no name in any language I had been taught.

The world dropped away. Not darkness. Not silence. The complete removal of the ordinary layer of experience that made it possible to function, to maintain the useful fiction that a single human lifetime occupied a meaningful scale. All of that simply stopped. And what was underneath it was everything.

I heard fire. Not a fire. The fire. Human hands coaxing heat from nothing at the edge of understanding, and the sound of it crackled through me with a freshness that should not have been possible at this distance in time. I heard rivers before they were named, before they were anything except movement and cold and the persistent carrying of things from one place to another, their currents moving through my awareness with the weight of everything they had ever transported. Prayer. Grief. Silt. The dissolved remains of the dead.

I felt the oceans as weight rather than water. As continuity. As the oldest available proof that the world held everything and offered nothing back, that every drop of blood ever lost to this earth was still here somewhere, changed in form but not in presence.

War cries from mouths that had been soil for two thousand years arrived still desperate, still insisting, still carrying the full weight of whatever had driven the bodies they came from to the places where they finally stopped.

The land did not grieve any of it. It held every blade ever unsheathed within its borders, every act of violence done on its surface or in its name, every promise sworn over stone in the dark and broken before morning. It held all of it with perfect fidelity and no interest in what I thought about the arrangement, and it was showing it to me now, and I understood with the part of me that had bypassed my own comprehension that this was not a gift.

It was a reckoning.

Through something much older than my own eyes I saw the darkness gathering at the edges. Not an army. Not a king with grievances and the re-sources to act on them. A hunger. Old and hollow and patient in a way that made everything human look impulsive, wearing the thin shape of a man over something that had long since stopped being one, moving to-ward the convergence beneath Hougun's stones because what pulsed there was the only thing remaining that could feed what it had become.

My palm was pressing hard against the stone. My own pulse beat against the rock and the rock's pulse beat against my palm and there was no longer any distinction between the two.

My eyes snapped open.

The glade was enormous. The trees at the edges were very far away. My breath scraped through my chest in ragged uneven pulls, loud in the silence of the clearing. I was on both hands, though I had no memory of the shift, and the earth beneath my palms was warm and still pulsing and had the quality of something that had just confirmed a decision it had reached a very long time before this morning.

I stayed there.

The stones did not change their glow. They were not waiting for my reaction. They had seen men kneel here and rise and go out into the world and do what was required, and they would see more after me, and my particular reckoning was simply the current entry in a record that stretched further back than stone could remember.

I rose. Slowly. I tested my legs. Tested the ground. Tested whether the world still had the same dimensions it had before I knelt. It did and it did not, and I let both of those things be true simultaneously because arguing with the evidence was a luxury I had never been able to afford.

Eryndor was watching me with the expression of a man who had just discharged a debt he had carried for longer than he could properly account for.

I looked at the stones. At my forearms where the glow had faded back to ordinary skin and ordinary veins. At the ground beneath my boots where the pulse still ran, constant and unhurried and entirely indifferent to the fact that everything I had understood about the shape of my life had just been restructured around it.

I thought about refusal. I gave it honest consideration, because anything less would have been dishonest, and I had never permitted myself dishonesty about things that actually mattered. I thought about walking out of this glade and back through Grizedale and treating this as a strange morning that had happened once and letting the distance accumulate.

The pulse ran through me, steady and patient, and it was not interested in my deliberations.

There was no version of that story where the darkness stopped gathering because I turned away. The ley lines did not need my belief. The hunger moving toward Hougun did not need my acknowledgement to keep moving. The only thing my refusal would change was whether I was present for what came next.

My hands closed at my sides.

My nails cut into my palms and the small clean pain of it pulled me fully back into my body, into the cold and the dark and the damp earth under my boots and the weight of the sword at my hip and the reliable reality of my own heartbeat.

Which was no longer entirely alone.

Eryndor's hand found my shoulder. Light. Barely there. The touch of a man with very little left, giving it anyway. The weight it carried had nothing to do with physical pressure. It was the weight of succession. One portion of something enormous being transferred from one set of hands to another because the world required it and the world did not ask.

I did not move away from it.

I stood with his hand on my shoulder and the earth's pulse steady beneath my feet and the stones glowing their slow, unhurried glow, and I did not make a speech. I did not arrive at a moment of blazing resolution. I simply stood there while the last of my resistance finished dissolving and felt the exact weight of what moved into the space it had occupied.

Not glory. Not purpose in any clean, uncomplicated sense.

War. The real kind. The kind that did not end when the battle did. The kind that lived in the ground and in the pulse at the wrist and in the bond between a land and the people willing to bleed for it. Running deeper than loyalty. Deeper than duty. So deep it had stopped having a name.

The visions from the stones had not fully released me. Twisted creatures at the edges of shadow. The shapes of forgotten gods pressing against the membrane of the world from the other side. Darkness coiling beneath Hougun's stones, circling the convergence with the patient certainty of something that intended to take what it wanted when the time was right. I felt the lineage burning in my blood with the heat of something that had been waiting to be recognised. The Emerald Guardians. Not a title. Not a name passed decoratively between generations. A function. A tether. A bond between flesh and ley line that predated any crown, that would outlast any throne, that was calling to me now with a directness that left no room for interpretation.

The wind found the glade and moved through me, carrying cold earth and iron and the distant ghost of ash from something that had burned on this ground long ago and left its evidence in the soil.

My heartbeat slammed against my ribs.

Not with terror.

With hunger.

That was the thing I had not expected. Not the weight of it, I had always been able to carry weight. Not the scale, I had long since made my peace with the scale of the world's indifference. But the hunger. The recognition. The specific quality of something clicking into alignment with another thing that had been waiting in the dark for it, and both of them going still at the moment of contact.

Eryndor felt the shift. His eyes had not left my face, and what moved across his expression in that moment was not quite relief but something adjacent to it. The particular quality of an ending that had arrived exactly as it was supposed to.

My shoulders squared. My breath evened without instruction. My fists closed at my sides with the slow and deliberate certainty of a man who had stopped deliberating.

I met Eryndor's gaze and held it.

I was not choosing. I understood that now with a clarity that the stones had stripped me down to. The road had been built before my birth. Everything that had made me, every terrible and necessary thing, every scar and every ghost and every night I had chosen to continue when stopping would have been easier, all of it had been the world's preparation. I was what it had made.

I had always been what it had made.

The land held me, selfishly, old and merciless and without the slightest interest in my comfort, the way it had always held me, the way it would hold me long after I was gone.

My nails pressed deeper into my palms.

This was not a weight.

It was power.

And it had always been mine.

CHAPTER TWO - THE TRIALS

The sweetness of wildflowers hit me first, thick and wrong, the kind of fragrance that did not belong to a place like this. I breathed it in and tasted the lie beneath it immediately. Beneath the flowers, beneath the cloying sweetness, something else pressed upward. Decay. Old stone. The particular cold of a place where something had been promised and the promise had rotted in place, year after year, until the rot itself became the only thing left.

I followed Eryndor deeper into the ruin.

His silhouette moved ahead of me, dark against darker stone, and his steps carried the particular deliberation of a man who had walked this path before and knew exactly what waited at the end of it. I did not ask. I had learned by then that asking Eryndor questions he was not ready to answer was a specific kind of waste. He would tell me what he wanted me to know when the telling served its purpose, and not a moment before.

The bones crunched under my boots before I saw them. Pale as old chalk, dry as secrets no one had spoken in decades, they snapped beneath my weight with a sound that the silence swallowed and gave nothing back. My jaw tightened. I kept walking.

Then I saw it.

The altar stood at the chamber's centre, and on it the Emerald Gem pulsed with the slow, steady rhythm of something alive. Not flickering. Not erratic. Steady, the way a heartbeat was steady, the way the earth's pulse was steady, deeply familiar in a way that reached past my ribs and settled somewhere I had no name for. It was not a relic. I understood that immediately, with the certainty of a man who had pressed his palm to the Whispering Stones and heard the world's memory pour through him. This was not something carved by mortal hands and left here to be found. This was a nucleus. A living centre. And the runes etched into the cage containing it glimmered faintly, resisting what they held, straining against it the way a body strained against a wound that would not close.

The pulse of the Gem moved through the cavern walls and into my ribs, coiling around my bones with the particular intimacy of something that had already decided it knew me. My breath came slower. My hands stayed still at my sides.

This was not an offering.

Eryndor's lips curved, and the smile was not kind. It was the smile of a man who understood that pain was the only honest teacher and had long since stopped apologising for the lesson.

"Guardianship isn't embraced," he said, his voice low enough that the silence had to lean in to hear it. "It's conquered. Wrested from the jaws of ruin, paid for in blood, and proven through effort that doesn't stop when you want it to."

I said nothing. The weight of it had already settled into my chest, pressing down on my sternum, tightening the space between my ribs. My grip on my sword was unnecessary in that moment, and I kept it anyway, knuckles white, because it was the one thing in this chamber that I understood.

Eryndor took one more step forward. His shadow stretched long behind him, cast by the green glow of the Gem. "Three trials await."

The words did not arrive as sound. They arrived as something physical, sinking into my skin the way cold sank into muscle, deep and slow and impossible to reverse.

"These trials will not test your strength," he continued, and his voice had taken on a quality I had not heard in it before, not command, not encouragement, but the finality of a thing being spoken because it was true and not for any other reason. "Not your endurance. Not what your body can survive. They will strip you down to the bone. They will scour away everything you believe yourself to be. And when they are finished, they will show you the soul you are willing to forge."

Three trials. Three ordeals designed not to test me, but to break me, to find out what survived the breaking, and whether that was enough.

The chamber pulsed around me. The stones hummed with an energy that did not sleep, that had never slept in this place, that waited the way only ancient things could wait, with total patience and total certainty. I felt it pressing against the walls I had spent years building around myself, finding the hairline cracks, applying pressure with quiet and terrible precision.

I breathed. I kept my feet where they were. And the Gem watched.

The first trial arrived without announcement.

The shrine closed around me. I felt it happen before I saw the evidence of it, felt the air thicken and the walls press inward, felt the oxygen shift into something denser and harder to move through. The incense from some long-extinguished ceremony still clung to the stone, heavy and cloying and bitter, and beneath it the acrid undertone of burnt flesh that no amount of time had managed to fully dissolve. I breathed it into my lungs and the taste settled on the back of my tongue and stayed there.

Then the fire came.

Not the ordinary kind. Not the useful kind I had lit in fieldcraft and survival and the cold practical necessity of staying alive through Cumbrian winters. This was spectral, heat without source, searing without reason, a blaze that engulfed me without touching me and still stripped the breath from my chest. The smoke was real. Dense and suffocating, it wound around my ribs the way a grip wound around a throat, methodical, patient, tightening by increments I could not track until I was already fighting for the next breath.

A village in flames.

I knew before the image fully formed what I was going to see, and knowing did not prepare me for it. The charred beams. The walls collapsing inward, shrieking as they fell. The faces. Gods, the faces, illuminated by the fire's particular cruelty, each one caught in a moment that had frozen for them and been moving without pause for me ever since. Their mouths open. The sounds not reaching me through the roar of the fire, not reaching me but somehow still inside my skull, filling every space the smoke had left, the dying and the anguish and the specific register of a human voice at the moment it understood it was lost.

Each one was a blade.

You failed them. The fire hissed it through the embers, through the sparks spinning upward like the souls of everyone I had not reached in time. You failed them, and you know it, and every day you have carried the careful, practiced fiction that you did what you could, and this place is done with that fiction now.

Cold coiled in my chest. Not the cold of the chamber. Colder. Deeper. Not the fear of the fire, not even the fear of death, which I had made my peace with in pieces over the course of more near-misses than I could accurately count. This was the other fear. The one I kept behind the walls. The one that did not announce itself in battle or in danger but surfaced in the moments of silence, in the dark, in the space between one breath and the next. The fear that the fire was right. That I had never been enough. That every life I had carried since was carrying weight that I had no right to bear.

I had been through pain before. I had been through the kind of pain that restructured a person, that took what they were and left behind something different, something harder and less certain of its own shape. I had not been through this. This was not pain, exactly. This was excavation. Claws raking through me for the specific purpose of finding what lived at the bottom, and whether it would survive the exposure.

My teeth clenched. My breath came in ragged pulls. My fists curled at my sides, nails into palms, the small clean pain of it the only thing I had full confidence was real. I did not kneel. I had not knelt before anything that tried to break me, and I was not going to begin here, in a spectral fire built from my own worst knowledge of myself.

I stood in the ashes of everything I had not saved. I breathed the air of the fire I had not extinguished. And I made the only vow that mattered in that moment, not a vow of heroism, not a vow of glory, but the specific, cold, unyielding vow of a survivor: nothing was going to take from me again. Not by violence. Not by guilt. Not by the slow, methodical erosion of a trial designed to find the place where I broke.

The fire held. And I held with it. And eventually, one of us stopped.

The second trial arrived differently.

It did not announce itself with fire or heat or the visceral immediacy of things I could name and face directly. It arrived as a vibration in the stone, an obsidian rhythm that moved through the floor and up through my boots and into my bones and began to hum in a frequency that bypassed my ears entirely and settled somewhere deeper. A pressure in my chest like an invisible hand with infinite patience.

The spirits did not speak in words. They spoke in what words tried to be and never fully managed.

The visions came in pieces. A serpent with scales the colour of deep water, coiling around a sun bleeding its last light into a sky that had no interest in holding it. A willow standing over bones that the roots had long since grown through and around and made into part of themselves. A child's laughter bouncing off the walls of a charnel house, sweet and hollow and wrong in the specific way that beautiful things were wrong in places built for the dead.

The air smelled of ozone and rotting lilies at the same time, their wilted petals releasing something thick and sweet that clung to the inside of my nose and would not leave. I breathed through it. I kept breathing through it. My brow was wet with cold sweat, the temperature of it a specific contradiction against the feverish heat of my skin.

This was not a riddle in the sense that required cleverness. I had navigated enough situations that demanded quick thinking and sharp calculation to know what that felt like, the particular quality of a problem that wanted the cutting edge of my mind applied to it. This was not that. This peeled me open the way a practised hand peeled skin from muscle, layer by layer, without any wasted motion, exposing everything I had kept folded away in the dark and quiet places.

The answer came slowly. Not as revelation. Not as a flash of understanding that illuminated everything at once. It came the way dawn came after the worst nights, incremental, grudging, bleeding its light across the sky one degree of grey at a time. And what it showed me was not a truth about the world or the ley lines or the nature of power.

It showed me myself.

Not the version I carried into rooms. Not the controlled, measured, deliberate self I had constructed over twenty-five years of careful maintenance. The other one. The one underneath all the carefully maintained structures. The one that had not saved everyone it should have saved, that had not been enough when being enough was the only thing that mattered, that carried every one of those failures in the specific place below the sternum where the ones that could not be processed ended up when there was nowhere else to put them.

I was not enough. I had never been enough, a realisation that settled into my bones like a persistant winter chill. No matter how many milestones I reached or how much of myself I poured into the expectations of others, there was always a phantom finish line that shifted just as I approached it. It was the exhaustion of running a race where the rules were unwritten and the prize was a validation that remained perpetually out of reach. Eventually, the weight of this percieved inadequacy became a mirror, reflecting not my failures, but the impossibility of filling a void that was never mine to bridge in the first place.

The trials, the land, the ley lines, none of it had chosen me because I was sufficient. I had been chosen in spite of being insufficient, and the relentless, irrational, exhausting refusal to accept that insufficiency as the final word, to keep trying anyway, to keep standing in front of the things that needed standing in front of, knowing I would come up short and standing there regardless.

That was the answer. Not my strength. My brokenness. My failure. The carrying of it and the continuing anyway.

The hallucination fractured. The whispers died. The images dissolved into nothing and the world came back sudden and unkind, and I staggered under the return of it, under the weight of what I now knew about myself with a clarity I could not unfeel.

I had passed. I thought I had passed. But it did not feel like that. It felt like a bone set wrong, like something that would heal into a shape that would ache in cold weather for the rest of my life as a reminder of the break. I was and was not the person who had walked into this trial. Whatever I had been before, I was carrying more of it now, more of myself, and it was heavier than anything I had ever been asked to hold.

Eryndor watched me with eyes that held the particular knowing of a person who had understood the outcome before the trial began. I did not speak to him. There was nothing to say that the silence was not already saying better.

I found the pool of water without deciding to look for it, stumbling through the ruins until the dark surface of it stopped me. It was still and depthless, a void that reflected perfectly and offered nothing back except the truth of what was standing over it.

A stranger looked up at me.

The golden remnant of the trial still faintly lit my irises from within, the last trace of the ley line's attention. My hair hung damp and tangled against my jaw, darker with sweat. The stubble had grown past what I remembered, and it aged me in a way that had nothing to do with the days it represented. But it was the eyes that held me there. The hollowness in them. The absence. The man I had been when I walked in was not the man looking back from the water's surface.

I stayed there for a long moment. Long enough that the stillness of the pool began to feel like a verdict. I did not fight it. The trial had already taken what it wanted. Fighting the evidence of it now was not something I had the resources for.

The third trial was already in the air when I straightened.

The wind found me through the ruins, hooked into my cloak with fingers that felt deliberate, that pulled with the specific force of something that wanted me to understand what was coming before it arrived. It carried cold and loss in equal measure, and it pressed against the cavity of my chest with a slow, merciless certainty that had nothing of the fire's violence and everything of its inevitability.

The deep hum came next, rising from beneath the stones, settling into my ribs and then deeper, into the bones themselves, filling the marrow. The manor beneath me was alive and aware and it did not demand. It did not beg. It simply waited with the patience of a thing that had been waiting for centuries and had no difficulty waiting a little longer.

Copper on the back of my tongue. The taste of what was coming, bitter and metallic and already present before the cost had been formally named. My mouth was dry. I could not swallow it away.

I heard them before anything else. The voices. Not the voices of warriors or soldiers or the men who had stood beside me in the battles that had brought me here. The voices of the ones I had sworn to protect. Quiet. Not demanding vengeance. Not calling for the specific reckoning that my sword hand understood. Calling for something else entirely. For the version of me that would have to exist after this moment, the one I had not yet become and could not yet see the shape of.

I dropped to my knees.

The silence that followed was not the silence of absence. It had weight. It had mass. It pressed down on my shoulders and the back of my neck and the space between my shoulder blades with the cumulative heaviness of every choice and every cost that had led me to this particular square of cold stone.

I pressed my palm to the earth.

It moved against my hand. Not dramatically. Subtly, the way a pulse moved against fingertips, the way the Whispering Stones had moved against my palm in the glade, with the specific warmth of something immeasurably old confirming that it had been paying attention. This soil had memory. It had held the weight of empires and absorbed the blood of generations and it knew, with the calm certainty of something that could not be surprised, what I was about to lose.

A hollow ache opened inside me. Not in the chest. Deeper. In the place that the Trial of Wisdom had already found and exposed, the place that did not have a clean name because it predated the part of me that had learned to name things. Something was being taken. Not asked for. Not bargained for. Taken, with the same quiet inevitability as the tide taking sand, grain by grain, without malice and without hesitation and without any interest in what the sand thought about the arrangement.

"You understand now, don't you?"

Eryndor's voice arrived soft and edged with something ancient, not a question but the specific quality of a statement made by a person who already knows the answer and is offering the other person the dignity of speaking it.

The truth settled through me the way a blade settled into a wound, precisely along the line of least resistance, final. The trial had not required a price. It had taken the possibility of return. There was no version of what came next in which I was the same person who had walked into this place. Some burdens were worth bearing even if they broke you. I understood that now. I understood it in the specific, physical way I understood things that had moved past the reach of argument.

Thunder answered from the horizon.

The Gem was in my hands, and it no longer felt like stone. It pulsed against my palms, alive, the way living things pulsed, warm and present and specific in a way that mere objects were not. A heart of starlight and shadow, the world's own soul cradled in bloodstained hands, and it caught my reflection back at me from its surface and showed me the question I had been refusing to ask.

Was I still the man who had begun this?

The scars of every battlefield I had walked through were etched into the Gem's surface, visible in the way memories were visible in old stone, worn into the material by repetition and weight. The Whispering Waste. The frozen cliffs of Serpent's Peak. The obsidian dark of the Labyrinth. Each had taken something and given something back, and the exchange had been profitable and terrible in equal measure. I had come through all of it. I was not whole. But I had come through.

I pressed the Gem against my breastplate.

Power did not flood into me. The word flood was wrong, too gentle, too manageable. It devoured. It poured through every vein I had as volcanic heat pours through fissures in the rock, not filling but consuming, scorching the channels it moved through and leaving them fundamentally changed in its wake. The taste of raw earth filled my mouth. The smell of forgotten magic, of every working that had ever been done in this place and every sacrifice that had fed the ley lines in the centuries before my birth, pressed into my lungs until I could not breathe anything else.

The roar that filled the chamber was not a voice. It was power itself, enormous and impersonal, and it shook the walls and shook my bones and reached down through the roots of the earth to the ley lines running beneath Hougun's foundations and it answered them, and they answered it, and through me the connection closed and the current ran and the ages of lost memory and every failed Guardian who had stood where I stood poured into me in a tide that was beyond unbearable and did not care.

I was drowning in the world's memory.

And then I was not drowning. I was holding it. All of it. Every age and every sacrifice and every line of power running beneath this land, and it was mine, and I was its, and the man I had been before I pressed my hand to the stone was gone, replaced by something that carried all of him and was also more than him in ways that did not yet have names.

Eryndor stood at the edge of the chamber, and he was flickering.

Not metaphorically. He was losing definition, the edges of him becoming uncertain, the solidity that I had taken for granted in every moment since Grizedale beginning to dissolve into something that was more memory than presence. The cold of it hit me through the storm of power still moving through my veins, cold and specific and wrong in a way that the power could not insulate against.

"No. I have so much more to learn" The words came out before I could stop it, quiet, not a command but a refusal that had nowhere to go.

He smiled. Not with relief. Not with peace. With the particular quality of a man who has known the ending for a very long time and has simply been waiting to arrive at it.

"Sacrifice is inevitable, Talon." The words tasted like ash in the air between us. Like the answer to a question I had not finished asking.

My fists closed at my sides. Everything I had just absorbed, all that power, all that memory, all that weight, and none of it was capable of stopping this. The calculation was already done and the outcome was already fixed and I had not been given a vote on any of it. I wanted to offer myself in trade. I wanted to find the thing the ley lines would accept in exchange for this one specific outcome. "What did I sacrifice?" The question tore out of my throat, raw, not composed, not measured, not the voice of a Guardian or a Lord or any of the things I had just become.

Eryndor's gaze met mine, and it was ageless, and it did not look away. His fingers found my wrist, firm, a grip that communicated everything his words were not going to finish. The smile that returned to his face was gentle with the specific gentleness of inevitability, the kind that had stopped being cruel because it had always been coming.

"I'll tell you," he said, and his voice was already becoming something the wind was doing rather than something he was producing. "When I return."

And then he was not there.

Not gone dramatically. Not swallowed by fire or shadow. Simply gone, absorbed into the ley lines the same way everything that had ever been part of this land eventually returned to it, quietly, without remainder, leaving the space where he had been so completely empty that it seemed impossible he had ever occupied it.

I stood in the howling silence of what remained.

The Emerald Gem burned at my chest, steady, unhurried, patient as the earth. I had the power. I had the manor. I had everything that the trials had promised and the victory that the battle would seal, and the hollow that Eryndor's absence had left in me was larger than any of it, larger than the power, larger than the cost, larger than the certainty now running through my bones.

I had never felt so completely alone.

Hougun Manor did not serve kings. It had never served kings. Yet it had chosen me, the exile, the man with nothing left, the one who had been stripped down to the bone by three trials and had not broken. Not a triumph. A burden. The most honest kind, the kind that arrived without fanfare, that did not look like what it was until you were already beneath its weight.

I caught the wrongness in my peripheral vision before I turned to look.

The stench of burnt earth and blood reached me before the gates did. It wrapped around me as I pushed through them, thick and cloying and absolute, the scent of what a place became after men decided it was worth dying over.

What had been a noble estate was a carcass. Charred stone. Skeletal hallways still smoking with the slow, determined patience of fires that had burned themselves out and left the ruin of their work behind. Agonised sounds threaded through the haze from somewhere in the debris, human and desperate and cutting through the noise of everything else with the particular insistence of pain that had no audience and no relief.

I had seen slaughter before. I had walked through the aftermath of battles and sieges and the specific kinds of devastation that men committed upon the places they had decided represented something worth destroying. None of it had prepared me for this, for a place that had belonged to me before I had claimed it, for the specific quality of violation that came with watching something you were responsible for be torn apart.

The rival lords circled at the edges of the destruction, their armour catching the firelight in flashes that had nothing of honour in them. They had not come for justice. They had not come for vengeance. They had come because they could smell the ley lines through the smoke and the blood and the ruin, could feel them throbbing beneath the soil the way a hunting animal felt the proximity of prey through the soles of its feet.

The Gem at my chest burned hotter with every step I took toward them. Its rhythm had aligned with something inside me that was past the reach of thought, something that did not calculate or hesitate or consider the tactical picture. Eryndor's voice moved through my blood like a thread, his presence absorbed into the power that was also now mine, grounding me in the specific weight of what this moment required.

The ground split under my boots before I told it to. Roots erupted from the cold earth with a violence that was not mine and was also entirely mine, thick and relentless, moving with the specific hunger of a land that had been patient long enough and had found someone through whom to stop being patient. They took the invaders into the earth, and their screams were swallowed the way the earth swallowed everything, completely and without return.

I moved through the battlefield with the Gem burning at my chest and the ley lines running through my veins like a second circulatory system, and my blade sang through the smoke-thick air with the guidance of everyone who had stood in this place before me and been broken by it, and I was not broken, not yet, possibly not ever again, and the distinction between my own fury and the land's fury had dissolved into something that I stopped trying to locate.

Then I felt it. The void in the chaos. The wrongness.

Daegrith.

The name arrived with a physical quality, cold and specific, and I found him through the smoke and the wreckage and the ruin before I had consciously gone looking. He had been someone else once. What he was now wore that person's face the way a fever wore the memory of health, as evidence of what had been lost rather than what remained. The corruption in him was visible to something in me that had not existed this morning, the ley line awareness moving through my blood cataloguing what it encountered, and what it found in Daegrith was wrong in every frequency.

The stench of him reached me first. Rot. Decay. The specific smell of power stolen from its source and not properly metabolised, festering in the body that had taken it with the slow, inevitable toxicity of the wrong kind of nourishment.

He laughed when our eyes met. The sound split the air like a blade drawn across stone, sharp and without warmth. He moved toward me, and his movements were wrong, his limbs responding to instructions that came from somewhere other than the natural mechanics of a human body, twitching at angles that made the eye refuse them.

Our blades met and the impact travelled up my arms and into my shoulders and the stone beneath us cracked with the force of it, and the ley lines shuddered from the collision in a way that I felt through every bone simultaneously. We moved through each other's strikes and parries with the grinding intimacy of two people who understood that one of them was not walking away from this ground, and the only remaining question was the order of events.

"Do you think you're different?" He spat the words between strikes, his voice carrying the particular bitterness of a man who needed me to be as lost as he was. "You'll fall just like I did."

I caught his next strike and turned it and pressed him back two steps into the rubble. My breath was ragged and my muscles were burning and the iron taste of my own blood where a strike had opened my lip was warm and present and entirely real.

"Maybe," I said. "But it'll be by my own choice."

The ground split beneath his feet.

I had not done it deliberately. Or I had, without going through the steps that deliberation required, the ley lines moving through me responding to whatever the land had already decided about Daegrith. A chasm opened, dark and absolute, judgment made physical, and from it the vines came. They moved with a purpose that had nothing of the natural world's randomness in it, specific and intentional, burrowing into his corrupted flesh with the specific hunger of a land reclaiming what had been taken from it.

He screamed. Not in defiance. In terror. The distinction was something I would carry.

His fingers found the crumbling stone at the chasm's edge, clawing for purchase, for the possibility of staying in a world he had spent everything to take. The manor had already decided. The vines constricted and the earth opened and the thing that had been a man and then a monster was simply gone, absorbed into the dark, reclaimed by the land with the same quiet inevitability as everything else.

The flutter of his red cloak was the last thing. Then silence.

The silence of a verdict carried out. Not peace. Something more precise than peace.

I stood in it with my breath coming in torn pulls and the Gem dimming against my chest, power spent, and my legs holding me through the last of the effort by some combination of the ley lines and the stubbornness that had gotten me this far and nothing more sophisticated than that. The manor was mine. The battle was over. Every god or creature or rival lord that wanted to test that understanding was welcome to arrive and find out what it cost them.

The tug at my cloak arrived so quietly I almost missed it.

I turned.

A child. Ten years old, perhaps, skin dark with soot, eyes wide and very carefully not crying, watching me with an expression I recognised from my own mirrors in the months after I had lost something I could not quantify.

"Is it over?" the boy asked, and the hope in his voice was the most difficult thing I had heard all day, threaded through the question like something fragile that a careless word could shatter.

I crouched. Brought myself to his level. Looked at him directly, the way I had looked at Eryndor in the clearing before everything changed, because the boy deserved the same honesty the old man had offered me.

"For now," I said.

He looked at the smouldering banners still clinging to the scorched stone above us, the remnants of something that had meant something to someone before the fire. "My father fought for you," he said, his voice carefully even in the way children's voices went carefully even when they were holding something larger than they had the capacity to hold. "He said you'd protect us."

The weight of that settled through me layer by layer. His father's name was among the ones I did not know, which was not a comfortable truth but was the truth, and there was a version of this moment in which I offered him something else. I did not take that version.

"I'll try," I said.

His chin came up with the specific resolution of a child deciding to carry something heavy. "One day, I'll fight for you," he declared, and then he was gone, absorbed back into the scattered crowd before I could find an answer.

I rose off the ground staring into the scattered crowd.

The battle's echoes faded. The survivors watched me from the rubble with expressions that I would have given a great deal to stop being able to read, awe and terror interlocked in a way that told me clearly that what they were seeing when they looked at me was not what I had been this morning. I was not a warrior to them. I was something else. Something with a category I did not yet have a name for and was not sure I wanted.

Eryndor's voice came through the breeze, faint as memory, carrying the particular quality of something that had been said a long time ago and was only now arriving.

"You see now, don't you? Power is neither a gift nor a burden. It's a choice. And that choice you bear alone."

"Were there others like me?" I asked the wind, feeling only marginally absurd about it.

The answer came, thin and distant. "Once. Long ago. He made his choice. And it changed everything."

"What happened to him?"

The wind shifted. The voice moved with it, away and toward somewhere else simultaneously. "Sacrifice is inevitable, Talon."

And then nothing. Just the wind.

I stood for a long time in the cooling dark with the manor looming at my back, scarred and standing, and the question that would not resolve itself pressing against the inside of my sternum. Had I saved Hougun, or had I become its next weight, the newest entry in a history of people who had poured themselves into its foundations and been changed beyond recognition in the process?

The survivors watched me from the rubble. In their faces, torchbearer. In their eyes, something that belonged to the land and not entirely to himself anymore.

I breathed. I turned and I walked back into the manor I had just won.

The halls were cold and full of dust and the particular quality of silence that belonged to spaces that had been waiting a long time for someone to return. The air moved against me as I walked deeper into it, not a draft, a presence, the manor exhaling its accumulated centuries of silence, thick with memory and expectation both. The shadows clung to the walls the way grief clung, familiar, shapeless, unwilling to be addressed directly. A low hum moved through the foundation and synced with my heartbeat the way the pulse beneath Grizedale had synced with it in the early morning before all of this began. The manor was not dead. It had been waiting.

And now it knew I was home.

I had vowed to restore this place. To protect it. To rule it. And by my hands, the days that followed proved I could. The halls came back to life under consistent attention. The lands grew productive. The people moved through the estate with the specific quality of safety that came from knowing the walls around them were held by someone who intended to keep holding them. My name carved itself into the shape of a hero, and I wore it the way I wore the scars on my forearms, underneath the sleeves, out of sight, because offering it to every room I entered was a specific kind of vanity I did not have the stomach for.

But beneath the golden surface of every day, the rot.

There was one act. One decision made in the cold calculation of necessity, in the place where my strategist's mind lived, the place that evaluated outcomes and selected the one that preserved the most lives and asked questions about method afterward. Lord Elmsworth. The look on his face when he understood what I had done. That look had not left me. It lived in the back of every room I occupied, in the corner of every mirror, in the specific quality of silence after people finished praising me for the thing they did not know I had done.

I had not just broken a man. I had broken the version of myself that had believed there were lines I would not cross, and that version of myself did not exist anymore, and the space it had occupied was now just space.

The villagers called me their hero, and the word wrapped around my throat the way a rope wrapped, beautiful and functional and specifically designed for one purpose. They believed it entirely, and their belief was the most suffocating thing in a life that had given me significant experience with suffocation. They saw the Lord who had delivered them. They did not see what the delivery had cost. They did not need to. That was not their burden.

It was mine.

And alongside it, Lord Blackwood, from Sudfolc, a man whose calculating mind used vast knowledge of science and chemistry to feign the supernatural, his aim was to overthrow the King of Sudfolc through a series of ritualistic assassination and manipulation, replacing it with a new world empire founded on fear.

I had stood against Blackwood before. Vowed, in the specific way that vows meant something before reality began to apply its corrections, never to become the kind of person who made use of the kind of man that Blackwood was. The vow had not survived contact with the political arithmetic of holding a manor against rivals who did not share my scruples. The pact existed now, inked in blood and necessity, and the cold voice in me that evaluated outcomes called it the only viable option, and the rest of me knew it for what it was.

An infection. Moving through everything I had built, slow and patient, corroding from the inside the way that the most effective poisons always operated.

The shadows moved closer in the grand hall, threading through the stone and the cold air, and the manor's ancient pulse moved against the soles of my feet with the steady knowledge of a thing that had witnessed every version of this before. It knew what compromises felt like when they embedded themselves in the walls. It had been holding this particular knowledge for centuries.

My reflection appeared in the cracked window at the corridor's end. I did not look away from it. I had never been able to look away from things I did not want to see. It was the one discipline I had never managed to break.

This was my empire. My legacy. Every room a monument not to the power I had gained but to the precise and terrible arithmetic of what that power had required. The people cheered outside these walls, and the cheering was genuine, and it deserved to be, and none of that changed what I saw when I was standing still and the noise stopped and there was only the silence and the reflection and the weight.

I had won Hougun Manor.

I was not sure, standing in the cold dark of its hallway with the land's pulse still running through my bones and Eryndor's absence still carved into the hollow beneath my sternum, that winning was the right word for it.

But I was here. The manor was standing. The people were safe.

For now, I had told the boy.

For now was all I had ever had.

CHAPTER THREE - THE DRAGON OF THE EMERALD CRAGGS

CUMBRIA HAD BEEN SHAPING ME SINCE BEFORE I HAD the language to understand what shaping was.

I had grown up beneath its storm clouds and inside its winds, in the kind of country that did not permit softness, that wore you down to whatever was actually underneath and let the rest blow away across the fells. Hougun Manor was part of that. It had never simply stood on the land. It had grown from it, its walls sweating with the memory of every battle fought in its name, its stones so saturated with defiance that I sometimes thought the defiance had entered me through the soles of my boots long before I understood what I was carrying.

The scent of the manor was something I had stopped noticing years ago and only registered now in the moments when it shifted. Old wood, always. The bitter edge of iron that had soaked too deep into the stone to ever fully leave. The ghost of smoke from fires burned so long ago the timber was dust and the ash was part of the floor. The corridors were never still, even when they were silent. The floor groaned under my weight with a sound that was less mechanical and more the expression of a very old thing accommodating a very persistent presence. The torches twisted in draughts that came from no identifiable source, and the light they threw was always slightly wrong, always slightly contested by the dark at the edges of every room.

And beneath all of it, beneath the stone and the soil and the accumulated centuries of everything Hougun had absorbed and refused to release, the ley lines pulsed. When I drew on them, the manor did not offer me power in the way a well offered water, patiently and in proportion to my need. It gave everything at once, with the fury of a dying star, with the complete and absolute commitment of a force that did not understand restraint, had never learned restraint, had never needed to. It did not yield to reason. It did not negotiate. When I held Hougun's power, I held the world by its throat, and the world pressed back with everything it had, and the cost of that exchange lived in me now in ways I was still learning to map.

I had sought knowledge across every dark valley and sharp-edged peak this land had to offer. I had found the druids, the ones who kept what others had chosen to forget, who guarded the old knowledge with the specific devotion of people who understood what happened when old knowledge went unguarded. They had spoken of the Emerald Gem in the specific tones of something real that had been spoken of so long in the register of legend that even its keepers had to remind themselves of the distinction. A fragment of the world's heart, tied to the abyss beneath the earth's skin, made by nothing human and intended for no human purpose.

And then fate, which had never once come to me cleanly, came with emerald scales and a voice like mountains deciding to move.

Myrcanthor the dragon of the Emerald Craggs

I had heard the name before I sought it. In the mouths of dying men who had encountered something they could not categorise and were trying to warn whoever found them. In the broken verses of poets who had gotten close enough to feel the air she displaced and had spent the rest of their lives trying to communicate the specific quality of that feeling and failing. She had been freed from time, the druids said, though that phrase did not fully parse for me until I stood before her and understood it in my body rather than my mind. Her wings stirred the Cumbrian mist the way weather stirred it, as a phenomenon of the world rather than a creature moving through the world.

She was not old in the way that ruins were old, or bones, or the way flesh yielded to the slow cruelty of years. She was old the way mountains were old. The way rivers were old. The way stars were old, the ones that had been burning before anyone had thought to give them names, that would still be burning after every name was forgotten. Time moved differently around her. It had learned to accommodate her rather than move through her.

Eryndor's words still burned in the front of my mind when I entered the forest, his voice carrying the specific weight of a man who had said the same thing to himself many times before he said it to me.

"You must seek her, Talon." He had looked old that morning, genuinely old, his body bowed by the years his conviction refused to acknowledge. "She will not suffer men."

My jaw had tightened. "Then why me?"

He had smiled, which was not an answer, except that it was. "Because you are not just a man." The smile had held. "Only she holds the secret to unlocking your gem's full, terrible power."

The forest pressed in close on either side of me, the trees standing the way old things stood, with the patience of organisms that measured time in centuries and found human urgency faintly incomprehensible. The Gem at my chest pulsed with a rhythm that was not quite my own heartbeat, slightly different in cadence, slightly different in depth, guiding me through the mist and the bracken and the ruins of civilisations that had not lasted long enough to leave anything except foundations. I followed it the way I followed the earth's pulse, with the specific trust of a man who had run out of better options.

Night dissolved into the grey uncertainty of dawn as the slope steepened beneath me, and the wind shifted from a constant presence into something with specific intent, something that pushed back against every upward step with the precise force of a thing that had been told to make this difficult. Eryndor's warning lived in the muscles of my legs with every stride. Myrcanthor would not bow to strength. She had seen too much of what strength looked like when it was separated from everything else and came knocking at her door. She had watched those men become the sediment of her lair floor. She would demand everything, and everything meant the things I kept in the locked rooms of myself, the ones I had not opened voluntarily since I was young enough to believe that vulnerability was survivable.

My breath came ragged and tasted of ice and copper. The path did not behave like a path. It writhed. Jagged stones jutted from it at angles that seemed designed to find the gaps in my boots and locate the specific tendons of my feet, and gravel gave way under my weight and fell into the abyss below with a sound that lasted long enough to suggest the abyss had significant depth. Every step sent pain lancing upward and I converted it, the way I converted most pain, into momentum. The cold had moved past the stage of being uncomfortable and entered the stage of being structural, working its way into my bones and making the simple mechanics of movement feel like negotiation.

The shapes in the trees were there before I identified them as shapes, registering first as a quality of wrongness in my peripheral vision, the specific sense of the observed. Eyes in the undergrowth, not reflecting firelight because there was no firelight, but present regardless, the kind of watching that had nothing behind it that I had any language for. Their whispers were not sound. They were a pressure in the marrow, a vibration at a frequency below what the ears processed, and it was more disorienting than any sound would have been because I could not locate the source or determine the direction.

The mountain was testing me. I understood that. It was doing what everything in this land did when something approached that it was not certain about, applying pressure to find the threshold, to discover where the thing broke or changed its mind and turned back.

I did not turn back.

Then the air changed.

A deep pulse moved through the stone beneath my feet, pressing up through the soles of my boots and into the bones of my feet and climbing, not stopping at my ankles or my shins but continuing upward, settling into my ribs and my skull and my blood with the specific quality of something that predated every other pulse I had ever felt. It was not a sound. It was pressure and rhythm and force simultaneously, and it pressed into me with a patience that suggested it had been doing this for a very long time and was entirely prepared to continue. And through it, beneath it, I felt her. Not saw. Not heard. Felt, the way you felt a storm before the first crack of thunder, the way you felt the sea's intention before the wave arrived.

She was there.

The plateau opened before me without announcement, a jagged expanse of stone carved by time and fire and whatever forces had been at work in this mountain before any human categorisation of forces existed. The air here smelled of scorched earth and something beneath that, something that my mind kept trying to classify and kept failing to classify, because it was not death, not decay, not fire in any ordinary sense. It was time. The specific smell of time in a place where time had accumulated undisturbed, heavy and absolute and pressing against the inside of my chest with a weight that made the ley line pulse feel gentle by comparison.

She moved.

The shadow uncoiled from the cavern with the specific speed of something that had decided to move rather than needed to, the distinction between capacity and choice evident in every inch of the motion. Fire and stone filled my lungs, the taste of ash settling on the back of my tongue before I had consciously registered the source. Then she was fully visible and the word visible felt inadequate, felt like trying to describe the ocean with the word wet.

Emerald and gold.

Her scales caught the pale light and did something to it that light was not supposed to do, bending it, sharpening it, returning it to the world as something other than what it had arrived as. The sound of her movement was soft and metallic and constant, the scales shifting against each other in a frequency that I felt in my teeth. She was vast in the way that was not simply a matter of measurement, in the way that made measurement feel beside the point. Her wings, still partly furled, bore the specific texture of things that had been tested by genuinely significant forces and had not broken, the scars across their membranes each carrying the precise quality of a story that had not ended well for the other party.

Her eyes found me.

Not found in the sense of located. Found in the sense of assessed, catalogued, measured against something I could not see and did not have access to the specifications of. They were gold, but gold was wrong, gold was a colour and these were something else that happened to appear gold, twin voids where time had learned to collect, where history accumulated and played out in the silence behind her gaze. They did not simply see me. They moved through me, through the flesh and the bone and the carefully maintained exterior, through the years and the choices and the ghost of Eryndor still living in the hollow beneath my sternum, through every locked room in myself. And they were cold with the specific cold of a thing that had been lied to before and had no remaining interest in making accommodation for the possibility that this time would be different.

A tremor moved through the cavern. Not from motion. From her awareness of me, the physical consequence of her attention concentrating.

Then her voice came, and voice was the wrong word, because what arrived did not use air the way voices used air. It erupted through the stone and the bone and the space between atoms with the force of a seismic event, and it was older than any language, older than the consensus that had produced language, older than the need for consensus. It did not speak to my ears. It spoke to whatever was underneath my ears, to the part of me that had been listening to the earth's pulse since the Whispering Stones and had not fully stopped.

"Why have you crawled here, mortal?" The words hit me like struck stone, each one a separate impact. "Do you seek power? Are you like the fools who rot beneath my lair? Or is greed coiling around your heart, whispering lies?" A pause, and the pause had its own weight, heavier than the words around it. "You are fragile, fleeting flesh. Yet you dare to stand before me."

The cavern closed in with her attention. The air thickened to something I had to actively move through, and the scent of scorched earth and charred bone pressed into my lungs with the insistence of a warning delivered by something that had not yet decided whether the warning would be its final communication with me.

The tremor in my breath was not fear. I wanted to be precise about that, even in the privacy of my own chest. It was the specific physiological response to standing in front of a force that could end me without inconvenience, combined with the specific fury of a man who had not survived everything he had survived in order to break in front of the one thing he had been walking toward since Grizedale. I did not flinch under her gaze. My feet stayed where they were. My hands stayed open at my sides, visible, deliberate, because the only language available to me in that moment was the language of what I chose to do with my body, and I chose stillness.

"I do not come for power." Each syllable came out of me like something hammered into shape. "I do not come to conquer." I held her gaze, those gold-void eyes that were measuring me against everything they had ever measured and finding the precise location of my edges. "I come to protect."

My voice did not shake. I was surprised by this, in the removed way I was sometimes surprised by my own body's decisions when they coincided with what I needed.

I told her about the rot. About the decay that had moved through Hougun's veins the way disease moved through blood, patient and systematic and entirely committed to its outcome. About the ley lines thrumming with sickness where they had once thrummed with the specific vitality of something alive and healthy. About the air of the manor, about the way its corridors had begun to twist away from what they had been into something that wore the shape of it and was not it. I gave her the grief of it, the words sharpened by something I did not want to name directly and did not need to, because she was already measuring me against the truth rather than the presentation of the truth and the distinction was either irrelevant or it was everything.

I told her about the broken people. The souls ground down beneath the spreading blight, the weight of it. The duty that bound me to this, which was not ambition and not pride but something that had entered my blood before I had the capacity to consent to it, that had been written into me at the Whispering Stones and before them in Grizedale and before that in the specific shape of everything I had survived and not managed to put down since.

The silence after I finished was absolute.

And then Myrcanthor moved.

Not with violence. Not with the speed of something attacking. With purpose, which was different and more frightening. A shifting of her vast body that was not dramatic but was completely intentional, the slow deliberate revelation of what power looked like when it had nothing to prove. She rose, and the cavern accommodated her the way the sky accommodated weather, because it had no alternative. Her wings spread and the darkness moved with them, gathered into her span, and the dust that fell from the ceiling in the displacement fell like ash and settled on my skin and tasted like the end of something.

The earth shuddered with her awakening. Her breath arrived against my face carrying the specific heat of scorched lands and blood-soaked fields and empires that had concluded badly, and the gold of her eyes narrowed, and her presence pulled the air from my lungs with the casual thoroughness of something that did not need my permission.

"To earn my breath." Her voice had changed. Soft now, which was worse. The devastation was still there but underneath the soft, which meant it was the kind of devastation that had moved past the need to announce itself. "You will face the Trial of the Earthbound Flame." A long inhale, slow and deliberate. "Fail." The word arrived barely above a whisper and landed like a blade between the ribs. "And your ashes will nourish the roots that bind this mountain to the world's bones."

I breathed out. Slow. Deliberate. Not defiance. Acceptance. The specific kind of acceptance that came from having already decided, before I climbed this mountain, before I entered this cavern, before I looked into those gold-void eyes, that whatever she asked for I was going to give it, because the alternative was not something I was going to choose.

The world split open into fire.

The earth convulsed beneath me before I had finished processing her words, the stone cracking apart with the force and the speed of something that had been waiting for a specific signal and had now received it. A chasm opened with a sound that was less explosion and more the specific vocal expression of something primordial expressing itself for the first time in a very long time. The heat that came out of it was not simply high temperature. It was intention. It gripped my skin with specific force, and the stench that came with it was scorched soil and rot so old it had moved past biological and into geological, a foulness that had been festering in the dark for centuries with no agenda except to wait.

From the abyss the vines came.

Thick as serpents, glowing with the specific green that the Emerald Gem also carried, though in an inverted register, in the register of threat rather than pulse. Their thorns caught the light from the crystal veins in the cavern walls and threw it back sharpened, and the sound they made moving through the air was a shriek that was less sound and more anguish, the specific cry of something that had no preference about what it destroyed as long as it destroyed something. I spun, and the nearest vine passed close enough to my face that I felt the air displacement before the pain registered across my cheek, warm and immediate and sharp with copper.

Blood hit the cavern floor.

I did not stop moving.

The crystals burst from the walls in the same moment, jagged and singing, their edges producing a sound that was halfway between a note and a scream, and the ground shifted beneath my feet in the specific way of things that had decided my weight was no longer welcome. I moved across it the way I had learned to move across unstable ground in the years when stable ground had been a luxury I could not rely on, with the constant readiness to redirect my weight at a moment's notice, reading the surface two steps ahead and trusting the reading even when it contradicted what my eyes suggested.

Then the fire.

Not the ordinary kind. Not the kind I could categorise and set at a managed distance in my mind. This was conscious, rage given form, emerald and gold spiralling into a storm of molten intent that did not consume so much as it evaluated. It swept over me with the force of a tidal wave made of judgement and the heat of it was secondary to the weight of it, the specific pressure of something ancient and entirely serious asking a question in the only register it had. The question was not in words. It was more fundamental than words. It was the question the Whispering Stones had asked and the Trials had asked and the earth's pulse had been asking since

Grizedale, the question that everything in this land kept returning to with the patience of something that intended to get an answer.

Are you what you claim to be? Or will you burn?

I held.

Not through strength, exactly. Not through the controlled fury I usually converted difficulty into. Through something more stripped down than that, through the specific residue of a man who had been scoured down to his essential components by three Trials and a night in a glade older than language and the loss of the only person who had ever looked at him with knowledge and not just approval. I held through what was left after all of that. Whatever name that had, I was standing in it.

Through the fire, Myrcanthor was visible.

She stood beyond the flames with the stillness of something carved from permanence, her scales shifting and pulsing and catching the fire's light and doing things with it that fire was not supposed to do. Her size was relevant and was also beside the point. Her wings were unfurled now, vast and veined with the specific texture of things that had been tested by centuries of genuine consequence, every scar a story about the last time something had thought it could break her. Her gold eyes were on me through the flames and they had changed quality, very slightly, in the way that things that were done measuring sometimes changed when they arrived at a number.

"You understand." The words crackled from her, suspended between something that was not quite a question and not quite a verdict, in the specific territory between doubt and something I was not certain I deserved yet.

My breath was ragged and tasted of blood and ash and the Gem at my chest was burning with a heat that I had learned to move toward rather than away from. I met her gaze. My spine held itself straight through a decision I was not aware of making.

"I don't seek dominion." The words came out stripped and honest in the way that words came out when there was nothing left to protect them with. "I seek accord."

Time held itself.

Not metaphorically. The cavern went genuinely still, the fire banked, the vines motionless, the crystals silent, everything in this space waiting on the outcome of the specific calculation happening behind those gold-void eyes. I stood in the centre of that stillness with my blood dripping from my cheek and the Gem burning against my sternum and the earth's pulse running through my boots, and I did not move, because moving would have been the wrong language for this moment.

"For that," Myrcanthor said, and her voice had dropped to a register that moved through the stone rather than the air, that I felt in my jaw and my ribcage and the soles of my feet simultaneously, "I pledge my strength." A breath. Long. Deliberate. Loaded with the specific weight of a commitment that was not made lightly and could not be unmade. "Not as a servant. As an equal."

The words did not echo. They embedded. Into the stone, into the air, into the ley lines I could feel running beneath the mountain's foundations. An oath of the specific kind that the world itself witnessed and held and did not forget.

She bowed.

The great dragon lowered her head, her crown of emerald and gold descending toward the cavern floor in a motion that was not submission but acknowledgement, the specific recognition of one force by another. I extended my hand, and when my skin met her scale the jolt that moved through me was not simply electrical or simply magical but both of those and something underneath both of them, the specific shock of a bond forming that had no language yet because it had not existed before this moment.

The sky trembled. I felt it through the mountain, through the stone, through the ley lines that ran beneath this place in their vast web of connection. The earth shook with the specific quality of things that were being recognised, the bond between us registering through the world's circulatory system the way any significant event registered, with the pulse of acknowledgement moving outward from the point of contact in all directions simultaneously.

Not magic. Not prophecy. Not the fulfilling of any specific legend or the completion of any particular destiny.

Unity. The simplest and most terrifying version of it.

She did not align with me because I had conquered her or because any ancient text demanded it or because the alternatives had been exhausted. She aligned because she had weighed me against everything she had seen in the centuries she had been watching men make choices and she had found something in me that was worth standing beside. The specific quality of that, of being chosen rather than claiming, settled into my chest with a weight I had not expected.

We returned to Hougun.

It was not a march. Nothing ceremonial, nothing that looked from the outside the way arrivals were supposed to look. It was a reckoning, the specific quality of two forces returning to a place that needed them and had been waiting with the patience of the ancient and the urgency of the dying. Myrcanthor's wings stretched wide over the land and her shadow moved across it like weather, and where her fire swept through the manor's corrupted spaces the rot did not simply die but fled, scrambling back from the specific combination of her fire and the Gem's pulse at my chest and the ley lines responding to both.

The darkness that had been working its patient way through Hougun's stones for years recoiled. Not because it was weak. Because what had arrived to meet it was older and more committed and had no interest in negotiation.

Her breath was wind and judgement. Her roar was not violence but cleansing, the specific quality of a sound that undid rather than destroyed, that stripped the corrupted layers away and left what had been underneath them before the rot had taken hold.

I stood in the courtyard with my shoulders carrying what they carried and watched her work, and I felt the balance she had spoken of during the descent, the thing she had articulated from centuries of watching power without that balance consume itself and the world around it. She had watched kings choke on what they had claimed. She had watched civilisations collapse from the specific internal weight of power held without the wisdom to proportion it. She had learned. And she was teaching me, not with instruction but with presence, with the daily accumulated evidence of what it looked like to be genuinely powerful and genuinely responsible simultaneously.

In the darkest parts of the nights that followed, when Eryndor's absence pressed hardest and the weight of the choices I had made at Hougun was most concentrated and the guilt that lived below my sternum was loudest, it was her voice that moved through the Gem and into my blood with the resonance of something large and permanent and entirely certain of its own continuity. Not comfort in the soft sense. Something more durable than that.

The bond had been forged in the fire of the Emerald Crags and sealed in the earth's acknowledgement of it, and it whispered through the ley lines beneath Hougun the way the ley lines whispered everything, constantly and without pause, available to anyone who knew how to listen.

I was no longer only a lord. I understood that now, not as a title or a designation but as a lived reality, a transformation that Myrcanthor had confirmed rather than produced. She was the last flame of the wild world, my sentinel, the constant in a landscape that had proven, repeatedly and without apology, that nothing else was guaranteed to remain.

And she had chosen to stand beside me.

Not because I had earned it in any way I could quantify.

Because I had stood in front of her fire and held, and she had been waiting a very long time for someone who could.

CHAPTER FOUR - THE SAGA OF BLADE ASHENFANG

TWO FORCES SHAPED WHAT I BECAME BEFORE HOUGUN Manor had a name for what I was. The first was Myrcanthor. I have already told you what she was. What she cost. What it meant to stand in front of her fire and not break, and what I carried back from the Emerald Crags in the bond we sealed in the earth's acknowledgement of us both. She was old in the way mountains were old, the way rivers were old, and she had watched enough men destroy themselves reaching for things they did not understand to know the specific quality of a man who was going to reach for them anyway.

The second had a name I had heard before I sought it. Whispered in corners where the light did not reach, spoken in the specific register people used when they were not certain the thing they were naming was not listening.

Ashenfang.

Not made for men. Not made for gods, exactly, though it had been born in the same event that made the world, in the place where molten fury met the newborn universe and the collision produced things that were supposed to remain theoretical. It pulsed with the rhythm of that original violence. Not sound, something underneath sound, the frequency at which creation remembered destroying itself in the process of becoming. It connected everything, life and death, destruction and rebirth, and it did not whisper of these things gently. It spoke of ruin first and glory second, and the truths underneath both were the kind that broke the architecture of the mind if you looked at them directly.

Even Myrcanthor said its name carefully.

We were in a stone-lit chamber, her vast form making the space feel finite in a way it had not before she occupied it. The shadows in the corners had relocated themselves to avoid her, which I had begun to understand was a thing they did in her presence, a form of structural acknowledgement. Her voice, when it came, had dropped below its usual register, below the level at which stone resonated, into something that pressed against the inside of my chest.

"To rule," she said. "To guard what is yours." She paused, and the pause was not hesitation but deliberate measurement, the specific beat of someone deciding how much to give me. "You must first face what lives within you. Your strength. Your shadow. Your fire."

I held her gaze. "That's not an answer."

"No." Her eyes did not move from mine. "It's a map."

That was all she gave me, and it was more than it sounded, and I spent the following days understanding that the information I actually needed was not the information she had declined to provide.

The altar was in a place I found through the Gem rather than through any practical navigation, the pulse at my chest leading me the way it led me through the Wastes, with the specific directional certainty of something that had decided the destination before I had. Ashenfang lay half-buried in scorched stone, and the first thing I registered about it was not its appearance but its presence. A low ember of living flame moved in its core, sending slow spirals of smoke into the still, heavy air, and it did not reflect the light available to it. It took that light in and gave nothing back, and the shadows around it had deepened in direct proportion to the depth of what it was absorbing.

It was not simply powerful. It was awake.

The veins of molten red across its surface moved like the surface of a cooling star, like something that had been burning for so long it had evolved past the need to look like burning. Beneath the fury, a rhythm. Not sound. Sensation. A heartbeat so old it predated the word for heartbeat, watchful and unforgiving in the specific way of things that had been disappointed before and had incorporated the expectation of disappointment into their fundamental character. The scent surrounding it was not iron, not rust, not the ordinary smell of steel. It was scorched bark. Embers from forests devoured before I was born. The specific smell of burnt blood soaked deep into soil that had no interest in releasing it. And under all of that, sulphur, the bitter residual trace of something the land itself had tried to bury.

Ashenfang did not rest. It waited. With the specific patience of something that understood waiting better than anything else because it had been doing it since before patience was a concept with a name.

Myrcanthor had spoken of Aerondor once, in the particular way she spoke of things she had watched rather than heard about. A titan among men, she had said, but the emphasis she gave the word titan was not about physical scale. It was about the quality of his will. He had not carried Ashenfang for conquest. He had carried it for correction. He had judged chaos and found it wanting and bound it with chains forged from the fire of the earth itself, and he had won, and in winning he had understood what he was holding with a clarity that most men who touched the blade never lived long enough to achieve.

He had seen its hunger. Not for victory, she said. For annihilation. The specific desire of a thing that had been born in the event that almost unmade the world and had never fully resolved its relationship with the memory of that near-unmaking. He had been wise enough and frightened enough, two qualities she seemed to believe were inseparable, to cast it into Caldera's Maw, the fissure at the world's heart where fire did not die, where it had slept for centuries in the company of things that burned and did not diminish.

When she said the blade's name again in my presence, I heard the silence shift. Not the silence of absence. The silence of something that had been waiting to be called by someone and had just heard the call.

Ashenfang had waited long enough. The question it was waiting to answer was whether I was worthy of it or merely another name for the long list of people it had destroyed in the process of finding out.

The weight of Hougun Manor had settled into my bones in the weeks following the battle. Not metaphorically. I felt it in my spine when I stood still, in the specific pressure of everything the title meant pressing down through the crown of my skull and lodging somewhere in the thoracic vertebrae, immovable and constant. My enemies, the ones with swords and the ones with patience, were growing bolder in the way that things grew bolder when they sensed that the thing opposing them was carrying more than it could comfortably manage. They were not wrong. The steel at my hip had begun to feel insufficient in a way I could not quantify precisely but could not ignore. It was the right size and the right weight and it had served me in every context I had ever needed it to serve me, and against what I could feel gathering in the deep places of the world, it was not going to be enough.

Myrcanthor said Ashenfang could rewrite reality. She said it the way she said most things, with the specific restraint of someone who was giving me the truth but withholding the part that would have changed my decision. I had learned enough about her by then to understand that this was care rather than deception, that the things she withheld were the things that had broken the people who received them before they were ready, and that she was betting on me being different.

I was not certain she was right. I went anyway.

The dark tomes that mentioned Ashenfang mentioned it the way the forest mentioned predators, with the specific language of things that had been encountered and survived by very few. Their pages carried the final words of seekers who had reached Caldera's Maw and gotten close enough to understand what they were reaching for, and the common thread in those final words was not bravery and not despair but something in between, the specific register of people who had been shown the cost in full and had reached anyway.

I understood them in a way I had not when I first read them.

The Ashen Wastes announced themselves before I could see them. The air changed first, the way air always changed in places where something significant had happened to the land and the land had not recovered from it, loading itself with the specific weight of scorched stone and a rot so old it had moved past biological, past geological, into something that had no category in any system I had been taught. The sky above the Wastes was bruised, purples and greys that had the specific quality of skin over old damage, and the wind did not move through it the way wind moved through ordinary air. It screamed. It threw embers that found the exposed skin above my collar and the backs of my hands with the specific targeting of things that had been doing this long enough to know where to look.

Smoke and iron settled on the back of my tongue and stayed.

The cave that housed the blade was not shaped by any process I had encountered before. It had not been carved or worn or gradually hollowed by patient geological force. It had been produced by an event, something that had happened here with such concentrated violence that the rock around it had simply reorganised itself in response. The walls pulsed with veins of fiery red that beat with a rhythm I was already familiar with, the heartbeat of Ashenfang moving through the stone the way the ley lines moved through Hougun's foundations, insisting on its presence through every medium available.

Beneath my boots the stone throbbed with heat that climbed upward through the leather and into the soles of my feet and settled in my ankles like a brand. Not random heat. Intentional heat. The specific warmth of something that was paying attention to what was walking across it.

The air buzzed with the specific electric quality of spaces where very old power had been concentrated for very long periods, minerals and mystery and the particular tension of potential that had not been discharged in longer than the stone could remember. Dust coiled upward in the still air as I moved through it, rising like something waking, and the ground cracked beneath my weight with the brittleness of ash compressed over centuries, releasing slow spirals as I stepped. The magma beneath was not distant. I could feel it through the soles of my feet the way I felt the ley lines, as a presence rather than a heat, biding its time with the specific patience of forces that had always moved on geological timescales and found my urgency, my human urgency, faintly beside the point.

The elementals found me before I found them.

I heard them first as the screeches of things in genuine fury, not the fury of things that were in pain but the fury of things that had a defined territory and had encountered something that should not be within it. Their liquid forms surged and flickered at the edges of my vision, living manifestations of everything the Wastes contained, wrath and flame given ambulatory form, hunting with the specific efficiency of things that did not need to think about what they were doing because they had been doing it since the Wastes were created. The sound they produced was not sound in the ordinary sense. It was pain delivered directly to the specific places inside the skull where thought lived, each note a precise reminder that I was in a realm that had no category for me and no interest in creating one.

I pressed on. Not through bravado, through the specific calculus of a man who had committed to an outcome and understood that stopping partway through was a different kind of death.

The heat wrapped around me the way Myrcanthor's presence had wrapped around the cavern, intimate and comprehensive, finding every gap between clothing and skin and making its occupation of those gaps permanent. Each breath came in searing and registered in my throat as evidence of somewhere I should not be. And beneath the discomfort, underneath the specific physical toll of moving through a place not designed for human survival, something else moved. Something that had been dormant and was not dormant anymore, ignited by whatever the Wastes were doing to me, jagged and electric and entirely mine.

The Trials of the Maw.

I knew they were coming the way I had known the pulse in Grizedale before I could name it, through the body rather than the mind, through the specific quality of the ground under my feet as I approached the edge of the volcanic chasm and looked down into the place where the world churned with its oldest violence.

The heat from the chasm arrived before I reached the edge. It rolled over me in waves, each one a specific temperature above the last, and the sulphur in the air went from an undertone to the primary note, acrid and bitter and coating the inside of my lungs with each breath in a way that would leave evidence. The rivers of fire below painted the walls in molten light, and the surface bubbled with the specific restlessness of something that was very close to erupting and had been very close to erupting for a long time and was not going to commit to either direction.

The ground beneath my boots trembled. Then something else trembled.

The Infernal Guardian came from the churning depths with the speed of something that had been there waiting and had now received the signal it was waiting for. It rose with the force of an event rather than a movement, molten and massive and entirely focused, its obsidian scales catching the chasm's light in the way Myrcanthor's caught morning light, by doing something to it that light was not supposed to permit. Magma bled from its limbs and hissed where it touched the ground, and the heat radiating from its form bent the air between us into a trembling distortion through which it was difficult to perceive it clearly, which I suspected was intentional.

I was small in front of it. I permitted myself to note this fact and did not permit it to mean anything.

"Only a spirit as steadfast as the Cumbrian Mountains can claim Ashen-fang." Its voice was thunder that had forgotten how to be only sound, each syllable reverberating through the cavern in a frequency that I felt in my back teeth and my sternum simultaneously. The words were not a threat. They were a specification. The specific standard against which I was about to be measured, stated plainly, without the courtesy of ambiguity.

The earth shuddered. The stone itself seemed to absorb the verdict.

I did not have time to process the specific quality of what I was facing before the fire arrived.

A tidal wave of molten fury, the specific fire of a place that had been burning since before the first human being stood upright and looked at the horizon and thought about what was beyond it. It devoured the air in front of it as it came, vacuuming the breath from my lungs before it reached me, and when it hit my skin every nerve in my body registered the information simultaneously. The metallic taste of my own blood mixed with smoke and the specific reek of scorched stone filled my mouth and my sinuses, and the flames howled with the particular sound of things that were not merely burning but intending to.

My muscles locked. My vision narrowed to the specific tunnel that it narrowed to in the moments when the body was trying to decide whether to fight or abandon the premise entirely. Oblivion reached for me, not as threat but as offer, as the specific temptation of the edge of consciousness when remaining conscious was costing a great deal.

The Emerald Gem pulsed against my chest. Cold. Not cold in the temperature sense. Cold in the sense of opposition, of something that had decided to stand on the other side of what was happening to me, providing resistance rather than comfort.

I struck it with my palm.

The shield erupted outward in an emerald pulse, a surge of raw energy that met the fire with the specific violence of two forces that had been heading for each other since before either of them had a name. Fire hit the shield and shattered into light, and the light scattered across the cavern walls in fragments, and for a moment the space was full of pieces of the fire that had wanted to consume me, broken into its constituent parts, each one still hot but no longer assembled into something with unified intent.

I stood with my knuckles white and my legs braced and my lungs burning from the inside and the Gem pulsing against my breastplate with a rhythm that had stopped being subtle. The heat still rolled over me in the aftermath. My arms were shaking with the specific tremor of muscles that had been asked to hold something larger than their ordinary brief.

A sound came out of me. Not chosen. Not shaped. Just the specific raw human declaration of a body that had held when it was not certain it could hold, that had made a decision about what it was and was insisting on that decision in the only register available at that particular moment.

I endure. I resist. I choose.

The darkness that came next was not the darkness of the chasm or the cavern. It was a different medium entirely, a living void with specific weight and specific temperature and the particular quality of something that had been here before and knew how to find the parts of me that ordinary darkness could not locate.

Time moved differently in it. It moved the way tar moved, slowly, with the specific resistance of a substance that had a different relationship to forward momentum than I did. The air, if air was the right word, pressed against me from all directions simultaneously, and the whispers that inhabited it were intimate in the specific way of things that had been inside the architecture of my own thinking for years and were now external. Half-familiar. Half-foreign. They sang in the frequencies I was most susceptible to because I had been the one generating them in the quiet hours since Grizedale.

The figure emerged from the void's deep centre the way the Guardian had emerged from the chasm, with the specific quality of something that had been there before I arrived and had simply been waiting for the right moment of arrival. A throne of bone. A cloak of blood, not metaphorical blood, specific blood, the specific colour and viscosity of blood from bodies that had had reasons for existing before they did not. And the sword in its grip, Ashenfang, dripping not with gore but with ruin, with the specific evidence of everything the blade became when it was held by the wrong kind of purpose.

The figure wearing my face did not look at me with contempt. It looked at me with recognition.

The whispers coiled tighter. Power, they offered. Legacy, they offered. Control, the final one, the one that landed in the specific place inside me where the refusal to be owned had been living since before I could name it. All of it, the entire catalogue of everything I had spent my life moving toward without admitting that I was moving toward it, offered in full, without condition, without the price that everything real had always carried.

I stood at the threshold of that offer and I felt it. I want to be honest about that. I felt the specific weight of what was being offered and I understood it in my body before I understood it in my mind, and the part of me that had been carrying Hougun and Eryndor's absence and the cost of every choice made in the cold calculation of necessity felt the offer arrive like something cold pressed against a burn.

But another voice was already there, quieter than the whispers but more specific, more located, not ambient but directed. Responsibility, it said. Compassion, it said. Choice. Real strength, not the kind that bent the world to its preferences, but the kind that stood inside the storm without becoming the storm, that held the blade without becoming the blade, that had access to everything the tyrant on the throne had access to and chose differently.

I held that distinction in both hands.

The scent of pine arrived. Clean, specific, the particular freshness of Cumbrian air after rain had moved through the valley and left the world smelling like the actual world. Warm wind against my face. Sunlight through the backs of my eyelids, the specific orange-warmth of it.

Everything the void had offered was still there. Still real. Still mine if I reached for it.

I snarled and broke the chains before I had consciously decided to break them.

The vision shattered. Not dramatically. The way things shattered when their structural integrity had been compromised and someone applied the specific force that the compromised point had been waiting for. The darkness fled from the periphery inward, collapsing toward its own centre, and what was left was the cavern and the heat and my own breath, ragged and alive and entirely mine.

I was not a tyrant. Not a butcher. The bone throne and the blood cloak and the familiar face wearing the wrong expression belonged to a path that had been offered and refused, and the refusal was mine.

The Trial of Strength arrived without intermission.

The Infernal Guardian came through the cavern wall rather than through the entrance, which suggested it had been waiting on the other side of it and had grown impatient with the delay. Its fists were larger than most men and they met the stone walls with the specific force of things that had no concern about causing structural damage to their own environment, hurling boulders that moved through the air with the unhurried mass of objects that had simply decided on a direction and could not be meaningfully argued with.

I was not a man in that moment. I was the accumulated sum of every war I had survived and every decision I had made in the moments between life and death, and that sum moved through the cavern with the specific economy of something that had been tested enough times to have developed instincts that bypassed deliberation entirely. I twisted. Ducked. Read the angle of the next strike in the quality of the Guardian's weight distribution and moved before the strike had finished forming.

When its blow came down I raised my blade.

Ashenfang met molten flesh and the sound that produced was not the sound of steel meeting ordinary resistance. Steel screamed and fire roared and the impact travelled up both my arms and into my shoulders and settled in my spine as evidence of the Guardian's absolute, unrelenting power. I pressed forward. Not because pressing forward was the tactically correct decision. Because retreat had never been the decision and was not going to become the decision here.

The cavern thundered around us, metal and fire and stone in a combination that had no analogue in anything I had experienced before, and each impact through my arms carried the specific shock of forces that were larger than my body was designed to manage. My muscles were screaming in the register below sound, the register of tissue being asked to do more than its architecture was built for. The Gem at my chest pulsed wildly, beating against my breastplate with the rhythm of something that had been waiting for this specific moment, and the ley lines moved through my veins with the specific current of everything I was connected to through Hougun's foundations and the bond with Myrcanthor and the earth's ancient pulse.

The moment came.

I felt it before I saw it, the specific shift in the Guardian's balance that indicated the gap between what it intended and what its body could deliver in the next half-second. I pivoted. The Gem's pulse surged up through my chest and into my arms and into the blade, and the emerald flames that erupted along Ashenfang's edge were not a technique I had deployed. They were a consequence. The blade and the Gem and the ley lines and everything I was made of converging in the specific instant before the strike landed.

Steel met fire. Fury met the specific resolve of a man who had already refused a throne.

Ashenfang carved through the molten titan with the certainty of something that had always known this was coming, that had been waiting in the forge at the world's creation for this specific strike at this specific moment against this specific thing. The blow split the Guardian's chest and the impact resonated through me like the Gem resonating against the Whispering Stones, as recognition rather than force. Its body did not explode. It shattered into molten shards the way things shattered when their structural purpose had been completed and the structure was no longer required.

It howled. Not in rage. In recognition.

Then silence.

The kind of silence that followed things that had been coming for a very long time. The air was thick with sulphur and scorched bone, and the embers fell slowly through it, each one flickering like the last breath of something that had finally finished. The cavern exhaled a final tremor and went still.

I stood in the wreckage, scorched and bloodied and breathing in the specific shallow way of a body that had been doing too much for too long and was still insisting on doing it. My legs held. I noted this with the remote, detached appreciation of a man cataloguing the immediate aftermath of something that had tried very hard to end him.

Before me, the obsidian altar. On it, Ashenfang.

Not waiting in the way it had waited before, with the patient hunger of something that had not yet decided about me. Waiting in a different register now, the register of something that had watched the Trials and had arrived at its own conclusions and was prepared to test whether those conclusions were correct.

I crossed the cavern to it. My boots scraped against scorched stone, each footfall echoing in the space that had just been full of the Guardian's dying sound and was now occupied only by my approach. The altar pulsed with dark living light, the veins of molten fire webbing through the blackened rock beating with the specific rhythm of Ashenfang's own heartbeat, which I had been listening to since I entered the cave.

The blade glowed with the slow radiant flicker of something that had been burning inside its own dark for centuries and had developed a relationship with the burning. Its light moved across the cavern walls in shadows that did not hold still, that moved with the specific restlessness of things that were not entirely confined to the surfaces they inhabited.

I reached out and closed my fingers around the hilt.

Searing. Steadfast. The blade breathed beneath my grip, alive and specifically aware, pulsing with a warning that was not hostile but honest. And then the eruption.

Power moved through me the way the ley line surge moved through me, except the ley lines had been the world's circulatory system and this was something older, something from before the world had learned to organise its power into systems. White-hot and absolute, illuminating every fibre of my being simultaneously, and the sensation was pain and pleasure in the specific way that things that were genuinely significant were both at once, unable to be categorised as only one or the other because neither category was sufficient.

My breath hitched. Waves of heat moved through muscles that had already been worked past their limits and demanded things of them that they had not agreed to. A deafening hum established itself inside my skull, occupying the space where thought usually lived and filling it with the specific resonance of Ashenfang's will, which was vast and ancient and not organised around human priorities. Iron filled my mouth. The air reeked of burning ozone and the specific smell of things that were close to changing state.

The blade fought me.

Not subtly. With the primal fury of something that had been waiting for centuries for someone worthy and was not yet certain that the verdict from the Trials was final, was testing the verdict by applying everything it had against the person who had just claimed the right to hold it. Its edge gleamed with hunger, the specific hunger of a thing that had been made in the moment the universe almost ended and had never fully resolved its relationship with endings. My knees buckled under the weight of the struggle, not the physical weight but the weight of will pressing against will, the specific contest between what the blade was and what I was and which of those things was going to determine the terms of this relationship.

Surrender was present. I want to be honest about that too. It was present as a real option, as the specific temptation of releasing the contest and letting the outcome settle wherever it settled, and I had been through enough by then to understand why people reached Ashenfang and did not come back.

The Emerald Gem flared.

Not in response to my intention. In response to the contest, the land's own power recognising the specific combination of forces and inserting itself into the space between them, the Gem's steady pulse meeting the blade's infernal fury with the specific quality of something that had been waiting for this meeting the way Ashenfang had been waiting for me. Forces collided in my chest and my arms and the space between my bones, chaos and clarity, fire and stone, threatening to tear the container of my body apart at its seams. Instead, they began to do something neither of them could have done separately. They interlocked. Not merged. Not resolved into something simpler. Interlocked, the specific arrangement of two forces that had opposed each other finding the configuration in which they reinforced each other instead.

Ashenfang was no longer only a weapon.

It was part of me, which is a thing I understood with my body rather than my mind, as a structural fact rather than a feeling. Refined yet ruthless, elegant and devastating, and the flames along its edge now moved like the ley lines moved, with intention rather than random fury, with the specific quality of force that had been given direction by something that understood what direction was for. Each movement of the blade sent the shadows of the cavern swirling in patterns that were not quite random, the untamed force within it now responsive to the context of the hand that held it.

Under my grip it throbbed with a heartbeat. Not mine. Not only mine. The dark steel and the living fire in concert, a rhythm that I would spend the rest of my life learning to listen to in the same way I had learned to listen to the earth's pulse in Grizedale.

Ashenfang had been forged at the edge of creation and the edge of oblivion simultaneously. It was not meant to be wanted. It was meant to be feared in the specific way that things were feared when they were real. Its obsidian edge held the memory of every war it had ever ended and every war it had begun, the whispers of every act of forbidden power that had tried to claim it, heavy with all of it, and none of that weight had transferred to me.

I had claimed it. It had accepted the claim. The distinction between those two things was everything.

I walked out of the Maw with the heat of the Wastes still clinging to my skin like armour, which was the right comparison because it had changed what I was made of in the same way armour changed what was underneath it, not by addition but by pressure, by the specific effect of being tested by something large enough to matter.

Ashenfang pulsed at my side with restrained force, and the restraint was the point. Not because the force was diminished. Because I was now the context in which it operated.

When I returned to Hougun, the blade changed what returning meant.

In battle it moved through shadow and left light in its path, the specific light of something that had decided on a direction and could not be diverted from it. Its arc through the air was not the arc of a weapon being swung. It was the arc of a force that had accepted direction from a hand it had decided to trust. Blood hissed on contact with the blade's heat, vaporising before it could tell the story of the encounter, and the stench of scorched flesh and burning leather marked my passage through every engagement with the particular finality of a verdict that could not be appealed.

But the weight of it.

Each time I gripped the hilt I felt the weight of Ashenfang descend into my bones not as the weight of the blade's physical mass but as the weight of its purpose, the crushing, specific, unrelenting weight of a thing that did not permit carelessness, that demanded I hold in mind simultaneously every life it had touched and every life it was about to touch and the relationship between those two categories. It was not a weapon for conquest. I had understood this before I reached for it. I understood it differently now in the way you understood things differently after you had held them and felt the specific temperature of what they were.

Every strike was measured. Every life taken was a reckoning rather than a victory, an oath fulfilled rather than an enemy overcome. In every clash I fought two wars simultaneously, the external one that left evidence in blood and broken stone, and the internal one between the warrior who understood that force was sometimes the only available language and the Guardian who understood that the use of that language always had a cost and always required accountability for that cost.

I bore both titles. I could not set either of them down. And between them, in the specific tension of carrying incompatible responsibilities simultaneously, the legends grew.

Ashenfang. An infernal blade of fire and judgment, awakened in the hour of greatest need. In the moments when everything else had been extinguished, when the darkness had accumulated to the point where human endurance had nothing left to offer it, the blade ignited with the specific light of my will, brilliant and burning and entirely committed, and the shadows that had been advancing with the patience of things that knew how to wait found something in the darkness ahead of them that was waiting back.

And beside me, as always, Myrcanthor. Not a relic of what the world had been but a living force of what it could sustain if sustained properly, soaring with the specific freedom of something that had chosen its alliances rather than being bound by them. Together we moved through the fractured realm, flame and steel, the wisdom of centuries and the resolve of a man who had held the Trial of Spirit's offering in both hands and set it down, two forces bound by choice rather than chains, which was the only bond that had ever held anything worth holding.

At the centre of my chest the Emerald Gem pulsed with the land's rhythm, anchoring me in the specific way that things anchored you when they were connected to something larger and older than any individual's need. It was a constant reminder of what I served, not power, which was easy to serve and destroyed everything that served it, but balance, which was difficult to serve and required constant vigilance and cost something real every time it was genuinely maintained.

I had not become a legend. I had become the thing that legends were built to contain, the specific human reality of a man who had access to everything and chose it less than he chose what it was for. And in the choosing, the realm held. It trembled under the weight of what moved through it and against it, but it held.

In my fight, the specific fight of a man who had refused a throne and picked up Ashenfang and returned to Hougun with both, hope did not merely persist.

It rekindled, one measured strike at a time.

CHAPTER FIVE – WHISPERS OF THE PAST

THE DAWN ARRIVED WRONG. I FELT IT BEFORE I OPENED my eyes, in the specific quality of the silence outside, the kind of silence that was not the absence of sound but the presence of something that had displaced it. Cumbrian mornings had their own grammar, the low conversation of wind through the fells, water finding its way down stone, the distant argument of birds. All of it was gone. What remained was a stillness so complete it had weight, a physical pressure against the skin, and beneath it the suggestion of something vast holding its breath.

I stood on the south-facing balcony with Ashenfang at my hip and my hands loose at my sides and I looked at what the dawn had done to the land I governed.

The fog had come down from the slopes and was not moving the way fog moved. It wound through the rugged hills with the specific deliberation of something that had chosen its path rather than been carried along it, swallowing the landscape in pieces, consuming rather than drifting. Coniston Lake's surface rippled below the mist line, and the ripples were wrong because there was no wind, because there had been no wind since before I woke, because whatever was moving the water was moving it from beneath.

The air tasted of damp stone and cold iron and the specific quality of embers that had not yet been kindled, smoke from a fire that did not yet exist but was already present in the atmosphere as a fact waiting to become itself. Silver threads in my dark hair caught what little light the morning had managed, and the breeze that briefly stirred them carried nothing except the confirmation of what I already knew.

Something vast had begun to move.

Myrcanthor's breath drifted beside me, slow and deliberate, coiling into the cold air in slow spirals that were more like exhalations of intention than the ordinary respiration of a living creature. Her golden eyes were on the treeline, where the skeletal boughs swayed in a wind that did not exist, in response to a pressure that was not atmospheric.

A tremor passed between us. Not motion, not thought, not language in any form I could parse, but a resonance in the bones, in the place where the bond between us lived below the level of communication. I had learned to read it the way I had learned to read the earth's pulse, not through translation but through the accumulated understanding of a thing felt many times until it became familiar.

The dread was physical. Metallic on the tongue. The specific electric charge in the air before a storm, except that this storm was not one that would pass.

I thought the question before I could speak it, and felt it move between us in the specific frequency of years of shared attention.

"Do you sense it as well?" Her voice came low and resonant, the kind of sound that moved through stone rather than air.

The thought was already rippling through me, weightless and thunderous simultaneously, the way the earth's pulse arrived, not through the ears but through everything beneath them. I kept my gaze on the treeline. The air had thickened around my lungs, not dramatically, not in a way I could point to, but with the specific, quiet suffocation of a presence that was not yet present but was also no longer absent.

"The mystical currents are restless." My voice came out lower than I intended, the murmur of a man careful not to disturb whatever was listening. "The earth weeps. Faint, but getting louder." I paused, because the next question was not really a question. "Can you feel it, Myrcanthor? The discord?"

The growl that came from her was not aggressive. It was geological. A low vibration that passed through the stone of the balcony and up through the soles of my boots and into the bones of my feet before it arrived at my ears, and her tail curled sinuous and taut around the battlement in a motion that was not restlessness but the specific tension of a sentinel that has registered the thing it has been watching for.

The scent of ozone came off her scales, sharp as prophecy.

The magic was wrong. I had known this for several days, had felt it through Ashenfang's pulse and through the ley lines running beneath Hougun's foundations, had been aware of the specific arrhythmic stutter that had replaced the normal rhythm of the power moving through this land. It moved through the foundations of the earth with the quality of a sickness, worming its way into the ley lines the way infection wormed its way into a wound, not randomly but with the specific progress of something that knew where it was going. Someone was wielding it. Not blindly. Not accidentally. With understanding and intent.

The footsteps announced themselves before their owner came into view.

Measured. Deliberate. Each impact on the glacial stone of the corridor carrying the specific weight of a man who had been carrying something heavy for a very long time and had learned to walk in a way that distributed the weight across the entire stride rather than letting it accumulate in any single moment. They struck the manor's floor with a hollowness that the cavernous hush amplified and swallowed in equal measure.

Rowan emerged from the dim corridor and the sight of him told me most of what I needed to know before he spoke. The steward of Hougun Manor had been worn thin by years of quiet vigilance, shaped by the specific erosion of a man who absorbed the troubles of everyone around him and had no system for releasing what he absorbed. He stood in the corridor's shadow with his weathered hands already moving against each other, a tangle of unease so habitual he would not have noticed he was doing it.

The silence between us stretched. Rowan let it stretch, which was not indecision but the specific care of a man who understood that some information required the right moment to enter a room, and was choosing the moment.

"My lord." Each syllable descended like something dropped into deep water, the impact absorbed by the depths before the surface had finished registering it. "The townsfolk have sent a warning." He paused. Long enough for the word warning to find its full weight. "The wells." Another pause, the construction of a sentence designed to arrive at its most terrible part last. "They undulate. No wind stirs the surface."

I watched his hands.

"The livestock will not tread near the manor's shadow." His voice held steady with the specific steadiness of a man who had decided to be steady and was executing that decision with considerable effort. "Their eyes roll white and hollow." He swallowed. "As if seeing what we cannot."

A faint shiver moved through his frame. The specific involuntary kind.

"They whisper of the restless dead."

The words landed with the specific quality of something that had been true before it was spoken and did not become more or less true by being spoken, but became unavoidable.

The air in the corridor had changed around us. Cold and clammy in a way that was distinct from the general cold of a Cumbrian morning, carrying the specific organic undertone of wet decay and something beneath that, something that moved beneath the decay the way the wrong magic moved beneath the ley lines, patient and purposeful and not of nature.

Beneath the stone the earth turned, not by spade or geological force, but by something that did not have a category in any framework I had been given. The silence did not return after Rowan's words. It lingered instead, thick with the specific anticipatory quality of a thing that was waiting for the next development with the certainty that the next development was already decided.

Deep below the manor, something that had been sleeping was not sleeping anymore.

Ashenfang responded before my hand reached for it. The blade pulsed against my hip, a living thing, the specific thrum of dragon-forged star-born steel recognising the twisted resonance of the magic moving through the land and answering it with the specific tone of something that had been built to answer exactly this. The dark steel shimmered faintly through the scabbard, its resonance moving up through my hip and into my side in a way that was less sensation and more the specific communication of something that shared my purpose.

The scent of scorched metal and old embers moved into my nose, mingling with the damp earthen musk rising from below.

"The crypts." The word dropped from me with the specific finality of a thing named that has been known for longer than the naming. It did not echo in the corridor. It simply occupied the space. Rowan's hands twisted harder.

"My lord." He cleared his throat, not from necessity but from the specific delay of a man buying the last moments before words that could not be taken back. "The villagers speak of lights. Unnatural ones." He paused. "Verdant flickers seething in the darkness."

Iron bloomed on the back of my tongue. The specific metallic taste that arrived when what I was hearing confirmed what I had already known at a level below conscious acknowledgement.

Rowan pressed on, because stopping was not an option and he understood that. "Some claim to hear voices rising from the abyss. Incantation."

My jaw clenched against the slow cold fury that had been coiling in my chest since I stood on the balcony and tasted the morning's wrongness. I exhaled once. Controlled.

Myrcanthor stirred beside me. Her wings unfurled with the specific deliberateness of something that did not move imprecisely, each motion intentional, and the air she displaced moved through the corridor in a wave that carried the specific charge of her presence, of the ozone and old magic that lived in her scales and the particular quality of light that crawled across them when she moved. The stone walls caught her reflection in fragments, ghost-fire moving through shadow.

"The preparations begin." Her voice cut through the corridor's accumulated dread with the specific cleanness of a thing that did not participate in dread.

My grip on Ashenfang's hilt confirmed what I had already decided. "I will investigate." The words arrived with the quality of a vow made in the presence of something that would hold me to it. I turned to Rowan. "Dispatch the sylphs. Guard the manor's edge. Nothing enters. Nothing leaves."

I breathed. Slow. The air was already loading itself with decay and shifting bones and waking magic, the specific combination of scents that told me the crypts had been changing for longer than this morning, that the wrongness I had been feeling for days had been building toward this particular confluence without my having the precise language for what it was building toward.

Now I had the language. I descended.

The crypts of Hougun Manor did not smell of simple death. Death was clean in comparison. What met me on the stairs was the specific accumulated rot of centuries, of things buried not merely because they had died but because they had needed to be buried, kept, contained, the scent of history and violence and the specific organic chemistry of promises pressed into stone over generations. Dust rose in spirals from each step, disturbed by my passing, and the walls sweated with moisture that was cold to the touch in the specific way of surfaces that had not been warm in a very long time.

Torches clung to the damp stone and fought their own private war with the dark, their flickering tongues casting shadows that did not resolve into anything definite and were worse for the ambiguity. The chill moved through the narrow press of the tunnel with the specific patience of things that operated on geological timescales and found my urgency beside the point. Each step carried the specific weight of descent, not only physical but something older, the descent of a man moving toward a truth he had been keeping at distance.

Above me, I could feel Myrcanthor's presence as an absence, the massive negative space of a force that was not following me into this particular dark, a silence in the bond between us that was not a withdrawal of attention but the specific stillness of something watching from a distance it had chosen for reasons I did not yet understand.

The tunnel pressed narrower. The thrum of the ley lines deepened through the stone, and the rhythm of them was wrong, arrhythmic, the specific stutter of power that had been interfered with, manipulated, fed from the wrong direction.

The gate.

Iron. Massive. Covered in runes that shimmered with a spectral green light that had no business being as faint as it was, the light of protections that had held for centuries beginning to fail at the specific molecular level of old certainties encountering sustained malice. The sigils were spider-webbed with fine fractures, their precision compromised, the power they contained hanging in the specific precarious way of things that are one more stress away from complete structural failure.

I dropped to one knee and pressed my palm to the cold metal.

It bit through my skin with the specific cold of iron that had been in contact with something beyond ordinary temperature, the cold of proximity to a force that consumed heat as a function of its own nature. The geomantic surge that moved through my palm and up my arm was raw and primal and did not bother with the usual gradient of building to intensity. It arrived at full force immediately, blinding, and beneath it, through it, past the gate and through the stone and into the dark where things that should have remained dead had been conducting themselves for what felt like a very long time, I felt it.

A presence. The specific quality of a thing that was aware of being felt.

"Talon." The sound did not arrive through air. It slithered through the iron itself, through the stone, through the cold that had been building in this tunnel since before I arrived, and it moved into my mind with the specific intimacy of something that had been in there before and remembered the architecture. "Lord of Hougun."

The name in that voice.

My breath caught in the specific involuntary way of a body that has received information it was not structurally prepared to receive. The air had changed around me, thickening with the specific foulness of ash coating the tongue, acrid and bitter, the specific taste of old graves and the secrets they had been asked to hold indefinitely. Rotting stone. The specific smell of something that had been sealed and had been working on its seal from the inside for years.

Daegrith.

The name was already in my throat before I had decided to speak it, because some names arrived rather than being chosen. It tasted of blood and grief and the specific rawness of a wound that had been almost healed for long enough that I had stopped cataloguing it and was now discovering it had not healed at all.

"Daegrith." My voice was the specific tangle of a man who had fought too many things to let his voice break and was currently engaged in that fight. The name tasted of everything I said it tasted of and also of the specific fury of someone who had paid a price for a burial that had not held.

The runes flared. Crimson first, the colour of the specific anger of old protections recognising a violation, bright and furious and fading immediately into the sickly green of something compromised at its source. Then the gate made a sound that was less noise and more the physical expression of stress beyond design parameters, a tortured metallic wail that passed through the iron and into the stone and up through my palm and along my arm and into my spine, and the cold dread it carried was not the dread of danger but the specific dread of confirmation.

I rose. Ashenfang was already in my hand, which was not a decision so much as a consequence, the blade's will and mine arriving at the same conclusion simultaneously.

"If you've crawled back from the void," I said, and my voice came out with the specific quality of fury that had moved past the stage of being hot, "it is not by my invitation." I let the words settle into the gate and the stone and whatever was on the other side of both. "This ends here."

The world shuddered.

The crypt walls wept. Thick fluid bled from the cracks, slow and cold, with the specific viscosity of something that was not water and had not been water, carrying the organic undertone of rot so concentrated it had become a substance rather than a smell. The air turned heavy around me with the specific suffocation of a space that was actively producing something rather than simply containing it.

Then the voice returned, and it was not a whisper anymore. It was weight. A storm given the specific shape of something that knew exactly where to apply pressure.

"The manor needs me, Talon." The words arrived with the specific force of something that had been waiting to say them and had calculated the exact moment of maximum impact. "The grimoire throbs. Its heart of chaos bleeds power beyond your pitiful comprehension."

My heartbeat was loud in my ears, the specific loudness of a body that was maintaining function under conditions it was not designed for and was applying additional resources to the problem. I did not move. My feet stayed where they were, my grip on Ashenfang stayed where it was, and the cold fury in my chest stayed exactly where it was.

"You twisted this land once, Daegrith." Each word came out with the specific deliberateness of iron drawn across whetstone, not slowly but with weight and intention. "I swore on my ancestors' graves it would never happen again." I let the silence after land. "Your schemes end now."

Laughter answered. The specific kind that had nothing of amusement in it, the rattling chuckle of bones grinding, of the dead remembering what aliveness felt like and finding the memory not quite functional. And then the air pressure changed.

"I am not your enemy, Talon." The words moved through the dark with the specific unhurried precision of something that had been composing this sentence for a long time. "Not this time. Open the door." A pause. Loaded. "And witness the truth that will shatter your world."

The words found the specific places in me where doubt lived.

I stood with my palm still carrying the cold of the iron and the geomantic surge fading through my arm and Daegrith's words working their way into the architecture of my mind, coiling tighter with each repetition, finding the hairline cracks that five years of recovery had left behind and applying pressure with the specific expertise of something that had intimate knowledge of the structural weaknesses.

The manor around me trembled. Not from outside force. The specific tremor of a building that was afraid of what it was containing. The ley lines screamed in the stone beneath my feet, their magic recoiling from the presence beyond the gate in the specific way of natural forces encountering something that violated the terms of the natural.

My fingers moved above the iron clasp.

My skin burned with cold. Wrong in the specific way of contact with something that had spent too long in the dark and had taken on the temperature of it permanently. Daegrith's words were still working. Festering. I could feel the doubt taking root in the specific places beneath my sternum where certainty usually lived.

I thought about everything the voice had told me. I thought about the grimoire and the approaching threat and the specific arithmetic of a situation in which the only available asset was one I had buried.

I wrenched the gate open.

The silence that followed was not the silence of absence. It was the silence of dread itself arriving, fully formed, into the space that the gate had been containing, pressing outward and inward simultaneously, occupying every frequency, devouring time.

And within it, waiting with the patient certainty of something that had known I would open the gate, something was there.

I emerged into the surface world and the air did not feel like relief.

My lungs rejected it at first, attempting to purge something that had embedded itself too deep to be displaced by ordinary air. The rot of the underworld clung to the inside of my airways with the specific tenacity of things that had decided on a residence and had no interest in vacating it. My vision swam at the edges in the specific way of a mind that had been asked to hold more than its ordinary complement and was still processing the excess.

The darkness had not merely been around me in the crypts. It had entered me. Had moved through the specific gaps that Daegrith's voice had found and made itself at home in the spaces it occupied. And within that darkness, Daegrith. Gaunt. Ethereal. The specific paradox of a presence that was simultaneously less than a man and more, a ruin shaped by hate across the years of its imprisonment, a husk of malice that had used the time to become more precisely itself.

A broken god shackled by his own damnation. His presence had been a void that consumed the light available to it, and it was not his appearance that had moved through me and lodged there but his words. "An enemy rises, Talon. They hunt the grimoire. If they succeed, this land will drown in a tide of blood and darkness." The specific cold of a voice that had nothing left to lose from honesty. "You cannot stop them without me."

Those words clung to my skin in the surface air the way frostbite clung, specific and localised and impossible to warm out by ordinary means. My resolve had the specific quality of glass under sustained pressure, still intact, but carrying the evidence of the force being applied.

Could I trust a spirit that had held Hougun's heart in its hands and had been poised to crush it? The stones of the manor remembered. I could feel it through my boots, the specific residual memory of near destruction still present in the bedrock, still warning anyone who knew how to listen. And beneath that warning, the specific problem of having no other viable move.

I exhaled. The taste in my mouth was iron and ash and the specific flavour of a decision I might not live long enough to understand the consequences of. The weight of it settled into my spine.

Myrcanthor materialised beside me.

She arrived like weather, less the movement of a physical object through space and more the sudden presence of a phenomenon. The wind at her heels carried sea salt and magic, and the magic clung to her scales with the specific quality of something older than the land itself wearing her as a garment. Her eyes found me immediately, molten emerald searching, dissecting, looking for the specific thing she needed to know without asking it directly.

"Speak." The command arrived as a low rasp, a vibration that moved through the carved stone and up through my boots before it reached my ears.

The wind clawed at my hair and my cloak in the specific way of wind that wanted something. My voice found its way out of me fractured and low, not from weakness but from the specific restraint of a man carrying more than he wants to put words to.

"Daegrith." Even the name was a specific injury in my throat, jagged and rusted. I swallowed. The taste remained. "He swears fealty. Pledges to protect this land."

Myrcanthor's gaze narrowed.

The silence between us was not empty. It was full of everything she had seen in the centuries before me, every promise given and broken, every alliance that had ended in the specific catastrophe of trust misplaced, all of it accumulating in the air between her eyes and mine with the compressed weight of a thousand unspoken judgements.

"And do you believe him?" Her voice was venom-laced and coiled, the specific fury of something that had been here before and had the scars to prove it.

My grip tightened on the stone railing. The sky beyond the manor had deepened to bruised purples and churning black in the specific way of skies that were reflecting something that was happening below them rather than around them. The wind lashed with a force that had nothing of weather in it and everything of the specific elemental response to power disturbed.

"I don't know." The words tore out of me with the specific rawness of a truth that had been under pressure and had finally found a gap to exit through. "But damned if we've any other hand to play."

The growl that moved through Myrcanthor's chest was not rage alone. I had learned enough of her in the years of our bond to distinguish the frequencies, and this one carried grief in it, and warning, and the specific quality of something that had seen this before and was being asked to watch it happen again with the additional insult of having been present for the original.

The stone groaned beneath her weight.

"Then let the bloodbath begin or end." The words arrived not as an oath but as something older. A prophecy wearing the clothing of acceptance. "This is not a fight for land." Her voice had honed itself to the specific edge of a blade that had been sharpened by betrayal rather than whetstone. "This is a battle for the soul of truth itself."

Beyond us, twilight bled across Cumbria in the specific way of light surrendering to something that had been patient all day and had now arrived at its appointed time. The storm gathered above the hills, vast and purposeful, its ink-black clouds churning with the specific violence of weather that had been given something to be angry about. Lightning carved through the sky in jagged lines, and below it the land moved, not in the way of geological event, but in the specific way of something alive and disturbed shifting against its own foundations.

Inside, the grand hall held the specific weight of imminent ruin.

I stood among my council in a chamber that had stopped feeling like a space the living occupied and had begun feeling like a space the living were visiting. The timbers above groaned with the specific voice of wood under sustained pressure from forces not listed in its architectural brief. The stone walls exhaled cold breath with the undertone of corruption waiting at the threshold for an invitation.

By the hearth, Rowan clawed at the rough stone with pale fingers that had already lost their colour, pressing his hands into the rock in the specific way of a man trying to locate something solid in a world that had stopped providing it. The fire behind him had become the wrong kind of eye, flickering with malevolent awareness rather than warmth, painting his hollowed face in the specific light of terror made external.

The scent of wood smoke had changed in the room. Not the comfort of a hearth. The funeral quality of it, thick and acrid, with the specific undertone of a grave left open in wet weather.

"My lord." His voice was dry and desolate in the specific way of a throat scraped raw by everything that had passed through it in the hours before this moment. He turned from the fire. His pupils had been swallowed by the specific darkness of eyes that have seen something they cannot categorise and the lack of category is the most frightening part. "The tombs." He swallowed. "They are awake."

The final syllable did not fade. It embedded itself in the stone and in the air and in the specific silence that followed, which was not the silence of nothing but the silence of everything pausing to confirm what had just been said.

I did not move. My gaze held him with the specific quality of attention that had been trained by years of needing to extract the complete truth from partial information.

Rowan's words moved into the room the way the wrongness moved through the ley lines, not through the air but through the substance of the space itself. I did not hear them. I absorbed them, felt them settle into the specific layer below conscious processing where the most important information lived.

The pressure in the room thickened. The specific pressure of the unspeakable being approached through approximation.

"The villagers consume themselves." His voice had been hollowed out, the specific acoustic quality of a vessel that had held too much for too long and was vibrating with the resonance of the emptiness. "Not whispers, my lord." He stopped. Started again. "Screams." He could not keep them on the same frequency as ordinary words, and he was not trying to. "Not human screams. Not wholly." He shuddered with the full-body violence of a man whose nervous system had received more than it was built to process. "Guttural. Fractured. Wrong. Sounds that clawed at the wind, as though agony had exceeded the capacity of the bodies producing it."

An image moved through my mind unbidden and vivid, the specific intrusion of information that had been building below conscious threshold and had now found its way to the surface. Twisted shapes at the edge of sight. Mist curling around them as they moved against the wind's direction. Living shadow with purposeful architecture.

Rowan's voice cracked into something that was not quite a sob. The fracture of a man who had endured beyond his design parameters and was registering the structural consequence. His hands found his cloak and held it with knuckles that had gone entirely white.

"Unnatural fires." His breath hitched between the words in the specific rhythm of someone maintaining speech through active effort. "Beyond the trees. An aurora bleeding from the earth itself. Not wild. Not random." His voice dropped to the register of things spoken to contain them rather than communicate them. "The ground breathes. It poisons the air." A pause that carried the weight of the word he was building toward. "It's sentient." The word arrived like something being let through a door that should have remained closed. "It listens."

A tremor tore through the manor. The foundations made the specific sound of stone under lateral force that it was not designed to accommodate, and dust fell from the rafters with the specific quality of things that had been disturbed from long stillness, and the timbers above groaned in the chorus of old wood remembering what stress felt like.

The hearthfire twisted. Recoiled, which was not something fire did, in the specific way of a thing that had encountered something it had reflexive understanding of and the reflex was retreat. Embers spat with the venom of things expelling a foreign body. The flames blackened at their edges.

Rowan's mouth moved. His lips formed words that his voice took a moment to follow.

"The children." Two words in the specific register of a man who had been trying not to say them and had run out of the ability to continue not saying them. His lips moved again. His voice came back barely above breath, carrying the specific weight of words that should not be spoken anywhere that could hear them. "Their screams pierce the veil of sleep." A pause long enough to hold everything that followed. "They are vessels, my lord." His voice was almost gone. "Vessels for voices that are not their own."

The silence that settled was not the peace of resolution. It was the suffocating thickness of a truth that had been fully spoken for the first time and now occupied the room with the permanence of things that could not be unspoken.

I knew, in the specific way I knew things that my body confirmed before my mind processed them, that this was no disturbance. This was war. The specific kind that began below the surface and arrived at the surface already fully formed.

Outside, the wind screamed against the windows with the specific desperate force of something trying to get in through a barrier it understood was keeping it out. The manor groaned, its bones trembling with the specific vibration of old stone encountering a force it had not been built to resist. Below the stone, in the specific dark of the crypts and the ley lines and the earth's deep channels, the thing that had woken was not waiting patiently. It was applying itself.

"The earth heaves." Rowan's voice had thinned to the specific quality of something produced by a man who was not certain he would still be standing when he finished the sentence. "The tombs rise."

What followed his words was not silence. It was presence. The specific arrival of something that had been approaching and had now arrived, pressing against the edges of the space with the patient certainty of something that had already decided the outcome and was simply waiting for the physical events to catch up.

The cold moved beneath my skin with the specific quality of something that had come through the gate, that had followed me from the crypts in a form I could not see, and was now coiling around the specific architecture of my doubt with the expertise of intimate knowledge.

I set my jaw. "And the ley lines? Any disturbances beyond the manor walls?"

Rowan hesitated. A shadow moved across his face in the specific way of a man who has one more piece of information and has been calculating whether delivering it will be the thing that breaks the room entirely. His eyes went briefly to the floor, to the specific polished stone that had been witnessing this conversation, and then returned.

"The sylphs bring ominous tidings." Each syllable carried the specific weight of someone who had been hoping to be wrong. "The magical current weakens at the woodland's southern edge. Near the ruins of Grizedale."

The name moved through the room the way Daegrith's name had moved through the crypt. Not sound but arrival. Grizedale, where the Whispering Stones had looked at me and found the thing they were looking for. Where everything had begun. The specific taste of that name was rot and the particular cold of a wound that the land had been carrying long enough that it had integrated it into its own tissue and could no longer distinguish it from the original.

I turned to Myrcanthor. Her massive head rested against the carved windowsill with the specific stillness of something that had been listening to this entire conversation from beneath the conversation's surface level, tracking the information that was not being said alongside the information that was. The storm outside moved in the molten emerald of her eyes, reflected and refracted, and she did not blink.

"It's consistent." Her voice was a low resonant hum that moved through the stone of the windowsill and into the wall and through the floor, threading itself into the foundation. "The ley lines converge beneath Grizedale. If they seek to shatter the land's essence, that is where they will strike first."

I tightened my grip on Ashenfang's pommel. The steel pulsed in the specific way of a blade that had been listening along with everyone else and had arrived at the same conclusion. I gave Rowan his orders, the sylphs to the ruins, watch the shadows, report anything that moved, each instruction delivered with the specific economy of a man who understood that time was already in shorter supply than the situation deserved.

Rowan vanished before the words had fully settled.

I turned back to Myrcanthor. The firelight between us was the specific warm amber of something that was trying to provide ordinary comfort in a room that had stopped being ordinary several hours ago.

"Do you hear it?" My voice dropped to the register of things said between two beings who did not require volume to communicate. "This is no mere tremor of the ley lines."

Her tail flicked once. The specific minimal motion of something that did not waste movement on anything except precision.

"I perceive it," she said. "And so do they."

Beyond the storm, beyond the trembling light of the manor's torches, something was listening. Had been listening. Was already moving in the specific patient way of things that understood they had time and had chosen to use it.

What moved through Myrcanthor's chest next was not a growl. It was a sound pulled from the specific depth of something older than her scale and claw, a groan that belonged to the veins of the earth rather than the anatomy of a dragon. "A presence stirs." The words moved through the twilight like smoke through cold air, coiling, slow, specific. "A foreign presence. A thing that does not belong."

The night exhaled around us. A hush that was not the hush of peace but the specific hush of things that had been moving and had now reached their positions.

I moved through the dim corridors toward the armoury, and the manor moved around me the way it always moved, with the specific awareness of a building that knew everything that happened within it and kept its own counsel about most of it. The armoury was not a room of steel and iron storage. It was a reliquary, the specific accumulation of every war that had shaped Hougun into what it was, objects that carried the weight of the decisions that had produced them, whispering from the walls in the specific language of things that remembered.

My breastplate's emerald-encrusted emblem caught the flickering light of the sigils and threw it back sharpened, the specific quality of an heirloom that was more than decorative. The magic in it pulsed with the ley lines' rhythm, the specific resonance of a connection that had been present since before I understood what connections meant.

My fingers found Ashenfang's hilt with the specific familiarity of a hand finding its way in the dark to something it has touched ten thousand times before. The sword moulded to my grip with the specific warmth of a blade forged in dragon's breath and tempered by the earth's oldest power, and it pulsed beneath my fingers with the specific alive quality of a thing that shared my purpose and was prepared to serve it.

The soft knock fractured the corridor's specific hush.

I turned sharply.

A shadow in the doorway, haloed by the lantern's attempt at light. The dim glow reached for her and found the fragile defiance etched across her face, the specific combination of features that told the story of a person who had been building armour for a very long time and had gotten very good at it and was still being held together by the effort of the construction.

Lira stood with the specific quality of a blade at breaking point. Storm-lit eyes that burned with a war she had not stopped fighting, and behind the composure, behind the control drawn taut across the raw ache beneath, the weight of a thousand things pressed and not released. Fear was there. Doubt was there. And the specific quality of a person who had been performing adequacy for so long in front of someone who never confirmed it that they had begun to perform it in front of everyone including themselves.

She wore red in the specific shade of war rather than morning, her cloak pooling around her boots with the quality of blood spilled in a fight rather than the gentle fall of fabric, a challenge hurled at fate rather than a choice made for comfort. The auburn in her braids caught the lantern's light in the specific way of hair that had been attended to with great care, each strand woven with the ritual precision of someone who controlled the things they could control. But the ends were damaged, and her fingers had not mended them, which was information about the distance between what she managed and what she permitted herself.

I had spent enough time reading people to read this one without her knowing she was being read.

"I did not intend to trespass." Her voice was tempered steel, the specific quality of control applied to something that wanted to be something else. "But I deemed it necessary that we speak."

I studied her. My gaze carried the specific quality of attention that did not offer reassurance as a byproduct and was not going to offer it here. I let the silence do its work.

"You must be Lira." My tone gave nothing except the fact of the statement.

She inclined her head and stepped forward into the armoury, into the scent of old steel and oiled leather and the specific dust of things that had been here long enough to have opinions about the present situation. She did not hesitate at the threshold, which told me something about her relationship with spaces that should have stopped her.

"Indeed. And you are Lord Talon." Her voice carried a quiet edge, drawn taut between defiance and something beneath the defiance, a hunger searching for something she had not named.

"If you've come to defend your father's sins, you'll find no mercy here." I remained exactly as still as I had been since she appeared. The specific stillness of a man who does not move toward things until he has information about what they are.

Her gaze did not waver. Not for the duration of a single breath.

"I'm not here to justify him." Her voice held with the specific quality of a blade laid flat against a throat. "But I am here because of his legacy."

"Enlighten me." Two words carrying the specific weight of all the words not included.

Her fingers moved to her mantle's edge, a motion barely visible, a tremor at the boundary of her control, the specific small breach in the armour's seal that she would correct in a moment and hoped I had not seen. She had calculated what to say next and the calculation was visible in the very slight pause before it arrived.

"My father's failures are his own." Her voice was steady with the specific steadiness of someone who had rehearsed this part. "I don't seek to lessen the weight of the ruin he left behind." She paused. Then gave me the thing she had been building toward. "But he loved this land, Lord Talon. So much that even in death he bound his soul to it."

The words descended into the armoury's accumulated silence with the specific quality of something landing in deep water, no splash, just the displacement of what had been there before.

Outside, the wind screamed against the stone with the specific urgency of a thing that had heard her and was responding. My eyes narrowed.

"And what is your aim, Lira?" My voice was a blade being examined rather than drawn, cold and precise and entirely focused. "To absolve him? Or to redeem yourself?"

She did not flinch. She stepped forward, shoulders squared with the specific deliberateness of someone who had decided before entering this room that she was not going to flinch, and was executing that decision.

"I seek neither." Her gaze locked with mine and held it with the specific quality of someone who had nothing left to lose from honesty. "I aim to protect what he could not." She let me hold that. Then she gave me the rest of it. "The grimoire stirs, Talon. If it falls into the wrong hands, it will not merely corrupt." A breath. "It will consume. This land. Your manor. Everything you hold." She did not look away. "It will burn."

My grip on Ashenfang tightened. The blade pulsed against my palm with the specific rhythm of a warning delivered through the only channel that never lied.

"Someone has secured the grimoire," I said. "No one can access it."

Lira's mouth tightened. A small motion, the specific compression of someone who has information that contradicts what they are hearing and is deciding how much of it to deliver.

"For now," she said. The two words carried the weight of everything they excluded. "But a force is coming, Talon. One far beyond my father's shadow." Her breath hitched. The single involuntary motion she could not prevent. "One that does not seek power." The pause she gave the next words was the specific pause of someone who needed them to land correctly. "It feeds on it. Craves it. And it twists it into a horror beyond comprehension."

The wind moved through the turret's arrow slits in the specific long, cold exhale of something that had been listening.

Myrcanthor was still on the window ledge where I had left her. Beneath her scales and the centuries of accumulated memory they carried, I knew, because the bond between us carried things that words did not, that a battle was being waged. She had not always been a creature of distance. There had been a time, buried deep enough that she did not refer to it directly, when she had acted, when she had lent her fire to kings and queens and whispered her wisdom into the ears of those she had believed were worth it, and every one of those investments had ended in the specific catastrophe of trust extended to things that could not hold it.

She had built her distance from that. Each betrayal had added a layer to the specific structure of her withdrawal, until the distance had become a kind of architecture, the only safe relationship with mortal history being the one in which she observed it rather than participated in it.

But the thing she could feel through the storm and the ley lines and the specific wrongness moving through the land's foundations was not a thing that the architecture of her distance could survive. She had tasted this before. Old. Familiar. The specific thing that came back again and again no matter what was done to seal it.

Her talons pressed into the stone of the window ledge in the specific way of something applying force to a surface that it needed to remain attached to.

She turned her gaze from the horizon, but the storm continued in the corner of her vision, the malignant flame on the far edge of the land that was not fire in any sense she recognised. Not wild. Not accidental. The specific flavour of it on her tongue was wrong in a way that went back further than her own memory, back to the specific wrongness of things that had been present at the world's near-unmaking and had never fully resolved the experience.

If she acted, she shattered the last wall between the protected distance she had built and the world she had built it against. If she did not, she watched. Again. While the land cracked and mourned and the people in it drowned because the things that could have helped them had decided that helping cost too much.

Talon. The magic that ran through Ashenfang and through the Gem and through the bond between them. Lira with her fire-eyes and the damage she was using as armour. The tombs awake. The veil thinning. The grimoire stirring with the specific appetite of something that had been waiting for the right hands.

She could not afford silence. The specific calculation was complete, and the cost of action was real, and the cost of inaction was worse in the specific way that the worse cost was always the one you lived inside rather than the one you chose.

Myrcanthor turned her head back to the horizon, the storm braiding through her spines like prophecy.

She would not rush to the war. She was not built for rushing. But when she came, she would not come quietly, and whatever was waiting on the other side of the thinning veil was going to find out what it meant to have been patient long enough that the last of the great dragons had run out of reasons to stay still.

CHAPTER SIX – THE GRIMOIRE AWAKENS

THE STORM HAD A MIND. I HAD LIVED INSIDE CUMBRIAN weather long enough to know its moods, the ordinary fury of a fell squall, the specific grinding persistence of rain that had decided on three days and intended to deliver them, the particular cold that came down from the peaks carrying ice in its lungs. I knew all of these. This was not any of these.

The rain fell in sheets that had direction, the specific directional quality of something applied rather than fallen, each impact on the manor's stone a separate percussion in a rhythm that was too consistent, too organised, to be the product of wind and chance. It had been building since before dark, and in the hours of its building I had felt it through the soles of my boots and through the walls and through Ashenfang's pulse at my hip, and what I had felt was intent.

The wind found the turrets and the gables and moved through them with the specific sound of a dirge, the low mournful resonance of air being forced through old stone at frequencies that the stone was not designed to produce. Shutters rattled with the urgency of things trying to communicate through the only medium available to them. The trees I could see from the study window were not bending in the way of trees accommodating force. They were bending in the way of things that had been pressed to their limit and were approaching the question of whether they would return from this or not.

Inside, the air crackled. The specific electric quality of a space that had absorbed too much charge from the storm outside and had stopped being merely a room and become an environment with its own weather. The lamps fought the dark with the desperation of small things contending with something very large, their flames twisting in drafts that came from directions I could not locate.

I did not look up from the map.

My hands were steady over its surface, the specific steady of twenty-five years of learning to keep my hands steady regardless of what the rest of me was doing. The map lay unfurled on the polished oak desk with the worn and tattered edges of a thing that had been handled with reverence for a very long time, that had absorbed the attention of every serious moment it had been present for and carried that absorption in the texture of its surface. It was not simply parchment. I had understood this from the first time I held it, had felt its pulse against my palms in the specific way that the Whispering Stones had pulsed, as the thrum of something alive that had decided to make itself known.

The ley lines traced across its surface in luminescent strands that shifted when I looked directly at them and held more still when I looked slightly away, the specific behaviour of things that did not want to be fixed. Where they converged, runes shimmered faintly, the specific faint shimmer of protections that were present but were not at full capacity, and the pattern of those convergences had been changing. Subtly. In the specific incremental way of things that moved when you were not watching and arrived at new positions between observations.

The map showed me Hougun's silhouette against the evening sky in stark ink, its spires carrying the weight of their history in every line. Nearby, the crumbled ruins of Grizedale lay in their shadow, overrun and absorbed, the specific quality of a place where something had been defeated and the land had been given the task of processing what remained. Sacred groves nearby, their roots pressing into soil that still pulsed with the specific rhythm of a time when the power in this land had not yet been organised into ley lines because it had not needed organisation, because it had simply been everywhere.

Lira stood across the desk.

She had been studying the map with a precision that had caught my attention before I had consciously decided to be paying attention to her. Her gloved fingers traced the ley paths with the specific care of someone who was not simply reading a map but recognising something they already understood, confirming information rather than discovering it. She moved across Grizedale's battered shape and her fingers lingered.

"This is where they'll strike first." Her voice was low and carried the specific weight of certainty arrived at through evidence rather than instinct.

"The convergence is weakest here. If they fracture it, the entire ley network collapses." She looked up from the map, and her gaze was the specific gaze of someone who has already considered every alternative and has eliminated them. "The barriers shatter. The wilds uncoil. Everything we've worked to protect crumbles to dust."

The words settled into the room with the specific weight of accurate things that no one wanted to be accurate.

Lightning split the sky outside the study window with the violence of a world trying to communicate something in the only register that would be heard. In the flash of it, the landscape beyond the glass erupted briefly into full visibility: trees bent at angles that should have broken them, rain blurring the horizon into a moving wall, and in that half-second of silver illumination I felt something that was not the storm.

Old. Watchful. Occupying the storm the way a predator occupied cover, using the chaos of it as concealment while it assessed the space it intended to move into. Not arrived yet. But not far. And fully aware that I could feel it.

I looked to Lira.

The shadows moved across my face in the lamplight, and I was aware that this was information about me she did not have, that my expression was in the dark and hers was not, and I let it remain that way.

"You know the ley lines well." I kept my voice at the specific register of a statement that was also a question that was also an accusation delivered as neither. "A peculiar mastery, considering your claims to stand apart from your father's legacy."

She held my gaze with the specific quality of someone who had been expecting this line of questioning and had decided in advance not to flinch at it.

Her jaw tightened. One small motion. The only concession her body made before her voice arrived, perfectly controlled. "Knowledge doesn't equate to guilt, Lord Talon." Not defensive. The specific precision of a person who had made this distinction so many times in private that they could deliver it in public without the rough edges. "My father taught me because he believed these places mattered." A pause. Not for effect but for accuracy. "His choices may have been flawed. Destructive, at times. But his intent was clear. To protect what we were all too willing to forget."

Outside, the wind made the specific sound of a thing that had been restrained and was no longer being restrained.

The glass trembled in its iron frame.

Myrcanthor's presence shifted beyond the window, vast and coiling, and the air in the study changed quality the way the air changed when a significant weather system moved overhead, not the weather itself but the pressure change that preceded it. Then her voice arrived, not through the room but through the specific channel of our bond, moving through my mind like smoke finding the lowest level of a closed space.

"Her conviction rings true." The words misted the rain-streaked glass in some quality I could feel against my skin rather than see with my eyes. Her emerald gaze was on Lira through the window, and the quality of that attention was dissecting, the specific attention of something that had been measuring people against the ultimate outcomes of their convictions for centuries and had developed high standards for the measurement. "But conviction can be a deceiver's mask. Passion obscures reality." A pause that carried the weight of specific historical instances she was choosing not to enumerate. "Trust is a perilous wager."

My knuckles had gone white against the desk's surface. The pressure of my own hands against the polished oak was the specific physical anchor of a man who needed his body to stay where it was while his mind moved through the calculation. The storm churned outside, and inside me something churned in the specific way of decisions that were going to have to be made without sufficient information, which was the only way decisions of this kind ever got made.

"Trust is irrelevant." My voice came out stripped of warmth by the specific process of removing everything that was not precision. "Only truth matters. And the truth demands action."

The words landed between us and held.

Lira did not look away from me. She straightened, the specific straightening of someone who had brought something to offer and was deciding to offer the whole of it.

"I can guide you to Grizedale." Not a plea. Not a negotiation. A statement with the specific quality of a fact she was making available for my use. "There are paths the maps overlook. Trails the trees guard. You cannot find them alone. You must be chosen."

I held her gaze and I held the calculation and I held the memory of everything I had paid to protect this land and the specific arithmetic of what I stood to lose if I got this wrong.

"And why," I said, letting the words carry the full weight of everything unsaid, "should I grant you passage?"

She gave me her answer without flinching toward it or away from it.

"Because what's coming doesn't kill." The room took on the specific quality of a space in which something important was being said, the way rooms
sometimes responded to the weight of language. "It unravels. It strips you
of meaning and hollows you out until you forget who you are." Her voice
held absolutely steady. "Not death. Erasure."

The distinction landed in my chest in the specific place that the Trial of
Spirit had found when it showed me the tyrant on the bone throne with
my face. The specific fear, not of dying but of becoming something that
would not recognise itself. I understood what she was describing in the register of personal acquaintance.

I did not tell her that. But I also did not dismiss it.

The first tendrils of dawn were already working at the horizon's edge when
we stepped outside, turning the sky the specific muted orange and grey of
a morning that had survived a difficult night and was not yet certain about
the day ahead. The storm had not stopped. It had simply shifted quality,
from the furious assault of the hours before dawn to the specific grim persistence of something that had committed to its course and was not interested in finishing before its business was done.

Our footfalls were swallowed by the wind before they could echo. Lira's
warnings moved beside me like things that had taken on physical form, the
specific weight of dread that was not unfounded but was not yet fully

shaped, pressing at the edges of every step. The wind recoiled from the words she had given us in the study the way Myrcanthor had described the wrongness beyond the manor's walls, as though even the air had preferences about what it carried.

The road ahead was not unknown so much as it was a different category of unknown, the kind that was not waiting to become known but had actively organised itself against being understood. A chill moved through me that was not the temperature of the air but the specific cold of certainty, the terrible specificity of knowing that what we were walking toward had the capacity to undo the thing that had survived everything else.

Rowan walked beside us and did not speak. Duty and dread were conducting their private war behind his eyes, visible in the specific tension of a man whose face was doing its best to hold two incompatible things simultaneously, and the cold sweat on his brow was the physiological evidence of how much effort that was costing him. Myrcanthor moved with us in the specific way she moved when she had made a decision she had not yet announced, the silence in her stride carrying the specific weight of something that had been considered and was not yet released.

"Leaving Hougun undefended is reckless." Her voice arrived like stone grinding against stone, each word placed with the deliberate weight of something she had been carrying and had now decided to set down in the open. Shadows moved across her massive face in the dawn's grey light, and in those shadows was the specific quality of worry that she was not accustomed to displaying.

I checked the fit of Ashenfang against my hip. The blade's weight was the specific weight of a vow made in fire and ley line energy, a pledge that had its own gravity independent of mine. "If Grizedale falls, the manor holds no significance." I turned to face them, and the storm light moved in my eyes in the way that things moved when they had already been decided and the decision had been made on the specific level below deliberation where the most important decisions lived. "We defend what lies beyond these walls. That is our purpose now."

Myrcanthor's gaze sharpened with the specific quality of an attention that had been ranging wide and had now narrowed to a point. Her head tilted toward Lira, who stood in the storm with her cloak soaked through and clinging to her in the specific way of wet clothing that had given up the pretence of protection and was simply present, a figure that the wind moved around rather than through, as though it had assessed her and decided not to bother.

"And what of her?"

Lira did not look at Myrcanthor. She held the horizon with her eyes and her jaw was set in the specific way of someone who has heard this question before in various forms and has stopped deciding how to answer it and started simply being the answer.

"Her stake is bound as deeply as ours." My voice held the specific quality of a man who has made a decision he cannot fully defend yet and is not going to pretend otherwise. "If betrayal lurks in her midst, it will be unmasked in time." I looked at Lira, and then at Myrcanthor, and the look I gave Myrcanthor carried everything I could not say directly about the specific nature of the arithmetic I had just completed. "But for now, we stand as one."

The growl that moved through Myrcanthor's chest was not anger. It was the specific sound of a force that had decided to accept a situation it had not chosen and was communicating the precise terms of that acceptance. It moved through the stone beneath our feet and registered in the soles of my boots as both acknowledgement and warning, and the two were inseparable.

"Then I will hold you to that." Not a promise. A blade in the shape of one.

Above us, the sky had become the specific sky of a storm that had been building toward something rather than building toward dissipation. Its belly swelled with light that was the wrong colour for dawn, and its voice rolled through the air in a continuous low frequency that I felt through my sternum before I heard it through my ears. The trees at the manor's edge contorted with the specific anguish of things that had rooted themselves in a particular place and were now being tested by forces that did not take root into account. The wind carried something on it beneath the rain, a presence moving toward us through the storm, using the storm the way the thing I had felt in the lightning flash had been using it. Patient. Methodical. Not yet here.

But coming.

And immune, entirely, to any preference we had about that.

We walked into it together, the four of us, into the specific unknown that was not waiting to be discovered but had been waiting for us to arrive at it, and the dawn light thinned around us as we moved away from Hougun's walls and toward the thing that Grizedale was holding at its convergence, and behind us the manor's stones were already absorbing the specific cold of a morning that was going to ask things of all of us that none of us had yet agreed to give.

CHAPTER SEVEN - THE JOURNEY TO GRIZEDALE

THE NIGHT SWALLOWED US BEFORE WE REACHED THE first tree line. Not the ordinary dark of a Cumbrian night, which I knew well enough to move through without a torch, reading the landscape by the memory of it and by the specific quality of starlight on wet stone. This dark had weight. It pressed against the eyes with the specific force of something that wanted to be impenetrable, and the fog that had come down from the slopes moved through the trees with an intention that had nothing of weather in it.

I rode Nocturne into it and felt the horse read it before I did.

He had carried me through battle noise and siege fire and the specific chaos of things that wanted to end us both, and he had done all of it with the particular steadiness of an animal that had decided fear was not a productive response to danger. But his ears pricked at something in the trees ahead, and his breath went shallow in the specific way of a warhorse that was not afraid but was paying the closest possible attention, and his massive body stilled beneath me the way it stilled when he had determined that forward motion was not yet the correct decision.

My gloved fingers found his flank. Not direction. Just acknowledgement. Something was here. He already knew.

Lira moved through the undergrowth to my left with the specific quality of a person who had been moving through difficult terrain in the dark for long enough that it had stopped requiring conscious attention, her bow across her back, her footfalls placed with the precision of someone who understood that survival in places like this required the ability to be still and moving simultaneously.

The forest spoke in the register I had learned to read since Grizedale. Wind-lashed branches carried the specific groan of old wood under pressure that was not purely atmospheric. An owl cut the dark with a single note and was then absent, which was information. The fallen leaves beneath our feet whispered the specific wet whisper of vegetation disturbed after rain, and beneath that, threaded through the smell of damp pine and cold earth, something else. Not a smell exactly. The suggestion of wrongness. The specific quality of an absence where something should have been present.

The oaks on either side had the specific age that made them look less like trees and more like intentions that had been standing long enough to accumulate bark, their gnarled limbs reaching at angles that looked like choices rather than growth, their bark carved into shapes that the torchlight I was not using would have resolved into faces and probably was better off not doing so. The shadows beneath them moved with the specific restlessness

of things that had been disturbed from a long stillness and were not yet decided about what to do next.

The path narrowed. Not gradually, the way paths narrowed when the
forest was simply dense. In increments that felt deliberate, the trees pressing inward with the specific quality of a thing closing around something it
intended to keep. The canopy locked overhead into the specific darkness
of a sealed space, ribs of old wood forming a vault that admitted nothing
from the sky, and beneath it the air had the compressed, pressured quality
of a space that held more than its volume should contain.

Then the tremor.

Subtle. Barely perceptible through the soles of my boots. Not seismic. Not
the ordinary movement of earth settling or water finding a new channel
beneath stone. This was a pulse. The specific arrhythmic pulse of something that was not the ley lines I had grown accustomed to feeling through
Hougun's foundations but was related to them in the way that a sick version of something was related to the healthy original.

Nocturne stilled completely. His breath went to nothing, his eyes showing
the specific white at the edges that I had only seen once before, in a battle I
preferred not to catalogue. He was not afraid. He was more precise than
afraid. He had determined that the information available required standing still and processing it before any other action.

I pressed my palm flat against his neck and felt the tension in every muscle
of his vast body, coiled and waiting.

"We go on foot." I kept my voice below the level of the forest's ambient noise. Not from fear of being heard but from the specific instinct of not adding unnecessary information to an environment that was already listening with more attention than I was comfortable with.

I dismounted. My boots found the wet earth and it gave beneath me with the specific yield of soil that had absorbed more than it should have, the scent of wet moss rising immediate and thick around my feet. I ran my hand one final time along Nocturne's neck, communicating what hands communicated when words were wrong for the moment, and turned into the dark.

Lira followed without instruction. I noticed her breath was steady in a way that required maintenance, the specific evenness of someone who had decided on a breathing pattern and was applying it against the cold thing uncoiling beneath her ribs, because I could see it in the set of her shoulders, the particular quality of held-together.

She touched the bark of the nearest oak as she passed it. A brief contact, fingers reading the surface, and then she stopped. Not entirely. But enough. Her hand pressed flat against the bark and I watched her face in the forest's dark and saw the specific expression of someone receiving information they had not expected and did not want.

"The wood is dead," she said, barely above breath. "It should pulse. There's nothing."

I knew what she meant before she finished. I had felt it through my boots, through the specific quality of the earth beneath us, the sick heartbeat of something that was the ley lines and was also what happened to ley lines when something had been feeding on them for long enough to change their fundamental character. The forest floor pulsed beneath us with the specific barely-perceptible tremor of something newly awakened, something that had been buried and was now stretching into the space it had been compressed into for so long.

"We need to leave. Now." Her voice came out tight and brittle in the specific way of words being held to a narrower register than the situation wanted to occupy.

"Are you certain." I already was. I asked it because the specific quality of her certainty and the specific quality of my own needed to confirm they were reading the same information.

She turned toward me, and in the specific quality of the dark between us the answer was in her face before she gave it as sound.

Then the forest stopped breathing.

Not a metaphor. The specific cessation of every ambient noise simultaneously, the owl gone, the wind gone, the branch-creak and leaf-whisper and distant water-movement all gone in the same instant, replaced by the specific absence of all of it, which was louder than any of it had been.

And into that absence, the sound came.

Not a growl in the animal register I understood. Not the territorial announcement of something that lived in these woods and had found us in its territory. This came from lower, from the specific frequency below the range of ordinary threat, a guttural breath torn from lungs that had long since ceased to be biological, rising from everywhere and nowhere simultaneously, carrying the grave-cold rot of something that had been sealed under earth for longer than the trees had been standing and had just finished the process of not being sealed anymore.

Then the stench hit.

Lira's breath caught beside me with the specific involuntary sound of a body receiving information through the most primal sensory channel available. Not the rot of flesh in the ordinary sense. Something older. The specific deep corruption of something that had been festering beneath the surface of reality for long enough to have changed the nature of what festering meant, carrying the reek of soil disturbed after centuries of enforced silence, of charred bone, of the specific acrid quality that preceded magic of the wrong kind when it finally broke its containment.

Then the eyes.

Twin red points in the dark beyond the nearest trees. Burning with the cold, steady light of something that had no relationship with warmth. Then another pair. And another. One by one they appeared in the specific patient rhythm of things that were not discovering us but revealing themselves to us in a sequence they had chosen for its effect.

They did not move. They watched.

Every instinct I had cultivated over twenty-five years of situations that wanted to end me screamed the same word, and my body held it, because running into this dark would have been the specific kind of decision that I would not get to regret.

Beside me, Nocturne's muscles shuddered with the contained force of a body that had decided on absolute stillness as its only viable option. His ears were flat. His breath was barely present.

The trees groaned. The branches shifted. No wind caused either.

My fingers closed around Ashenfang's hilt and felt the blade respond the way it responded when the wrongness was the specific kind of wrongness it had been made to answer. The dragon-steel hummed against my palm with the low, hungry vibration of something that had been waiting for a reason to move.

From the dark beyond the red eyes, a shift. Enormous. Awake. Oriented toward us with the specific directional intention of something that had finished deciding whether we were prey.

The whisper began low. Not in the air but in the specific place inside the skull where sound arrived before the ears processed it. A voice that was not a voice. Curling through the spaces between the trees like smoke finding ventilation. "You should not have come."

The specific cold that moved through my blood was not fear of the words. It was the recognition of a category of threat that predated the categories I had been trained to navigate.

"Wyrmhounds." Lira's voice came out half prayer and half identification, her bowstring already drawn in the specific motion of someone who had gotten to the equipment before the decision was fully formed. Her fingers were steady around the wood, but I could see in the quality of the light what it was costing her to make them steady.

They came from the treeline in the specific way of things that had never needed to fear anything and had therefore never learned the aesthetic of approaching. Six of them, slithering into the clearing between one breath and the next, obsidian forms that the dark kept trying to absorb and kept failing, their red eyes pulsing with a rhythm that was wrong in the specific physiological way that the wrong ley line pulse was wrong. Saliva dripped from their maws, black and viscous, hitting the earth and hissing where it landed with the specific chemistry of something that did not belong in contact with living soil.

The stench intensified. I tasted it on the back of my throat, rot and old corruption and the specific foulness of magic that had been forced beyond its designed parameters.

Ashenfang cleared the scabbard before I had finished the decision to draw it, the obsidian blade catching the specific moonlight that reached through the canopy and making something different of it, fractured silver that moved along the edge with more intent than reflected light had any business possessing. The hum in my grip was the specific hum of a weapon that remembered every darkness it had ever been drawn against and had developed opinions.

"Behind me." My voice came out stripped of everything except the specific authority of a command that was not negotiating with the situation.

Lira was already moving. "I fight beside you." Not defiance for its own sake. The specific declaration of a person who had assessed the situation and arrived at the same tactical conclusion independently. Her arrow sang off the string before I had fully registered that she had drawn it, the head carved from dragon bone, and it hit the nearest Wyrmhound with the specific sound of something that had been aimed with the accumulated purpose of a great deal of contained fury.

There was no time to speak again. They were already upon us.

The Wyrmhounds did not charge. They flowed. The specific movement of things for which flesh was a suggestion rather than a structure, their forms shifting as they covered the ground between us in a way that bypassed the ordinary relationship between distance and time. Then they were simply there, a mass of black and bared teeth, and the air twisted around their presence with the specific quality of reality trying to organise itself away from contact with them.

Ashenfang's first arc lit the clearing.

The crescent of its path left a trail of moonlit fire through the dark and met the first skull with the specific concussive force of a blade that had been made for exactly this category of encounter. The skull burst with an explosion of ichor and steam, and the death cry that followed was the specific sound of something that had been animated by the wrong kind of energy departing that energy, a wet gurgling dissolution into the dirt, and the stench of burnt flesh wrapped in twisted magic rose into the cold air and settled into my lungs and stayed.

Lira's second arrow drove home somewhere to my right with the specific decisive sound of something that had been placed rather than simply fired, and the beast's shriek was the sound of bone structure failing from the inside, sharp and then ragged and then absent as the undergrowth accepted what collapsed into it.

Then the world became specific and immediate and nothing outside of it mattered.

Steel clashed against bodies that were not entirely physical and the impacts that came back up my arms and into my shoulders carried the specific information of forces operating in more registers than ordinary flesh. Claws found the gaps in my guard with the specific efficiency of things that had been doing this since before I was born and had had centuries to develop their approach. My breath came in the specific short pattern of combat breathing, every exhalation timed to the work, and the forest floor beneath my feet became the specific stage of blood and shadow that every real fight became, where each second was its own entire world and the one before it was ancient history.

I moved without elegance. Ashenfang moved with purpose. Each swing was survival calculated in the quarter-second available to calculate it, each contact a transaction between my resolve and the wrongness I was trying to end, and the ley line energy moving through the blade added a specific dimension to every strike that I felt as heat up my arms and as light at the edges of my vision.

Beside me, Lira fired with the specific rhythm of someone who had found the exact pace at which desperation and precision reached equilibrium, and every arrow struck something, and every something that was struck made one fewer demand on my peripheral attention. We did not fight heroically. We fought the specific way of people who understood that dying here was the worst available outcome and had organised their bodies around preventing it.

And then silence.

Not the good kind. The specific profound absence of combat noise after combat has ended, the hush that was not peace but the specific acoustic quality of a space in which something very loud had just been replaced by nothing. My chest heaved. The silence pressed against my mind with the weight of the specific contrast between the last sixty seconds and this moment.

We were standing. Both of us. Bloodied and scarred and still drawing breath.

The last Wyrmhound convulsed into a pool of black ichor that the earth hissed against and rejected, steam rising from the contact, and the stench of its dissolution was its own specific category of horror, death and decay stripped of everything biological and left with only the wrongness.

I dropped to one knee and dragged Ashenfang through the wet grass, not in triumph but in the specific ritual of a blade that needed its surface cleared of what it had accumulated, because leaving the ichor on the steel felt like leaving an argument unfinished.

Lira moved through the aftermath with the specific quiet efficiency of someone collecting what they had expended, retrieving arrows from the places they had come to rest. The dark leaned toward her as she moved through it, and I noticed it without intending to, the specific quality of the forest's attention toward a person who moved inside it with the ease of familiarity.

"Competent." The word arrived from somewhere below deliberation, low and without preamble.

She stilled. Her fingers tightened around an arrow's shaft, and then slowly, with the specific deliberateness of someone choosing a response rather than simply having one, a smirk found its way across her face.

"The sentiment's mutual," she said. Dry. Level. Sharp enough to draw something if mishandled.

Something crossed my face that I would not have permitted if I had been paying attention to what my face was doing. The specific unguarded flicker of a man whose defences had been occupied by six Wyrmhounds and had not yet fully redeployed. I turned it forward before it could be examined.

"We move."

The forest accepted us back into itself as we pressed forward, and it was not the same forest we had entered. It had thickened with the specific quality of a thing that had been watching what just happened and had formed opinions about the visitors. The trees loomed with a new proximity, their twisted limbs extending across the path with the specific reach of things that had decided to participate rather than simply exist. The thorns that lined the narrowing track pulsed faintly with their own dim life, roots crossed the path at the specific ankle-seeking angles of things that were not simply growing but placing.

Nocturne shuddered behind us, a sound he had been holding since before the Wyrmhounds and was only now releasing, a thin anxious sound that the silence swallowed before it could travel. He stayed where I had left him. I did not go back.

Lira moved ahead of me through the dark with the specific ease of a person navigating a space that their body recognised even when their mind was occupied with other things, each step placed without visible deliberation, her bow held loosely but with the specific readiness of something one motion from purpose. She moved the way the forest moved, fluid and without announcement.

I watched her without deciding to watch her.

"You've been here before." Not a question. The specific quality of a statement that was also an invitation for information I had not been given and had decided to request indirectly.

The hitch in her stride was barely perceptible. A single step that was slightly different from the ones around it, and then she glanced back, and her expression had the specific quality of a person who had expected the question to arrive eventually and had prepared for it and was discovering that preparation was not the same as readiness.

"Once," she said. The word landed with the specific weight of a thing that was standing in for more. Then the space around it. Then: "Many years ago."

My gaze stayed on the back of her head as she turned forward again. "With your father." The blade-edge of implication, laid flat rather than swung.

Her shoulders tightened. One small involuntary motion. The specific contraction of muscles that had been holding something at distance and had been briefly reminded of the effort required. Her pace did not change.

"Indeed." The word came out the specific dry and brittle quality of paper under pressure. "Grizedale was an obsession of his. He believed the ruins held revelations." She paused. The specific pause of a person deciding how much of the next thing to give. "He was very certain of that."

The memory in her voice was not soft. It was the specific quality of a thing that had been handled so many times that it had worn smooth, been examined from every angle, and had not resolved into anything easier than it had always been. A child following her father through these woods when the woods were different and she was different and neither of them knew yet what it was all going to cost.

"Revelations of what nature." I kept my voice at the specific register of someone asking because they needed to know, not because they wanted to.

She slowed her pace to match mine in the specific motion of someone who had decided the next thing required looking at rather than speaking away from. Her eyes found mine in the dark, and they carried a specific storm behind the glass of composure.

"He believed the ley lines were sentient," she said, and her voice had taken on the particular quality of words spoken in the register of things that had once been confided rather than declared. "Not merely conduits. A consciousness. Aware. Watching."

I considered the Whispering Stones. I considered the specific moment in the glade when the land had looked at me and confirmed what it had already decided. I did not dismiss what she was saying.

"And your belief."

"I don't dismiss it." Each word placed with specific deliberateness. "The ley lines hold immense power." She paused. "But power of that magnitude always exacts a price."

I opened my mouth for the next question and the air changed.

Not the wind. The weight of the air itself, shifting from the specific pressure of a cold night in a compromised forest into something categorically different, pressing into my chest with the specific quality of a force that was not atmospheric but was occupying the same space that atmosphere occupied. Ancient. Alive. Breathing with a rhythm that had no relationship to anything biological and yet registered as breathing, unmistakably.

Then the sound.

Not a roar. Not a voice. Not a scream. A deep, resonant hum that moved through the air and through the earth beneath my boots and through my chest simultaneously, vibrating in bone and tissue with the specific frequency of something that was not sound but was using sound as the only available medium for its expression. The strings of an instrument no instrument could produce, played by hands that did not exist.

"Proximity." Lira's voice barely survived the air. Her fingers found her bowstring with the specific motion of someone whose hands had moved before their mind had issued the instruction.

Ashenfang exhaled light. A soft flickering glow that was not my decision, the blade responding to the energy now pulsing through the clearing around us, drawing from it, resonating with it, becoming something beyond its ordinary character in the specific way it became when it was in proximity to forces that had been operating since before its own forging. I felt it in my grip, the transformation from metal to conduit, the extension of the ley lines flowing through my hand.

And then Grizedale was there.

Not arrived at. Revealed. The ruins rose from the dark the way wounds manifested in flesh that had been hiding them, a jagged scar on the earth's surface, broken pillars clawing upward against the sky, the specific skeletal remains of something that had once been organised and had been comprehensively disorganised by forces that did not respect the organisation of the living. The glyphs and symbols covering the monoliths glowed with the specific sickly green of magic that had been fed from a source it was not designed to feed from, and the vines coiling around the shattered stones were not the ordinary vines of reclamation, the specific patient work of living things absorbing what had been left behind. They moved. Slowly. With intent.

Life did not take root here. The air was the specific sterile wrongness of a place that had been comprehensively rejected by everything that required living conditions to exist. The earth beneath my boots recoiled from my weight in a way that was not the ordinary give of wet ground but the specific quality of soil that had been changed at a fundamental level.

"This place screams wrong." Lira's voice was barely breath, the specific compression of a person keeping sound contained because she had not yet determined what she was containing it from. Her knuckles had gone white around the bow. Her arms held their tautness with the specific quality of a wire that was one more increment of tension from snapping.

The air pressed close and foul, rank with rot and wet soil and beneath those the specific deeper corruption of something that had been infected rather than simply decomposed, the reek of ruin that had moved past biological and into something that had no taxonomy in the natural world.

I felt it through my skin before I felt it as thought. A prickle of something that had been here long enough to have become part of the ruins themselves, slithering beneath the surface of the air, coiling through the specific pathways of my nervous system with the intimate knowledge of something that had been inside these walls for centuries and understood the architecture of a person better than any person understood themselves.

Ashenfang felt cold. Not temperature. The specific cold of a blade that was encountering something it was not certain about, and the uncertainty was itself information.

"Stay close." My voice scraped the specific register of a sound that was not for Lira but for the ruins themselves, the specific declaration of a presence that was not leaving.

We went deeper. Each step carried the specific quality of descent, the earth softening and pulling at my boots with the specific hunger of ground that had been changed by what had been done here and had developed preferences about what stayed. The runes pulsed their sickly green in rhythmic waves, not the steady glow of ancient protections but the specific arrhythmic pulse of something that was being fed and was expressing the satisfaction of feeding.

Lira tasted it before she said it, the specific intake of breath that preceded the ash on the tongue, the acrid burnt-bone quality of the air in the ruins' heart.

Then the whisper.

A slithering at the specific edge of audibility, the threshold between hearing and the suggestion of hearing. A movement in the shadow at the periphery of sight, too fluid, too boneless, in the specific wrong way.

I turned hard, the specific controlled pivot of a body that had already processed the threat before the conscious mind had finished formulating the response. Ashenfang was in my hand. My voice cracked the silence with the specific authority of a command delivered to something that needed to understand it was being addressed.

Something shifted at the edge of the ruined space, enormous and deliberate. Lira's breath held in the specific way of someone who was not going to waste what was available to them on anything except the bowstring she was drawing.

The air curdled. More than blood. The specific metallic reek of ley lines that had been opened like veins and were bleeding into the atmosphere, crackling with the raw electric quality of power that had been contained and was no longer contained.

"Did you see that." My voice came out a low growl, the specific roughness of instinct and certainty combining.

"We're not alone." Her voice barely above breath. Then, after a pause that carried the specific weight of someone completing an assessment they did not want to complete: "And whatever it is, it's hungry."

It came from the ruined throat of a broken archway, slithering rather than stepping, and the description of its form was the description of something that form was insufficient to contain. Rags and shadows wrapped around a shape that was never quite the same shape for long enough to be a shape, each tattered edge coiling and uncoiling with the specific motion of something that wore the suggestion of physical presence as a courtesy extended to the observers rather than a fact about its nature. Its hood was a void. Its movements were the specific fluid grace of something that had no bones to constrain it and no nervous system to hesitate.

The reek arrived with it. Grave-cold rot and the specific deeper hunger of something that had been starved for centuries and had recently found a food source and was not interested in moderation.

Lira's sound was involuntary in the way that only the most primal responses were involuntary, stripped entirely of the composed exterior she had maintained across everything else we had faced, and the specific quality of what replaced it was not weakness but the honest acknowledgement of a category of threat that bypassed every learned response she had built.

"God's teeth." My voice came out raw, torn from a throat that the air was resisting. "What is that."

I had been through every kind of battle this land had offered and several that it had needed to import for the occasion. I had held Ashenfang against the Infernal Guardian. I had stood in the fire of the Emerald Crags. I had opened the gate and faced Daegrith's presence in the crypt's dark. My body was a record of everything I had survived by continuing to function when function was the last available option.

This thing shattered something with its presence alone. Not my body. Something more structural.

"A Shade." The word came out the specific taste of bile and recognition. "But not ordinary." I made myself finish it because giving a thing its name was the only available weapon when all other weapons were undeployed. "An abomination. Born from what was done here."

Its head snapped toward us.

The hiss that followed was not sound. It was the specific ripping of something that existed in the register below sound, the grinding of obsidian against bone, the death-cry of a star collapsing, delivered directly to the place inside the mind where the concept of safety lived and had been quietly developing since childhood. It struck, and the specific wound it left was not physical but was also not metaphorical.

Ashenfang screamed through the darkness in a silver arc and passed through the Shade with the specific clean resistance of a blade meeting nothing, no impact, no flesh, just darkness unravelling around the edge and reforming behind me with the speed of something that had never had to pretend it was bound by the physical laws that governed everything else.

The stench that arrived with the reformation was a tidal wave of wrongness that invaded every sensory channel simultaneously and settled into the back of my throat with the specific permanence of something that intended to stay.

The Shade laughed. A jagged shriek that was the specific sound of a knife made from madness and sharpened on every scream it had ever produced, delivered not as noise but as wound, embedding itself in the specific part of the mind that processed sound and doing something to the architecture there that I was going to be examining later if later happened.

Lira's arrow vanished into the Shade's form with the specific absence of impact, and when the sound came it was the specific wrong sound of an arrowhead meeting stone, and I turned to find the shaft embedded in the cold moss-slicked wall of the ruined temple behind where the Shade had been standing.

The cold that moved through my blood was not fear. It was the specific working of a tactical mind arriving at the conclusion that what it had been doing was not going to produce the required outcome, and that this conclusion needed to be reached faster than the Shade's attention cycle.

The runes.

The specific green pulse of them was not architectural. It was the specific light of something being fed, the energy moving through the sigils with the arrhythmic quality of the wrong ley line pulse, the same signature I had felt through Hougun's foundations when the corruption had been working on the land, concentrated here, directed here, being drawn from the ley lines beneath Grizedale and channelled into the Shade with the specific efficiency of a designed system rather than an accidental one.

"The runes." My voice came out desperate with the specific urgency of a realisation with a time limit attached. "They're feeding it. Draining the ley lines. Sever the connection."

Lira moved.

No deliberation. No pause for the fear that I could see still occupying the set of her jaw and the quality of her breathing. She converted it into motion the way I converted things into motion when there were no better options, using it as fuel, and she was already at the nearest rune pillar before I had finished processing that she was going.

Her dagger flashed in the sickly green light with the specific quality of something that had been drawn for the exact purpose it was about to serve. Her cry tore through the unnatural silence with the raw human quality of something that had decided to declare itself in a place that wanted it absent, and her blade drove into the stone and into the glowing sigils and the specific sound it produced was the sound of something having its supply severed.

The rune convulsed. Shuddered. Went dark with the specific abrupt absence of a light source that had not been intended to extinguish.

The Shade howled.

Not a sound but a rupture in the specific fabric of the air, a shriek of dying power that was also the sound of the connection between the rune and the thing it was feeding being cut, raw and broken and carrying the specific quality of something losing what it had been using to maintain its coherence in a world it was not supposed to occupy.

I moved into it.

Ashenfang swung the specific pendulum of a blade that had been waiting for the moment when what it was moving against had been made vulnerable, and when steel met shadow this time it met it differently, met something that had lost the specific protection of the ley line energy that had been holding it together in the world, and the impact erupted in a searing white-hot blaze that lit the ruins from the inside and then reversed, contracted, imploded with the specific violent inward collapse of something that had been assembled from wrongness and was now having the wrongness removed.

Then nothing.

The specific profound nothing of a space in which something enormous had been present and was not present anymore, the absence carrying the outline of the shape that had occupied it, filled now with the stench of extinguished sorcery and the specific ringing quality of air in which something had screamed and stopped screaming.

Lira's back pressed against the cold stone of the pillar and her fingers trembled with the specific fine tremor of hands that had been performing precise movements under impossible conditions and were now expressing the feedback of what that had cost. She breathed in ragged pulls, each one the specific sound of a person confirming they were still able to breathe.

"By the gods." Her voice was stripped entirely, the specific rawness of a throat that had been used as a channel for a war cry and was now being asked to produce ordinary speech. She looked at me and the question behind the words was the specific question of someone who needed confirmation that the category of threat they had just survived was the only one. "Tell me there aren't more of those."

My grip on Ashenfang had not released. The blade still hummed with the specific vibration of a weapon that had not determined the threat was resolved. My eyes moved through the ruins, through the broken pillars and the pulsing runes and the specific quality of wrongness that still saturated the air here, and I arrived at the answer that the evidence was providing before I had decided whether I wanted to give it.

"More." My voice was low with the specific quality of a word that was also a calculation. "This isn't a nest, Lira." I let the full weight of what I knew settle into the words before I released them. "It's a cancer. Whatever's twisted these ley lines is gorging on this place. It grows stronger with every death."

She pushed herself off the pillar with the specific motion of someone who had made a decision about what their body was going to do regardless of what their body was currently communicating about its preferences. She was pale. The tremor in her hands had not stopped. But she met my eyes with the specific quality of someone who had looked at the full picture and had arrived at a conclusion that the full picture demanded.

"Then we cauterise the wound." Her voice had found its level again, not steady through the absence of what she was feeling but steady through the specific decision to use it as fuel. "We eradicate it."

I turned fully toward her. The ruins burned at the edges of my vision. The weight of the dying land pressed through my boots and into my spine and settled in the specific place where every other weight had also settled, and in her face I saw the specific thing I had not expected, the same weight, carried differently, but the same.

I exhaled. "Together."

The word held between us with the specific quality of a thing that had moved past the register of tactics and into something neither of us was going to examine until later.

Above us, the storm had become something else.

On the obsidian pinnacle of Hougun Manor, Myrcanthor watched.

The wind was alive with the specific force of something that had been given a direction and was executing it without apology, raking across her scales with the specific violence of a storm that had been fed by the same source that was feeding everything wrong tonight. The clouds above Grizedale rolled with the specific sickly green of ley line energy corrupted and concentrating, festering in the sky above the ruins with the visible wrongness of weather that had been produced by something that did not understand weather.

She tasted it. Burning ozone and corruption, the specific bitter quality of power that had been extracted from its source and was oxidising as it moved through the air, turning rancid. Her emerald eyes narrowed against the storm and found what was beneath it.

A shift in the world's specific fabric. A crack in the place where impossible things waited before clawing through. The breath before the next event.

"Talon." His name was barely above the howl of the storm. But she said it with the specific quality of someone naming something they were about to move toward.

Her scales rippled with the specific unease that lived in her now, her tail striking the cold stone with one sharp lash. The sky split with a sound that was not thunder, the specific sound of something that had been building pressure finding its release in a direction that had nothing of weather in it.

Her breath left her in a slow exhale. "What hellfire have you unleashed."

The emerald fire in her tail pulsed with the specific wildness of power that had lost its regular rhythm, matching the twisted drum of the dying ley lines she could feel through the stone beneath her and through the air above her and through the bond between herself and Talon that had never required proximity to transmit information about state of emergency.

Her wings spread.

The specific dark cathedral of them, gleaming scales catching the corrupted light of a storm that had no right to be, vast enough to change the quality of the air around the manor's pinnacle. She had been watching. She had been calculating. She had been running the specific arithmetic of risk and certainty and the cost of action against the cost of inaction, and the arithmetic had finished.

The growl that built in her chest was not rage. It was the specific sound of a decision that had passed through every stage of deliberation and had emerged on the other side of it as something simple and absolute.

"Hold fast, my friend." Her voice was a prayer in the specific sense of words directed at someone who needed to receive them before the delivery vehicle arrived. "I'm coming."

One leap. The specific commitment of a force of nature into a void that it was prepared to fill, the defying of the distance between where she was and where she was needed by the simple fact of moving through it at the speed that a dragon moved when purpose had removed everything except purpose.

Lightning tore across the sky around her descent. The wind built her silhouette into the specific shape of something that was not weather and was not flight in the ordinary sense but was the specific combination of those two things that a dragon became when she had decided.

Lira's breath caught beside me a half-second before I heard the wing-beat, the specific sound of something enormous approaching at a speed that compressed the air ahead of it into a presence before the physical fact arrived. Then Myrcanthor descended through the storm's heart and the specific quality of her arrival changed the nature of everything in the ruins, because the wrongness of this place had been unopposed and was no longer unopposed.

No words exchanged. None were the right language for this moment.

We jumped together.

The ground ceased. The ruins ceased. The specific weight of everything that had been pressing through my boots and into my spine for the last several hours ceased, replaced by the specific sensation of vast muscle beneath me and the specific cold of altitude replacing the specific cold of corrupted ground, and the wind that arrived at this height was clean in a way that the air in the ruins had not been clean, carrying nothing except the raw truth of a Cumbrian storm.

I dug my fingers into the ridges of her spine and felt the specific living energy beneath her scales, the ley lines and the bond and the force that was older than both of them, channelling through her with the specific ease of something moving in its natural medium.

Beside me, Lira made a sound. Not the sounds she had been making in the ruins, not the sounds of the specific war she had been fighting against terror and exhaustion and the weight of everything she carried. The wind took it almost immediately. But I heard it.

Laughter.

The specific rare quality of a sound produced by someone who has been held down for long enough that finding the ceiling removed is something the body expresses before the mind can apply discretion to it. Not performance. Not relief in the ordinary sense. The specific sound of a woman who had been carrying ghosts since before she arrived in my armoury and had, for the specific duration of a dragon flight above a corrupted storm, been somewhere those ghosts could not follow.

I did not remark on it. I looked forward, into the high cold air above Cumbria, and breathed the specific clean quality of it, and for that precise duration I was not Lord of Hougun Manor and not Bearer of Ashenfang and not the man who had opened a gate to Daegrith and was still waiting to find out the full cost of that decision.

I was simply in the sky.

Then Hougun Manor materialised through the mist ahead of us, rising from the horizon with the specific quality of something that had been waiting with complete patience for as long as we had been away, a dark and brooding shape against the edge of a sky that was not finished with what it had begun.

Below, the ley lines pulsed in the specific frantic rhythm of a body in distress, the desperate signal of a land that had been losing blood for too long and needed something to stop the bleeding.

The sky had given us a breath.

The earth was calling us back to what the breath had been in preparation for.

And it was not going to wait.

CHAPTER EIGHT - THE SHADOWS OF THE LEY LINES

WE CAME BACK TO A MANOR THAT HAD CHANGED while we were gone. Not in ways I could point to immediately. The walls were the same walls, the stones the same stones, the spires the same dark shapes against a sky that had not improved in our absence. But the quality of the air around Hougun had shifted in the specific way of places that have been subjected to something while their inhabitants were elsewhere, a wrongness that was not loud but was absolute, pressing against the skin from the outside rather than rising through the floor from below.

No one spoke on the descent. There was nothing in the specific language of what we had survived that translated into ordinary speech, and the silence between us had the particular quality of people carrying things that required both hands.

The land around the manor had deteriorated.

I registered it incrementally as we descended, the specific accumulation of wrong details that the eye kept trying to attribute to the storm and kept failing to attribute to anything natural. The oaks at the valley's edge stood rigid in the specific way of things that had been frozen mid-motion rather than simply standing, their branches extended at angles that the wind had not produced because the wind had not been involved, their bark carrying the specific quality of having been changed from the inside rather than worn by the outside. The great oaks that had always moved in the specific patient language of old trees had become monuments to something they did not have the vocabulary to express. Their charred-looking limbs had not burned. The damage was of a different kind, the specific hollowing of things that have had what animated them extracted, leaving the structural form behind as evidence of what had been taken.

The rivers below were wrong in the specific way of water that had stopped having a relationship with movement. Not still in the way of a windless day. Still in the way of water that had been persuaded out of its nature by something that had gotten into it at the source.

The stars above were wrong. Not absent, but diminished, their light arriving at the earth with the specific quality of light that had passed through something that did not want it to arrive at all, faded and filtered, reaching the ground as a ghostly approximation of what it had been at the source.

Hougun Manor had become something other than what it had been. The mist that wrapped around its foundation did not drift in the way of ordinary mist. It coiled, slow and specific, with the particular patient intelligence of something that had decided on its route and was executing it, bleeding through the manor's walls at the specific seams where old stone met older foundation, gnawing at the cracks with a persistence that had nothing of weather in it. The trees in the courtyard stood as the oaks stood, rigid and specific in their wrongness, their charred limbs reaching at the sky in the frozen posture of things that had been screaming when they stopped.

The sickly green luminescence moved through the woodland around the estate in a slow rhythmic pulse that was not the pulse of life. It had the specific arrhythmic quality of the corrupted ley lines, the sick heartbeat of something feeding, and its steady throbbing against the dark was the most unsettling thing about the landscape, because it was patient, because it was not frantic but methodical, because it was the specific light of a presence that was not yet fully present but was working toward it with the confidence of something that had not yet encountered meaningful resistance.

Lira's fingers tightened around Myrcanthor's scales with the specific force of someone using physical contact as the only available anchor. I could see it in the quality of the grip, the white of her knuckles visible even in this light, the specific pressure of a person who needed to remain attached to something solid while the solid things were changing.

Her breath came in the specific controlled rhythm of someone who had decided on a breathing pattern and was applying it against the cold thing that had taken up residence beneath her ribs somewhere in the ruins of Grizedale and had not left.

"Time is dwindling." Her voice was barely above the storm's ambient noise, just a thread of sound carried on the wrong kind of air. But it arrived with the specific weight of words that had been compressed rather than casual, words that contained more than they were saying.

My gaze held the horizon. "Is your talent for stating the obvious here to stay." My voice was low and scraped, steel on whetstone. "Or is it simply reserved for me." It was not a question and both of us understood that. The specific edge in it was not entirely directed at her, but she was the nearest available surface for the thing that had been building in my chest since before the ruins.

The ghost of a smirk in response. No warmth in it. The specific expression of someone who understood the dynamic and was choosing not to escalate it at this particular moment.

We descended into Hougun in silence, and the manor received us the way it received all significant events, by adjusting its own quality to match what had arrived.

The torches in the great hall fought the dark with the specific desperation of things that had been fighting for longer than their fuel should have lasted, their flames twisting in drafts that came from the specific wrong directions, guttering and recovering and guttering again in the pattern of things that kept being interrupted by something they could not see. The shadows in the corners had the specific quality of accumulation rather than simple absence of light, as though they had been building while we were gone and had gotten considerably further along.

Ashenfang lay on the weathered table, and even in its resting position it consumed the light around it in the specific way it consumed things when the wrongness in a space had reached a level that activated whatever it was that lived in the steel beneath the ordinary properties of steel. Its hum was barely perceptible as sound, but I felt it through the table and through the air as a low, steady vibration that had been calibrated to the specific frequency of what was wrong in this room.

They had gathered while we were gone.

The Sylphs drifted near the arched windows with the specific restlessness of things that needed to keep moving and had been restricting themselves to the minimum necessary movement for an extended period. Their forms flickered in the way they flickered when something was pressing against the specific barriers their existence maintained between this world and the things that wanted to be in it. They shimmered with the specific trembling of an existence under sustained pressure, each Sylph a fragile thing that was aware of its own fragility in a way that was new, or recently intensified, and was working to conceal how much that awareness cost.

The Boggarts clung to the table's edge with their long bony fingers, their sharp darting eyes moving across every shadow in the room with the specific pattern of creatures that had been tracking something and had lost the thread of it and were attempting to reacquire. Their low layered voices twisted together in the specific sound of things that were speaking to themselves rather than to each other, the urgent sotto voce of the genuinely disturbed.

At the table's far end, the Wyrms lay coiled in their vast and ancient arrangement, their smooth gleaming scales catching the torchlight in the specific way of things that had been paying attention since long before the torches were lit. Their golden eyes were half-closed on me with the specific quality of an attention that was not observation but excavation, as though what they were looking for was inside rather than on the surface. The air around them carried the specific scent of rich earth and the particular quality of presence that belonged to things whose wisdom predated the words used to describe wisdom.

None of them spoke. Their silence was the specific silence of things that had gathered because something had called them, and were waiting for the person who had the fullest picture to speak it.

I stood at the head of the table and let the weight of the room settle into my spine and then pushed it down to the soles of my feet and spoke.

"We are besieged." The words were not a revelation to anyone in this room. They were a naming, the specific act of putting the precise shape of the situation into language so that what followed had the right context. "The corruption spreads across our realms. The ley lines are failing." I let the next part carry the specific weight it deserved. "If we do not act, everything we have bled for will be consumed by the darkness we seek to repel. And it will be forgotten."

The air in the hall moved in response to the words in the specific way of air that had been waiting for the right shape of sound to act as a catalyst.

Elara drifted forward.

She had the specific quality of a Sylph who had been carrying her information since before we returned and had been building toward the moment of delivery with the particular dread of a person who knew the information would change the room and had not yet resolved their own relationship with that knowledge. Her form shimmered with more fragility than I had seen in her before, a flicker at the edges of her existence that suggested the barriers she maintained were under more sustained pressure than they had previously encountered.

She did not speak in the ordinary way. Her voice arrived as a resonance, the specific frequency of information delivered through the stone and the air simultaneously, felt in the bones before it was processed as sound. "My lord." The title carried the weight of an old formality used as a structural support. "The ley lines are haemorrhaging." She gave those words the specific space they required to fully arrive. "Grizedale was merely the prelude."

The specific cold of that word. Prelude.

My fingers found Ashenfang's hilt. The leather was damp in a way that I could not attribute to sweat or weather and did not try to. "Where else."

Elara's glow faltered. A visible contraction, the specific withdrawal of a light source that has registered something it does not want to illuminate. Her form wavered with the particular quality of a thing that was about to say something it could not unsay. "Castlerigg." She paused. The torches stuttered around her. "Sunstone Vale." Another pause, longer, the specific duration of a person giving the next thing its full gravity before releasing it. "And the crypts beneath this very manor."

The silence that arrived after was not empty. It was the specific full silence of a room that had been holding a collective breath and had just been told not to exhale yet.

The Wyrms shifted. Not dramatically. The specific micro-movement of vast bodies that had been perfectly still and had registered something that made perfect stillness no longer the correct response. Their golden eyes did not widen. They narrowed, which was worse, the specific narrowing of things that had been waiting for a confirmation they had been hoping would not arrive.

The Boggarts' voices shifted register, their layered whispers climbing from the low urgent murmur of things tracking something into the specific higher frequency of things that had found it and did not want to have found it. Their bony fingers ceased the rhythmic tapping and pressed flat against the wood.

The Sylphs retreated incrementally toward the windows, the specific minimal movement of things seeking proximity to an exit.

The silence pressed against my skin from all sides, the specific silence of a chamber that understood what had just been named and was responding with the only language available to a room of stone and old air.

"Then we begin here." My voice cut through it with the specific quality of a decision that had been made before the words arrived. "Whatever lurks in those crypts, we end it. Tonight."

Lira moved. A single step forward, and the torches responded to her proximity with the specific violent flicker of flames encountering something that disrupted the ordinary relationship between fire and air, their light sputtering before recovering to a dim half-presence that was barely distinguishable from the dark.

She stopped.

The shadows at the room's edges shifted in the specific way I had come to recognise as the manor adjusting to information it had been waiting to receive.

The air grew heavier. Not the accumulated damp of an old building in a wet climate. Something specific, something that pressed from the inside of the air rather than the outside, coiling into the specific corners of perception and settling there with the particular patience of things that had been waiting for exactly this moment to make themselves felt.

Lira exhaled. The specific sound of a breath that had been compressed for longer than one breath should be compressed, released at the moment when continuing to hold it was no longer an option.

"There is another truth." Her voice was low and brittle in the specific way of words that were being said for the first time after having been held for a very long time. "And it will change everything."

The heaviness in the room shifted. The torches did not flicker. They held, which was worse, the specific stillness of things that had heard a threshold being approached and were paying attention.

A heartbeat. Long enough to be specific about its length.

"My father buried more than bones within the crypts." She did not rush the next part. She gave it the space its weight required. "A fragment of the Grimoire of the Void."

The room detonated.

Not physically. In the specific register of a space in which a truth has been released that was larger than the space's ordinary capacity to contain it.

The torches went from still to violent in the single interval between her last syllable and the room's response, their flames dancing in every direction simultaneously before guttering to near-nothing, leaving the hall in the specific half-light of a space that had been comprehensively disrupted.

A deep resonant groan moved through the manor from below. From the foundation. From the crypts specifically, as though the name of the thing they contained had reached it through the stone and it had responded to being named.

The Sylphs shrieked in the specific way of beings whose primary defensive architecture had just registered a threat at the precise level it had been designed to respond to, their voices merging into a terrible harmonic that was more sensation than sound, burrowing into the specific frequencies of the nervous system that processed wrongness and activating all of them simultaneously.

The Boggarts recoiled from the table with the specific motion of creatures that had been holding positions and had received instruction to abandon them, their quicksilver energy collapsed into the specific frantic movement of pure panic, their voices dropping from urgent whisper to desperate guttural curse, the kind of words that had been developed specifically for use in the dark against things that listened.

The Wyrms did not move. Their stillness was the specific stillness of prophecy, of things that had known and had been waiting for the knowing to become shared. Their golden eyes no longer narrowed. They were simply open, holding something in their depth that was not rage and not despair but the specific combination of recognition and inevitability that was more chilling than either.

I felt it through the stone. A pulse. Not the ordinary pulse of the ley lines beneath Hougun's foundations. Something that had moved, shifted its weight, as though what was below us had heard the name of what it was and had adjusted its relationship to the boundaries that contained it.

My grip on Ashenfang was specific and forceful and the leather was slick against my palm in the way it went slick when the blade was registering something through its own channels that it wanted my hand to know about.

"Silence." The single word landed with the specific weight of a command that had come from somewhere below the ordinary register of authority, from the place where the lord of this manor met the bearer of Ashenfang met the man who had pressed his palm to the Whispering Stones and had been told what he was carrying without being given the option of declining it. The torches flared in response with the specific violent brightness of flames that had received a directive.

My eyes found Lira. The specific quality of a gaze that was not merely looking but delivering information directly, bypassing the intermediary of polite expression, carrying the full weight of a calculation being conducted in real time against a person standing six feet away from it.

"You withheld this." Not a question. Not quite an accusation. The specific statement of a person arriving at a fact that has been present in the room longer than he has been aware of it.

Lira's spine did not bend. It was one of the things I had been cataloguing about her since the armoury, the specific quality of her response to being challenged, the reflex of straightening rather than retreating, her breath coming as controlled fury rather than defensive apology. "I did what I thought was right." Her eyes met mine and held with the specific quality of someone who has prepared for this conversation and who is also genuinely uncertain whether the preparation is going to be sufficient. "You think you have all the answers? That your anger changes what's already in motion?" She stepped forward, one step, closing the specific gap between challenge and confrontation. "If I had spoken sooner, what would you have done? Run straight into the crypts? Burn down the world to find the truth?"

My jaw set. The specific truth of it was that she was not entirely wrong, which was considerably more infuriating than if she had been entirely wrong. The room shuddered around us. The torches sank lower, their flames shrinking in the specific way of fires that were removing themselves from proximity to the heat between two people that had nothing to do with combustion.

The Boggarts had retreated to the specific deepest shadow available to them. The Sylphs had become barely perceptible at the windows, their voices thinned from mournful wind to the specific quiver of things that were making themselves very small.

"You thought it was inconsequential." Each word came out the specific weight of something that had been hammered rather than said. My knuckles were white against the hilt. "Do you understand what you've done. What you've risked."

"Yes." Her voice cracked on the word in the specific way of something under too much compression finding its exit point. "I do. I understand it better than you ever could."

I stepped forward. She did not step back. The torches flared with the specific violent brightness of flames feeding on the energy between two people who were a breath apart and neither of whom was retreating.

"Then why," my voice came out raw and ragged with the specific quality of something teetering on the specific edge of a thing I did not want to go over, "did you wait until now."

"Because it didn't matter." Her voice was a specific sharp thing. "Not until the corruption began feeding. Not until it started pulling at me, twisting my thoughts, corrupting my very essence. Not until I felt it from the inside." The specific rawness of those last words was different from the rest, the specific sound of words that had not been rehearsed because she had not expected to say them.

The cold that moved through me was not the cold of the manor. It was the specific cold of a new piece of information arriving in the middle of a confrontation and requiring immediate, separate processing.

"Pulling at you." I let the words out slowly, each one the specific weight of a question that was also an accusation that was also a calculation. I leaned forward, the specific controlled lean of someone who has decided on a precise distance. "What. Did. You. Do."

Her breath hitched. The specific involuntary catch of a body that has been asked a direct question it was not prepared to receive directly. "I don't know." The words came out the specific texture of something that was not entirely true and both of us registered it as such simultaneously. She swallowed. Pushed through it. "I feel it. I always have. And now it feels like me."

The specific implications of that settled through me in layers, each one colder than the one above it.

"You had no right to withhold this." The words came out the specific quality of something past fury, something that had moved through fury and come out the other side into a colder, more precise register. Betrayal was too simple a word for it. It was the specific feeling of a calculation you had been running discovering that one of the variables had been different from what you had been told it was, and the recalculation arriving at a result you had not been prepared for. My grip on Ashenfang was absolute, the leather slick beneath my palm.

She did not yield. She stepped toward me in the specific motion of someone who has been retreating from this moment for long enough and has stopped retreating. "I did what I thought was right." Her eyes were burning with the specific fire of conviction that had been forged in places I had not been present for. "And you think your anger is going to change what's already in motion? If I had spoken sooner, you would have run straight into the crypts. You would have burned down everything to find the truth and in the process, you would have destroyed the only person who knows where to look."

My jaw locked. The room shuddered around us. The walls pressed inward with the specific quality of a building that was responding to the pressure in its great hall in the only language available to stone and old mortar.

The Boggarts hissed from the deepest shadow and then were silent. The Sylphs had become nearly invisible at the windows, their presence reduced to the specific vibration of things that had made themselves as small as possible.

Then a growl.

Not produced by the air. Produced by the stone, moving through the floor and up through the soles of my boots and into the bones of my legs before it arrived at my ears, low and deep and carrying in it the specific resonance of something that had been patient for as long as patience was strategic and had arrived at its limit.

Myrcanthor.

Her wings spread from the perch above us with the specific deliberateness of something that did not need to make itself larger to fill a room but was choosing to make itself visible anyway. Her emerald gaze moved between Lira and me with the specific quality of an attention that had been watching this entire exchange and had been calculating the precise moment of intervention.

She descended.

The hall trembled with the specific vibration of mass and intent combined, the air shifting with the scent of ember and old storm and the particular quality of magic that was older than the ley lines and had not lost any of its potency with the years. Her massive head lowered until both Lira and I stood beneath the full weight of her presence, which was the specific weight of centuries of witnessing this exact category of human failure and having arrived at the position that it needed to stop.

"Enough." The single word arrived as absolute force through stone and air and bone simultaneously, the specific word of a being that did not raise its voice because raising its voice was not the mechanism of authority it used.

My fingers twitched against Ashenfang's hilt. Lira's breath came fast and shallow. Neither of us spoke.

Myrcanthor's gaze moved between us with the specific unhurried quality of something that had already assessed everything it was looking at and was now delivering the results of that assessment. "You will not fight amongst yourselves." The specific gravity of it was not a request. "The enemy you need to face is beneath your feet. And it has been listening to everything you just said."

The silence that followed was the specific silence of two people who had been mid-war and had been interrupted by something large enough to make the war look like a local event. Lira exhaled. A long breath, the specific sound of something releasing rather than surrendering, the distinction being that she was choosing to release it rather than having it taken. Her shoulders adjusted by a fraction. The fire in her eyes was still there. But its direction had changed.

My jaw was still tight. The cold fury had not dissipated. But Myrcanthor was not wrong, and I had never had the specific luxury of being unable to hear truth when it arrived, regardless of how it felt to receive it.

My head inclined. One small motion. The specific acknowledgement of a man who had not changed his mind about what had been done but had accepted the present moment's constraints.

"Then it's settled," Myrcanthor said, her emerald eyes holding the specific quality of something that was not quite relief and was not quite satisfaction but existed in the register between the two. "We go to the crypts. Together."

The council dispersed in the specific quiet of a gathering that understood the gathering had concluded. The Sylphs dissolved into the manor's corridors. The Boggarts slipped into the specific shadows they had been occupying. The Wyrms withdrew with the specific slow deliberateness of things that moved on geological timescales when they were not being asked to move faster.

No more words were raised. The specific truth that had been released into the room remained in the room, occupying the air and the stone and the spaces between us as we turned toward the crypts and the thing beneath them that had been waiting, with the specific patience of something that had been sealed for a very long time, for exactly this moment to become available.

The chamber tightened around our departure. The shadows closed in the specific incremental way of things that had been given permission by some authority I could not see. The air trembled with a quality that was not temperature but presence, the specific presence of something that had been below the stone for centuries and had recently finished deciding that it was time to stop being below the stone.

Beneath Hougun Manor, something that had a name I had not yet spoken aloud waited with the specific patience of inevitability.

And we went to meet it.

CHAPTER NINE – THE CRYPTS OF HOUGUN MANOR

THE OAK PANEL HAD BEEN WAITING IN THE EASTERN wing for centuries, patient in the specific way of things that had been given a purpose and had not yet been called to serve it.

Rowan had shown me this place years ago, in the specific hushed tones of a man who understood that some knowledge was too significant to be committed to paper, too dangerous to be shared with anyone who had not been bound to it by necessity. The sigils etched into the wood were not decorative. They had been burned in rather than carved, branded into the grain with the specific intent of things placed by people who understood that the difference between a carving and a brand was the difference between a symbol and a seal.

My gloved fingers found the runes and the cold that came back from them was not the cold of old wood in a cold manor. It was the specific cold of something that had been waiting in the dark for so long that it had acquired the temperature of the dark.

I spoke the words. The spell wound from my lips and into the glyphs with the specific intimacy of a key meeting a lock it had been made for, merging with the dormant force in the wood, and the response was immediate.

The groan that followed moved through the oak and the stone and the specific bones of my sternum before it reached my ears, low and mournful with the quality of something that had been holding a position for a very long time and was being relieved of it against its preference. The panel shuddered. Then it split, peeling back from the frame with a sound I did not want to have heard, something wet and specific, the sound of material giving way that should not have given way.

Beyond it: dark.

The spiral staircase descended into a blackness that did not lighten as my eyes adjusted, that had something in it that actively resisted being seen, and from it came the air of the crypt, the first assault of damp and decay and beneath that a reek more specific, more ancient, the specific smell of blood that had been spilled so long ago it had become part of the stone and was now being exhaled back into the world after centuries of absorption.

I exhaled. My breath was visible in the cold that came from below, the specifi c cold of a space that had its own climate independent of the seasons above.

My fingers found Ashenfang's hilt. The leather pressed back against my palm with the familiar temperature of a grip worn into the shape of my hand, and I held it there for a moment, feeling the blade's low pulse against my fingers, the specific vibration of something that had registered what was below us and was communicating its assessment.

I met Lira's gaze. Sharp. Holding.

"Stay close." My voice came out low and steady with the specific quality of a warning that was not for her comfort but for our survival. "Stray from me and your fate will be sealed."

The look she gave me was not entirely a smirk and not entirely a threat, occupying the specific territory between those two things with a precision that suggested she had spent time in that territory. Her fingers tightened around her dagger's pommel, the worn leather biting into her grip. "Your warnings are wasted." Her voice was the specific sound of something dragged across stone. "I was forged in these ruins long before you ever dared to tread them."

My expression did not shift into anything she could read. Ashenfang cleared an inch of its sheath, the dark blade catching the sickly phosphorescence from below and doing something to it that light was not supposed to permit. "If that's true." I left the rest of the sentence where it was, in the silence, where it had more room to work.

"Forward."

We descended.

The staircase spiralled into the earth with the specific geometry of a thing designed to disorient, each turn identical to the one before it, the carved stone beneath our boots damp and slick with the specific slickness of surfaces that had never dried in the years since they were last touched. The sound of our steps was swallowed before it could echo, the dark consuming each footfall with the specific appetite of spaces that had been sealed for long enough to have developed a relationship with silence they were reluctant to relinquish.

The air thickened with every turn. Not the thickness of dampness or age, though both were present, but the specific thickness of something pressing from the inside of the air rather than accumulating in it, wrapping around my ribs with the particular patient quality of things that were searching for the specific places to apply pressure and had not yet finished their assessment. The ley lines pulsed beneath the stone, and their pulse was wrong in the specific way I had learned to recognise, the arrhythmic stutter of power that had been interfered with, fed from the wrong direction, twisted from its natural current into something that served a different purpose.

Beneath the stutter, something else. A heartbeat that was not the ley lines and was not mine and was not Lira's. Deeper. Specific. Wrong.

The chamber opened below us without announcement.

It was colossal in the specific way of spaces that were not intended to be comfortable, vast and suffocating simultaneously, the air dense with an age that pressed against the lungs with the specific weight of centuries of accumulated silence. The walls were carved with faces, the hollow-eyed dead of Hougun's generations, their features frozen in expressions that had nothing of peace in them, caught in the specific moment of understanding rather than sleep. Their stone sarcophagi lined the walls with the specific arrangement of things placed with intention, and the expressions of the carved figures above them matched the expressions of the dead inside them in a way that suggested the carver had known what they were looking at.

Then the light.

From the chamber's farthest point, a verdant glow pulsed from an altar of dark stone, and the rhythm of it was the specific rhythm I had been feeling through the floor for the last twelve steps, the heartbeat that was not the ley lines but was feeding on them, drawing the power through the stone in long sick pulls and converting it into the sickly green that threw itself against the carved walls and made everything it touched wrong.

I stopped.

The shard rested on the altar's surface, and the energy coming from it was not a presence in the way that the Whispering Stones had been a presence, or the way Myrcanthor's awareness was a presence. It was an invasion. It moved through the ley lines the way infection moved through blood, with the specific directional purpose of something that had found a circulatory system and was using it as a delivery mechanism for something the system had not been designed to carry.

"You feel it." My voice came out barely above the ambient hum of the crypt. Not a question.

Lira's fingers had found her dagger's hilt before I finished the sentence. She breathed in shallow pulls, the specific breathing of someone rationing what they took in from air that had been compromised. The realisation settled into her face in layers, the specific way of someone who had been holding a belief and was watching it be dismantled piece by piece against their will.

"Its power." Her voice found its steadiness a beat after she started speaking, the specific recovery of someone catching their footing on uncertain ground. "It's stronger than I imagined." She paused. "My father swore it was dormant."

I held her gaze with the specific quality of an attention that was not gentle. "And you believed him."

She straightened. Her spine found its specific resistance, the reflex I had catalogued since the armoury, and she squared her shoulders against the weight of what I was not saying. "He wasn't always the man you knew, Talon." The rawness beneath the control was specific and involuntary, the sound of something that had been kept at distance for a long time and was being brought into proximity by the circumstances. "He loved this land. Fiercely. Just as you do."

My breath came slow and controlled and sceptical. "Then tell me why a man who loved this land buried a fragment of the Grimoire of the Void beneath its bones." I let the words settle. "One does not bury a truth like this unless they fear the shape of what it might take."

Lira moved toward the altar with the specific deliberateness of someone who needed to be moving in order to keep talking. The green light reached for her face and found it, throwing her features into the specific shadows of a person standing too close to something they had been trying not to fully look at. "He understood the ley lines better than any of us." Her voice had dropped to the register of things spoken in confidence rather than declaration. "He believed the fragment could stabilise them. Control their volatility." A pause. "That it was not a curse but a key."

My grip on Ashenfang tightened. The shard pulsed again with the specific

quality of something that was aware of being discussed. "And what happens when the key becomes the lock. When the thing he thought he could
control decides to take control instead."

She did not answer. In the specific silence of the crypt with the shard's
heartbeat filling the space between her not-answer and my question, the
answer was already present.

Then a voice came.

Not through the air. Through the specific register below air, threading
through the stone and the cold and the specific channels that the wrong
magic had carved through the ley lines, arriving not at the ears but at the
place behind the teeth where the tongue lived, slithering into perception
through every surface simultaneously.

"And still you stand, naive girl." It was a rasp, the specific sound of something that had been a voice and had been changed by the process of existing without a body. It scraped like rusted iron against stone. "Clinging to
your father's misguided convictions. Blind to his ruinous folly."

The words crawled. The specific sensation of them was not sound but
contact, each syllable a thing that pressed against the inside of the skull and
looked for the specific cracks it could work into. The air thickened with
the specific quality it thickened when something was using it as a medium
for force rather than for breathing. The stench of damp stone and old
decay surged into my throat with the particular intensity of something
that had been waiting to announce itself.

Ashenfang felt wrong in my hand. The familiar weight had shifted, the steel colder in the specific way of metal that had registered something the bearer had not yet consciously processed. Sweat at the back of my neck, cold and immediate. My pulse hammered with the specific urgency of a body that had identified a threat category it had not previously encountered and was calculating at speed.

"Show yourself." The words came from a place that was not entirely rational but was not entirely wrong either, the specific demand of a man who needed whatever was happening to have a shape he could orient toward.

The silence that swallowed the demand was the specific silence of something that had been waiting to be spoken to.

The vortex tore open near the altar without building toward it, a direct transition from nothing to something that should not be. Shadow coalesced with the specific wrongness of matter that was not obeying the ordinary rules of matter, the cold that arrived with it not temperature but the specific cold of a space that had been drained of something that warmth required to exist. The stench hit simultaneously, burnt sulphur and the specific deep decay of things that had been fermenting in conditions that should have destroyed them.

Then it took form.

Daegrith.

Not the man I had known. Not flesh, not the specific weight and presence of a living person occupying space. What stood in the crypt was the specific distillation of everything a man became when the things that made him human had been consumed by the things that made him powerful.

His face retained the structural remnants of former refinement, the noble bones that had once carried authority, now twisted into something that wore the bones as costume rather than containing them as body. His mouth was too wide, the specific too-wideness of a wound rather than a feature. His eyes burned with the cold specific fire of embers that had forgotten what warmth was and were simply hot now, simply consuming, the hunger in them patient and total.

Corrupted energy spat from his form in the specific arcs of power that had exceeded its container, lashing against the crypt walls and leaving scorch marks that glowed and faded in the rhythm of his breathing, which was not breathing but its structural equivalent. The ley lines below us pulsed with the specific agony of something being force-fed, their natural current overridden and replaced with the rhythm of his hunger.

The taste of metal and rot settled permanently on the back of my tongue.

Then Lira made a sound.

Sharp. Fragile. The specific sound of a person whose defences have been breached by something they were not prepared to encounter in this form. She stumbled back a half-step, the colour leaving her face in the specific rapid way of blood retreating from a surface that has received a shock. Her breath came in the shallow pulls of someone whose chest had been compressed by something that was not physical. Her fingers moved at her sides with the specific useless motion of a person whose body had not yet received instructions and was generating its own.

"Father?" The word arrived barely above breath, the specific quality of a word that had been held back for a long time and had escaped rather than been released.

Daegrith's head tilted. Slowly. The specific deliberateness of something that had planned this moment and was taking its time with it.

Then he laughed.

The sound was the specific sound of bone grinding against stone, of fibre cracking in frozen conditions, of a voice that had been dragged through depths that voices were not designed to pass through and had been changed by the transit. Not a sound of amusement. A sound of arrival.

"Lira." He stretched the syllables with the specific care of a blade being drawn slowly, each phoneme a separate point of contact. "My daughter." The word daughter had been filed to an edge. "How touching that you've come to stand before my masterpiece." The specific venom in the warmth was the most chilling thing about it, the performance of affection over the reality of something that had stopped caring about her specifically and had started caring about what she represented. "To witness the culmination of my work."

Lira's breath came sharp and ragged with the specific quality of a person in the process of a reckoning they had been avoiding for a very long time and had just run out of space to avoid. But beneath the sharpness, something else. Something that had been in her since Grizedale, harder and more specific than anything the fear was producing.

"This wasn't your plan." Her voice cracked on the words but did not break, the specific sound of something that was bending under load and had not decided to break. "You craved the ley lines' protection. Not this."

The temperature dropped with the specific speed of something that does not need to transition.

Daegrith stepped forward.

The laughter that preceded the step was the specific sound of bones scraping, of dead winds in a space that should not have wind, and it moved through the stone and the air and the specific channels of the body that processed threat simultaneously. His eyes burned with the particular hunger of something that had been waiting for this confrontation since before it had the capacity to want things and had developed the want retrospectively.

"Protect." He rolled the word in the specific way of something tasting something it finds contemptible. "What a fragile, childish delusion." The scent that came from him was burning ruin, the specific smell of scorched fate, of things that had been reduced to their component ash and were being breathed back into the air. "I do not shield. I consume. I shape. I reign."

The air vibrated with each word. Not metaphorically. The specific physical vibration of speech delivered through a medium that was not entirely air, that had something of the stone in it, that was using the ley lines as a secondary channel alongside the acoustic one. The metallic taste in my mouth intensified to the specific flavour of blood that had not been drawn yet but was being prepared for.

"You, with your feeble grasp of meaning." His voice dropped to the specific register of something that did not need volume. "Should know this truth better than most." The shadows curled around the words with the specific quality of things that had been given direction. "Sanctuary is a lie. Only absolute power carves a place beyond the reach of ruin."

The ground trembled beneath him with the specific tremor I had been feeling since we entered the chamber, intensified now, the heartbeat of something that had been feeding and had reached a level of satiation that was changing its character.

I roared.

Not a considered response. The specific raw sound of a man whose body had decided to make a declaration before his mind had finished composing one, the howl of something that had been compressed for too long in too much wrongness and had found the pressure point at which compression reversed into force. My voice hit the crypt walls and came back changed, the stone lending it frequencies it had not had when it left.

"Your reign ends here, Daegrith. Your ambitions die with you."

Daegrith's form trembled in the specific way of something that had received unexpected resistance and was recalibrating. The amusement in his eyes shifted to the specific expression of something that has been humoured long enough and has decided to stop humouring. The grin curdled. The gold in his eyes flickered with the specific quality of flames encountering an obstacle and considering how to move around it rather than through it.

When he spoke again, his words did not come as sound but as disease, moving through the air with the specific quality of something that had been weaponised for exactly this purpose, settling into perception through every available channel simultaneously. The decay that came with them was old and specific, the specific rot of things that had been buried and had been working on their containment from below for a very long time.

"Foolish mortal." The rasp wound through the crypt in the specific way of something that had found the ventilation of a space and was using it to distribute itself. "Do you truly believe you can halt the inevitable."

The ground shifted beneath us with the specific quality of earth that had received an instruction. Not geological movement. Intentional movement. The earth pressing up against the soles of my boots with a force that was not seismic but aware, the specific pressure of something that had been told to make itself felt.

"The shard is awake." At his words, the air constricted in the specific way of something drawing itself inward before releasing outward, the ley lines below us pulsing with sudden violent intensity, their rhythm no longer the sick stutter of the corrupted but the specific frantic thrashing of something being forced. "Its power surges through the veins of this world." His grin stretched beyond the geometry of a human face. "Bending. Twisting. Yielding to me."

His form wavered at the edges, the specific flickering of something that existed in more registers than the visual one, splintering and reforming with the quality of a signal passing through interference. His voice dropped to the specific register of a whisper that had the weight of avalanche.

"Feel it, boy." The presence of him swelled, not physically but in the specific way of something that occupied more of the available attention than its physical dimensions accounted for. "Feel the earth shudder at my will. This is just the start."

The floor split.

The crypt convulsed with the specific violence of a constraint that had been held too long releasing all at once, the stone cracking along the seams of old ley line channels, and from those cracks a burst of emerald light erupted with the specific force of pressure that had been building since before we descended. It tore through the dark, searing, the specific quality of light that had been produced by something that was not light's ordinary source but was using light's channels.

The runes embedded in the floor blazed with the specific intensity of channels that had been overfilled, their carved veins pulsing with the frantic rhythm of arteries under too much pressure.

Lira gagged. The air had curdled with rot and brimstone, the specific acrid combination of sulphur and the metallic edge of magic that had been forced beyond its designed parameters, and it clawed down her throat with the specific physical insistence of something that did not want to be breathed but was the only available option. The ground buckled beneath her with the specific quality of stone that had lost confidence in its own structural integrity, and the shockwave hit her before she had finished processing the warning, the specific force of something that had been building in the stone and had found its release point.

She hit the stone floor with the specific sound of a body meeting a surface that had no give. The edges of the crypt's shattered floor cut into her skin and the blood that followed was the specific bright red of fresh damage against pale stone.

She pulled herself upright with the specific determination of someone who had decided before they fell that falling was not going to be the last thing they did.

"Destroy it." Her voice came out raw and furious with the specific quality of a person who has resolved the question they have been considering and has arrived at the only available answer. "The shard is feeding. It's bleeding the land dry."

I did not need her to repeat it.

The truth had been pressing against my chest since I first felt the shard's pulse through the ley lines, the specific weight of something that was not theoretical but had been happening in the specific physical substance of the land I was responsible for, and it pressed now with the specific urgency of something that had run out of time for consideration.

I met her gaze. "Now."

The word was not a command. It was a vow made with the specific finality of things that could not be unmade once made.

Ashenfang pulsed in my grip with the specific urgency of a weapon that had been brought into proximity with something it recognised as its purpose and was ready for the resolution of that proximity. Its dark surface shimmered with the reflected green fire of the crypt, and in that reflection I could see the shard above the altar, trembling in the specific way of something that had been feeding and had registered the intention of what was coming toward it.

Daegrith's laughter rolled through the crypt walls with the specific quality of something that was not afraid of what was coming and wanted me to know it, his vast shadowy form coiling by the altar with the specific patience of something that had been here before and had survived being here before.

He appeared as the specific distillation of what remained when everything human had been stripped away and something else had grown into the vacancy, his eyes twin voids absorbing the flickering green light with the specific hunger of things that converted what they consumed into more of themselves. His voice did not rise because rising was not required.

"Fools." The word moved through the air with the specific toxic quality of something that had been carefully composed for maximum penetration. "You grasp at shadows, flailing against the inevitable." He paused with the specific timing of someone who had been delivering verdicts for a very long time and understood the value of silence before the most significant one. "The shard is no mere weapon. It is hunger. It shaped me. Unmade me. And it will claim you both, piece by screaming piece."

The doubt crossed my gaze before I finished suppressing it. The specific involuntary flicker of a mind that had received information it could not immediately counter, lasting the duration of a breath, and then my grip tightened around Ashenfang and the doubt was converted into something that moved in a different direction.

Ashenfang blazed with the specific green fire of something that had been brought into direct opposition with the thing it had been made to oppose, its surface shimmering with the specific resonance of a blade that was drawing on the ley lines through the bond between the Gem and the manor's foundation, channelling the same power that the shard was feeding on but using it differently, using it the way it had been intended to be used.

The web of energy holding the shard above the altar was visible now, the specific threads of corrupted ley line power forming a structure that had both architecture and vulnerability, and the vulnerability was in the runes that formed its anchor points.

Lira's breath came in the specific shallow pulls of someone who had been trying to process too much for too long and had arrived at the edge of what processing could manage. Her eyes had taken on the specific quality of a person being spoken to from inside their own mind, the shard's pulse finding the specific channels of her father's influence that had always been open in her and using them as a medium.

Then he spoke directly to her.

"You were always meant for more, my child." The voice arrived not through the air but through the specific internal channels that a father's voice used when it had been spent long enough in the architecture of a person to know where the load-bearing walls were. The cold of it was specific, the temperature of fingers against her jaw, of a hand that had once been gentle and was now something else that remembered how to perform gentleness. "Lira."

Her name in his specific inflection. The one she had heard before things changed.

She turned.

Not by decision. By the specific pull of a gravity she had been pretending did not exist since before we entered the crypt.

Daegrith's eyes found hers with the specific quality of eyes that had known exactly where she would be standing when this moment came. What looked back at her from his face was not the man who had taught her the ley lines, but it was wearing the structure of that man's features, and the structure was enough.

"You know the truth." Each word found the specific place in her that had been left open for it. "This shard is not just a fragment. It is the heart of a fallen god. A key to a realm beyond imagination. It is our legacy." His smile unfolded with the specific slowness of something that had been rehearsed. "Embrace it, Lira. It is yours by right. Together, we shall rule this crumbling world."

The taste of ash filled her mouth. I could see it in the specific quality of her stillness, the way she had stopped moving in the particular way of someone who has encountered something that requires the full available processing capacity and has redirected it all to a single point.

She was remembering. I could see the specific work of it in her face, the way old knowledge moved through a person when it was being retrieved under duress, the memories of her father's teaching and the specific moment when those teachings had curdled into something else, when the philosophy of balance had become the doctrine of domination and the man she had followed had become something she had been following away from rather than toward.

The ghost of the father she had loved was still in his face. The specific haunting of it, the structural remnants of a person she had adored, pressed against the reality of what was standing in front of her.

"Lira." My voice tore through what she was in the middle of with the specific force of something that understood it might not be enough but had no other available option. "Focus. Before it's too late."

Her breath hitched. Her eyes shut with the specific violence of someone slamming a door, and a shudder moved through her body with the full-body quality of something being physically expelled. The copper taste of bitten lip, the specific small shock of self-administered pain used as a reset.

"The runes." Her voice was barely above the shard's rising vibration. "They're feeding it. Sever them." She swallowed. "And we sever its lifeblood."

"It's a suicide run." The words came from the specific cold honest part of me that had been running the calculation and had arrived at the same result each time. I tightened my grip. "But it's better than oblivion."

Daegrith's form writhed with the specific quality of something that had been maintaining a shape through effort and had decided the effort was no longer worth it. His body twisted and distorted, the human architecture dissolving into the specific chaos of something that existed across more dimensions than the visual one could represent, flickering between states with the speed of something that had stopped pretending to be contained.

When he spoke, it was thunder through stone.

"You dare." The words cracked through the chamber with the specific force of something that had been held back and was no longer being held back. "After I resurrected you from the ashes. After I gifted you power beyond your feeble imaginings."

The runes blazed with the specific intensity of channels receiving more than their design parameters allowed. The shard thrashed above the altar in the specific violent motion of something that had registered the threat and was attempting to respond to it. Magic surged through the crypt in waves that were not temperature but had the same physical impact as temperature, each wave pressing against the specific surfaces of the body that registered environmental data.

The stench of burnt magic and sulphur had moved past the sensory threshold and had become the air itself, the specific air of a space in which the ordinary relationship between atmosphere and breathability had been suspended.

Lira's obsidian dagger gleamed with the specific cold light of something that had found its purpose. Her hand was not steady but it was not retreating, the specific fine tremor of someone who had made a decision and was in the process of committing to it before the part of them that was still afraid could complete its argument.

"You used me." Her voice was the specific low brittle sound of something that had been a wound for a very long time and had just been opened all the way. "Your ambition was the fuel. My life was kindling."

Daegrith's rage arrived as a wave of force, not emotional, physical, the specific shockwave of a presence that had organised all of its available power into a single directed outburst. It crossed the chamber in the instant before Lira moved and arrived a fraction too late.

She plunged the dagger into the pulsing rune with a cry that was the specific sound of someone releasing everything they had been holding in a single act of concentrated will, the cry of a daughter ending something she had been mourning for longer than she had admitted, raw and final and entirely hers.

The rune convulsed. The specific spasm of a mechanism having its connection severed, and then it died in the way the rune in Grizedale had died, the light snuffed with the specific abruptness of a circuit broken.

The shard screamed.

Not sound. The specific rupture of something that had been connected to its power source and had had the connection cut, the shriek of dying power moving through every available channel simultaneously, acoustic and ley line and bone, arriving in every part of the body at once with the specific quality of something that could not be processed fast enough to be endured sequentially.

I moved into the sound.

Ashenfang carved through the runes in the specific arc of a blade that had been waiting for the moment when what it was moving against had been made vulnerable. Where the blade passed, the sigils hissed their specific protest, the channels failing in sequence, the energy that had been moving through them reversing and collapsing back toward its source.

The shard detonated.

Not with the specific quality of an explosion, which was an outward event. With the specific quality of an implosion, an inward collapse, everything the shard had accumulated pulling violently back toward its own centre before the centre could no longer hold it, a violent consumption of itself that produced a light and a force that were not separate phenomena but the same phenomenon expressed through two different channels simultaneously.

The blast hit every surface in the crypt and every surface hit me.

Stone met my spine with the specific immediate reality of a hard surface meeting a body that had been moving fast and had met a harder thing faster, the pain arriving in the specific sequence of impact events, breath first, then nerves, then the cold bloom of blood at the back of my skull against the floor.

Somewhere in the distance of the chaos, Lira's scream. Sharp. Cut off.

Then nothing.

The specific nothing of a space in which something enormous has concluded.

I came back to consciousness through the specific gradual process of a body that had decided to continue and was reinstating its systems in order of importance. Breath first. The specific ragged quality of lungs that had been impacted and were re-establishing their rhythm. Then pain, catalogued quickly, ribs, skull, the back of my sword hand, nothing that was going to prevent the next decision. Then the smell, ash and old blood and the specific scorched air of a space in which a large amount of magic had been violently discharged and was now dissipating.

I turned.

The altar was a blackened ruin of its former specificity, the dark stone cracked and scorched, smoking from the specific seams where the rune channels had been. The shard was gone, and gone was the right word because there was no residue, no fragment, no evidence that anything had rested on that surface, only the specific absence of the green light that had been pulsing since we descended.

"Gone?" The word rasped from me with the specific quality of my own voice stripped of everything except the functional minimum required to produce it.

Lira moved in the peripheral dark. Her hands scraped against the broken stone with the specific sound of someone locating themselves through touch because the other senses had not fully reinstated. She coughed in the specific rattling way of a chest that had been compressed and was reassessing its capacity. When she rose to her hands and the trembling was visible in every limb but she rose, the specific determination of someone who had already decided that falling was not the ending.

"I believe so." Her voice was the ghost of itself, held together by will alone.

Then the silence changed.

Not the absence of sound. The specific arrival of the particular silence that preceded Daegrith.

"This is merely a setback." The voice moved through the crypt with the specific quality of something that had not been destroyed but had been displaced, coiling through the air in the specific way of a presence using the available medium rather than requiring a physical form to express itself through. It found my throat with the specific intimacy of something that knew exactly which channels to use. "You cannot extinguish me, boy. The ley lines are my lifeblood." The pause that followed was the specific pause of something choosing its last syllable with precision. "And I shall return." Another pause. "Stronger."

The silence that fell after was not the silence of victory.

It was the silence of a promise delivered into the specific bones of the crypt and left there, where it would remain regardless of what we did with the surface.

I exhaled. The specific long exhale of a body that has finished one phase and has not yet begun the next, standing inside the brief interval between them with the full weight of everything that had just happened settling through the layers of exhaustion into something more permanent.

The altar's blackened remains. The crypt's scorched stone. The specific quality of air that had been changed by what had passed through it and would carry that change indefinitely.

Daegrith's words still moved through the specific channels they had found in my bones. I turned to Lira. Her skin had gone the specific pale of someone who had been through something that took colour with it when it left. Her jaw was set with the specific quality of a resolution that had been found in the ruins of everything that had preceded it and was fragile precisely because of what it had cost to find.

"We leave." My voice was low and stripped, the specific sound of a man who had nothing left to perform it with but who had enough left to mean it. "Now. Before he returns."

Her nod was barely perceptible. But it was the specific nod of someone who had understood before I finished the sentence and was already standing.

"Agreed." The word tasted of ash and the specific bitterness of things named that could not be unnamed.

The ascent was the specific agony of upward motion through a body that had been comprehensively addressed by the events below, every step a negotiation between the determination of continuing and the accumulated evidence of what continuing cost. The stone resisted with the specific quality of things that had been given a purpose and were reluctant to release what they had been given. The air clung with the specific quality of burnt magic that had been absorbed into every surface and was now being exhaled back into the narrow staircase with each step we took through it.

The victory was the specific fragile victory of people who had survived rather than triumphed, and both of us knew the difference.

Behind us, or more precisely below us, in the specific dark of the crypt where the altar's blackened stone still breathed the ghost of green light, Daegrith's promise sat in the stone and waited.

Stronger, he had said.

And the specific quality of that word, its patience, its certainty, its complete absence of doubt, pressed against the back of my neck all the way up the spiral and into the cold air of the living world above.

Where it stayed.

CHAPTER TEN – THE JOURNEY TO SUNSTONE VALE

THE PALE SUN BARELY REACHED US. IT HUNG LOW AND wrong above Hougun Manor, its light filtered through the sickly green mist that had settled over the estate in the hours before dawn and had not lifted. The rays that made it through were the specific grey-gold of light that had been contaminated by what it passed through, casting shadows that moved with a quality I did not attribute to wind or cloud but to something that found shadows useful.

The morning held nothing of its ordinary character. No servants on the cobblestones. No distant kitchen sounds. No birdsong. The specific silence of a place that has stopped its ordinary functions and has not explained why pressed against my skin from every direction, settling on the chest with a weight that was not metaphorical.

I stood in the courtyard with Ashenfang at my hip and my eyes on the distant peaks, their silhouettes swallowed to their bases by the mist. Sunstone Vale. A land where power moved beneath the earth in channels old enough to have no names for their original purpose, raw and indifferent, a place that had a specific relationship with the unprepared that tended to be conclusive.

Rowan's steps crossed the cobblestones behind me with the specific sharpness of a man whose news had weight he had been carrying for some distance.

"The Sylphs and Wyrms have gathered, my lord." His voice was the specific murmur of a man accustomed to delivering information in rooms that were listening. "They stand ready."

My jaw set. "And the Boggart folk."

The hesitation before his answer had its own specific quality, the pause of someone who had hoped the question would not be asked in that particular order. "They refuse." His voice dropped lower. "The miasma is too potent. They say the journey ends in ruin."

I exhaled slowly through my nose and pushed the bitterness down through deliberate effort, the specific internal work of a man who had promised himself things about how he governed and was being tested on those promises. I had sworn I would not rule through fear. I had told myself that loyalty coerced was not loyalty but a debt with violent interest. The temptation to reach past that conviction and simply compel them was physically present, a specific pressure in my chest that I held there and did not act on.

My fingers closed into a fist until you could see the white of the knuckles visable under my skin.

"Then we go without them." The words were leadened by everything I was not saying with them, the specific gravity of a compromise that had been made against my own principles and would cost something I could not yet calculate. The taste of iron lingered on the back of my tongue.

I needed them. Their skills were not peripheral but specific to this kind of work, rooted in old knowledge that had no substitute in anything else we were bringing. But their fear was not a thing I could argue with because it was not irrational. It was rooted in truths I had contributed to. That knowledge sat quietly in me, specific and unresolved.

Rowan lingered with the specific quality of a man with one more thing to say and uncertainty about whether this was the moment for it. "And Lady Lira?"

The shift in the air around the name was immediate and involuntary. My jaw tightened in the specific way of muscles responding to something before the conscious mind has caught up. "She's coming." Iron in the words. But underneath it, the specific strain of conviction applied to something that was not entirely certain, a mask held in place through force rather than because it sat naturally.

I had pushed her toward a past she had spent years constructing a distance from. I had called forward the things she had buried. The specific awareness of that twisted in me the way blades twisted in wounds when the wound was not in the body.

Lira stood near the stables with her arms crossed in the specific way of someone who was holding themselves together through the physical act of creating pressure against the outside of their own ribcage. Her breath came shallow and deliberate, measured, the specific breathing of someone managing an internal environment by controlling what entered it.

The Sylphs moved on the air around her, their voices carrying just below the threshold of words. She did not need to hear the specific content. The tone was enough, and it always had been. They knew what she carried. They could sense it in the ley lines the way an infected body could be read through the blood that moved through it. Her father's work moved in the world's channels still, in the specific way of things that had been introduced into a system and had integrated themselves into its operation before anyone understood what they were integrating.

No matter how far she had run from it, no matter how many times she had made the specific deliberate choice to be someone other than her father's continuation, it followed in the channels of the world itself. She was not imagining the worst possibility. The worst possibility was that by standing here, by bringing herself into proximity with the ley lines at their most vulnerable, she was not breaking the cycle.

She was becoming it.

The Sylph's voice arrived without preamble. "You should not have come." Soft as displaced air, sharp as the specific cold of a blade drawn from its scabbard. It moved through her ribs and found the places where it would hurt most.

The defiance rose in her as it always rose, specific and immediate, the reflex of a person who had been told no so many times they had built a personality partly from the act of disregarding it. But underneath it, colder and more honest, was the specific truth that she had almost run this morning. That she had stood at the manor gate with her hand on the latch and had spent fifteen minutes that she had told no one about conducting a private war with herself about the direction she would walk through it.

"I'm here to help fix this." Her voice came out harder than she had intended and slightly less steady than she wanted, the specific sound of words being said by a person who needed them to be true and was not entirely certain they were. The lie in them was not in the intention but in the confidence. Because beneath the stated purpose was the specific other thing. She wanted to be done with the inheritance. To have it out of her blood. To find the end of the road that her father had put her on without her consent and discover there was something beyond it that belonged only to her.

The Sylph's glow dimmed in the specific way of a light source withdrawing from something it had assessed as wrong. "You unsettle the balance. You always have." Her form pulsed with the particular agitation of something that had been tolerating a presence and had reached the limit of that tolerance. "To be rid of you."

The words found the specific places that words like that always found. Not through the ears but through the older pathways, the ones that had been taking in that category of information since childhood and had learned to route it directly to the places where it would do the most comprehensive damage. She was a fracture in their order. She had always known this. The question she had never fully answered was whether that made her wrong to be here or whether being wrong to be here was simply the cost she paid for being anywhere at all.

Before she could complete the calculation, my presence arrived between them.

"Enough." Low and specific and not arguable. "Lira is with us. If you can't accept that, leave."

My fingers had the specific fine tremor of hands that had been holding something very tightly for a very long time. She could see it. She was one of the few people who looked at me carefully enough to see it, and I was not certain how I felt about that.

The Sylph's unease thickened in the air with the specific quality of truth that had been stated and had not been accepted, hanging between us like an accusation that had been officially declined but had not therefore disappeared. She hesitated with the specific hesitation of a being deciding whether to press an argument it knew it would not win in the immediate term. Then, with a hiss of displaced air that carried more information than any words she had chosen not to say, she turned and was absorbed into the mist with her kin.

Lira exhaled in the specific way of someone who had been holding something and had been relieved of it and had not yet decided whether the relief was warranted or whether the thing would come back heavier. "You didn't have to do that."

"Yes. I did." The response came out immediate in the specific way of things said before the deliberative part of the mind could suggest alternatives. But my gaze moved to the mist where the Sylphs had gone, and my shoulders carried the specific tightness of a man who had made a choice and was already feeling the weight of what it had displaced. "We don't have time for division." The hollowness in the words was something I could hear myself, the specific sound of a justification that had not fully convinced its speaker.

She looked at me with the specific quality of attention that contained more than its surface suggested. "Thank you." The words were fragile in her mouth, the specific fragility of gratitude that understood itself to be inadequate.

I did not answer. The silence I gave her instead was heavy with the specific weight of things I was not saying, which included but was not limited to the fact that I was not certain I had done the right thing and the fact that I was not certain she was not the liability they claimed and the fact that I had chosen her presence over the Sylphs' trust and could not yet calculate what that choice was going to cost.

I turned to Myrcanthor.

Her emerald eyes held the specific quality of attention that had seen too many iterations of the thing happening between us to be surprised by any of them. She watched the gathered warriors with the cool assessment of something that had been measuring human resolve against the specific weight of what resolved humans were asked to carry, and had developed a statistical model with a grim baseline.

"Sunstone Vale is a day's journey," she said, her voice the specific resonance of something that used stone as a secondary vibration medium. "The path will not be kind. The corruption has spread. It will fight you at every turn."

"Let it try." The words came out the specific quality of someone who meant them but who also carried the specific awareness that meaning something was not the same as being right about it. The tremor that moved through my voice on the last syllable was involuntary and specific and I hoped it had been swallowed by the morning air.

Myrcanthor's gaze did not move from my face. "Have you." Not a question. The specific two-word delivery of a being who had watched men claim readiness before and had developed a particular relationship with the gap between the claim and the reality.

"This isn't just a battle, Talon. It's a test. The land does not trust easily." The pause she gave those words carried the specific weight of personal knowledge. "And neither should you."

My grip on Ashenfang tightened until the leather bit into my palm. "What are you saying." The wind took the question before it could accumulate in the air, which was the specific mercy that the morning offered.

Her tail swept the cobblestones in a slow arc, the displaced dust rising in spirals that caught what little light the morning was willing to offer. "The ley lines are alive. They beat with the pulse of the land. If you falter, if you let doubt fester, they will feel it." The emerald in her eyes sharpened to the specific quality of something cutting through low visibility. "And so will your enemies."

The doubt moved in my bones with the specific subterranean quality of things that lived below the level of speech. Every compromise I had made in the name of survival. Every sliver of my own honour that I had spent to keep us breathing for another day. I had not confessed any of it, not to her, not to Lira, not to the specific quiet of nights when the only honest conversation was the one I would not speak aloud.

"I won't falter." The words arrived with the specific quality of things forged rather than found, shaped under pressure rather than discovered naturally.

"I hope not." The specific cold of that reply raised the specific physical response at the base of my neck.

She turned her gaze to Lira. The quality of that attention was different, the specific recalibration of something that had been assessing one kind of problem and was now assessing another.

"And you." Her voice dropped. "Will you stand when the shadows of your father's sins rise to greet you? Will you fight, even if survival demands you betray everything you believe in."

Lira's hands closed into fists at her sides. The specific controlled pain of nails into palms, used for the specific purpose of producing a clarity that the situation was not otherwise providing. The question wrapped around her in the specific way of things that had been asked of her so many times internally that having it asked aloud was not a new experience but was a more exposed one.

She had spent years trying to outrun the specific thing being named. She had not been running from her father's memory but from the specific possibility that the running itself was evidence that the thing she was running from was already present.

"I'm not my father." The words arrived with the specific quality of things that were true but were wearing thin from repetition, that had been said so many times in so many specific moments of doubt that their structural integrity had been compromised.

Myrcanthor did not look away. "No. But his imprint lingers, whether you choose to see it or not." The near-whisper of the final part carried the specific weight of something that was not cruel but was honest in a way that cruelty could not improve on. "Will you be his echo or his undoing."

Lira's jaw locked. Something moved through her in the specific direction of spine rather than chest, upward rather than inward. "My destiny is mine to forge." The thread of steel beneath those words was thin but it was there, and it was specific to her and not to anything she had inherited.

The flicker in Myrcanthor's eyes was brief and specific, the particular satisfaction of something that had been testing structural integrity and had found more than expected in the least expected place.

"Excellent." She lifted her head and the mist parted in the specific slow way of something that had been occupying a space and had been asked politely to move. "Then let us proceed. The Vale awaits. But its heart is failing. We go not just to reclaim it but to restore what has been lost."

The frost that met us when we left the manor was not weather. It was specific, the kind of cold that occupied the same physical register as temperature but was produced by a different mechanism, seeping into the skin with the particular persistence of something that had a destination in mind and the destination was the bones.

I took the lead with Ashenfang at my hip, every step measured against a surface that was providing less traction than ground should provide. Lira flanked my movement with the specific economy of someone who had been moving through dangerous terrain long enough that efficiency had become reflex. Myrcanthor moved through the space that large forces moved through, which was the space made available to them by the specific courtesy of everything that understood what they were. The Sylphs hovered above in their flickering formation. The Wyrms moved through the undergrowth at the edges with the specific fluid silence of things that breathed different air from humans and had always found the comparison somewhat unflattering.

The woodland had been changed.

The canopy that closed above us as we pressed forward was not the specific living darkness of old trees at close growth. It was the specific charred absence of canopy, the skeletal remains of what had been, their gnarled limbs reaching in the specific direction of things that had been reaching for something and had stopped being able to reach mid-gesture. The bark had split in ways that bark did not split from natural causes, the wounds weeping with the specific viscosity of something produced by the wrong kind of chemistry.

My breath hitched on the first inhale of the forest air. The stench was specific, sharp and putrid, the specific combination of rot that had moved past the stage of decomposition and had entered a stage that biological processes did not account for. It coated the back of my throat and stayed. The taste of it was metallic and old, the specific flavour of blood that had been in contact with something it was not supposed to be in contact with and had been changed by that contact.

Beneath my boots the ground was wrong. The specific wrongness of earth that had lost confidence in its own solidity, brittle in places, yielding in others in a way that had nothing of the ordinary wet yielding of saturated soil. The ley lines beneath it should have been providing the specific background pulse I had learned to read through my boots since the Whispering Stones. What I felt instead was the specific arrhythmic throb of channels that had been fed the wrong thing and were struggling with the ingestion.

Myrcanthor moved ahead in the specific way of something hunting rather than travelling, her head sweeping in slow deliberate arcs, her emerald eyes reading information that was not available to my vision. She stopped often. Each stop carried the specific quality of an assessment being made against criteria that were not verbal.

"This is not mere corruption." Her voice carried the specific resonance of something that had encountered a category of wrongness and was naming it precisely. "The land is not just sick. It is dying."

I met her gaze. The specific weight of what she had just said settled through me in layers, each one colder than the one above. "Then we act before it draws its last breath." My voice had the specific quality of resolve applied to a situation that was revealing itself to be larger than the resolve that had been prepared for it.

Above us, the Sylphs moved with the specific disrupted grace of things that were using their full capacity to remain functional in an environment that was actively working against their functionality. Their iridescent forms flickered with the specific rhythm of flames in a draft, not extinguishing but not burning cleanly, each pulse of their light slightly weaker than the one before.

One broke formation.

Elara descended with the specific urgency of a being that had been carrying something for the duration of a flight and had arrived at the moment of having to put it down. Her wings, which I had always observed as entirely composed of their own specific structure, bore hairline cracks that caught the foul light in a way that made the damage legible. She drifted toward me with the specific quality of approach that contained bad news and knew it.

"We shouldn't be here." Her voice had the specific texture of dry leaves in still air, barely present but carrying what it carried nonetheless. The wrongness she was describing was not geographic but fundamental, the specific wrongness of beings structured around one kind of magic finding themselves in the presence of its direct antithesis. It moved through the ley lines the way an invasive substance moved through clean water, changing the quality of everything it touched.

She had made a vow. Her ancestors had codified it into the specific architecture of what her kind were. They watched, they guided, they did not interfere with wild ley line magic. She had broken that in agreeing to this. The specific weight of that transgression had been present in her since before we left Hougun, and I had chosen not to address it because addressing it would have meant addressing the fact that I had asked her to break it.

"We're not turning back." My voice came out the specific quality of a command that had been generated not by certainty but by the absence of a viable alternative, and both of us knew the difference. I held the direction of the horizon because looking at her in this moment would have required acknowledging things I had not finished dealing with.

Her gaze moved past me to Lira.

I watched Elara's expression change with the specific incremental quality of a face that has completed a calculation and is in the process of deciding whether to share the result. Her assessment of Lira was not new, had been present since before we left, had been the specific source of the tension I had been navigating since the courtyard. The ley lines recoiled from Lira's presence in the specific way of systems that had encountered something they categorised as a foreign body and had organised a response. Elara had told me this. I had heard her. I had chosen to proceed anyway.

The guilt that settled in Elara's chest was visible in the specific quality of her stillness, the particular kind of motionlessness that came from a person who had arrived at a specific uncomfortable truth about their own participation in an outcome they had anticipated.

"I'm standing right here." Lira's voice came from behind me, low and quiet and carrying the specific edge of someone who had been listening to a conversation about themselves and had reached the end of their patience for the courtesy of pretending not to. Beneath the challenge was the specific rawness of a person who had been fighting to be seen as something other than her inheritance and was watching that fight be undermined in real time.

Elara's form shimmered with the specific conflicted quality of a being that was holding two true things simultaneously and finding the combination untenable. Her distrust of Lira was not irrational. Her knowledge of the ley lines' response to Lira's presence was empirical. But she had also brought Lira here. She had made that recommendation. She had permitted herself the specific reckless hope that it would be different this time.

"Enough, Elara." My voice came out with the specific fraying quality of control under sustained pressure, the first audible crack in the mask since we had left the manor. I turned to her, and the specific quality of what I gave her in that look was not reassurance because I had none available. It was need. "Enough."

She gave me nothing. No comfort, no guidance, no softening of what she knew. She had brought this into being and she knew it and the knowledge was in her face with the specific legibility of guilt that had not yet found a way to become anything else.

Then, without a word that would have been adequate, she was gone. A shimmer of iridescent motion in the fog and then the specific absence of her, felt more clearly than her presence had been.

Lira looked at me. I did not meet it.

The forest closed around us in the specific incremental way of things that were not simply dense but active, each step forward producing a corresponding tightening from either side, the roots and shadow working in the specific concert of something with unified intent. Twilight bled into a darkness that was heavier than the hour warranted, the mist between the warped trees curling with the specific quality of something that had found the spaces between them useful.

My breath caught.

A pulse moved through the air with the specific quality of something that was not sound but occupied the same perceptual channel, pressing against the inside of my ribs from a direction that was not physical. Deep. Primal.

The specific sensation of standing at the edge of a hidden drop and having the body register the depth before the eyes confirm it.

The silence had changed character. It was not the silence of absence but the silence of presence, the specific hush of something that had been making noise and had stopped because it had reached a position from which it did not need to.

I stopped. My hand came up in the specific motion of someone communicating through the body because the voice was not the right medium for this moment.

Lira froze mid-step. The specific quality of her stillness was different from ordinary stillness, the coiled kind, every muscle already calculating.

"What is it." Her whisper was barely sound.

My nostrils flared with the specific involuntary response of a body gathering the available chemical information. Metallic. The specific tang of blood that was not fresh and not old but somewhere in the specific middle range that meant near. "This stillness." My voice came from the specific low register of someone who was trying not to add more sound to a situation that was already listening. "It's wrong." I turned my head in a slow arc, reading the dark between the trees with the specific patient attention of someone who had learned that what killed you was usually what you had decided was not there. "It reeks of ambush."

The sound that came from the woods was not a growl in any register I had encountered in living things. It moved through the bark of the bare trees first, setting them trembling before it arrived in the air, a low specific resonance that pressed against the rib cage from below rather than from the front. Then another, deeper, with the specific quality of something much larger than a wolf's throat producing a wolf's vibration, and the ground's answer was immediate and specific, the tremble of an earth registering a weight that exceeded the ordinary parameters of the wildlife that should have been here.

Myrcanthor's head snapped up. The specific vertical narrowing of her pupils to slits was not a response to changed light. It was the specific response of predator senses registering the proximity of something it was not accustomed to considering prey.

The mist shifted with the specific quality of something moving within it that was using the mist as cover rather than simply occupying the same space. Her growl was wet and low and it moved through the ground rather than the air, the specific warning sound of something that had already decided on a response and was communicating that decision to its allies.

"Our solitude is shattered." Her voice was the specific quality of stone being cleaved, each word a separate impact.

They emerged from the tree line in the specific way of things that had been assembled rather than born, their bodies carrying the evidence of forces that had reshaped them beyond the tolerances of their original design. The corruption was visible in the specific details, the wrong angles of limbs, the specific stretching of skin over structures that skin had not been designed to accommodate, the open lesions weeping the particular black sludge of magic that had been processed by biological tissue and had changed both itself and the tissue in the process. Their fur was not the fur of animals but the specific residue of fur on something that had been an animal and had become something that wore the animal's remaining material.

The stench arrived ahead of them in the specific wave of something that had the composition of rot and burnt carrion and the acrid undertone of corrupted magic, and it found the back of my throat and settled there with the specific permanence of things that do not leave.

Their eyes. Twin points of cold red, not the hot red of fever or fury but the specific cold red of a fire that had been removed from any relationship with warmth and retained only the quality of burning. They did not hunger in the way of animals. They burned with the specific hunger of corruption, which was different in kind from biological need.

"Stay close." My voice came out the specific raw quality of instinct before intention. Ashenfang answered before I had finished the command, the emerald fire erupting along the blade with the specific sound of a force being released from containment, driving the darkness back in the particular violent way of light that had been made from something that understood darkness personally.

The creatures flinched from it. But they did not bleed. Their wounds seethed with the specific rejection of flesh that had been reconfigured around something other than biological integrity, the wounds not closing but not producing anything ordinary.

"Sylphs, to the air. Wyrms, hold the flanks. Now." The Sylphs became motion, streaks of silver tearing through the dark with the specific efficiency of things that had always been most dangerous in the vertical dimension.

The Wyrms uncoiled with the specific lethal synchronicity of ancient things that had been asked to do what they were made for.

The Wyrms tasted the air with their tongues in the specific way of things reading chemistry rather than vapour, and what the chemistry told them produced the specific low angry hissing of beings that had identified the source of a wrongness they had been tracking for weeks.

Lira stepped into position beside me.

Her skin had the specific pale quality of blood having retreated to the core in preparation for something demanding, but her hands were steady around the twin daggers with the specific steadiness of controlled will rather than calm, the kind that required ongoing maintenance and was maintaining itself.

"Any brilliant ideas." Her voice carried the specific thin quality of humour applied over something that was not humorous, stretched tight over a deeper register that was entirely serious. "Besides the obvious."

I kept my eyes ahead. The specific darkness where the next wave was forming. "Survive, Lira. That is the plan."

Four words. The specific weight of four words that did not pretend to be more than they were, that stripped the situation down to its actual available content. No strategy that was not survival. No promise that was not that we would be alive to make more promises.

The silence after them was the specific silence of two people who understood they were the same amount of afraid and had chosen not to say so.

The first wolf erupted from the dark before I had finished processing its approach, its body moving with the specific wrongness of something that did not need to observe the physics of muscle and tendon but was using them anyway as a courtesy. The stench of it arrived a fraction before the body did, rotted sinew and old blood and the sour specific chemistry of a carcass that had been reanimated by something that did not care about the biology of the process.

I met it with Ashenfang in the specific way of someone who had been taught by Myrcanthor that the body did not need the mind's permission to do what it had been trained to do.

The blade screamed through the air with the specific quality of steel that had been made in dragon fire and knew what it was meeting. It found the wolf's throat and passed through it with the specific resistance of zero, no tendon, no bone, only the particular hiss of something between states of matter that was not expecting the specific frequency of Ashenfang's fire.

The wolf's body folded with the specific motion of something that had been held together by something other than biological coherence and had had that something removed. It collapsed into grey ash before it completed the fall, the specific fine ash of magic that had been cancelled rather than destroyed, and the residue spiralled upward in the air and was carried away by a wind I could not feel.

No time for the specific clarity of having achieved something.

From the tree line they poured. The horde had the specific quality of an argument being made by volume rather than by individual instances, each creature a repetition of the same wrongness, jerking forward with the specific rhythm of things that were being animated from a central source rather than from individual biological intention. Their claws found the ground with each staggered stride in the specific sound of something that was impersonating purposeful movement without having the underlying architecture for it. Their eyes burned with the specific patient cold fire of something that was not running out of patience because patience required a kind of relationship with time that they did not have.

Talon and Lira moved.

Not strategy. The specific improvised efficiency of two people who had been in enough situations where stopping to plan was the specific mistake that got you killed and had developed the reflexes to operate without it. Ashenfang carved through the dark in arcs that left the specific trail of emerald fire against the night. Lira's daggers found the specific angles that daggers found when held by someone who had been trained in the specific geometry of close-quarters survival and had exceeded the training.

Each beast fell the specific way of things that dissolved rather than died, the ash spiralling up and being carried into the mist with the specific indifference of a world that was processing the results of the battle without commenting on them.

But for each one that fell, two more found the specific gaps in the tree line.

My muscles had the specific deep ache of things that had been doing too much for too long and were communicating this through a channel I could not silence. The creatures did not slow. They applied the specific mathematics of attrition, which was not a mathematics that favoured us.

The cold despair found its specific location beneath my ribs and established a residence I could feel with each breath. I forced it down. Not because I had dealt with it but because there was no time.

"We're not winning this fight." The words came from the specific honest part of me that had stopped lying to itself sometime in the last three minutes. "Retreat. To the woodlands. Now."

No one questioned it. The specific relief of a decision made by someone else when you have used everything you have to maintain the appearance of having more.

What followed was not rout. It was the specific brutal rhythm of withdrawal while maintaining contact, every step backward purchased with a specific cost, Ashenfang continuing its arcs while my legs moved in the opposing direction, the specific physical contradiction of fighting and retreating simultaneously.

Lira wove through the specific gaps between the creatures and comrades with the particular fluid efficiency of someone for whom the geometry of violence had become a second language, her blades speaking in the specific dialect of survival rather than victory.

Myrcanthor surged upward with the specific violence of a large force choosing to become airborne at speed, her wings cutting the fog into the specific pieces of something that has been divided by something sharp and powerful. The winds her ascent produced expanded outward in all directions in the specific way of weather made rapidly by a specific local cause, and in the brief window of visibility it created, the specific silver of the moonlight touched the battlefield and showed us what we were dealing with and we kept moving.

We broke through the tree line into the clearing with the specific momentum of people who have stopped being able to control the pace of their exit and have become committed to it.

The snarls faded.

The specific quality of silence that followed was not peace. It had weight and presence and the specific quality of something that had paused rather than concluded. The mist did not retreat. It settled around the clearing's edges with the specific patience of something that was waiting for a signal it had not received yet.

My chest heaved. The war drum of my pulse behind my eyes refused its specific invitation to slow down. I let Ashenfang find its sheath through the specific muscle memory of someone who had done this more times than they had counted, the blade's warmth still present in the palm of my hand as a specific reminder that the warmth meant it had not finished.

"Is everyone all right." My voice had the specific frayed quality of something that had been used extensively at volume and was now being asked to produce quiet and finding the transition difficult.

The murmured responses moved through the gathering with the specific collective quality of a group that was accounting for itself and finding fewer absences than it had feared, which was not relief but the specific relief-adjacent sensation of discovering the worst had not yet occurred.

The Sylphs hovered in the specific dimmed formation of things that had been in contact with something corrosive and were still processing the damage. The Wyrms held the clearing's edge with coils drawn in the specific way of things that had not decided whether the retreat was complete.

Lira wiped her blade with a specific focused motion that did not entirely account for the specific tremor in her hands, the fine involuntary evidence of a body that had been functioning at maximum and was now registering the cost.

"That was anomalous." Her voice was flat with the specific flatness of analysis applied to something that the analytical part of her had decided was the safest register to use. Her eyes held the specific quality of attention fixed on the place where the wolves had vanished, watching for the specific signal of return. "Unprecedented."

"Indeed." My voice had the specific tension of a word being used as the minimum viable response, everything under the surface continuing to churn. The tree line was specific in its wrongness, standing unnaturally still, the gnarled limbs carrying the specific quality of things that had stopped moving because something had asked them to rather than because nothing was moving them.

It's not over.

"Myrcanthor." She descended with the specific seismic grace of a massive thing descending deliberately, the heat of her passage curling the fog into distorted waves, embers trailing in the specific spiral of something burning at temperature and leaving evidence. Her emerald eyes scanned the dark with the specific intensity of something that was reading information rather than simply looking.

"The contagion spreads faster than we feared." Her voice carried the specific flatness of information delivered without comfort. "These creatures were not the storm." She paused in the specific way she paused when she was giving the next thing room to arrive. "They were the wind before it."

I drew a single slow breath against the specific tightening of my spine. My body had already metabolised the exhaustion of the last engagement and was communicating specific opinions about the prospect of the next. I gave it the specific response of continuing.

"We move." The sharpness in my voice was the specific sharpness of purpose that had replaced the capacity to pretend it was something more eloquent. "The Vale is close. We don't stop now."

Sunstone Vale rose ahead in the specific quality of a destination that had been acquiring mythic weight with every mile of approach, its peak veiled in silver mist, half-present in the specific way of things that existed at the intersection of the physical and the liminal. Not a place we were moving toward. A threshold we were approaching from the outside.

Behind us, the woods held the specific quality of something that had not finished with us, its shadows lingering with the specific extended quality of things that had been asked to perform a function and had not yet received the signal that the function was complete.

The weight of it was not the weight of history or of the land or of the specific accumulated wrongness of everything the journey had brought us through. It was a specific weight that asked more than the sum of its visible parts, that pressed in from directions that did not have names, that had the specific quality of a test that had not declared its grading criteria.

Each footfall was specific and deliberate against a surface that was offering less than it should. Ashenfang's specific faint glow cast gold and green over the cracked ground in the specific rhythmic flicker of something that was still alert, still oriented, still telling me things through the medium of its own pulse.

Above us, the Sylphs hovered in their specific dimmed formation, their radiance flickering with the specific pattern of things that had been having something siphoned from them and had not yet found the source of the siphon. Their light was being taken. That was specific and legible and I filed it.

Lira's breath caught with the specific involuntary quality of a body receiving environmental information faster than the deliberate systems can process it. "This feels wrong," she whispered, and the specific quality of the whisper was not for me but for the air itself, said because not saying it felt like a lie.

The forest leaned in with the specific quality of attention rather than movement, the windless dark between the trees swallowing the sound before it could carry.

"Utterly wrong." My voice came out hoarse, the specific roughness of something that had been saying things for too long in too much bad air. My eyes found the mist at the clearing's edge where the specific tendrils moved with the quality of things that were aware of being observed. Not weather. Not forest. A border or a wound.

"Stay sharp." My fingers tightened around Ashenfang's hilt in the specific reflex of a hand that had decided it was not letting go. "If those things return." I did not finish it. They all held the specific completion of that sentence in their own bodies, in the places where fear lived that were not the places where fear was spoken.

"They won't return." Myrcanthor's voice was the specific cold of stone in deep shadow. She gave the words their specific space. "They were merely the vanguard. The true danger lies beyond."

My jaw tightened. "Explain." The word arrived with the specific quality of something that needed the information and was specifically not ready to have it.

Her emerald gaze fixed on the horizon with the specific quality of eyes that were reading something the rest of us could not see. "This blight does not merely corrupt flesh." The weight of centuries in her voice was not decorative. It was specific and it was real. "It defiles essence. It unravels the soul itself."

The air shifted. The words had done something to the specific frequency of it.

Then the whispers came.

Not from a direction. From everywhere that had edges, from every space between things, curling into perception with the specific quality of a sound that had learned the specific channels through which doubt moved in a person and was using them. They did not have words at first. They had only the specific suggestion of words, the intimation of language operating just below the threshold at which it could be parsed, pressing at the soft places with the specific patient pressure of things that had all the time available to them.

The sound that cut through them was the specific jagged note of something scratching a surface that should not be available to scratching, nails on the inside of a mind, a shriek that was not external but arrived in the specific place where external things were processed and was indistinguishable from them.

I felt Ashenfang respond in my grip with the specific change in temperature and vibration of a weapon that had been calibrated for this category of threat and was communicating its readiness. But the readiness was in a language I did not fully know how to use against the specific thing producing the sound.

Lira stiffened with a specific full-body quality of someone who had felt the sound find the specific place it had been designed for. "What is that." Her voice came out the specific sound of a person trying to prevent a complete sentence from carrying all the weight it was threatening to carry.

No one answered. The specific quality of that silence was the most honest thing said in the last several minutes.

Myrcanthor's jaw tightened in the specific way of a face that had registered something it had hoped to avoid and was not surprised to find. "The incorporeal." Her voice was low and specific. "The fracturing of the ley lines draws them forth. They sense the imbalance." A pause with the weight of what she was not saying. "And they feed."

The whispers became a chorus in the specific way of things that had been individual voices and had achieved a collective identity, and the collective identity was louder and more specific in its reach, each layered sound finding a different specific location to press. They moved through reason the way water moved through failing stone, finding the cracks that had been forming since before the journey began and applying the specific patient pressure of things that had infinite time and no other purpose.

"Ignore them." My voice came out the specific raw quality of will being applied against something that was working on the part of me that will was supposed to protect. "Forward."

Above, the Sylphs faltered with the specific quality of forms losing their internal coherence under sustained external pressure, their glow stuttering in the specific pattern of flames being introduced to something that was consuming their fuel from below. Then a shriek tore through the clearing, not the sound of the whispers but the specific human-adjacent sound of a being experiencing something happening to it that it was not designed to survive.

One Sylph spiralled in the specific motion of something that had lost its orientation, her once-serene face carrying the specific terror of a person who had become aware of something closing around them that has no physical form to fight. "They're ensnaring us," she screamed, and the specific raw quality of it was not performance, it was the specific sound of a being reporting information about its own immediate dissolution. "They're dragging us into the abyss."

"Concentrate!" My voice cracked into the chaos with the specific force of something that had been compressed and was releasing. "Resist. Do not let them in." But the words had the specific hollow quality of commands I could not be certain I was obeying myself.

The shadows in the mist acquired the specific quality of silhouettes without sources, flickering shapes that moved with the specific wrongness of things that were wearing the geometry of human forms without understanding what those forms were for. Their hollow eyes burned with the specific cold red I had seen in the wolves, and their faces carried the specific quality of expressions that had been frozen in the specific moment of their unmaking.

The Sylph broke formation.

Her descent was specific and targeted, her wing trailing the specific frantic light of something that had lost control of its own trajectory and was converting the fall into direction. Her extended finger was specific in its aim.

"This is her doing." The voice carried the specific weight of a conviction that had been building for the duration of the journey and had been waiting for the specific permission of a crisis to become declaration. "The corruption follows her. It grows stronger in her presence."

The words did not fall. They embedded. In the specific way of things that found the places they were already partly true and confirmed them.

I felt Lira's breath catch behind me with the specific involuntary quality of a body receiving a blow it was not fully braced for. The specific cold dread in her was not the dread of an accusation she had never considered. It was the specific cold dread of an accusation she had been considering in private and had been trying not to confirm.

She had built her life on the specific work of fighting the thing being named. She had sacrificed the things that people sacrificed when they had decided to be the undoing rather than the continuation of something, friendship and peace and the specific comfort of a life lived away from the sharpest edges. And here was the specific possibility that the thing she had been fighting had been inside the perimeter the whole time.

The thought struck her with the specific force of a thing that had been circling her for years and had finally landed.

"Enough." I stepped between them with the specific motion of a body that had decided before the mind had finished the sentence. My stance was the specific rigid geometry of someone who had drawn a line and was standing on it. But the certainty was not entirely behind it. I could feel the specific place where it was not entirely behind it.

I knew what Lira was. I had seen what she could do and I had seen what she carried and I had chosen both times to proceed. But the whispers had found the specific crack that the Sylph's accusation had confirmed, the specific possibility that my choice had been motivated by something other than tactical wisdom, and they were applying the specific patient pressure of things that had found a structural weakness and had infinite time.

The Sylph's luminescent eyes burned with the specific fury of a being that believed what it was saying and could not understand why the person it was saying it to was not responding to truth with truth. "You're blind, Talon." Each syllable hit with the specific weight of something honed on certainty. "She'll doom us all."

The question moved through me with the specific quality of a thing I had been keeping in a specific locked place. Was she worth the risk. Not as an abstraction but as a specific calculation against a specific ledger of what the risk was costing.

For one specific moment, my hand moved toward Ashenfang's hilt. The specific fine increment of motion that preceded a decision. A single life. The rest would survive. The whispers provided the specific framing with the specific efficiency of things that had been doing this for longer than I had been alive and had gotten very good at the packaging.

My knuckles went white.

Myrcanthor's roar shattered the night in the specific way of something that had been watching the specific deterioration and had identified the precise moment of intervention required. It did not echo. It arrived and it remained, displacing everything else from the available space, leaving the specific ringing quality of something that had been said and could not be unsaid.

"Enough." The single word carried the specific authority of something that did not need volume because it was the only thing willing to name what was happening. "This infighting will destroy us. The spirits feed on fear, on anger. You give them fuel and they will tear us apart from within."

My hand released the hilt.

The specific shame of having moved toward it in the first place settled into the specific place where things I would not speak about lived and would continue to live.

Lira's jaw had the specific quality of stone that has been under pressure for a long time and has not broken. Her hands closed at her sides in the specific controlled grip of someone who had decided what their body was going to do while their mind was occupied elsewhere.

Lira. Her name was in the specific place where I kept the things I regretted that I had not yet resolved.

"Myrcanthor is right." My voice carried the specific strain of someone saying a true thing that is not the full truth, where the omission was not a lie but was something I would have to account for later. The doubt behind the ribs was specific and would not be dissolved by saying the correct thing aloud, because the doubt was about what I had almost done and the correct thing could not retroactively address the almost.

We moved. Because moving was the specific thing available that was not standing in the specific wreckage of the last several minutes.

"Stay close. Don't listen to them. Don't stop moving." My voice had the specific quality of a command that was also an instruction to myself. "We'll get through this." The words felt the specific hollow of things said to maintain forward motion rather than because they were true.

Lira's eyes found mine with the specific quality of someone who was choosing to believe something and was aware of the choosing. I returned her gaze with the specific expression of someone trying to give her what she needed while knowing what I had almost done.

The mist pressed in with the specific incremental quality of something taking territory. The whispers had become specific voices now, not ambient suggestion but the particular voices of particular people, shaped from the specific material of memories that only I had access to, using that material with the specific expertise of things that had been inside the architecture of my mind long enough to understand where the load-bearing walls were.

Eryndor. The specific quality of my mentor's voice carrying the specific words of my mentor's dying, the specific accusation in them, the specific truth of them. You failed me. The specific way the words found the specific place they had always found since I left him in the forest.

And then the calculation. One Sylph. The rest survive. The whispers offered it with the specific packaging of mercy rather than sacrifice, the specific framing of necessity rather than cowardice.

My fingers moved toward the hilt for the second time in as many minutes.

Lira's breath caught with the specific quality of someone whose own internal battle had suddenly produced a specific development they had not anticipated. "They're inside my head." Her voice came out with the specific rawness of information delivered in the specific register of the person who could not afford to process it emotionally but needed it communicated. "They're using his voice."

Her father's voice. The specific weapon that had been built from material she had never been able to fully clear from the available architecture.

I stopped. The whispers continued but at a specific distance from the decision they had been about to produce. "Daegrith's voice is a weapon." My voice came from the specific part of me that had not been compromised in the last several minutes. "That's all it is. It holds no power."

Her nod was the specific nod of someone who was not certain but had decided to proceed as if they were, which was often indistinguishable from certainty in terms of its functional outputs. "Easier conceived than achieved." The specific strain of those words was honest in a way that did not require any addition.

Myrcanthor held her position with the specific quality of something that had been waiting for the moment to pass and was watching it pass without comment, her presence the specific anchor point around which the chaos had been organising itself.

We emerged from the specific worst of the woods with the specific quality of people who were still accountable to each other for what had happened inside them. The whispers receded as the tree line thinned but did not disappear, their specific residue settling into the available space between us the way all significant things settled, quietly and permanently.

The sound of our breathing was the specific sound of people who had been tested and were still standing and were not yet sure what standing meant.

The ley lines pulsed at the Vale's threshold with the specific steady rhythm of something that had been watching and was neither welcoming nor refusing, simply present with the specific presence of things that had existed before the crisis and would exist after it.

"Is anyone wounded." My voice had the specific fraying quality of the end of a very long effort.

The responses moved through the gathering in the specific low tones of people accounting for themselves against a baseline they had not been certain of.

Myrcanthor's eyes held the specific quality of things that were still assessing. "This was merely a prelude." The words carried the specific weight of something that had been true from the beginning and was only being stated now because the evidence had become sufficient. "The Vale is near, but the blight thickens with every step. It will not let us pass unchallenged."

The specific weight of that pressed through my jaw into the bones of my skull. The next thing after everything that had just been the next thing. I gave it the only available response.

"Then we prepare for the inevitable." My voice was the specific steady of purpose that had replaced everything else because everything else had been spent. "Forward."

We pressed on.

The specific quiet stretched between us as the mist thickened ahead and the ley lines' pulse grew in my boots and the weight of Sunstone Vale began to accumulate in the specific way of things that were about to demand everything we had left, which was less than what we had brought with us but more than what the whispers had believed we would retain.

Lira's footsteps followed the specific careful rhythm of someone who was carrying more than the distance required and was calibrating each step around it. Her eyes found my back at the specific intervals of someone who was not certain whether the person ahead of her was the person she had trusted at the start of this road.

I felt the specific quality of that uncertainty without turning to address it.

Finally, after a silence that had its own specific arc, I spoke without turning. "Their opinions." The words came out quietly in the specific tone of something that had been held and was being offered rather than delivered. "Hold no power over you."

The scoff she gave back was the specific brittle sound of someone releasing pressure through the only valve currently available. "Convenient for you."

Her voice carried the specific cold edge of someone saying the true thing rather than the comfortable one. "You don't carry the weight of their accusations. You don't hear them with every step. You don't bear the weight of what they believe I am."

The words landed between us and stayed. The specific staying of things that were true and that both parties knew were true and that could not be resolved by the person they were directed at and also could not be ignored.

We walked on.

The mist ahead thickened. The ley lines pulsed with their specific desperate rhythm. Behind us, in the specific dark of the forest we had come through, the silence that was not silence held the particular patience of something that had not finished.

CHAPTER ELEVEN – THE SUNSTONE VALE

"THEY DOUBT YOU," I SAID, AND THE WORDS CAME OUT measured in the specific way of things being held at a distance while still being delivered. "But their suspicion alone does not make them right."

Lira stopped. Not gradually. The specific abrupt stop of someone who has been moving and has encountered something that makes movement feel dishonest. I turned. The stillness between us had the specific quality of a question that had been waiting to be asked and had found its moment.

"Doesn't it." The words came out low and raw with the specific quality of something that had been held back and was being given partial release, not a full opening but a controlled one, still breathing through the structure of her composure even as the structure was showing specific small failures. Her breath formed mist in the cold air. In the specific light available I could see, for the first time, what existed behind the defiance. Not weakness. Something more specific than weakness. The particular quiet struggle of a person who had been fighting a private war for so long they had forgotten what it looked like from the outside.

"My father's corruption poisoned everything he touched." Her voice was soft with the specific softness of things spoken carefully because the alternative was not speaking them at all. "The Sylphs' fear isn't misplaced." A pause that carried the specific weight of something true that she would rather not have had to confirm. "They see him in me. They see what I might become."

I exhaled slowly, the weariness settling in the specific way of something that had been building since before this conversation and was choosing now to make itself fully felt. My hand moved through my hair with the specific frustrated motion of a man who had said the same true thing too many times and was losing confidence in its architecture.

"You are not your father." Firm. Practised. The exact words. The same ones she had said to herself in the specific dark of every night since before I knew her.

Her eyes came up to mine with the specific quality of someone searching for something they needed to find rather than simply looking at a person. She held me in it. The silence stretched with the specific tightening quality of something being tested.

Then her expression shifted. Not dramatically. The specific small collapse of something that had been maintaining a performance and had decided, for this single moment, not to.

"You don't believe it either." The specific quiet of those words. Not accusation. Something more precise. The naming of a truth she had seen in me that I had been managing. "Not entirely."

"Lira." Her name came from me as the specific sound of a man reaching for something before it moved out of reach.

But she had already begun to step back. Not in fury, not with the specific violence of someone storming away from an argument. The deliberate withdrawal of someone who had decided that the current distance was more honest than the current proximity, and was choosing honesty, and doing it slowly, with the specific control of a person who understood exactly what she was doing and why. The chasm between us widened in the specific way of things that were not being closed.

I did not follow. The specific weight of words I had not said settled in my chest with the heaviness of things that were going to stay there.

Myrcanthor's presence arrived in the space Lira vacated, her emerald eyes tracking the retreat with the specific quality of attention that had been watching this dynamic since before the words that had just been exchanged were spoken. There was no surprise in her expression. There was the specific weight of something confirmed rather than discovered.

"Self-doubt clouds her judgment," she murmured, the sound of it reaching me with the specific resonance of something said through stone and air simultaneously.

I watched Lira until the forest absorbed her, the shadows reaching for her in the specific way they had always reached for her. The weight of it pressed against my ribs with the specific quality of something that had been there for a long time and had just found a more specific location to settle.

"She's not alone in her doubt." The words came out quieter than I had intended, from the specific place below the register of things I usually said aloud. I hesitated. What was underneath it was cold and specific and had been sitting in me since the clearing where my hand had moved toward the hilt. "My trust in her, Myrcanthor." The pause. "Is not whole."

The dragon turned her massive head toward me with the specific slow deliberateness of something that had been waiting for this admission and was giving it the full gravity of its arrival. A breath left her, warm and particular, the specific warmth of something that had been living for centuries and had accumulated a different relationship with heat than ordinary things. It moved over me with the specific quality of something grounding rather than comforting, which was the specific kind of thing she offered.

"Trust is not born from certainty, Talon." Her voice was the specific resonance of thunder that was also language. "It is a choice. A leap into the unknown. To trust is to embrace vulnerability." She held the pause with the specific weight of something that knew what it was saying cost the person hearing it. "And without it, your cause is already lost."

The frown that settled across my face came from the specific place where her words had found the specific architecture of my defences and had identified the load-bearing element. "I cannot lead this company if I am constantly questioning her," I said, the frustration specific in its quality, the frustration of someone who understands they are wrong and has not yet found a way to stop being wrong. "The Sylphs—"

"Lira is at war with herself." She did not let me build the argument. "Just as you are." The specific directness of those four words and what they named. "You bear the weight of leadership, of the impossible choices before you. She bears the weight of her past." She paused with the specific timing of someone who has one more thing to say and is placing it with precision. "These struggles, if left unchecked, will break you both."

I turned away from her. My fingers found Ashenfang's pommel and closed around it with the specific grip of someone using a familiar object as an anchor against a current they could feel pulling. "You make it sound simple," I said, and my voice came out with the specific tautness of something that had been compressed too long.

Her expression did not soften into dismissal. It softened into the specific quality of a being that had seen more versions of this than I had words to count and had not become indifferent to any of them. "This is anything but simple." A pause. "But unity is our only shield. The blight will not destroy us by force alone. It will unravel us from within. If you surrender to doubt, we are already lost."

The specific truth of it settled through my jaw and into my teeth and down through my spine into the soles of my boots, which were on the specific ground of the place I had sworn to protect. It burned with the specific quality of iron being given a specific shape. Slowly, against the specific resistance of everything in me that wanted to continue doubting because doubting felt like control, I nodded.

"I will try." The words arrived with the specific quality of things that were as much for me as for her. I was not entirely certain which of us I was reassuring.

"That is the most we can ask for." Her emerald eyes found Lira's fading silhouette at the forest's edge. "But do not delay, Talon. A shattered bond is a wound that does not mend." The words arrived with the specific precision of a blade finding the exact gap in armour it had been built for. They were about Lira, but the wound was in me, and it had been there since before I had a name for what had cracked to produce it.

I had not noticed the specific moment when Lira had become something other than another warrior beside me. It had happened in the specific accumulative way of things that did not announce themselves, each instance individually deniable, only legible in retrospect. Her silence had a specific quality that matched something in mine. Her footsteps fell in the specific rhythm of someone accustomed to moving through hard terrain without making it harder than it already was. She had carried the specific weight of her inheritance without using it as a reason to stop carrying other things, which was the specific kind of strength I had always been able to recognise and had never admitted to admiring.

I had spent years with the specific conviction that attachment was the vulnerability that preceded betrayal. That every bond was a future chain. But she was not that. She was the specific thing I had no prepared category for, which was more frightening than every category I had prepared for.

She unsettled me in the specific way of things that could see through the architecture I had built. That was the specific danger of her. Not her power. Not the inheritance she carried. The fact that in the specific moments when she was not performing anything, when the battle was over and the silence had not yet decided what to become, she was more present than most people managed in their loudest moments.

I thought I had concealed it. I had not.

She stood at the clearing's edge where the fog curled around her in the specific patient way it had always found her, her arms crossed in the specific way of someone who had given up the pretence of warmth and was simply present. She did not turn when I approached. Her voice, when it arrived, was the specific brittle quality of something that had been waiting to break cleanly and was determining the right fracture point.

"What next." Two words carrying the specific compressed weight of everything that was not being asked in them.

I stopped at the specific distance that was not far enough to be dismissive and not close enough to be presumptuous. I did not offer strategy. I did not offer command. I did not offer the specific words I had been composing since Myrcanthor told me not to delay.

"Forgive me."

Her head turned with the specific quality of someone whose expectations have been so completely disrupted by what has just been said that the body responds before the mind has processed it. "What." The word came out with the specific quality of disbelief that was not theatrical but genuine, the specific incredulous quality of someone who had prepared for every version of this conversation except this one.

The apology held in the air with the specific stillness of something that had been said with the full weight of its meaning and was not going to be qualified.

"I'm sorry for what I've done." Each word arrived the specific pace of something being released rather than delivered. "I have treated you as an obstacle rather than an ally. That was unjust."

The silence that followed was not empty. It had the specific quality of a space in which two people were holding something at the same time and neither was yet certain what to do with it. The earlier sharpness in her expression moved through several stages, each one the specific quality of a defence that had been prepared for a different kind of incoming and was recalibrating.

When she spoke, the sharpness had been replaced by something older and more specific. "Your distrust is evident." The accusation was not aggressive. It was the specific quiet of something that had been observed accurately and was being confirmed.

I exhaled with the specific raw quality of breath that had been held against resistance and was being released against pride. "I strive for faith." The words were not smooth. They were the specific honest roughness of something said by a man who was telling the truth about a struggle he had not resolved. "I want to believe that I can be better. That I can earn your trust." The pause was specific. "And I ask you to do the same. Mutual reliance is all we have. Without it, we are lost."

She held me in her gaze with the specific measuring quality of someone who had had bridges cracked under them before and was assessing the structural integrity of what was being offered before she put weight on it. The silence was the specific length of a genuine assessment rather than a performance of one.

Then a sigh. The specific long exhalation of someone releasing something they had been carrying in the specific muscles of the shoulder and the jaw.

A nod. Slow. Reluctant. The specific nod of a person who had decided to proceed and was not pretending there was no cost to the decision.

"Agreed." The word arrived with the weight of something that was both acceptance and reservation simultaneously. Then the specific curl at the corner of her mouth, not amusement, the specific expression of someone who was going to give ground and was announcing the specific terms of the giving. "However. Blind obedience isn't in my nature."

Something moved across my face that was not quite the smile it was adjacent to, the specific brief ghost of something that had been absent from my expression for longer than I had tracked. "I wouldn't expect it." Low and specific, with the edge that had stopped being hostility and become something else without either of us declaring the change.

The specific quality of what was between us shifted. Not resolved. The specific tension of something unfinished that had accepted its own state and was continuing to exist within it. The pressure in the air lightened by the specific degree that honesty lightened things when it was genuinely offered and genuinely received.

Lira relaxed her posture by the specific fraction of someone who had not fully relaxed but had stopped actively bracing. She turned to face the others.

"Let's move." Clear. Steady. The specific voice of someone who had made a decision and was done deliberating about it.

We caught up with Myrcanthor and the others, our pace the specific side-by-side rhythm of two people who had just negotiated something and were proceeding in the knowledge of what it had cost both of them. The Sylphs hovered in their specific watchful formation, their whispers a low continuous hum that carried the specific tone of beings that had not yet been persuaded of anything but were prepared to continue observing. Their suspicion was legible and specific. It was not resolved. But it was no longer the immediate threat.

Myrcanthor's voice broke through with the specific quality of something that had been calibrating the moment to say the most important thing.

"We're at the edge." Her massive shape cast shadows across the path ahead with the specific quality of things that existed at a different scale from the rest of the landscape. "Sunstone Vale is near. But the darkness is strongest there." She gave the final part its specific space. "Brace yourselves for the worst."

My gaze found Lira's for the specific brief interval of an exchange that did not use words and did not need to. Then I turned to face Myrcanthor with the specific quality of resolve that had been reassembled from components rather than found whole.

"We are prepared." The specific quality of a declaration that was also a challenge to whatever had been waiting to hear it. "Let this ordeal reach its end."

The summit took the specific work of a climb that had been designed by the geology and the corruption in equal measure, each in different ways. The path was treacherous in the specific ways of terrain that had been changed by what had been done to it, roots twisted at the specific ankle-seeking angles of things that had been ordinary roots and had been reorganised by something that had different priorities, loose rocks crumbling with the specific failure of material whose integrity had been compromised from below. The air as we climbed carried the specific rot of things that had been dying for a long time and had reached the specific stage of the process where dying was indistinguishable from the presence of death itself.

Beneath my boots, the ground pulsed. Not seismic. Not the weather-produced trembling of saturated soil. The specific pulse of ley lines that had been wounded and were still beating with the particular desperate rhythm of something that had not yet been permitted to stop.

Then the summit. And the world that opened below it.

None of us found words for it immediately. The specific quality of a silence produced not by the absence of things to say but by the presence of something that temporarily made language feel inadequate.

Sunstone Vale.

What stretched before us had been paradise in the specific way of places that had been shaped by the specific convergence of ley line power over centuries, the land organised by that power into something that served it and was served by it. What remained was the specific ruin of that relationship. The earth was cracked and shattered in the particular pattern of ground that had been drained rather than simply damaged, haemorrhaging power through the specific visible veins of ley energy that stretched across the land like capillaries in a body whose blood pressure had collapsed. Their glow flickered with the specific rhythm of things that were still trying.

The sunstone crystals that had been the specific material expression of this place's power lay shattered. Their brilliance was gone. In its place, the sickly green of corrupted ley energy pulsed in the specific slow rhythm of something feeding rather than radiating, thick and suffocating in the air above the shattered stone, the specific quality of a presence that had replaced something rather than simply occupied the space left by its absence.

The stench beneath my boots was specific: burnt stone and a deeper fouler layer that had no comparison in anything I wanted to compare it to. The land was not simply dying. The specific quality of what had been done here was consumption. Active, ongoing, not yet complete.

"Myrcanthor." Her name arrived from me as the specific quality of a word doing multiple things simultaneously. "What force has wrought this ruin."

Her emerald eyes moved across the desecrated landscape with the specific quality of eyes that were cataloguing rather than witnessing, the ancient intelligence in them doing something colder and more specific than grief. "The blight has infected the heart." The weight of prophecy in those words was not performative. It was the specific weight of something she had been watching approach for longer than I could calculate.

My boots found the cracked earth and I stepped forward with the specific movement of someone pressing toward the thing they needed to understand. "Can it be reclaimed."

The hesitation that followed was the most frightening thing she had given me yet. The specific rarity of Myrcanthor pausing before an answer, her talons finding the brittle ground with the specific depth of something seeking purchase in a surface that had lost its integrity. "Perhaps." The single word arrived with the specific care of something being handled rather than delivered. "But the ley lines are fragile now. Unstable. Volatile. Any attempt to mend them risks incalculable peril."

The hush that settled was not peace. It had the specific quality of a breath held before the next development.

Lira's voice arrived from behind me with the specific fragility of something that was small against the scale of what we were looking at. "And the alternative."

"The nexus will shatter." No hesitation this time. The specific finality of a door closing. "And when it does, the blight will be unleashed. Free to consume all without restraint."

I turned to the others with my expression carrying the specific quality of resolve that had been assembled from components that were running low. My grip on Ashenfang was the specific grip of a man who had made a decision and was anchoring himself to it through the physical contact of familiar steel. "We have come too far, lost too much, to falter now."

Then the sound came.

Guttural. Wet. The specific sound of something that had a throat but was using it for a purpose that throats were not designed for, a death rattle pulled out and given direction rather than simply released. It moved through the cracked ground before it moved through the air, the specific physical transmission of something too large to be contained in sound alone. The stench arrived with it in the specific wave of rot and bile and corrupted magic, the particular combination of smells that had no reference point in anything biological.

The ground trembled with the specific rhythm of footfalls that belonged to a scale I did not want to correctly calculate.

My hand had the specific grip of a man whose body had already begun its preparation while his mind was still completing the assessment. "Weapons." Not a command. A statement of what was already happening.

It tore itself from the ruined earth with the specific violence of something that had been contained and was no longer accepting containment, its emergence the specific rupture of a surface that had been holding something it could not hold. The form that assembled itself as it rose was the specific horror of wrong proportions, a size and a configuration of limbs and bone that was not the result of biology but of something having been done to biology, flesh stretched over a structure it had not been designed to cover, the wounds where the bone pushed through weeping with the specific black sludge I had seen in the corrupted wolves but in vastly greater quantity. Its eyes were the specific cold red that I had catalogued since the forest. They did not burn with hunger. They burned with the specific cold of corruption that had found its full form.

Lira's dagger was in her grip before I had finished the specific assessment. Her breath came in the specific shallow pulls of someone who was doing the same calculation I was doing and was arriving at the same results. "By the gods." Her voice carried the specific quality of words said because not saying them would have been a different kind of dishonesty. "What is that."

Myrcanthor spoke. Her voice had changed from its ordinary resonance to something lower and more specific, worn at the edges in a way I had not heard from her before, as though what she was saying was costing her something she had budgeted for this specific category of loss. The green light moved across her scales in the specific way of something finding the gaps in a surface it had been testing.

She had seen the rise of kingdoms and the specific slow dissolution of everything that made them. She had felt the world groan with the particular complaint of something that had been asked to hold too much for too long. And this before her was older than her grief about it, older than her capacity to place it in context.

"A guardian." Her voice came barely above the specific sound the air made when it moved around something large. "A protector. Now only a husk. Consumed by the very blight it was forged to resist."

The specific tragedy of those words found the specific place in me where tragedy settled. This was not an enemy. It was a monument to what the blight did to the things that opposed it, which was to hollow them out and wear their shape as armour against the next thing that tried to oppose it.

Then the roar.

Not a sound. A force. The specific physical force of something that had been compressed into audio form but had not lost any of its material quality in the conversion, arriving against my chest and my ribs and the bones of my face with the specific concussive quality of proximity to something enormous expressing rage. It tasted of sulphur and rusted iron and the specific chemistry of magic that had been turned against its own nature.

The ground cracked in the specific pattern of earth receiving a weight it had not consented to bear, fissures crawling outward from each point of contact, and the creature's claws found the wounded soil with the specific depth of things that had been given too much mass and not enough restraint. Each step dragged the specific stench of grave soil and centuries of accumulated wrongness in its wake.

My jaw locked. The scar beneath my eye throbbed with the specific rhythm of the ley lines beneath the shattered earth, a physical syncing with the land that Ashenfang had been producing in me since I claimed it. I did not move. My hand closed around the hilt with the specific certainty of a decision that had already been made and was simply being enacted.

"Hold." The word erupted from me with the specific raw quality of a command that had come from below the part of me that considered its words before releasing them. "By the ashes of our ancestors, hold the line. It must not reach the nexus."

The Sylphs moved above in the specific desperate grace of beings using their full capacity to be what they were in conditions that were actively working against it, weaving a lattice of light that held for the specific duration of their combined effort and then held less as the creature's presence pressed against it with the particular weight of something that had more patience than they had power. The light of them dimmed in the specific sequential way of stars disappearing before a storm.

Below, the Wyrms coiled in their specific defensive geometry, their obsidian scales catching the sickly green in the particular way of surfaces that were reflecting something they had not been designed to reflect. Their hissing was the specific sound of ancient creatures that had never encountered the thing in front of them and were registering that specific unfamiliarity with every available channel.

Lira moved. The specific fluid efficiency of someone who had found the geometry of the battlefield and was working within it with the particular economy of a person who knew they could not win this at range and was working toward the specific angles where she could be most effective. Her auburn hair across her face, the specific sweat and the specific blood and the specific expression of a person using everything they had and finding everything they had was not enough to constitute victory.

"It's unstoppable." Her voice came out with the specific rawness of honesty admitted in the middle of a fight, the particular acknowledgement of something being named rather than surrendered to. "We need a new plan. Now."

My blade found the creature's limb with the specific arc of a strike I had committed to completely. Ashenfang's emerald fire erupted along the edge and the severed flesh hit the cracked ground with the specific sound of corrupted material meeting the surface.

Then it grew back.

The specific horror of watching it reassemble, tendrils of muscle finding each other with the particular purpose of things that had a directive and were executing it, the limb rising renewed with the specific mockery of a body that had been given a different relationship to damage than the one I understood.

My knuckles went white. The specific cold fury of a man who had just been shown the specific futility of the approach he had available and had not yet located the correct approach. "Myrcanthor." My voice stripped to steel. My eyes found her above. "Obliterate it. Now."

Her eyes blazed with the specific cold fire of something that had been waiting for permission it should not have needed and had now received it.

The torrent that left her jaws was the specific green fire of something that had been produced by centuries of existing at the intersection of magic and dragon biology, rushing forward with the particular force of something that had never before been unleashed at full capacity at something it was not certain could be destroyed. The light it produced was the specific blinding white of complete saturation, the world reduced to pure brilliance for the specific duration of the inferno's peak. Then the specific sound of the creature's response, not the dying sound of something being destroyed but the specific sound of something being wounded and continuing.

The stench of burning corrupted flesh moved through the air with the specific chemistry of a fire that had been given the wrong fuel, and through the dimming of the aftermath the creature endured, its form scorched but its structure intact, the corruption running in channels too deep for fire to fully reach.

"It's a cancer, Talon." Myrcanthor's voice had the specific quality of something arriving at a conclusion it had been building toward since before we reached the summit. Her gaze moved from the creature to the nexus, which pulsed with the specific sickly yellow of something that had been golden and had been changed. "As long as the nexus breathes, this thing will rise. Again. And again."

My jaw set. The specific quality of a decision forming from the available materials. "Then we cut out the tumour." The words arrived from the specific part of me that had finished the calculation and was done waiting for a better option.

The ground disagreed.

The earth buckled with the specific violence of a body that had been forced to contain something it could not contain and had reached the end of its capacity, rolling beneath us in the particular way of geological structures making a decision about their own integrity.

"Lira, prepare the—"

The ley lines erupted.

The specific detonation of energy that had been coiled in the channels beneath Sunstone Vale reaching some specific critical threshold and releasing it in the single interval between one breath and the next, the sky fracturing into the specific blinding quality of pure unfiltered magic in its most raw and untethered state, and then the specific consuming darkness of the aftermath, not night, not shadow, the specific void of a space that had been so thoroughly emptied by the release that it was taking time to re-establish its relationship with light.

From that darkness the creature rose with the specific renewed quality of something that had been fed by the release rather than diminished by it, its form carrying the specific seething fury of a thing that had been hurt and had found its hurt converted into purpose.

The scream it produced was the specific world-breaking quality of sound that had moved beyond the register of the ordinary and into the register of things that changed the quality of the air they moved through, cracking the specific silence of the Vale and the specific quality of the sky above it in the same unbroken action.

"We're losing time." Myrcanthor's voice carried the specific raw quality of something I had never heard from her before. The specific fraying of the edge that had always been immovable in her voice, the particular note that I had been certain she did not have available. The specific fear of something that had not been afraid in a very long time and was afraid now. "The nexus is fracturing. This is a death sentence."

Her scales carried the specific dull quality of something whose surface had been changed by the corruption that had been pressing against it since before we arrived, the encroachment visible in the specific way that damage was visible on things that had been designed to resist it and were discovering the limits of the design. The blight moved through the Vale in the specific widening pattern of veins spreading from a single wound.

The ground split beneath us with the specific groan of earth giving way to something it had been asked to hold for too long.

I turned to Lira. The specific quality of my gaze was the most direct thing I had given her since the apology. "Your father's forbidden knowledge touched the ley lines." Each word arrived with the specific urgency of something being said with all the available time accounted for. "This broken web of power. Can it be repaired. Can you stop it before it swallows everything."

The question hung between us with the specific weight of a blade suspended by something very thin.

Her breath caught. The specific involuntary quality of a body that has received information it needs a moment to process. Her fingers curled, trembling with the specific fine tremor of someone who was at the specific intersection of everything they had been avoiding and the only available path forward.

The doubt arrived in her face with the specific legibility of something that had found the crack in the composure and was moving through it. Then something shifted. In the specific direction of down rather than away, the settling of something into its foundations rather than the crumbling of them. The inheritance she had been running from was specific and real and it contained specific knowledge that she was the only person present who had access to, and the specific horrible clarity of that arrived in her expression as the thing beneath the doubt rather than the replacement of it.

Her father had wielded what was in the ley lines like a blade. He had understood them at the specific level of someone who had spent everything to understand them, and what he had sacrificed to gain that understanding was the specific list of everything that had made his life worth the living. She had spent years running from that knowledge because of what it had cost him. But she was not him. She had just said so. And the specific test of whether that was true or simply something she said was whether she could use what he had given her without becoming what he had become.

Her jaw tightened. Something in her eyes that was the specific quality of steel in the process of being shaped.

"I'll try." The words came from the specific place where ash and old fear lived, carrying all of that, not pretending otherwise. Then she was gone.

She vanished into the storm of corrupted magic with the specific quality of someone who had made a decision and had moved past the point of it before the observer had fully processed the decision being made. The sickly light swallowed her and the specific quality of the air where she had been was the particular absence of something that had been present and was no longer.

I was dragged back into the fury before her name had finished forming in my chest.

The battle erupted around me in the specific way of things that had been waiting for the specific moment when the largest threat had been addressed and had now been given the field. Steel found the specific corrupted flesh with the particular hiss of fire meeting material it was designed to oppose. Screams moved through the smoke in the specific register of beings that were carrying more than their bodies were built for. The ground beneath me had the specific quality of something that had stopped being neutral and was participating in the conflict.

The Wyrms roared with the specific fury of ancient things that were fighting something that should not exist and were using every specific quality of what they were to fight it. Their breath carried the specific stench of sulphur and ruin and the particular heat of something that had been contained in biology for centuries and was being released at maximum capacity. The corrupted magic pressed back with the specific intensity of something that had been fed by everything this land had contained and was not yet empty.

We did not fight for the specific glory of it. We fought for the specific seconds that Lira needed.

She ran across the Vale's broken surface toward the convergence point with the specific efficiency of someone who had shed everything that was not essential to the next thirty seconds. The battlefield became sound behind her, the specific muffled roar of something she had left on the other side of a decision, her boots striking cursed ground with the particular urgency of someone who was very aware of the thing they were racing against.

The convergence point pulsed ahead of her with the specific wounded luminosity of something that was still trying to be what it had been made to be and was failing at the specific rate of its own destruction. She dropped to her knees before it with the specific controlled descent of someone who could not afford to stumble and did not. Her fingers trembled as she reached toward the fractured sunstone, the specific fine tremor of hands that were close to something that had claimed everything her father was.

The warmth that came back from the stone was old and specific, the warmth of something that had been warm for as long as the land had existed and was now warm in the particular way of things that were close to ceasing. The cracks in its surface bled the specific unstable magic of something that had been overfilled and was releasing what it could no longer hold. Her hand rested against it and the world trembled with the specific quality of a large thing responding to a very specific touch.

She closed her eyes.

His teachings arrived not as memory but as revelation, in the specific way of things that had been present but unprocessed and had found the right conditions to become legible. The madness she had always attributed to him stripped away to reveal the specific knowledge underneath, the obsession justified by what it had found, the ruthlessness explained by what it had cost to find. She felt what he had felt in the specific way of someone who had inherited the sensitivity without having to pay what he had paid to develop it.

The ley lines writhed beneath her palms. They were not passive channels. They were the specific active presence of something that had been wounded and was screaming for the particular kind of help that could not be described in ordinary language and could only be provided by the specific person who understood the frequency of the scream.

They did not want control. They wanted wholeness. Or they wanted the specific mercy of an end. And she was the specific person who had to decide.

The whisper that left her was not for anyone present. It was the specific private declaration of someone conducting a final reckoning with themselves in the only moment available for it. "I am not like him." The words came from the specific place where everything she had built her identity on lived. "This power will not claim me." Her palms pressed flat against the broken stone.

The stone answered.

The specific steadying of something that had been flickering, the pulse of the convergence point finding a rhythm and then finding a stronger rhythm, syncing with the specific heartbeat of the person touching it in the particular way of things that had been waiting for someone with the right frequency to present themselves.

Then the scream. Not from her. From the stone itself. From the magic that had been waiting for exactly this specific person at exactly this specific moment to give it the direction it could not find on its own.

The aberration shuddered.

Its massive form began the specific process of dissolution that was not death but the particular removal of the thing that had been animating it, the corrupted power withdrawing from the tissues it had been inhabiting, leaving them with the specific collapse of things that had been held together by something other than biology and had had that something removed. It thrashed with the specific desperation of something that was losing the argument it had thought it had already won.

The nexus had made its decision.

The scream that tore through the Vale was the specific sound of a thing being unmade rather than simply destroyed, the particular cry of something that had been assembled and was being disassembled, each component returning to the state it had been in before the corruption found it. Then it was not there. The specific clean absence of something that had occupied space and no longer did, not dissolved so much as rejected, the world refusing its continued presence with the particular finality of a decision that had been made at the deepest available level.

The light that followed was specific in its quality. Golden. The particular warm gold of the ley lines as they had been before, before the corruption found the specific gaps in them and worked its way in, pouring across the Vale in the specific wave of something returning to its own nature after an extended period of being forced to be something else. It moved over the land with the particular quality of restoration rather than replacement, finding the specific cracks in the earth and filling them rather than covering them.

Darkness recoiled from it with the specific quality of something that had been depending on the absence of light and was now being denied that dependency. The air changed in the specific way of air that had been carrying the wrong thing for too long and was being relieved of it, the specific clean quality of breath after something foul had passed through a room and the room had had time to recover.

The specific earth shiver of the land reorienting to its own pulse, to the particular rhythm it had been before something else had overwritten it. The stench of rot lifted in the specific incremental way of things dissipating rather than stopping, the specific clean arrival of air that tasted of nothing except what air was supposed to taste of.

Lira staggered back from the convergence point with the specific motion of someone whose legs had given the maximum available and were no longer able to negotiate the terms of the next step. Each breath came in the particular gasps of someone who had been channelling something much larger than their body and was discovering the cost in real time.

I caught her before she completed the fall.

The specific weight of her against my arms was the specific weight of someone who had given everything and was discovering that everything had a mass. I held her with the specific quality of someone who was not letting go, which was different from simply holding, different in every specific way from the category of contact I had been maintaining with the careful distance of a man who had decided that distance was a form of safety.

My voice arrived with the specific roughness of someone who had used all of the available polish on things other than this moment. "You triumphed." The words arrived not as assessment but as recognition, the specific acknowledgement of what I had watched her do and what it had required and what it had changed in the specific calculus of everything I had doubted about her.

Her eyes opened. The fire in them was the specific fire of something that had not been extinguished by what it had been through. The smile that found her face was small and the specific kind of real that only came from exhaustion honest enough to strip everything else.

"Together," she said. The specific quality of one word carrying the specific weight of everything that had been negotiated and survived and decided in the hours that had produced this moment.

The others gathered with the specific quality of people who had arrived at the end of something enormous and were standing in the particular hush of the aftermath, the final glow of the restored nexus casting the specific long shadows of late battle across the shapes of people who were still breathing and were not certain what to do with that fact.

Myrcanthor looked across the restored Vale with the specific quality of eyes that had seen too much to be fully comforted by what they were seeing, even when what they were seeing was genuinely beautiful. Her jaw held the specific tension of something that was not finished.

"This is only the beginning." Her voice was low and specific in its weight, not the weight of despair but the particular weight of accuracy. "The ley lines remain exposed. The balance is not yet restored."

I nodded. My hand found Ashenfang's hilt in the specific way of a hand that understood the touch was a statement about what came next rather than a preparation for an immediate action. The danger was specific and real and had not concluded simply because this part of it had.

"Then we finish what we started." My voice carried the specific quality of something that had been said as a vow before it was said as a sentence, already binding before the words were complete.

The wind took the words across the reborn Vale with the specific quality of wind that had been waiting to carry something worth carrying. Below us, the land breathed. The specific long exhale of something that had been holding its breath for longer than breath was meant to be held, and had been given, by the specific person who was the only one who could give it, the particular permission to breathe again.

CHAPTER TWELVE - ECHOES OF THE NEXUS

THE GOLDEN LIGHT WAS WRONG. I UNDERSTOOD THIS before I could articulate why, standing in the specific aftermath of Sunstone Vale's restoration with the nexus pulsing its new warmth across the cracked earth and feeling the wrongness of it in my spine rather than through my eyes. The light was real. The healing was real. The ley lines beneath my boots had shifted from their specific arrhythmic screaming into something that approximated their natural pulse. All of that was true. And the air still carried the specific weight of something that had not finished with us.

The silence was wrong in the same way. Not the silence of absence, not the silence of rest, but the specific silence of a presence that had reorganised itself from loud to quiet without departing.

Something was still watching us. Still waiting for us to make our move.

Lira sat on a broken log at the clearing's edge with her hands in her lap and her fingers curved in the specific position of hands that had been gripping something enormous and had been asked to let it go and had not yet fully processed the instruction. Before her, the shattered Sunstone crystal pulsed with the specific weak rhythm of something that was still trying, a heartbeat that kept finding the next beat and could not be certain of the one after. The exhaustion in her was not in the muscles alone. It was in the specific deeper register of a person who had been scoured out from the inside, who had had something very large pass through them and had found hollows where certainties used to be.

The corruption had not left her.

She could feel it in the specific way she could feel the ley line pulse through the ground, not external but integrated, coiled in the specific place beneath her sternum where the worst things settled and stayed. It had moved through her to reach the nexus and it had moved back through her on the way out and it had left residue in the specific channels it had used, the way water left mineral traces in stone after it passed through. Her hands tightened in her lap. The taste of metal and old decay persisted on the back of her tongue with the specific permanence of things that had decided on a location.

I approached with the specific care of someone reading the quality of the silence around a person before deciding whether to disturb it. Ashenfang hung at my side with the specific dull quality of a blade that had spent everything it had and was resting in the way that things rested when they were not sure they had recovered. My steps were gentle against the new-healed earth, which still had the specific fragility of a recently closed wound.

"You need to rest." My voice came out low with the specific quality of something being offered rather than commanded. "What you did surpassed anything I could have asked for."

She did not respond immediately. The exhale she gave instead was the specific long exhalation of someone who had been holding something at tension for too long and was releasing the tension without releasing the weight. Her eyes came up to mine with the specific shadowed quality of exhaustion that had moved past the stage of being corrected by sleep.

"This is an insufficient fix." Her voice was barely above the ambient sound of the Vale settling. Not resignation. The specific accurate assessment of someone who had been inside the mechanics of the problem and knew exactly where the remaining fault lines were. "The nexus holds. Just barely." She swallowed and the taste of ash and spent magic was visible in the specific quality of the swallow. "What happens when the next one fails."

I knelt beside her. The ground beneath my knee had the specific give of earth that had been changed from the inside out and was still accommodating the change. "We will face it." The words arrived with the specific quality of certainty being applied to a situation that did not entirely deserve certainty, the specific conscious decision to believe something because the alternative was worse. "As we have this one. Together."

She repeated the word with her lips barely moving. Together. It arrived in her mouth with the specific hollow quality of a sound that had been true once and was being tested against the current circumstances.

Myrcanthor's presence dominated the clearing's edge in the specific way that she dominated spaces when she chose not to announce herself but to simply be fully present in them. Her wings were folded. Her massive frame was the specific dark of something that absorbed the moonlit Vale's golden light rather than reflecting it. Her emerald eyes moved across the landscape with the particular survey of something that had been alive long enough to read a land's face the way I read a battlefield, not what it showed but what it was not showing.

When she spoke, it was not triumph. It was the specific solemn register of something that had decided to be honest rather than comforting.

"Even though the nexus is safe," she said, and the particular weight she gave the conjunction told me what was coming before the rest of the sentence arrived, "the wound is getting worse. The contagion is suppressed. It is not extinguished."

The golden light across the Vale did not dim. But the specific quality of what I saw it doing to the landscape changed, the warmth of it suddenly insufficient to the specific cold of what she had just named.

The wind shifted. It moved through the golden mist at the tree line and pulled it back in the specific slow way of something deliberately revealing what it had been covering. Shadows at the tree line parted for a specific brief interval, a glimpse of something on the other side of the visible.

Then footsteps.

Measured. The specific deliberateness of someone who had been moving toward this moment for some time and had decided on the pace of their arrival.

Rowan stepped into the clearing's light and the journey was in every specific detail of him. His cloak bore the particular dust of roads covered at pace, frayed at the edges in the specific way of fabric that had been through sustained use without respite. The sharpness that had always lived in his eyes had been replaced by something cloudier, the specific haunted quality of eyes that had seen things they were still in the process of categorising. He stood with the specific rigid quality of a man who had decided to be upright regardless of what his body was suggesting.

"You survived." Not a question. Not relief that we had survived this ordeal. The specific delivery of a fact that he had decided to say aloud for reasons that had nothing to do with uncertainty and everything to do with needing to confirm it outside his own mind.

Lira's breath caught with the specific involuntary quality of someone who has been surprised by their own response to a thing. Something passed across her face in the brief unreadable interval between the response and the composure. Then she gripped the cracked Sunstone beside her with the specific force of someone using physical contact as an anchor.

"And you abandoned the manor." Her voice was quiet. Not accusation. The specific quality of understanding that had been extended to cover something it found difficult to cover, the particular tone of someone who was naming a truth and was choosing not to weaponise it.

The words held in the air with the specific heaviness of things that had been said and could not be unsaid and were carrying more than their literal content.

Rowan exhaled. The specific duration of a breath that has been held against multiple pressures simultaneously and is being released against all of them at once. "The manor hasn't fallen." His voice was low with the particular undertone of a man who knew the next word he was about to say was the most significant one. "Not yet." His gaze moved from Lira to me with the specific quality of eyes delivering a warning they did not know how to soften. "But it stirs, Talon."

The words settled with the specific weight of things that arrived at the worst possible moment and knew it.

He continued, his voice steady with the specific steadiness of someone who had decided to say the difficult thing completely rather than stopping at the threshold of it. "If the ley lines breathe anew here, then we have not finished." The question arrived quietly but with the specific unyielding quality of something that had been building since before he entered the clearing. "What dire consequences await Hougun Manor."

I looked at Myrcanthor first. Then at Rowan. "Will the taint return to claim it."

The silence that arrived was the specific quality of silence before something structural fails, the particular hush of the world gathering itself before a significant event.

Myrcanthor's tail swept the cracked earth in a slow arc and the tremor it produced moved through the brittle soil with the specific quality of something confirming what it found there. She answered slowly, with the specific reluctance of something that valued accuracy more than comfort but had not lost its awareness that accuracy sometimes cost the person receiving it. "The possibility exists."

The words settled through the gathered company in the specific way of truths that had been half-suspected and were now confirmed, each person absorbing the weight at their own specific pace.

She continued before the silence could calcify. "The ley lines are interwoven. The collapse of one nexus will inevitably destabilise the others." Her emerald gaze found the horizon where the nexus's golden light reached the specific edge of the illuminated territory and met the dark that was waiting beyond it.

I was on my feet before the sentence had fully completed, the specific movement of a body that had made a decision at the level below deliberation. "Our position is untenable. If the contagion still festers, locating its source is paramount."

Myrcanthor did not answer immediately. Her gaze locked onto the flickering nexus with the specific quality of something that was consulting an older source of information than the ones available in speech. When she spoke, her voice carried the particular weight of centuries of accumulated understanding encountering something that exceeded its own categories. "This is beyond mere corruption." The exhale that followed moved through the stone at her feet, audible through the ground rather than the air. "These ley lines, these conduits of power, predate the land itself." Her eyes found mine, and the depth in them was the specific depth of something that had been looking at the same question for a very long time and had not finished. "And even I do not fully understand what they are capable of."

The wind moved through the Vale with the specific cold of air that had come from somewhere other than the local atmosphere, carrying the quality of distance and something beneath distance. The specific feeling of an unseen force pressing at the periphery of perception. Not yet arrived. But oriented toward us.

Rowan's fingers twisted in the specific restless way of hands that needed to be doing something that the current situation did not permit. "Explain." His voice was the specific tight thread of a man who had been carrying uncertainty for too long and was requesting the specific information that would allow him to convert it into something manageable.

Myrcanthor paused. The specific rarity of it was its own form of information. Her massive eyes held the flickering glow of the ley lines in a way that mirrored their specific uncertainty, the light shifting in registers that I could not fully track. "The old sagas speak of a force bound to the very creation of the ley lines," she said, choosing each word with the particular care of someone building something that needed to hold weight. "Not a guardian. Not a god. But older than the first application of either category." She gave that its space. "A force that did not simply reside alongside the ley lines but within them. Intrinsic to their nature. As essential to them as breath is to a living body."

The corruption's persistence had the specific quality of something that was not simply decay but appetite, not random but directional, and the direction it had been pointing toward since before we arrived in the Vale was now legible in a way it had not been when we were still fighting the immediate shape of it.

Lira's breath hitched. The specific involuntary quality of a body that has received information it was not finished processing and has registered the incompleteness. Her gaze came up to find Myrcanthor's face with the particular urgency of someone looking for the specific confirmation of the thing they already feared most.

"Did we wake something."

The words arrived with the specific quality of a stone dropped into dark water. Not loud. But moving outward in all directions from the point of impact.

Myrcanthor exhaled, and the sound moved through the earth rather than the air. "The nexus is not merely a conduit." Each word carried the specific deliberate weight of something being said in full awareness of its consequences. "It is a gateway. A portal." She paused with the particular duration of someone giving the next thing the space it needed to arrive at its full weight. "By stabilising it, we may have done more than close the wound." Another pause. "We may have drawn a presence through. Something that should have remained dormant."

The silence that followed was the specific silence of a group that had been holding the category of what we had done as victory and had just had the category reclassified.

A door once opened.

I tightened my grip on Ashenfang's hilt in the specific way of a hand that needed the specific warmth of the blade's familiar pulse against the specific cold that had arrived in my chest. "Then we must find the source." The words arrived as the specific declaration of a decision that had been made before the full cost was visible, because waiting for the full cost had never once been an available option.

The Sylphs had not moved from the golden mist at the clearing's edge. Their shimmering forms were the specific barely-distinguishable quality of things that had been present throughout the whole conversation and had been conducting their own separate calculation about everything they had heard. The silence they maintained was not empty. It had the specific accumulated quality of judgment that had been building since before Rowan arrived and had found additional material in everything said since.

Their stares pressed against Lira's skin with the specific quality of something that had weight but no physical form, the particular suffocation of being assessed by multiple consciousnesses simultaneously and finding the assessment uniformly negative.

Then a voice, the specific delicate quality of something that had decided not to use its full capacity because the message it was delivering did not require volume.

"She is bound to this." Soft. But with the specific certainty of a verdict rather than an opinion. "The defilement runs in her very essence."

Lira stilled. The specific quality of a body that has been moving and has received a signal to stop. Something moved through her eyes with the particular brevity of pain that had found an entry point and had moved through it before the defences could organise. Then her voice came back cold, the specific cold of something that had been through fire and had decided on a response that fire could not touch.

"My hearing's perfectly fine."

The Sylph's glow pulsed with the particular rhythm of something that was not moving and was not yielding. The specific stubbornness of a being that was entirely convinced of its own accuracy.

I stepped forward with the specific weight of presence inserted between two things that were approaching a point of irreversible damage.

"Enough." No room in it for negotiation. "Lira's actions preserved the nexus. Without her, none of us would have survived."

The Sylph's luminescence dimmed by the specific fraction of something that had absorbed an argument it could not immediately refute but had not changed its fundamental position. "She did safeguard it." The concession arrived with the particular reluctant quality of a truth being given against preference. "But at what cost." The pause was the specific pause of a being that had been building to the actual question and had now arrived at it. "We do not understand her. Even she does not understand herself. How long before she becomes what we fear."

Lira was on her feet before the sentence completed. The specific movement of a body that had found a threshold and had crossed it, her posture the rigid quality of something that had stopped accommodating the position it was being asked to accommodate. Her hands were closed at her sides, the specific white of knuckles that had nails pressing into palms. The power beneath her skin had the particular quality of something that was present and was being contained and the containment was costing her something I could see in the line of her jaw.

"I don't know what I am yet." Her voice was fierce with the specific fierceness of something that had stopped performing certainty and was being honest about its own complexity. "I don't know the full weight of my father's influence. But I refuse to carry the guilt of crimes I have not committed."

The air held for a specific interval. The Sylph's form wavered in the particular way of something whose certainty has encountered something it could not fully categorise, whose confidence has found the specific obstacle of a person refusing to be the thing being projected onto them. The Vale around us was colder in the specific way of the dying light rather than the temperature, the realisation that Lira's relationship with herself was as unresolved as anyone else's relationship with her.

Myrcanthor advanced with the specific slow authority of something that did not need to hurry because its presence was itself the argument. Her wings shifted with the particular sound of something promising two things simultaneously. "The nexus demands harmony." Her voice moved through the brittle ground and into the bones of everything present. "Distrust among you will only hasten your downfall."

The Sylphs bowed their heads in the specific unison of beings that had received a directive from something with sufficient authority to constitute a directive. Their glowing forms receded like the specific fading of mist when it has been given a reason to disperse. Graceful. Silent. The specific unspoken warning of things that had withdrawn but had not changed.

I exhaled and looked at Lira. She held herself with the specific quality of a blade that has been struck against something harder than itself and is in the specific moment of finding out whether it has survived the impact intact. Her shoulders carried the tension of things that had been held too long.

"You do not need to prove yourself to anyone." My voice found a register I did not use often, the specific softer register that came from the place where I kept things I was not performing.

She held very still for a specific beat. Then: "I do not seek validation." A breath. The particular pause of someone choosing the right word from among several that were available and less accurate. "I seek to conquer my own doubts."

The specific honesty of that statement held in the air between us in the way that specific honest things held, not comfortably, but with the particular weight of something true.

The golden glow of the nexus faded as we moved deeper into the Vale, the specific incremental dimming of something that was losing its battle with what surrounded it, its light flickering with the particular quality of a flame being pressured from below rather than from the sides. The air grew dense with the specific accumulation of something that was not visible but was occupying the same space as visibility and was substituting its own quality for what light should have been providing.

Myrcanthor turned toward the fading crystal with the specific sharpness of a large head making a movement that smaller things made when their instincts had overridden their deliberation. The specific quality of her face as it found the nexus was unreadable in a way that was itself information, the particular blankness of something that was processing something very significant very quickly and was not yet ready to present the processing.

"It begins." The two words arrived without the specific context that would have made them less frightening.

I was beside her before I had finished deciding to be, my grip on Ashenfang finding the specific pulse of the blade that had been sensing the change in the Vale's fabric before I had consciously registered it, the weapon communicating through its own channels that something in the air had fundamentally altered. "What begins."

The dragon's gaze did not move from the nexus. "The resurgence." The specific single word of it rippled through the already fractured silence with the particular quality of a stone finding a specific frequency in cracked glass.

The ground trembled. Not the geological tremor of shifting earth. The specific pulse of something beneath the geology, something that used the earth a s a medium for its communication rather than as the source of its movement.

"A hunger stirs beneath the ley lines." Her voice had the specific tightness of something she had been hoping not to have to say. "A god that has slept for far too long."

The hush that arrived was not the peace of safety. It was the specific silence of the moment before something irrevocable, the particular pause of the world gathering itself before it changed.

I nodded. The specific single motion of a man who had arrived at the only available position. "Then we face it. No matter the cost."

Lira moved. A step forward, the specific step of someone whose exhaustion had been displaced by something with more force than exhaustion, something that had ignited in the specific place where purpose lived and had overwritten the fatigue. Her eyes found mine with the particular quality of steel finding its mirror in other steel. "United, we stand."

"As one." The words arrived from me as a vow rather than a statement, carrying the particular difference between the two, which was the difference between a description and a commitment.

Behind us, the nexus pulsed with the specific weak rhythm of something that had given everything and was still trying, its golden luminescence the particular fading quality of embers that had decided not to go out entirely but could not make specific promises about how long that decision would hold.

I decided that we should keep moving.

The Vale ahead had changed from what it had been when we arrived. The specific decay that had been there before our battle had been joined by something new, a quality added rather than simply continued, the particular progression of corruption that had been suppressed in one area finding additional expression in the area ahead. Blackened vines coiled over the skeletal remains of what had been living earth, their surface slick with the specific organic sheen of things that had been altered at a biological level, curling and twisting with the particular quality of things that were aware of us and were expressing that awareness through motion. The trees that remained upright were the specific grotesque sentinels of things that had been hollowed from the inside, their bark split in jagged wounds that wept the particular sickly resin of a corruption that had passed through the living wood and left evidence of its passage in the tissue.

The air burned the specific back of my throat with the particular acrid quality of decay that had moved past the biological stage and into something that did not have a name in the categories of ordinary rot, carrying the metallic undertone of corrupted magic that had been here long enough to have become part of the atmosphere.

The ground convulsed beneath us in the specific way of earth that had lost confidence in its own structural integrity, the parched surface splintering in cracks that opened with the particular speed of things that had been waiting for the specific load that we represented. Pebbles fell into a chasm ahead that had not been there when we arrived, swallowed by the specific darkness of a depth that was still being determined.

The land was breaking, not with a sudden crack , but a slow, rhythmic groan that vibrated through the soles of my boots.

Myrcanthor stopped with the specific abruptness of a massive creature receiving information through senses that operated at a different speed from the visible. Her wings unfurled with the particular sound of large things displacing heavy air, pushing aside the stagnant atmosphere with the specific force of something that needed to see what was around her rather than simply what was in front. Her talons found the trembling ground and the tremor that came back up through them was legible to her in a way it was not legible to me.

Her emerald eyes swept the fractured earth with the specific careful precision of something that was reading a language I did not have. The ley lines beneath us pulsed with the particular hungry quality of channels that had been overdrawn and were still demanding more than the system could supply, their glow flickering in the erratic rhythm of a heartbeat that had been compromised.

"Be careful." Her voice was the specific low resonant growl of something that had arrived at a warning by a route that included information we did not have access to. "This ground is untrustworthy. It does not merely crumble." The pause before the last word was the particular pause of something choosing precision over comfort. "It hungers."

The wind moved through the skeletal trees with the specific hollow mournful quality of air passing through spaces that had been designed for something else, the particular sound of absence made audible. The stench of burnt stone and the fouler underlying rot pressed into the specific channels of my sinuses and settled there with the particular permanence of things that intended to stay.

Ashenfang's pulse against my palm was the specific reliable constant of a blade that was oriented toward what was ahead and was communicating its assessment through the only medium available to it. I was listening.

Lira exhaled in the specific slow way of someone rationing what they were taking in from the compromised air, her breath misting in the unnatural chill that had established itself in the Vale ahead of us. She looked at the fractured terrain with the particular assessment of someone who had already made their decision and was confirming it against the available evidence. Then she looked at Myrcanthor.

"Then let's not linger." Her voice was steady with the specific steadiness of something that had been maintained through effort and had not yet been given permission to stop being maintained.

We moved forward. Into the land that was watching us with the particular attention of something that had been waiting for us to arrive and had specific plans for what happened next.

The ley lines beneath my boots shifted from the particular weak pulse of the nexus's aftermath into something with a different character, a dissonant vibration that was not the sick arrhythmic stutter of corruption and was not the healthy pulse of power in its natural state, but was a third thing that I did not have a category for yet and that scraped against my bones with the specific quality of something that was communicating rather than simply being present.

The Sunstone crystal's feeble glow was still visible behind us, the specific diminished light of something that had given everything available and was operating on whatever was below everything. Above, the Sylphs moved with the particular restless flickering of forms that had lost their steady luminescence and were pulsing in the specific broken rhythm of things that were struggling to maintain their own coherence in the presence of what was ahead.

Rowan's breath had the particular uneven quality of someone whose body was responding to environmental information at a pace ahead of his deliberate composure. His fingers touched the blade at his hip in the specific checking motion of someone confirming that the thing they would reach for was still there. His gaze moved across the shadowy horizon with the particular darting quality of eyes that had been trained to look for specific threats and were currently finding the entire horizon threatening. "We need to leave." His voice was the specific fragile thread of someone saying a true thing that they already know will not be acted on. "The world feels twisted."

Myrcanthor did not turn from the shaking nexus. The specific total stillness of her attention on it was its own form of answer to the question that had not yet been asked. "Retreat is impossible." The words came from the deep register of something that had thought this through to its conclusion before anyone else had started. "The stabilisation is not yet complete. If we abandon it now, we do not delay the darkness." The pause before the next part was the specific duration of something choosing the most accurate word available. "We invite it." Her wings shifted, the specific displacement of air sending dust spiralling in the particular patterns of something communicating through its movement. "If we turn back now, we do not run from the blight. We become its heralds."

The hush fell with the specific weight of an absolute.

The ground quivered. The ley lines pulsed with the particular desperate quality of something that was still functioning but was communicating the specific urgency of its difficulty.

Rowan's jaw held the specific tension of two things in direct conflict being resolved in real time. The reluctant nod when it arrived was the particular concession of someone who had been overruled by the quality of the argument rather than by force.

The Sylphs above flickered with the specific pattern of forms that had been maintaining themselves at a level the current atmosphere did not support, their radiance pulsing in the particular broken rhythm of things that were spending more than they were taking in. Their watchfulness toward Lira had not changed. It had the particular quality of something that had become more specific rather than less, sharpened by everything that had happened since the nexus restored itself.

Lira stood at the nexus's edge with her arms crossed and the fractured Sunstone's weak light reflected in her eyes in the specific quality of someone who was looking at something without seeing it, whose attention had moved inward toward something she was trying to understand. The ley lines beneath her feet were doing something specific. I could see it in the quality of her stillness, the particular way she had stopped moving with the slight weight-shifting motion of a person who was standing and had acquired the particular quality of a person who had become rooted.

The pulse of the lines had found the specific rhythm of her heartbeat and was matching it.

Then she exhaled with the specific quality of a realisation taking physical form in the breath, the weight of it pressing cold against her ribs in a way that was visible in the specific adjustment of her posture.

"Talon." Her voice barely disturbed the specific hush of the clearing and still carried the particular weight that made me pivot with my stance already shifting to its guarded configuration. "What is it."

She hesitated. The specific hesitation of someone for whom saying a thing aloud will make it real in a way that it is not yet real, and who is calculating whether the reality is preferable to the uncertainty. "I feel something." The words arrived with the particular charged quality of something that had been held and was being released. "Like a presence." She swallowed. "It's reaching."

All available attention directed to her. The specific quality of a group that has been organised around external threats finding that the next significant development has arrived from an unexpected direction.

Myrcanthor's head lowered with the specific deliberate quality of something bringing its full sensory capacity to bear on a point. Her emerald eyes found Lira's with the particular boring intensity of something searching for truth beneath the surface of words. "A summons," she said. The specific single word that reframed everything. "Describe it."

Lira's breath stilled. The specific stillness of someone looking for language to fit an experience that predated the available language. "Elusive," she said at last, and her voice had the particular quality of something being admitted rather than stated. "Like something is reaching out. Tugging at me. Not with force." A pause. The specific duration of someone finding the right word. "A message."

The sharp hiss that cut through the charged air was the specific sound of outrage finding its minimum expression. A Sylph drifted forward with the particular agitation of something that had been listening and had reached its threshold. "Ridiculous." Her luminescence pulsed with barely restrained force. "The nexus is inert. A conduit, not a living force. It does not beckon."

The denial was the specific absolute kind. But in the depths of Myrcanthor's gaze something shifted with the particular quality of something finding an opening rather than a conclusion. "Is it." Her head lifted toward the weakened nexus, toward the frayed ley lines that were pulsing in the specific pattern of something that had been through a great deal and was still trying to communicate. "These currents of power predate our lifetimes by aeons. They have shaped worlds. To assume they do not think, do not remember, seems a failure of understanding." The particular measured weight of those words found the specific places where easy dismissal lived and dislodged them.

Lira swallowed. The nexus's pulse was still in her bones in the specific way that a thing persisted after direct contact, integrated rather than simply remembered. And beneath the fractured ground, something dark and specific moved with the quality of something that had been dormant and was no longer dormant.

My grip on Ashenfang found its specific white-knuckled position. "If the nexus is reaching for Lira, then what does it want." My voice was low with the particular edge of a question that was also a warning. "What does it crave."

Rowan's voice arrived with the specific careful quality of someone testing an idea against the air before committing to it. "Perhaps it's her bloodline." The words entered the specific atmosphere of the clearing with the quality of something that had been submerged and had found its way to the surface. "If Daegrith wielded an affinity for the ley lines, if that bond was passed through blood, perhaps the nexus remembers."

The ripple that moved through the Sylphs was the specific physical response of beings that had heard a thing confirmed that they had been hoping to have refuted. Their whispers built with the particular tide-before-storm quality of things that were approaching a collective determination. One voice emerged with the specific brittle quality of dry leaves. "If she is tied to Daegrith, then she is tied to the blight. We cannot trust her. We dare not."

The hush that descended was the specific suffocating kind.

I moved into it. "Enough." The word arrived as the specific strike it was intended to be. "We've dissected this argument enough times to bleed it dry. Lira saved the nexus. She is not our enemy."

The Sylphs fell silent with the particular quality of silence that was not agreement but was the specific acknowledgement that the argument had been halted rather than won. The distrust remained in the air with the particular weight of something that had been stated and could not be unstated, curling in the cold spaces between us.

Lira's fists had tightened with the specific gradual quality of something building rather than snapping, her nails finding the specific places in her palms where the pain was most useful for focus. Her gaze was on the nexus with the particular quality of something that needed a fixed point while everything around it moved.

The ground shuddered. The specific quiet warning of a tremor that was not geological, moving through the cracked earth in the particular waves of something that was building from below rather than shifting from the side.

Myrcanthor's head snapped upward with the specific speed of instinct rather than decision. Her wings rustled. Her nostrils flared with the particular quality of something tasting the air for information it had been specifically waiting for and had now found. Her voice arrived low and urgent with the particular quality of something that was usually unshaken and was not currently unshaken. "It's awake."

Lira staggered back from the nexus with the specific motion of someone who has been standing near something and has received a signal too large for the body to absorb without physical response, her breath coming in the particular short pulls of someone whose chest has been compressed by something that is not external. "What fresh hell is this."

The Sunstone was no longer flickering. It was burning. The specific quality of something that had been weak and had found a source and was now drawing on it with the full capacity of what it was, its golden light blazing through the Vale with the particular intensity of something that had been a dying ember and had just been given fuel. It beat with the specific rhythm of a living heart, not the weak intermittent pulse of before but the strong particular beat of something that had been waiting to be this and had now been given the conditions.

The ley lines responded. The specific murmur beneath the earth became the particular crescendo of something that had been speaking at a frequency below what we had been able to register and had found a way to make itself heard at full volume. The air thickened with the particular metallic taste of magic at its most raw and most uncontained, pressing against the tongue, humming against the skin with the specific electric quality of something that was operating outside its designed parameters and did not care. Reality bent. The specific inward fold of the world's fabric drawn toward the nexus's impossible light with the particular gravity of something that had decided where the center was.

The group reeled with the specific physical response to forces that were not weather and were not combat but were the particular fundamental forces of the world being rearranged around a point. "This is unnatural." My voice came out strained with the particular quality of something pushing through resistance. Ashenfang ignited in my hand with the specific emerald fire of a blade that had made a decision before I had made a decision, the glow pushing back against the closing chaos with the particular force of something that had been made for exactly this category of confrontation and was doing what it was made for. "Hold formation."

And the Vale exhaled.

Myrcanthor uncoiled with the specific massive urgency of something that had been holding its position and had determined that the position was no longer tenable. Her wings spread with the particular vastness of something that was not simply large but was making itself present in the specific way of things that understood their own scale. Her emerald eyes blazed with the particular reflection of the broken Sunstone throwing its light across her scales in the specific patterns of something that had changed. She placed herself between us and the pulsing nexus with the particular deliberateness of something that had chosen a side and was expressing that choice physically.

"A power has been unleashed." Her voice was low with the particular tautness of something barely restrained. "I warned you this was never just a wellspring." The specific weight of having been right about a thing one had hoped to be wrong about. "This is a portal."

The specific chill of that word moved through the gathered company with the particular ripple of something that had been suspected and was now confirmed.

"A portal to where." Rowan's voice carried the particular quality of a question that was afraid of its own answer.

Myrcanthor's gaze held the nexus with the specific unblinking attention of something that was reading information arriving faster than it could process. The tremors built beneath us toward the particular crescendo of things approaching a specific threshold.

Then detonation.

The nexus erupted in the specific way of something releasing everything it had accumulated rather than simply failing. The golden light that burst from it was not the warm comfortable gold of restoration. It was the particular searing white of a force that had exceeded the capacity of its con-

tainer and was making that fact physical, burning the specific places behind the eyes where ordinary light did not reach, filling the air with the
taste of ozone and something beneath ozone, the particular raw flavour of
power at the moment before it became something other than power.
Reality bent. The specific inward warping of the fabric of the world at the
nexus's immediate vicinity, gravity finding a new relationship with itself
for the particular duration of the detonation.

Then the light collapsed around us.

The void that followed was the specific absolute kind. Not darkness. The
particular absence of everything that darkness was made in contrast to, the
specific experience of a world that had been robbed of its operating assumptions in the same instant. The ley lines dropped from their crescendo
to the particular faint whisper of something that had spent itself completely and was breathing in the specific shallow way of things that were
determining whether they were going to continue.

"What just happened." My voice was the particular sharp quality of a man
who needed information and was going to have it.

Myrcanthor's reply arrived with the specific careful precision of something
choosing every word against the criterion of accuracy. "The nexus has sta-
bilised." A pause with the particular weight of a thing being held before
the thing that complicated it. "But the pattern is different."

Lira moved toward the nexus with the specific slow quality of someone
moving through a medium that had acquired resistance, each step requiring the particular conscious commitment of a person who was walking
against something that was pushing back. The darkness that pressed

against her bones was specific and hungry and oriented toward the nexus in the particular way of things that had found a direction and were following it. "I feel it." Her hands flexed at her sides with the specific involuntary quality of someone whose body was registering something that her conscious mind was still in the process of understanding. "The pull is stronger. Like a magnetic force."

I was between her and the Sunstone before I had decided to be, the specific protective placement of a body that had made a decision before the deliberative mind caught up. "Stop." The particular sharp cut of a command delivered against something I could not see or name but could feel through the specific quality of Ashenfang's pulse against my palm. "We don't know what we're dealing with."

Myrcanthor's eyes found me with the particular calculating quality of something that had already determined an answer I had not yet reached. "Perhaps." The specific measured counterpoint to my urgency. "She alone may possess the means to understand it. If the nexus seeks her, there is a reason."

My jaw tightened with the particular quality of someone whose resolve had found the specific point where it wavered against something he trusted more than his own caution. I did not trust the force in the nexus. I did not trust whatever had come through. But Lira. The particular dangerous weight of that trust. With the specific reluctance of a man who was making a decision he might regret and was making it anyway because the alternative was worse, I stepped aside. "Be careful." The words came out with the particular quiet desperation of someone who had run out of other things to offer.

Lira exhaled with the specific quality of someone who had been holding something and had been given permission to put it down, though the permission had not eliminated the thing being put down. Her pulse was visible in the particular beat at her throat as she reached for the fractured Sunstone, the specific rhythm of someone approaching something that had been waiting for them specifically and had not been waiting gently.

The moment her fingers made contact, the world removed itself.

The violence of it was specific: not pain but the particular total displacement of every sensory channel simultaneously, the vision fragmenting into the specific chaotic combination of blinding light and absolute dark, her nervous system receiving more than it had been calibrated to receive and attempting to process it through every available pathway at once.

She saw.

The ley lines in their birth state, the specific raw and unshaped channels of the world's original power spiralling through the bones of the earth like the veins of a living thing that had not yet decided what it was, carrying the particular breath of the earth before the earth had been categorised into land and sea and sky. The pulse of the Sunstone. The specific hum of existence before existence had been divided into its component parts. And at the core, not a force. Not simply magic. The particular quality of a presence that was alive in the specific register that predated every category of alive that she or I or Myrcanthor had ever used.

The visions splintered. The specific rush of whispers carrying things that had never been spoken because there was no language adequate to them, knowledge of an age and a scale that the human mind was not designed to contain, arriving through the channels that Lira's heritage had opened and filling them with more than they had been designed to hold. Then, with the specific abruptness of something that had delivered its message and was finished, it ceased.

Lira staggered with the specific motion of someone who has been holding an enormous weight and has suddenly had it removed and has discovered that their body had reorganised itself around the holding and does not immediately know what to do without it. Her breath came back in gasps. Her eyes opened on the particular quality of eyes that have seen something they will not fully process for a long time.

"It's alive." Her voice was the specific fraying quality of something holding together at its minimum. The words themselves barely. She swallowed, the specific physical effort of someone finding the exact description of what they had encountered in the vocabulary available to them. "The ley lines. They are sentient."

The specific weight of those three words arriving in the particular quality of the aftermath silence. Her companions held in the stillness with the particular quality of people who have had a category they have been using to organise their understanding retroactively invalidated, the specific creeping horror of a truth that changed the meaning of everything that had preceded it.

Myrcanthor's wings folded in the specific motion of something that had moved from a defensive posture to a calculating one, the particular control of a predator that had identified something significant and was now assessing rather than reacting. When she spoke, her voice had the specific low measured quality of something building an argument from a foundation of grave certainty. "If this is true, then what we have disturbed is no mere force. It is a will." The pause. "And a will is far more dangerous than the darkest of curses."

The Vale tightened around us. The specific quality of a space that had been simply present and had become attended, the air acquiring the particular weight of something that had no shape but was filling the available space with itself. The ley lines beneath our feet had dropped below the threshold of audibility. They whispered in the specific register of something that had decided to be patient, which was more frightening than their previous screaming had been.

I moved the group with the specific curt motion of someone whose instincts had outpaced the deliberative process, each step away from the Sunstone's fractured heart placed with the particular conscious care of someone who understood that the ground they were moving across was not neutral. My senses extended outward with the specific futile reaching of something that was looking for a threat in a situation where the threat was not organised the way threats were supposed to be organised.

Lira's steps followed with the particular lightness of someone whose physical reserves were near their floor but who was continuing anyway because continuation was the only available option. The truth of what she had touched moved in her in the specific way of things that had been integrated rather than simply experienced, wound around her chest with the particular inescapable quality of knowledge that had entered the architecture of a person and become part of it.

The Sylphs flickered above with the specific broken rhythm of forms that had been struggling since the battle and had not recovered, their agitation the particular quality of beings that were registering the new information about the ley lines and finding it deeply incompatible with the categories they had been using to understand the world.

Rowan broke the silence with the particular careful quality of someone testing the ground before placing their full weight on it. "If the ley lines have awareness." He stopped. The specific hesitation of someone who had identified the weight of the thing they were about to say and was deciding whether to say all of it. "Then does that mean they can think. Feel."

Myrcanthor turned with the slow particular quality of something that had been waiting for that question. The fading light of the Sunstone found her scales in the specific way of something that was not quite strong enough to illuminate fully but was trying. "Not as you understand it." The particular thoughtfulness of something building a distinction that mattered. "The ley lines do not think in the way mortals do. Their awareness is woven into the fabric of existence itself. It is instinct. It is memory. It is will." Her gaze moved to Lira with the particular quality of something that had been arriving at a specific conclusion for a long time and had now arrived. Rowan followed her gaze, the specific discomfort in his expression the discomfort of someone who had understood before being told. "And yet they chose to reach out to you."

The silence after that had the specific weight of a blade suspended.

Then a voice. The particular cold brittle quality of air through dead branches. "Because she's bound to the blight."

A Sylph drifted lower with the particular trembling quality of something that was afraid and was naming the source of its fear. "The ley lines resonate with the corruption in her blood, just as they once did with her father." Not an opinion. The specific delivery of a verdict.

Lira stopped mid-step. The ground beneath her felt the specific fragile quality of something that had been tested too many times, and she understood the specific metaphor of that in a way that pressed against her from the inside. She turned with the particular slow deliberateness of someone choosing how to face what was being said rather than simply responding to it. Her gaze found the Sylph with the specific quality of something colder and more dangerous than rage. "Enough." Her voice was the specific calm of something that had moved past the stage where volume was necessary. "Your distrust is expected. I will not bear false condemnation."

She straightened, the particular small lift of her chin that was not arrogance but the specific declaration of someone who knew exactly where the boundary was and was standing at it. "I know my own heart. If you doubt it, that is your burden to carry. Not mine."

The Sylph hovered in the particular uncertain quality of a being whose certainty had found a specific obstacle. The glow of her pulsed with the specific quality of dying light clinging to its last intensity before the exhaustion of it.

Then it flared. "You are the architect of our calamity!" The particular venom of something that had been controlled and was no longer controlling itself. "Your father—"

"I am not my father's legacy." Lira's voice exploded with the particular quality of something that had been compressed for long enough and had found its release point, reverberating through the Vale with the specific physical force of sound produced by someone who had stopped performing restraint. The land responded in the specific way that lands responded to things said with complete conviction in their presence, the wind moving with the particular quality of something that had been given direction. Her fists were closed, her nails in the specific locations in her palms, but she did not step back. "I did not inherit his corruption. I did not choose this fate. And yet I stand here, fighting for this world, bleeding for it just as you do."

The specific weight of those words in the charged air. The Sylph's glow faltered with the particular flickering of a candle encountering a draft, the certainty she had held unravelling from the specific place where Lira's declaration had found it.

"Enough. Now." I stepped between them with the specific placement of someone who had made a decision about where the line was and was putting their body on it. My fingers rested on Ashenfang's pommel with the particular quality of a gesture that was a promise rather than a threat. "This infighting is a luxury we cannot afford. While we stand here bickering, the true enemy moves unchecked. If we allow division to fester, we have already lost."

The Sylph hesitated with the specific quality of something that had been about to speak and had found the argument insufficient to justify continuing. Her glow dimmed. The withdrawal was the particular reluctant withdrawal of something that had not changed its position but had decided to hold it somewhere other than here.

Lira exhaled. The specific hollow sound of fire draining away from the place where it had been burning, leaving the particular weary embers of someone who had held the position and was now accounting for what holding it had cost. The exhaustion arrived back in her body with the specific quality of something that had been waiting while she was too occupied to feel it.

I looked at her. The particular quality of my gaze was not the gaze I used for strategy or assessment. "Are you all right."

The laugh she gave was the specific quiet brittle sound of something that was not really a laugh but was the sound adjacent to one that the body produced when laughter was the wrong thing and silence was also wrong. "I am standing. That is enough." She turned before I could respond, the specific movement of a soldier who has decided that the conversation has reached the limit of what she is willing to give to it, and has ended it through the body rather than through words.

The group pressed forward. The unspoken weight of what had passed between us trailing in the specific way of things that did not disappear when the conversation containing them ended.

The Vale ahead was the particular disfigured landscape of something that had been subjected to corruption and had not been fully restored by what we had done at the nexus. The blackened vines coiled with the specific awareness of things that were registering our approach and were deciding what to do with the registration. The trees were the specific grotesque sentinels of things that had been hollowed out and were still standing. The air was the specific thick accumulation of decay and the acrid sharper note of corrupted magic that had been in the tissue of this place long enough to have changed the tissue and the air together.

The ground convulsed. The specific violent splintering of earth that had lost confidence in its own structure, cracks racing through the parched surface with the particular speed of things that had been waiting for the specific load that we represented. The chasm ahead was the particular new absence of ground that had not been there when we arrived.

The land was breaking. Beneath it, something was stirring with the specific patient quality of things that had been waiting and had now determined that waiting was no longer required.

Myrcanthor stopped. Her wings spread with the particular urgency of something receiving information through channels that did not wait for the deliberative mind to catch up. Her talons found the trembling ground and the specific information that came back through them moved through her body in the particular way that the ley line pulse moved through me. Her eyes swept the fractured earth with the specific careful precision of something that was reading a landscape's failure mode.

"Be careful." Her voice had the particular resonant growl of something that had been given information it was not permitted to withhold. "This ground is untrustworthy. It does not merely crumble." The specific pause. "It hungers."

The wind through the skeletal trees was the particular hollow sound of something moving through spaces that were the wrong shape for what they had become. The stench of burnt stone and the fouler underlying rot found the specific channels and settled in them with the particular permanence of things that had decided on a residence.

Ashenfang's pulse against my palm was specific and continuous and orienting. I was listening to it the way I had learned to listen to the earth's pulse, as the most reliable available information about what the next thing was likely to be.

Lira's breath was the particular thin mist of cold air in a place that had not retained warmth. She looked at the fractured terrain, at the specific evidence of a land that had stopped welcoming anything that walked on it. Then at Myrcanthor.

"Then let's not linger." Her voice found the specific steadiness that was the particular achievement of someone who was maintaining it through will rather than because it came naturally in this moment.

We moved forward. Into the particular dark of a land that was watching us approach and was not watching with anything that resembled welcome.

CHAPTER THIRTEEN - INTO THE HEART OF DARKNESS!

ROWAN'S ATTEMPT AT LEVITY DIED BEFORE IT REACHED US.

"Is that all?" The words left his mouth and collapsed immediately into the specific silence that had been present since before he spoke, devoured by a weight that was not the absence of sound but the presence of something that used silence as its medium. It pressed against my ribs from the inside rather than the outside, which was the specific quality that distinguished it from ordinary dread.

I knelt and pressed my fingers to the cracked veins of ley energy in the ground.

They should have hummed. They should have moved through my fingertips with the particular vital quality of the land's pulse, the specific warmth of power that had been restored to its proper channels. What I felt instead was the specific fading quality of something that had been burning and was now burning less, the flicker of an ember that had not been fed and was making the particular decision about whether to go out. Not fractured. Not simply damaged. Draining. My voice arrived low because anything louder felt like a lie. "It's not just fractured. It's draining. Something is leeching it dry."

The sharp inhale from one of the Sylphs was the specific involuntary sound of a being receiving information that contradicted its most fundamental assumptions. She hovered with her luminous form doing the particular flickering of something that had been stable and had encountered an instability, her wings the specific twitching of nerves that had been cut. "Impossible." The word arrived with the hollow quality of a person who was saying impossible and knew they were wrong. "The nexus should have strengthened them. Not stolen their lives."

Myrcanthor moved with the particular slow deliberateness of something very large that had decided to be deliberate rather than reactive, opening her wings by the specific fraction of a being testing the available space for something it had not yet named. The light that had been playing across her emerald scales had changed quality, leaving the specific shadows in the specific cracks in her scales that did not belong to ordinary shadow. Her expression had become unreadable in the particular way of faces that were processing something they would not share until the processing was complete.

"Unless," she said, and her voice was the particular low vast quality of thunder that was still several miles away but was moving toward you, "a hunger is feeding on them."

The words moved through the air with the specific quality of things that had not simply been spoken but had been placed, and the placement was intentional. Something in the space around us reorganised itself around those words. A presence that had been ambient became specific. Listening.

Her gaze found Lira with the particular weight of a question that had been formed before it was spoken.

"Your vision," she continued, her voice the specific tempered quality of something that had decided to ask rather than accuse but had not abandoned the possibility of accusation. "Did you see anything parasitic. A corruption feeding on the ley lines."

Lira's breath hitched in the specific involuntary way of a body receiving a question it had been hoping to avoid. The phantom heat from the nexus was still in her skin, not warmth but the specific quality of something that had been inside the skin and had left its character there, a stain, a brand, the particular residue of a presence that did not release cleanly. The taste in her mouth was the specific combination of burnt earth and bile, the particular acrid quality of decay mixed with something older than decay. She swallowed, and it did not leave. It would not leave.

"I don't know," she admitted. But the words came out with the specific texture of partial truth, the particular quality of something that was not quite a lie and was not quite honest. Because she felt it as she said it. The weight of a gaze from something that was not in the chamber with us. Pressing against the backs of her eyes from the other side, watching through the specific membrane of reality that this place had thinned to something approaching transparency.

The air had acquired a quality I could not attribute to the physical chemistry of the space. It was specific and heavy in the way of something that had taken up residence in the atmosphere and intended to remain. Lira's breath came in the particular shallow pulls of someone managing their intake of a compromised medium, her body rigid with the specific tension of someone who had understood something and was not yet prepared to say it.

The vivid afterimage of what she had seen in the nexus moved behind her eyes with the particular persistence of things that had entered through a channel other than the ordinary visual one and were not subject to the ordinary process of fading. It had seen her. In the specific way that things saw you when they had been waiting for you specifically. Not a general awareness. Recognition.

It was not simply feeding. It was devouring. The specific distinction between the two was the distinction between something that had a limit and something that had decided limits did not apply. It could swallow the essence from the bones of the world and would not be satisfied, because satisfaction was not a category it had ever learned.

A silence too heavy descended. Not the absence of sound but the particular waiting quality of something that had arrived at a threshold and was applying pressure to it from the other side.

I moved before the thought had finished forming. The crack of my knuckles as my fingers closed into fists was the specific sound of a body organising itself for something it had not yet named. One breath, sharp, with the particular bite of iron that accompanied the specific physiological state preceding violence. I was on my feet with Ashenfang in my grip before the deliberate part of my mind had caught up.

"We're running out of time." My voice had the specific quality of a blade drawn rather than a sentence spoken. "This isn't decay. This isn't a collapse. This is intent." I looked at Lira, then at the nexus, then at the specific pattern of the bleeding ley lines beneath our feet, channels that had been restored and were now losing what they had been restored to at a rate that suggested direction rather than entropy. "And if we don't find the source soon—"

I didn't finish. They felt it. The breath of the unseen, pressing through the specific thin place in the air that had been thinning since before we arrived and had reached a particular proximity to something on the other side.

Not wind. Not the movement of anything physical. A presence. Vast. Oriented. Using the space between reality's layers to observe us in the specific patient way of something that had been doing exactly this for a very long time and found nothing unusual about the length.

Then the ground pulsed. Once. Twice. The rhythm was the specific wrong rhythm, the particular cadence of something that was not the land's heartbeat but was using the land's channels to make itself felt, a slow deliberate pulse that moved through the stone and into the bones of my feet and up through my spine with the particular quality of a message being delivered through the only available medium.

Myrcanthor's wings twitched. The specific tightening of something that had moved from passive observation to active readiness without transitioning through the intermediate stages. Her emerald eyes moved across the dark with the particular narrowing of pupils finding a frequency rather than a location. Muscles tensed along her flanks in the specific preparation of something that had decided the thing it was preparing for was real. "Stay close." Her voice was the particular rolling quality of thunder that had been given language. "The deeper we go, the more the air will resist us. The closer we come to the epicentre—" the specific pause of something choosing its words against the criterion of accuracy, "the more it will fight back."

Above, the Sylphs had lost the particular fluid grace that defined them. Their glowing forms danced in the specific wild pattern of flames in a draught from an unknown direction, the particular agitation of beings that processed the world through magical sensitivity and were receiving too much information from a source they could not locate. Even they, with centuries of attuned existence, were registering the weight of this as wrongness rather than information.

The Wyrms had coiled into the specific geometry of things that had been uncoiled and had received a reason to coil, their golden eyes carrying the particular quality of ancient beings that had been unshaken by the rise and fall of civilisations and were encountering something that was shaking them. Not rage. Not combat-readiness. Something adjacent to the thing that ancient things felt when they recognised that something older than them was in the room.

The chasm.

It opened before us with the specific jagged quality of a wound rather than a geological feature, its edges crumbling into the particular darkness of a depth that had not been formed by natural processes. The earth trembled with the particular quality of a vast force breathing through the medium of the stone rather than the air, a slow exhalation from something below whose intake I had not registered and whose capacity I could not calculate. Then came a sound from the darkness. Low. Dragging. The specific wrong quality of a growl produced by something that had never been a living thing in any category I had been taught, a rasping exhale of something that had been buried and was in the particular process of becoming unburied, slow and deliberate and not concerned about who heard it.

The perfect calm that came over me was the specific deadly calm that preceded the specific category of action that bypassed deliberation entirely. My pulse found the particular rapid quality of blood being moved by a body that had made its decisions. Muscles at tension. Every channel of sensory information fully open. The sound continued to move through the darkness in the particular dragging way of something that used sound as an announcement rather than a communication, telling us it was there rather than telling us anything about itself except that it was vast and patient and had decided we should know it was there.

The darkness was not simply dark. It was the specific thickened quality of an atmosphere that had been changed by the presence of something that consumed rather than simply occupied, the particular rot-and-damp combination of a smell that had its origin below the biological register, beneath ordinary decay, in something that had been producing this specific chemistry for longer than decay had been a category.

I drew Ashenfang. The emerald fire that came from the blade was the particular fragile brave quality of light making a statement about itself in a context that was actively working to make the statement irrelevant, a single flicker against a specific consuming void. "Tell me you heard that." A low snarl barely above breath. But I knew they had heard it because the specific quality of the silence that followed their hearing it was different from any preceding silence.

Then again. A growl from below the surface of the world. Not a warning from a creature. The specific vibration of something vast becoming aware that it had company. Patient. The particular patience of a thing that had been waiting for this specific moment and had incorporated the waiting into its fundamental character.

Myrcanthor felt it in the specific deep channels of her ancient biology, the particular resonance of something old recognising something older. Her wings did not spread in fear but in the particular readiness of something that had fought things that ended worlds and was now reading the specific signature of something that had outlasted them. She had burned gods from the sky. She had watched empires become geology. But this had the specific quality of something that had been present when the gods were young and had outlasted their burning.

She unfurled her wings in the particular slow deliberate motion of something making a statement rather than a preparation. Obsidian membranes stretched to the particular width of things that had been designed against the specific scale of significant threats. The air shifted with the specific acrid electric quality of something that had been given a direction by her readiness. Talon tasted metal at the back of his throat. Not blood. The particular metallic quality of the air itself responding to what was being communicated through her presence. "Stay close." The specific curl of her voice from her throat was the particular quality of something that had decided to be quiet because volume was not the relevant variable. "Whatever hunts us." Her claws raked the fractured ground in the particular scraping motion of something that needed physical contact with the surface it was standing on. "It does not kill for survival." The air quivered with the specific quality of something being named that had been present before it was named. "It kills because it enjoys the end."

Then footsteps. Each impact on the earth had the specific quality of something that had mass that exceeded what should produce that impact, the particular hollow coffin-lid resonance of weight on hollow ground. The ground pulsed below each footfall. A slow, wet tremor with the specific quality of something that was not seismic but digestive, the particular motion of earth responding to something moving through it from below.

Myrcanthor moved forward with the specific commitment of something that had decided the direction was forward regardless of what forward contained. The air around us thickened with the specific tar-like quality of something that had substance despite being invisible, pressing against skin and forcing itself into lungs with the particular persistence of something that had been instructed to resist our progress. The taste of rust and decay settled on the back of my tongue with the specific permanence of things that had decided to stay, old blood left to its own devices in a sealed space, the particular sour chemistry of something that had been there long enough to become part of the atmosphere.

We tightened formation with the specific instinctive movement of bodies that had determined that the available space should be minimised. Ashenfang's cold fire, Lira's daggers, Rowan's hammer, all of them carrying the particular weight of things that had been made for specific categories of threat and were now in the presence of something that exceeded those categories without negating them.

The earth exhaled. A guttural shudder moving through the stone with the specific quality of a body whose internal mechanics had been disturbed, the pulse beneath us erratic with the particular sick rhythm of something that was no longer operating under its own agency. Corrupted vines pulsed through the dirt with the specific organic wrongness of things that had been altered at a level below biology, their glow the particular sickly green of power being used for a purpose it was not designed for.

My grip on Ashenfang was the specific iron quality of hands that had made a decision and were expressing it through the only available medium. The blade whispered through the void with the particular quality of something that had been made to sever things and was in the presence of things worth severing. The runes along it pulsed with the specific feverish quality of magic that was in the presence of its antithesis and was responding with everything available to it.

"Ready yourselves." Nothing more was needed.

The silence had the particular bloated quality of something that had accumulated too much of itself and was pressing outward against the available space. We moved forward in the specific quality of people who had understood that the alternative was worse. The air clung to us with the particular quality of damp cloth against skin, except the cloth was not cloth but the specific residual presence of something that had already been here and had left its character in the atmosphere. The stench of primordial rot found the particular channels of the nasal passages that normal rot did not reach, something beneath biological decay that had a specific wrong quality suggesting it had never been biological in the first place and was producing this chemistry through different means.

Then the ground trembled with the specific quality of something breathing through the earth itself, a slow rhythmic pulse drawing air from below in the particular way of a vast darkness inhaling through the medium of the stone. Tasting. The specific quality of something that tasted the air before it decided what to do with what the air contained.

Myrcanthor froze.

The specific quality of that freezing was the worst thing that had happened to me in the last several minutes, which was saying something. A dragon. A war titan. A being that had been present at the burning of gods. Frozen. Not in the particular way of things surprised or things afraid. In the particular way of things that had recognised something and were processing the recognition and the processing was not going well.

Her talons found the broken ground with the specific digging quality of something that needed an anchor. Dread. The particular raw primal kind that bypassed the analytical systems entirely and arrived in the body first.

Then the growl. Not from her. From the air. A slow dragging rasp with the specific quality of something that had no biological source and was using the available acoustic medium out of courtesy rather than necessity. It moved through them not through the ears but through the particular channels that registered threat at the frequency below sound, settling into the marrow with the specific vibration of something that was communicating rather than simply sounding.

The shadows around us contracted. Not the ordinary contraction of shadows when light was added. The specific intentional contraction of something alive that had decided to make itself smaller in preparation for something.

"It's here." Myrcanthor's voice had the specific raw quality of something that had been forced through a throat that was fighting against producing it. Her emerald eyes burned with the particular quality of defiance that existed not because it was strategically sound but because it was the only available response to something this large. Her pupils had contracted to the specific razor-thin slits of something that had identified a threat and was measuring it against every category it had available. "The convergence."

Her wings spread with the specific spreading of things that bore wounds. The ley lines beneath us screamed in the particular way that things with no capacity for sound screamed when forced past their design tolerances, the green light of them pulsing through the cracks in the ground like a failing heartbeat visible from the outside.

Rowan's voice had the specific brittle quality of something that had been a strong thing and had been in contact with too much wrongness for too long. "Convergence?" The word barely formed before it was swallowed by the specific absence that had replaced the ordinary air, not silence but a vacuum of the particular kind that ate sound rather than simply not producing it.

His hands were at his hammer with the specific fumbling quality of fingers that had been made slick by the particular physiological response to something that exceeded the ordinary parameters of fear. White knuckles. The particular useless defiance of a grip on something that had no application against what was coming.

The light died. Not the gradual dimming of something losing power. The specific ripping quality of something being removed by force.

Myrcanthor turned to me with the particular quality of something that had run out of alternatives to honesty. Her emerald eyes cast the specific quality of light on the broken ground that made the terrain look like something that was having a specific reaction to the light rather than simply reflecting it. "The ley lines." She exhaled, and the sound carried the particular weight of something that had been alive for centuries and was mourning on a scale that centuries of living had calibrated her to. "They writhe." Her massive body had the specific tension of something that was aware of something beyond sight. One talon lifted, pointing at the land, the air, the particular fabric of reality around us that had been twisting since before we descended. "Here, they do more than move. They convulse. They consume. They bring things that should not be."

The earth exhaled beneath us. Not metaphorically. The specific physical movement of ground that was acting as the respiratory system for something below, the particular wrong sensation of standing on something that was breathing.

I pressed the words past my clenched teeth with the specific forced quality of words that were being made to exist against the resistance of everything in me that knew they were a mistake. "A nexus. Unknown." The question felt wrong the moment it existed. The particular coiling sensation in my gut was the specific physiological response to having done something that could not be undone by naming it. A thing that large, that old, that patient. How had it stayed silent. How had it stayed hidden. How had it accumulated this specific scale of presence without anyone who studied the ley lines encountering it.

Myrcanthor did not answer immediately. She stood with the particular quality of something that had received a verdict and was waiting for it to finish settling. Her wings partially open, held at the specific angle of something that was not defending but acknowledging. The sky above us had the specific bruised quality of something that had been subjected to forces for which it had no structural preparation. The air pressed with the specific quality of invisible hands applying weight from multiple directions simultaneously. When she finally spoke, her voice did not need volume because it was already inside everything in the space.

"It was never silent." A pause with the particular duration of something that had been true for as long as she had existed and was being said aloud for the first time. The ley lines shuddered beneath the specific resonance of her voice in the ground. "We just refused to listen."

We moved forward. Each step had the specific quality of steps taken on a surface that should not be producing the particular tactile feedback it was producing, too smooth, the particular absence of the ordinary texture of worn stone, the specific quality of something that had been licked clean rather than eroded. The roots that pushed through the cracked earth pulsed with a frequency that was the ley lines and was also something feeding on the ley lines and the two had become sufficiently integrated that the distinction was no longer visible from the surface.

The specific wrongness of walking on something alive was the particular crawling quality beneath the soles of my boots that had nothing to do with temperature.

One Sylph descended with the specific strained quality of a being that had been maintaining its form under conditions that were actively working against it, landing on a twisted branch with the particular quality of someone using all available steadiness just to remain present. Her voice was the particular quality of wind through the hollow of a dead thing. "It lies just beyond." But the words had the specific wrong quality of something being shaped around an absence rather than a presence, as though the air had decided what the words would be before she did.

A shadow unfolded in the distance. Tall in the specific way of things that had height as a function of what they were rather than as a dimension of their physical structure. It moved with the particular quality of something that the eyes kept trying to track and kept losing, not because it was fast but because it operated in a different relationship to visual continuity than the things the eye had been trained to follow.

A sound tore through the air.

Deep. Guttural. The particular death rattle of something that had been buried too deeply for too long and was now in the specific process of un-burying itself, the slow exhalation of something that had been under pressure and was releasing that pressure through the available channels. The ley lines responded to it in the specific way they responded to things that threatened their existence, which was to scream through the stone in the particular frequency that I felt through my boots as distinct from their ordinary pulse.

The world began to split along the specific lines of least resistance.

Lira moved forward. Not by decision. The specific quality of movement that was happening to her rather than being produced by her, her body responding to a pull that had not asked her permission, her feet finding the particular direction without the involvement of the deliberative systems that would have suggested against it. Her breath had the specific hitched quality of a person whose respiratory system had registered something her conscious mind was still trying to categorise. "The ancient power." The words arrived from her mouth with the specific forced quality of things being said by something other than the person whose mouth they were exiting from, dragged from her lips by the same force that was directing her feet.

She swallowed. The taste was wrong. And then something arrived in her skull that had not come through her ears. Not a whisper. Not a thought. The specific intimation of something that had found the particular internal channel it was looking for and was using it without announcing itself as a visitor.

Her fingers twitched at her sides with the specific involuntary quality of nerves receiving signals from a competing source. Her pulse had the particular quality of something that had stopped responding to her own biology and had found a different rhythm to match.

"Lira." My voice broke through whatever was happening inside her with the specific quality of steel struck against stone. She jerked, the particular full-body quality of someone emerging from a specific depth they had not noticed entering, her breath coming back in the shallow rapid pulls of someone realising how shallow and rapid it had become.

I studied her. The particular sharpness of attention that had been reading people's specific states since before I had language for what I was reading. "Are you well." Low. Careful. The specific edge of the question was not the edge of the concern but the edge of the assessment underneath the concern.

The pressure on her chest was visible in the particular quality of her stillness, the specific way she was holding herself together through the deliberate application of will to the structural integrity of her composure. She forced the words past the specific burn in her throat, past the taste of ash and old bile that had settled there since she touched the nexus and had not lifted. "I'm fine."

The specific quality of that lie was audible to both of us. To all of us.

Myrcanthor moved forward with the particular purposeful quality of something that had identified the next necessary position and was occupying it. Her massive body displaced the air with the specific quality of something moving at a scale that air found it necessary to accommodate. She stopped at the edge of the chasm. Her gaze found the specific darkness below, and in that darkness I could see reflected in the particular quality of her eyes something that she was looking at and I was not.

"Here." The word arrived with the particular weight of a verdict, a judgment, a specific announcement of something that had been confirmed rather than discovered. The brittle earth shuddered beneath the specific vibration of her pronouncement through the stone. "The nexus of power."

I inhaled and the scent of burnt stone and damp earth and something beneath both of them, the particular acrid quality of charred flesh that had never been flesh in any ordinary sense, filled the specific channels of my lungs. My grip on Ashenfang found its particular white-knuckled quality. The blade was warm in the specific way of something that had registered what was below us and had been registering it for longer than I had.

Below, the ley lines pulsed in the particular quality of their corrupted state, the specific sickly green of something that had been changed from the inside out, shifting and writhing with the particular motion of things that had always been still and had been given a different instruction.

The carvings on the walls had the particular quality of stone that had been made wrong in its formation rather than changed by time, the specific texture of something that had been grown rather than carved. Watching. Moving in the particular peripheral way of things that remained still when directly observed and changed when the observation was indirect.

Lira exhaled. The sound had the specific wrong quality of something that had been produced by a different mechanism than breathing. "It's pulling me in." The words arrived with the particular quality of something being said about a thing that was already happening, a report rather than a concern.

I was at her arm before the sentence completed. My grip was specific and firm with the particular quality of something establishing an anchor against a current that was already operating. "Stay back." The warning was sharp in the specific way of things said by someone who has understood the threat faster than they can articulate it.

Myrcanthor's great head turned toward us with the particular quality of something that had been waiting for this specific development to occur. "The descent is possible." Her voice had the particular heavy certainty of something that had already run the calculation. "But the ley lines reach their full power here. Whatever lurks beneath. It is no longer sleeping."

The specific weight of those last four words settled through the gathered company in the particular way that significant truths settled, not loud but permanent.

I exhaled with the specific slow controlled quality of someone managing their own response to something they would prefer to respond to differently. "We go together."

The descent had the specific quality of a passage that had been designed by something that understood how to produce maximum discomfort in the particular ways that mattered most. The ground grew slick with the specific moisture of something that was not water, carrying the particular smell of blood and decay combined in the ratio of something that had been bleeding for longer than blood was meant to bleed. The walls of the chasm tightened around us with the specific incremental quality of something that was doing this deliberately, matching our progress with their own compression, pulsing with the particular rhythm of the ley lines except wrong.

The glyphs on the walls had the specific quality of things that moved when they were not being watched. Not a trick of torchlight. The particular purposeful motion of symbols that had a relationship with observation and had decided to conduct themselves differently in its absence.

Then the voices. A hushed murmur with the specific quality of voices that had been produced at a frequency below audibility and had found a way to be heard despite that, the particular sensation of whispers in the specific registers that were not acoustic but were experienced as acoustic regardless. They built with the specific escalating quality of things that had been restrained and were finding the restraint insufficient.

Rowan's voice had the specific cracked quality of something structural failing. "What is this place." His words had the particular fragility of things said by someone who had decided that saying something was preferable to the specific quality of the silence that would otherwise occupy the space.

Myrcanthor did not look at him. Her gaze held forward with the particular fixed quality of something that was using all available processing for what was ahead and had none to spare for reassurance. "A sanctuary." The word curled with the particular quality of something spoken without any of the content the word would normally carry. No reverence. Only the specific weight of dread that had found a category it fit into and was resting there. "Crafted by those who first wielded the ley lines."

The air had the particular resistance quality of something that had developed a position on our presence and was expressing that position through its physical properties. Lira reached out and her fingers found the carvings, and the heat that shot up her arm was the specific heat of something that had been produced by a source that had no relationship with temperature in the ordinary sense, burning from beneath the flesh rather than against it, a heat with the particular quality of recognition rather than combustion.

She snatched her hand back with the specific involuntary quality of a body that had made a decision before the mind had processed the information. Her pulse hammered against her ribs in the particular rapid way of blood responding to something that the cardiovascular system had classified as an emergency.

The symbols twisted. Not in the particular way of shadows on moving surfaces. The specific autonomous motion of things that were alive and were doing what alive things did, which was move according to their own priorities.

"They match the inscriptions in my father's tome." The words arrived with the specific quality of something said by a person who had understood what they were looking at and had delayed saying it while they confirmed what understanding it meant.

The cavern exhaled.

The walls groaned with the particular quality of stone accommodating something it had not been built to accommodate, and the specific quality of that groan moved through the space as both sound and sensation simultaneously. The glyphs pulsed with the particular shift from illumination to intention, the specific quality of something that had been passive and had received a signal, their green light finding the particular rhythm of a heartbeat that had always been there and had now decided to make itself audible.

The air thickened in the specific wrong way. Burnt ozone and the particular foul quality of rot that had been in a sealed space long enough to develop its own character mixed with the specific metallic tang of something that had been blood-adjacent for so long it had become indistinguishable from it. It stung the throat with the particular quality of something that had been designed to sting throats.

Ashenfang was in my hand before I had finished making the decision to draw it. The blade hummed with the particular quality of something that had been made to detect the specific category of wrongness that was present here and was detecting it comprehensively. My knuckles were the particular white of something that had found its grip and was not releasing it. "Explain." My voice had the particular scraping quality of steel on stone. One word with the particular weight of everything the one word had to carry.

Lira hesitated. Not from doubt. The specific quality of someone who understood that what they were about to say was going to change the specific architecture of everything that had been built on the existing understanding. The knowledge pressed against her ribs from the inside with the particular quality of a thing that needed to be said and was waiting for the courage to be said. Her eyes found mine with the specific communication of someone who was about to give something they could not take back. "My father." It arrived as both a confession and a curse in the particular way those two things were sometimes the same thing. "He was obsessed with the ley lines. With their origins. If these inscriptions match his writings, then he must have known of this place." The pause. The specific duration of someone placing the next words with full awareness of their weight. "He might have used it."

The implication moved through the space between us with the specific quality of something that had too many limbs for the room it occupied.

The cavern reacted. The air convulsed with the particular quality of something that had been listening and had heard something it could use. The smell of rot intensified to the specific quality of something that had been waiting for a particular chemical signal and had received it, filling the mouth with the bitter taste of flesh that had been in darkness long enough to develop an identity separate from the original organism. The ley lines in the walls pulsed with the particular frantic quality of something that had been holding a rhythm and had received an interruption.

Myrcanthor's wings closed with the specific tight quality of something that had made a decision about the available space and had decided to occupy less of it. Her frame had the particular tensed geometry of a predator that had identified something. Her voice, when it came, was the specific growl of something that had access to truth older than war. "If he left his mark here, then his magic still lingers. And magic that lingers does not rest. It festers. It calls to something."

A sound filled the air. Low, dragging, with the specific quality of something that was not skittering or scraping but was the particular motion of a vast thing adjusting its position in the available space just beyond the boundary of where the torchlight could follow it. Rising from the depth with the particular patience of something that had done this before and would do it again.

I turned with the specific speed of instinct. Ashenfang flared with the particular emerald fire of something that had identified its target. "We keep moving. If there are answers here, we take them. Before whatever hunts us does." My eyes found every available angle of the passage with the specific rapid assessment of someone mapping a space they expected to become a battlefield.

The passage stretched forward with the particular quality of a dark that had substance.

The altar chamber opened around us with the specific quality of spaces that had been waiting for a particular moment to reveal themselves and had decided this was that moment. Its walls had the specific living sheen of surfaces that had been in contact with something organic for so long that the distinction between stone and flesh had been compromised, a particular slick quality that had no analogue in anything I wanted to compare it to. The ley lines' glow bathed the space in the particular fevered quality of light that had been produced by something wrong and was carrying that wrongness in its illumination. At the centre, rising with the specific quality of something that had been placed rather than grown, stood the pedestal, the specific geometry of something made for a single purpose, split by a jagged fissure that pulsed with the particular sickly green of a wound that had been bleeding for centuries and had found a rhythm in the bleeding.

Lira moved forward. The specific quality of movement that was not hers, that had found the particular channel her body offered and was using it, her feet carrying her toward the pedestal with the particular directional certainty of something that had been oriented toward this destination since before she was born.

The air around her had the specific thick quality of burnt stone and charred depth, a particular combination of decay and something that had once been vital and had been converted into something else. It filled her lungs with the particular quality of something that was occupying the space usually occupied by air while not providing what air provided.

The ley lines hummed with the particular slow sick wave of something that had been forced out of its natural rhythm and was expressing that forcing in every available pulse. And beneath that, a heartbeat that was not the ley lines and was not human and had the particular quality of something very old that had been waiting in the specific patience of geological time. "This is it." Her voice was barely there, the particular raw quality of something that had been hollowed out by what it was looking at. "The source. The thing that's been calling me."

The cavern exhaled. The walls shuddered with the particular quality of something that had been structural and had found a different purpose. The crack in the altar split wider with the specific motion of something that had been contained and was deciding not to be contained anymore. The chamber breathed with the particular slow heavy quality of something that had all the time available to it and was not hurrying.

Lira did not belong here. The thought arrived with the specific quality of something that had been true for a long time and had found the right moment to make itself known. Not fear. The specific quality of recognition from the inside, the particular sensation of a place that had always known you and had been waiting for you to arrive at the correct position to be claimed by it.

Her hand found the pedestal and the specific quality of what happened was not heat in the temperature sense but in the particular sense of something forcing its way through the skin from below, revelation rather than combustion, truth arriving through the channels of touch with the particular violence of something that had been waiting for exactly this contact.

The energy surge was everything and nothing the body was designed to process simultaneously.

She saw.

Not visions. Not the particular organised presentation of memory or imagination. The specific raw quality of truth arriving through every available channel at once, the ley lines in their birth state moving through the bones of the world with the particular vital quality of something that had not yet been taught what it was, the pulse of the Sunstone, the specific hum of existence before it had been divided into its component categories. And at the core, the particular quality of a presence that was alive in the register that predated every category of alive that had ever been applied to anything, that had been present before the first application of any category.

It turned.

Not with physical motion. With the particular quality of attention that was vast enough to be directional without being directional in the way of bodies, the specific reorientation of a consciousness that had just found a specific thing it had been looking for.

It saw her.

Lira's scream did not arrive through her throat or her lungs. It arrived through the particular channel that connected her to the ley lines, through every channel that her father's work had opened in her, through every specific opening that her inheritance had left available, the particular full-body expression of a soul that had been found by something it was not equipped to be found by.

The force wrenched her back into her body with the particular violence of something that had to use force to accomplish what should have been easy, slamming her consciousness into her own flesh with the specific impact of a blade driven into material. She hit the stone floor and her body had the particular convulsing quality of something that had received too much through channels not designed for that volume, vision blurred by the specific overwhelming quality of her nervous system attempting to process what had just passed through it.

I caught her before the fall completed. My grip on her had the particular firm quality of something that understood that steadiness was the specific thing required and that providing it was the specific thing it could do.

Rowan's voice arrived from the particular distance of someone who had been on the periphery of what had just happened and was working to understand it from the outside. "What did you see."

Lira's head came up with the particular slow quality of something operating against significant resistance. Her lips trembled with the specific fine tremor of something in the process of producing words from material that had been through what her nervous system had been through. The particular paleness of her skin was the specific paleness of blood that had retreated to the core for reasons that the body had decided were beyond the ordinary criteria for retreat. Her fingers were still curved in the particular position of someone holding something that was no longer there.

"A power older than gods." Her breath had the particular shuddering quality of something that was not fully hers yet. Each word carried the specific quality of something being pulled from a source that was still very close to what had just happened. "And I think." A breath. The particular quality of a pause around something that she was deciding whether to say. "I think it knows my name."

The rot that came afterward was the specific quality of something that had been in existence before rot had a definition. Not the familiar decay of things that had lived and ended. The particular quality of something that had never been in the category of the living and was producing this chemistry through different means entirely, a festering that had been operating in the specific conditions of its own particular darkness for ages, sweet and sick in the particular combination that the body registered as something worse than danger.

Rowan gagged with the specific involuntary full-body quality of a system that had been presented with something it was not designed to metabolise. "Gods." The word came out raw with bile. "What in the abyss is that."

The air shifted with the specific quality of something that had been ambient and had become directional, the particular drawing-inward quality of a darkness that had perceived something it wanted. And then the whispers arrived not in the ear but in the particular internal space where thought lived, bypassing the ordinary acoustic channels entirely, arriving through the specific channels that the ley line connection and the blood connection and the inheritance had left open in Lira.

They had no language that any living thing had ever used. But they had the particular quality of something that had always known her, that had been waiting with the specific patience of a thing that understood time differently, that had watched her father work and had understood that the work was the specific preparation for this moment.

Lira's nails found her palms with the particular digging quality of someone using pain as the specific tool for maintaining their location in the present moment. The pull on her consciousness was the particular unbearable quality of something applying force to the specific place where the self was connected to itself.

"Lira," it said. Not from the cavern. Not from the fissure. From the particular internal space that had always been hers and was currently occupied by something that was not her. The voice had the particular quality of something assembled from the echo of forgotten things, the specific frequency of a corpse that had never stopped vibrating. "You were always meant to come back to us." Something broke in her at the particular internal location where things broke when the breaking was not external but structural.

I moved before the sentence completed. My grip on her arm was specific and immediate, the particular anchoring quality of something that understood what was being attempted and was refusing to permit it. "No." The word arrived raw with the particular desperation of something that was also a command, a refusal, a declaration made against something that was already in the process of happening. "Whatever this is, you are not its pawn."

The thing in the fissure responded. The particular sound of wet bone splitting, of teeth finding each other in a specific grinding motion, the particular wet rasping quality of a hunger that had waited past the specific point where waiting had changed its character into something more specific than patience. It had the particular quality of finding something amusing, which was worse than finding something threatening, because amusement meant it did not consider us a specific danger.

The pedestal erupted.

Not in fire. In the particular quality of despair given physical expression, a blinding green light exploding in the chamber with the specific violence of something that had been held and was no longer being held, a whirlwind of dark energy tearing at reality in the particular way of something that had always been beneath reality and had decided to come through rather than continue existing beneath. The ground convulsed with the particular shattering quality of foundations failing, stone breaking with the specific sound of things that had been structural and had received more than they were designed for. Then it screamed.

Not from a throat. The specific quality of a sound that had its origin in the ley lines themselves, the particular tearing quality of something ripping through the medium of reality rather than through the medium of air, a sound that did not resonate in the ears but in the particular cavities of the skull and the chest and the specific places in the anatomy where things that should not be felt were felt regardless.

Reality twisted. The walls had the specific liquefied quality of something that had lost its relationship with solidity. The carved glyphs moved with the particular autonomous quality of things that had received new instructions, reshaping with the specific purposeful motion of something that was changing its own language.

From the heart of the light, a shape assembled itself.

The specific quality of its wrongness was not in any individual feature but in the totality of its presence, the particular impossibility of a thing that had been assembled from materials that had never been intended to constitute a form, vast and dark as obsidian and broken in the specific way of something that had been constructed from the remnants of things better left unconstructed. The sickly green veins pulsed beneath the surface of it with the particular quality of something that was the ley lines and was also what was consuming the ley lines and the two had become sufficiently integrated to be indistinguishable. Its shadows had the specific intentional quality of things that were not shadows produced by the absence of light but shadows that had been given a directive.

It opened its eyes.

Not eyes. The particular abyssal quality of two openings that led not to the interior of a being but to the specific quality of nothing that was somehow worse than nothing, that had the particular burning quality of hatred that had been in existence long enough to become structural rather than emotional. The weight of its gaze had the particular quality of something that was applying pressure through the specific medium of being looked at.

Rowan's breath had the particular strangled quality of someone whose respiratory system was attempting to cope with something that exceeded its usual brief. "Gods." The specific whisper of a person who had run out of the category of adequate response. "What is that."

Myrcanthor did not blink. The specific total stillness of her was the most frightening thing in the room. A dragon. A being that had burned gods. Still. Not in the particular way of things that had been stopped. In the particular way of things that had recognised something and were giving it the specific quality of respect that recognition sometimes required. "A Sentinel." Her voice had the particular quality of stone fracturing from within. "Or what's left of one."

Then the creature screamed.

The particular violation of the air by that sound was not acoustic. It was the specific quality of a sonic void, an inward collapse of the available space around the sound rather than an outward expansion, a black hole assembled from agony that pulled at every living thing with the particular hunger of something that fed on the specific quality of existence. It was not simply pain. It was the particular quality of erasure, the unmade quality of identity being separated from its attachment to itself, nerves firing in the specific order that produced the particular sensation of the self becoming less certain of its own edges.

I dropped to one knee. My teeth found each other with the specific grinding quality of something maintaining structural integrity against a force that was testing it. Ashenfang in both hands, its light the particular guttering quality of something fighting against a consuming dark rather than simply existing in an ordinary dark.

Lira had both palms at her temples with the specific urgent quality of someone trying to maintain the boundaries of their own skull against a force that was finding the seams. Her breath came in the particular broken quality of something that was not entirely under her management. The thing's pulse was inside her. The specific grotesque quality of a resonance that mimicked her own heartbeat with the particular intimacy of something that had found the specific frequency of her existence and was matching it. Not communication. Feeding.

The chamber had the particular warped quality of a space that had lost its relationship with the ordinary dimensions of space, buckling and folding with the specific quality of something that had been asked to accommodate the impossible and was losing the argument. It was not an enemy. The specific quality of what it was moved through me as I looked at it. An event. A category that contained its own logic, its own temporality, its own specific relationship with the ordinary rules of the world, which was a relationship of having decided those rules did not apply.

Rowan's grip on his hammer had the specific bloodied quality of something held past the point where the skin maintained its integrity. "We can't fight this." The specific fragile finality of words that had understood something before the rest of the person had caught up to them.

Lira did not move. Her hands trembled with the particular quality of something that had found the specific frequency of what was present and was vibrating in the resonance of it. Her feet had the specific quality of feet that had stopped moving not from paralysis but from understanding. It had been waiting for her. The specific dawning quality of that knowledge settling through her, the particular terrible clarity of it, the understanding that her father's obsession had not been aimless but directed, and the direction had always been this specific point in this specific place at this specific moment.

The air fractured again with the particular quality of something that did not have to build toward impact but arrived at it directly. The specific impact of it was not physical but the particular grief-weaponised quality of something that had assembled its force from the specific accumulated weight of every buried nightmare in every person in the room simultaneously, personalised in the particular way of something that had access to the specific contents of each of them. It reached into me and found the particular things it was looking for and it spoke in those frequencies with the specific knowledge of something that had always had access.

It moved. With the particular quality of something that had never been constrained by the category of physical movement, tearing itself from the wound in the earth with the specific violence of something that had grown past the size of the wound it came from and was making the wound accommodate it rather than the reverse. Reality strained with the particular quality of something being asked to contain something it had not been designed to contain.

It had no face in the particular sense of a stable arrangement of features. It had many faces in the particular sense of something that existed in more states simultaneously than any individual moment could represent, its form assembling and disassembling in the specific continuous motion of something that had never been required to commit to a single state. The two vast voids where the eyes were had the particular quality of things that were not merely seeing but the specific activity of peeling, the particular unravelling of the self that happened when something with sufficient access looked at you with sufficient attention.

The stench had the specific quality of something that had been present before smell was a category, the particular combination of burning and rotting and something beneath both that I had no word for, the specific chemistry of things that had been forgotten long enough that they had changed their relationship with existence itself. Old prayers that had never been answered. Gods that should not have been named. Things that were prayed against rather than prayed to.

I felt Ashenfang waver in my grip with the specific quality of something that was made of specific materials and had encountered something that those materials were not designed to be proximate to. My body had the particular quality of something that had fought at the edge of the abyss before and was now standing in the abyss and was discovering the specific distinction. My veins had the particular ice quality of something that had lost its relationship with the blood's ordinary temperature. My lungs had the specific stone quality of something that had forgotten the ordinary mechanics of inflation.

Rowan's hammer had the particular quality of something that had become irrelevant while still being held. His voice had the specific thick guttural quality of a sound produced despite the body's preference not to produce it.

Lira felt the shadows reach for her with the particular recognising quality of things that had always known she was there and had been waiting for the specific proximity that would permit contact. She heard her father's voice in the particular internal space where his teaching had always lived, the specific echo of his obsession given the particular clarity of things spoken from beyond the point at which they could be taken back.

True magic always demands a cost. This was the specific cost. She had always known. She had known in the particular way of things known before they are understood, carried in the blood before the mind had the language for them.

Myrcanthor stood motionless. The particular terrible quality of that stillness was the worst thing I had ever seen from something that had flattened mountains. Not fear. Recognition. The specific quality of something that had identified what was present and was running the calculation about what identification meant in this specific context.

When she spoke, her voice had the particular wrong quality of something that had been a vast and ancient thing and had been changed by proximity to something vastly older. "This is not a battle we can win." The specific quality of that sentence was not a command. Not a warning. The particular quality of something that had arrived at a truth and was saying it out loud because there was no longer any reason not to. Not retreat. The specific quality of a sentence that understood that retreat was not available because there was nowhere to retreat to.

Then the thing in the dark moved. Its maw opened with the particular quality of something tearing through the available fabric of space rather than through biological tissue, a jagged chasm ringed with the specific motion of things that gnashed without pause, the particular quality of a portal rather than an opening. A doorway in the specific sense of something that led to a place that was not a place in any category that had ever had a name.

It lunged.

The darkness detonated outward with the particular surge of something that had been given a direction and was committing to it completely. Sentient, with the specific quality of appetite given the particular gift of volition, a storm that had decided on a target. Not merely force. Hunger that had been waiting long enough to have developed strategies.

I lifted Ashenfang before the darkness reached me but the darkness was already everywhere it was going to be before the lift completed. Its emerald eyes had the particular swelling quality of something that was not seeing but devouring, the specific quality of wounds that had been given a visual organ's function while maintaining a wound's essential character.

Lira threw herself clear with the particular urgency of a body that had made a decision before the mind had finished the question. Her hands produced the particular frantic quality of magic from someone who had been drawing on sources that had been drawing on her in return for too long and was now spending what was left at speed, the ley lines wailing in the specific frequency of something that had reached the end of what it could give without ceasing to be what it was.

She understood. In the particular clarifying quality of the moment when everything that had been obscured by hope and necessity and the ongoing commitment to not yet knowing became visible simultaneously. They were never meant to win. They were meant to resist. The specific distinction between those two things had the particular weight of something she was going to have to live with after this.

If after was still a category that applied.

Myrcanthor screamed. The specific particular quality of agony from something that had not made that sound in the centuries it had been alive, a sound that moved through the floor and up through my boots and into my chest and settled there with the specific weight of something I was going to carry. One side of her body convulsed with the particular quality of something happening from the inside out, the obsidian limbs erupting through her scales with the specific violence of something that had found a channel and was using it completely. The corruption moved through her veins with the particular blackening quality of something that had gotten past every defence she had and was working with the efficiency of something that had been waiting for exactly this access.

Her scales, which had always been the particular eternal quality of things that would outlast everything, curled away with the specific quality of ash. Not poisoned. The particular specific quality of being unmade. The slow merciless undoing of all she was.

Something broke in my chest at that specific sight. Not strategically. Not as a calculation about our odds. In the particular place where something broke when something that had seemed permanent proved to be not permanent, when something that had been a constant in the world revealed its contingency.

Then instinct.

Not thought. Not strategy. The specific particular quality of rage that had found its purest form, the particular righteous fury of something that had burned past every intermediate stage and arrived at itself completely. Ashenfang screamed in my hand with the specific quality of something that had been waiting for exactly this permission, the emerald fire erupting along its length with the particular all-in quality of something that had no more reason for restraint.

I felt the ley lines surge through my bones with the particular quality of something that had been wounded and was using the wound as a channel for every available force, crying out in pain through me and I became the particular expression of that crying, their fear my fury, their torment the specific material from which my vow assembled itself.

I roared. Not a battle cry. The specific quality of a promise made in the particular language of the body when words are insufficient. And drove Ashenfang into the pulsing core.

Steel met corrupted magic with the specific quality of two things that had always been moving toward each other finally arriving at contact. Reality cracked with the particular quality of something that had been refusing the contact and could no longer refuse it. Not from force. From refusal. The specific quality of the world's rejection of what had been placed in it.

Emerald fire exploded outward with the specific quality of a dying star expressing itself completely, tearing through the creature's essence in the particular way of something that had been built to oppose exactly this, the specific character of Ashenfang finding the particular character of what it was severing and applying everything it had to the severing.

Silence. The specific absolute quality of absence. Not peace. The particular hollow of something that had been consuming everything and had stopped consuming, leaving the specific quality of a space that had been full of the wrong thing and was now empty of everything.

Then Myrcanthor's voice. The specific commanding quality of something that had found its way past the corruption's erosion to what had always been underneath it. "Talon! Find its core! Its vile heart! Destroy it now!" Not a plea. The particular quality of a final act of will from something that was using everything it had left to produce it.

She had seen it. A pulse. The specific quality of a wound in the fabric of existence, a rupture that was the creature's actual source rather than its presence, a void trying to reconstitute itself through the particular medium of the available ley line energy.

I ran. Through ash. Through the specific shattered quality of the bones of something that had been built a very long time ago. Toward the particular beating quality of everything broken. Rowan was beside me, his hammer moving with the particular quality of something that had found its specific purpose and was committed to it, bone-crushing fury clearing the specific path that needed clearing. Lira, her form moving through the shadows with the particular grace of someone who had always known how to navigate the specific spaces between light, her magic erupting with the particular quality of someone spending the last of what they had because the last of it was what the moment required.

The shriek arrived with the particular primordial quality of something that had existed before shrieking was a category and was producing it anyway, tearing through the available space with the specific quality of something that had run out of the patience it had cultivated for ages and was expressing the loss of that patience through the only available channel.

I lunged. Ashenfang blazed with the particular quality of something that was not simply steel anymore but the specific expression of the ley lines' pain and Myrcanthor's rage and every life that had been bent by what this thing had done and was doing, the dragon's fury reborn in the particular form it needed to be in for this specific act.

The core quivered with the particular grotesque quality of something that was not expecting this specific force applied at this specific angle and was discovering that its certainty had been premature. Too late. The blade drove into it with the particular inevitability of something that had been moving toward this moment since before either of us had a name.

The impact was apocalyptic in the particular quality of something that was not a physical explosion but a structural one, the specific quality of a thing that should not have been being told so by the mechanism that had been made for exactly that purpose. Reality cracked not from force but from the particular quality of something that had always been wrong being corrected with everything available.

Emerald fire devoured. Not flesh. The specific twisted festering malice at the thing's core, the particular concentrated wrongness of something that had been assembling itself from the world's damage for ages, torn apart by the specific light of something that had always been its opposite.

Silence. Absolute. The particular hollow of annihilation rather than peace, the specific absence of something that had been comprehensively present and was now comprehensively not. A void in the shape of what had been there.

Then its voice. Not from the chamber. From the particular internal space where such things found their channels. The specific cold amusement of something that had found the entire encounter instructive. That laugh. The particular quality of something that had not been in pain but had been fed, and found the feeding interesting, and was communicating something specific about what the feeding had produced that I was not yet equipped to understand.

I barely had time to breathe before the voice struck me. My body turned on the specific instincts of something that had moved through combat long enough to move before thought. Where I had stood a heartbeat be-fore, the world expressed its opinion in the particular violent way of stone vaporising and earth screaming and the floor splitting with the specific quality of something that had received more than it was designed for from the inside.

Lira threw herself clear. Her eyes had the particular wide quality of horror and understanding arriving simultaneously. Her hands blazed with the particular frantic quality of magic from someone who was spending the last of what they had and understood that it was the last. The ley lines wailed with the particular quality of something that had reached the end of its endurance and was expressing that end through the only available register.

And then Myrcanthor screamed again. The particular quality of a dragon's cry that had been shaped by suffering rather than by battle, moving through the night with the specific quality of something that had not been produced in centuries and would not be forgotten. Her vast body collapsed under the particular weight of something inside it, the corruption consuming her from the specific inside with the efficiency of something that had found the perfect host.

She thrust her body between us and the advancing dark. Not a gesture of power. The particular quality of something that had run out of power and was offering what remained of it as a different kind of resource. "Find its core," she had said. The specific quality of a command produced by a being that was using its last available will to give direction to something that might be able to act on it.

We carved through the remaining darkness together. Talon and Rowan and Lira. Through ash and the specific shattered quality of civilisations that had been here before us and had not survived the same specific encounter. Toward the particular beating heart of everything that had gone wrong.

The killing blow had the specific quality of something that had always been heading toward this moment. The impact that followed was not the ending. The particular subtle quality of the creature's response, the way it did not die so much as conclude this particular phase, the specific quality of its laughter as it changed, was the information that mattered. A death rattle that was also a transformation. A final convulsion that was also a statement.

Then the silence that was not peace. The particular quality of a silence wrapped around the world's bones and pressing inward, the specific quality of aftermath in a context where aftermath was not the same as conclusion.

I took a ragged breath and the taste of ash was the particular persistent quality of something that had decided to stay rather than dissipate with the creature that had produced it. My hands had the specific tremor of things that had been doing too much for too long and had been presented with a moment of stopping and were not certain what to do with the stopping. Ashenfang's phantom heat moved through my bones with the particular quality of a weapon that had done what it was made for and was resting in the specific way of things that were not finished but were between.

The ground had the particular blackened quality of something that had been subjected to what we had all just been subjected to and had not recovered. The sky, visible through the cracks in the cavern roof, had the particular smouldering quality of something whose last light was the specific light of a world that had come very close to something it was not prepared for.

Lira sat on the cold stone floor with her arms around herself in the particular holding quality of someone who was determining the specific integrity of what was left after what had just passed through it. The ley lines beneath her had the particular diminished quality of things that had given what they had to give and were now in the specific process of discovering whether there was anything left.

Rowan stood facing away with his fists at the particular bloodless quality of someone who had been holding something too hard for too long and had not released the grip even when the battle ended. The particular wit that had been his specific defence against the weight of things was the particular absent quality of something that had been stripped away by contact with something that stripped away the inessential.

Myrcanthor stood with the particular fractured quality of something that had always been whole and was encountering the specific experience of not being whole. The corruption had left the particular blackened quality of its passage across her scales, the dark veins the specific visible evidence of something that had been inside the architecture of something eternal and had changed it. The particular splintered quality of something at her ancient core that had endured everything and was now in the process of discovering that this specific thing had been different from everything.

I swallowed with the particular raw quality of something that had been in contact with too much for too long and was still processing the contact. This was not a victory. The particular taste of that recognition was the specific taste of something true and unwanted. The air had the specific lingering quality of a presence that had concluded this phase and was not therefore absent. It pressed with the particular quality of something that had been here before us and would be here after us.

That laugh. The particular quality of something finding the entire encounter instructive in a way that implied the instruction had been taken. The ley lines shuddering with the particular quality of things that had felt something too large for the available structures and were still feeling it.

Rowan's voice arrived with the particular hoarse quality of something that had been through everything that had just happened and was still required to function. "We move." The specific quality of a statement that was also a command that was also the only remaining available option.

One breath. The particular burning quality of lungs that had been in contact with this air for too long. One step. Then another. The nexus awaited. The particular cold specific quality of the thing I had understood since the creature's laughter settled in my bones and refused to dissipate.

The worst was not behind us.

CHAPTER FOURTEEN - THE SHATTERED VEIL

THE BATTLE'S SILENCE WAS WRONG IN THE PARTICULAR way of silences produced by the violent cessation of sound rather than its ordinary absence. Where the clash of steel and the roar of fire and the specific crack of magic had filled every available frequency, now only the heavy smoke that curled through the ruins remained, carrying the particular sharp sting of burnt flesh and the specific copper of blood-soaked earth. It coated the tongue with the particular persistent quality of things that had decided to stay. Beneath it all, the ley lines shuddered through the stone with the specific recoil of something that had been through too much and had not yet determined whether it was going to survive the experience.

Myrcanthor lay across the broken terrain with the particular quality of things that had been vast and had been made small by something larger than their vastness.

I knelt beside her and my hand found her flank with the specific pressing quality of someone confirming a truth they were hoping to have refuted. The heat that came back through my palm was wrong. Not the particular living fire of dragon-kind that I had always felt through the bond, the specific warmth of something enormous and ancient and entirely certain of its own continuation. This was the specific quality of decay that had been given a temperature, a sickness that had settled into the flesh and was moving with the particular patient quality of something that had no reason to hurry. It slipped between my fingers with the specific oily quality of dying magic, the particular sensation of power that had been changed from its natural state into something that could not be used for anything except its own dissolution.

Her breath was the particular thin ragged quality of something that had always produced vast sound and was now producing barely enough to be audible, smoke and blood at the corners of her jaw with each exhale, the specific evidence of an interior damage that was expressing itself through the only available channels.

Lira's voice broke the silence with the specific quality of something that had been held as long as it could be held. "She's dying." The words arrived rough and raw with the particular grain of grief scraped through sound, not performance but the specific honest expression of someone who had understood something and could not make themselves not understand it.

Rowan's body did not flinch but his eyes produced the particular betraying flicker of a man built from the specific materials of iron and war encountering something that those materials did not fully address. The particular whitening of his knuckles beneath dried blood and grit. The air around us had the specific weight of death combined with the particular worse weight of resignation, the particular suffocating quality of people who had started to believe that the possible territory had been exhausted.

"Then we find a way." His voice had the particular steel-sheathed quality of something that had decided on its position and was not going to be moved from it by the available evidence. Because there was only one direction and it was going to demand more than blood. The particular more-than-blood quality of what it was going to demand was something none of us had yet quantified.

The nausea that moved through me was the specific heavy crawling quality of something that had found the channels of my body and was using them as a medium for information I had not requested. Not simply the physical response to corruption adjacent to me. An invasion. A force finding the specific places beneath my ribs where the body kept its most fundamental operations and pressing against them with the particular desperate quality of something that was hungry at the specific level below the word hungry, the particular quality of wanting that had been wanting for so long it had become structural.

It was not trying to damage me. The specific quality of its intent was worse than damage. It was trying to claim me, to take up residence in the particular internal spaces that were currently occupied by myself and displace what it found there.

My fingers pressed harder into Myrcanthor's burning flesh.

The world ruptured.

The blast of light that tore through the gloom was the specific quality of something that had no ordinary source, no flame, no sun, no magic in the register I had been trained to use and recognise. It was the particular quality of creation stripped of everything that had been added to it since the beginning, the specific raw undiluted quality of the breath of gods and the particular scream of the first star finding its own light for the first time. The air convulsed around it with the specific electric quality of something that had found the particular frequency at which the atmosphere became something else, and the ozone was thick in my lungs with the particular acrid quality of air that had been fundamentally changed.

The earth buckled beneath me.

Then the hum. Not a roar. Not a scream. The particular deep resonant quality of something that used sound as a secondary medium for a primary communication, moving through bone and stone and the specific channels that connected my body to the ley lines and through those channels to everything those ley lines touched. It did not belong to beast or man or dragon. It belonged to the particular category of world-sounds, the specific register of something that used the world as its instrument.

The ley lines responded to it with the particular bowing quality of things that had recognised something and were acknowledging it the only way available to them.

I did not move. Did not speak. Because the specific quality of what was moving through me was not a victory. The particular cold clarity of understanding arrived through my body rather than my mind, settling in the bones with the particular quality of a debt whose terms had not been fully disclosed but whose existence was now irrevocable.

Emerald fire erupted from the seams of my armour.

It moved with the specific quality of something that had been given a direction and was committing to it completely, snaking down my arm in twisting ribbons of the particular green that lived in Ashenfang and in the Gem and in the specific frequency of the ley lines when they were operating as they were designed to operate. It found Myrcanthor's wounds and entered them with the particular consuming quality of something that had not come to soothe but to purge, burning through the corruption with the specific relentless quality of something that was constitutionally opposed to what it was burning through and had been given sufficient force to act on that opposition.

The sickness fought back. The particular writhing quality of a corrupted thing being separated from its host, shadowy tendrils finding the light and slashing at it with the particular desperate quality of something that had settled itself deep enough to believe it was permanent and was discovering it was not. They hissed. They curled. The specific quality of their dissolution was not the dissolution of things defeated but the dissolution of things being expelled from something they had believed was theirs.

And then Myrcanthor convulsed.

Her colossal body arched with the particular quality of something that had been compressed and was releasing, her roar splitting the specific silence of the battlefield with the particular quality of sound that had been produced before language existed, the deep baritone quality of something that used sound not to communicate but to simply be, primal and raw and older than any word I had for it. The darkness within her screamed with the particular quality of a parasite understanding that it was being removed from a host it had claimed, clawing against the light with the specific desperate fury of something that had not expected to encounter this particular resistance.

I felt the burning move through me with the specific quality of something passing through rather than residing, my nerves alive with the particular fire of a force using my body as a channel for something too large for my body's ordinary capacity. My breath stuttered with the specific quality of something whose respiratory system was being asked to maintain function through conditions not listed in its design parameters. My vision fractured at the edges in the particular way of sight responding to something that was happening at a level below the visual.

The Gem was not healing. The specific quality of what it was doing was transfer. Power surging from me into her with the particular quality of something that had identified where it needed to be and was moving there through the most direct available route, which was through me. Defiance and debt. The specific combination of those two things existing simultaneously in the same channel.

Then silence. But the particular quality of a silence that had been preceded by something so large that the silence was less an absence and more the specific void left by the thing's passage.

Convulsive shudder. Rupture. The darkness tore away from her with the particular quality of something that had been wrenched rather than simply removed, breaking into the specific fine particles of dust and memory, scattering with the particular quality of things that had been solid and had been forced to become otherwise. The air trembled with the specific quality of something that had been in it and was now not in it, and the world produced the particular exhale of something that had been holding its breath for the specific duration of the corruption's presence.

Myrcanthor stilled.

The particular quality of that stillness had a different character from the stillness of before. Before had the specific quality of something approaching an ending. This had the particular quality of a threshold held open, the specific breath-before-breath quality of something about to begin.

Then light. The particular golden quality of something that was not the sickly green of corrupted ley lines but the specific warm gold of power in its natural state, flooding from her core with the particular quality of molten dawn finding every available channel, pouring through torn sinew and mending it with the particular quality of something that was not simply repairing damage but reestablishing the fundamental architecture of what she was. The corruption hissed in the particular retreat of something that had been present and was being made not-present, curling into the specific vapour of something that had no coherence without the host that had been sustaining it.

Her scales emerged from the process with the particular quality of things that had been dulled and had been returned to themselves, shimmering with the specific forged-emerald quality of something that had been reconstituted at a level deeper than the surface, power pulsing beneath the surface with the particular renewed breath-quality of something that was alive in a more specific sense than it had been even before the corruption found it.

Myrcanthor awoke.

Not simply healed. The particular quality of what she was now had something different in it, some specific addition produced by what she had been through and what had been done to bring her back, a reforging in the particular sense of something having been broken down to its components and rebuilt into something that had kept everything essential and had added something else. Her gaze found mine and the twin infernos in her eyes had the particular quality of something that had always burned and was burning now in the specific register of something that had recently confirmed its own capacity to burn. The ground trembled beneath the specific quality of her return.

I collapsed.

My breath tore from my lungs with the particular ragged quality of something whose respiratory system had been doing more than respiration for the duration of the transfer and was now being asked to return to its ordinary function and was finding the transition difficult. Each inhale was laced with the specific pain of something that had been used as a channel and was still registering the passage. My heart staggered with the particular uneven quality of something whose rhythm had been disrupted and had not yet returned to its own frequency.

Lira caught me. The particular quality of her arms finding me before the fall completed, her voice breaking around my name with the specific sound of something that had been held through the entire previous sequence and was finding its first honest expression in this moment. Her hands had the particular quality of something doing two things simultaneously, one pressed to my cheek and one over my chest, the specific quality of someone trying to determine whether what they are holding is still there.

Myrcanthor moved before either of us had found our next breath.

She rose with the particular quality of something that had been prone and had decided to be otherwise, wings unfurling with the specific quality of things torn from time, the last shadows of the corruption clinging and being shed with the particular ease of dust dismissed by the specific authority of something that had decided it was done accommodating them. Her gaze found mine and the quality of it was the particular knowledge-quality of something that had seen everything about me and had made its assessment.

When she spoke, her voice moved through the ruins with the particular quality of thunder that had been given the specific form of law. "The obligation is settled." Not gratitude. Not forgiveness. The particular immovable quality of an accounting completed. An exchange had been made with the specific character of something carved into the structure of existence rather than agreed between parties.

Talon understood. The particular settling quality of her words in the specific places in his bones where things that were irrevocable settled.

Around us, the others had the particular quality of something frozen between the moment before and the moment after, their faces carrying the specific quality of people who had been present for something that had reorganised their understanding of the available territory. Wide eyes carrying not awe but the particular specific combination of reverence and the specific creeping quality of dread that accompanied witnessing a power that had always been larger than the context it had been occupying making itself fully known.

The ley lines, which had been struggling with the particular desperate quality of things that were trying to maintain function under conditions that exceeded their tolerances, had stilled. The specific quality of that stilling was not the stilling of rest but the stilling of something that had received an instruction from something with sufficient authority to give instructions to ley lines.

Power as old as the bones of the earth had spoken. The particular quality of what followed was the quality of things that had been in the presence of such a speaking and were adjusting to the specific implications of having been present.

I swallowed against the particular dryness in my throat. My pulse had the specific slow methodical quality of something maintaining function through deliberate effort rather than ordinary automaticity. I had called the Gem. It had answered. But in the particular quality of its answering, it had woken something that had been asleep beneath the specific surface of what I thought I understood about what the Gem was and what it was connected to. A whisper moved through the particular internal space where such things moved, not a sound but the specific quality of cold breath finding the most sensitive available surface.

Nothing is freely given. The particular cold specific quality of that certainty settling through me. And the cost. The particular quality of something still to be calculated but already irrevocable.

Myrcanthor ascended with the particular quality of something that had been returned to itself and was now occupying the full extent of what that self entailed. Scales catching the available light with the particular quality of forged emeralds under the specific quality of sunlight that only existed at the specific moment of a world's reorganisation around a significant event. And yet beneath the particular majesty of her ascent, the specific weight of what had been woken pressed against my chest with the quality of something that was not yet named but was already present.

The reckoning was coming. It always did.

My breath found the specific slow controlled quality of something that had identified the next necessary task and was organising itself for it. The force that now moved through me in the wake of the Gem's use had a different quality from anything I had used before, a vaster quality, the particular feeling of something that was not simply my power but creation's echo, the specific resonance of something that had been present since before the categories existed and was expressing itself through the available channels.

The Emerald Gem pulsed against my chest with the particular slow quality of something that had answered a call and was in the specific quiet after the answering, each flicker of light carrying the particular quality of a breath rather than a burst, the wordless connection that had always been present expressing itself now in a register that was different from its ordinary register. It had always been there. But this was different. Not guidance. Answer.

Myrcanthor's gaze, when it found me, had the particular quality of eyes that had looked at a man and had seen the specific layers underneath the man, the particular knowledge-quality of a being that had been watching long enough to read what was underneath the surface presentation. There was something in her expression that I had not seen from her before, a particular quality of quiet that had depth to it, the specific quiet of something that had felt the sacrifice from the inside.

Around us, the ley lines pulsed in the specific broken-prism quality of something that had been changed at a level that expressed itself in every frequency simultaneously. The light they produced fractured and re-formed in the particular ways that did not correspond to any physics I had been taught, each pulse sending a specific tremor through the available air and the specific quality of the air itself bending what the eye processed and twisting the particular distance between things.

Rowan's voice had the specific hushed quality of something that had been brought as low as it could go without stopping entirely. "Unprecedented." The word arrived with the particular brittle quality of something that had been used to have categories for things and had just encountered something that exceeded its categories.

The ground beneath us had the particular liquid quality of something that had lost its relationship with solidity as a default state. Our shapes reflected in its surface with the particular twisted quality of reflections produced by something that was not interested in accurate reproduction, our bodies stretched and broken in the specific way of things seen through a medium that has been compromised at the level of its fundamental physics.

The sky had the particular violently wrong quality of something that had been subjected to forces it had not been designed to accommodate, deep violets bleeding into burnt gold with the particular smearing quality of colours that had lost their boundaries, storm clouds with the specific writhing quality of something that had been given too much life for the form it was using to express it.

Myrcanthor's voice arrived with the specific tight quality of something that was controlling itself around a fear it had almost never been required to express. "The ley lines. Their power is unfolding. Reality itself is coming undone."

A fissure split the air with the particular quality of something that was not acoustic but logical, the specific sensation of reason developing a crack through which the unreasonable was now visible. The terrain beneath our feet and the atmosphere around us and the specific current of time had all acquired the particular quality of things that had been anchored to laws of existence and had found those laws insufficient.

Ashenfang in my hand was the specific cool anchor of something that maintained its own relationship with solidity regardless of what was happening to everything around it. Its steel was the particular familiar quality of the only thing in the available sensory field that had not been compromised by what had been done here. "We must move." The urgency in my voice was the specific urgency of someone who understood that the available time was contracting in proportion to the available reality. No time for the particular luxury of wondering what we had woken.

The emerald blade's glow had the particular weakened quality of something that had given everything available to it and was operating on whatever remained below everything, its light carrying the specific character of something that was still present but was using the minimum necessary to maintain presence. The corruption that moved through the land had the particular quality of a wound that had found a new expression, pressing against flesh with the specific invasive cold quality of something that had decided it deserved access to the interior.

My grip found the particular white-knuckled quality of commitment. "We press on." My breath misted with the specific quality of air that had been wrong for long enough to have changed temperature as one of its symptoms. "We need to find the root of this before it finds us." Each step had the particular deliberate quality of movement through a medium that had stopped being neutral.

Beneath us the ground trembled and breathed with the particular quality of something alive that had not previously been alive, an undulating surface with the specific mirror-quality of something that reflected rather than supported, showing us the particular distorted versions of ourselves that the corrupted medium produced.

Lira faltered. Her breath had the specific caught quality of a body that had received information through the visual channel that it had not been prepared to receive. The reflection that held her attention had the particular wrong quality of her face without her in it, her features present in their specific arrangement but carrying the specific cracked porcelain quality of something that had lost its structural integrity, dark veins of corruption spreading through the fractures with the particular quality of something that had always been there and had been waiting for this specific quality of light to make it visible. Hollow pits where the eyes should have carried the specific quality of depth that was the self.

A scream had the particular quality of something that tried to find her throat and found it occupied by silence instead.

"Talon." Her voice had the particular barely-there quality of something using the minimum necessary breath.

"Lira." My voice was the particular low-weighted quality of something that had identified where she was and was providing a location for her to return to from wherever the reflection had taken her.

She tore her gaze from it with the particular quality of someone whose body had to participate in what should have been a purely mental decision, wrenching herself back from something that had been holding her with its specific quality of recognition. "Nothing." The particular too-quick quality of the lie. The specific ashen taste of it on her own tongue.

The whispers returned. But different. The particular wrong quality of what was different was that they were not the hissing taunting whispers of something that wanted to corrupt. The specific quality of what came now was the particular quality of voices that had been in the dark for a very long time and had found something that might be able to hear them.

A sound like dry leaves in a breathless wind but carrying beneath the acoustics the particular quality of voices that had been disassembled into their component frequencies and were trying to reassemble themselves through the available medium. Not malicious. Not mocking. The particular quality of things begging. The specific register of desperation that was worse than threat because it carried the particular implication that what was asking had once been something that did not need to beg.

Lira's arms wrapped around herself with the particular quality of someone trying to produce a physical response to a sensation that had no physical source, trying to shake off the particular phantom-touch quality of something that was pressing against her in the specific channels where things that were not physical made themselves felt.

A voice with the particular fragile quality of glass approaching its own breaking point threaded through the suffocating air. "Save us." The particular raw quality of the next voice, the specific sound of something that had been in agony for longer than agony was designed to last. "Please. Abandon us not."

Rowan halted mid-step. His staff had the particular violent-shaking quality of something that had encountered a resonance it was not designed to accommodate, the runes along it flickering with the specific erratic quality of something recoiling from an unidentified source. "Did you hear that." His voice had the particular barely-there quality of someone who was asking a question they already knew the answer to and were hoping the confirmation would not come.

Myrcanthor's emerald gaze swept the empty air with the particular sharp quality of blades finding a target. "Indeed." The particular iron-caution quality of her voice. "But tread carefully. The blight twists all things. Voices. Memories. Even echoes of the dead."

Rowan's expression had the particular torn quality of something that was being pulled between the specific organ that processed logic and the specific organ that processed grief, and the two had arrived at different conclusions. "Their voices," he breathed, with the particular delicate quality of someone handling something they were afraid to damage. "So real."

"They are not." My voice came out cold with the specific quality of a blade rather than a judgment, the particular clean cut of something that had made a decision and was not entertaining alternatives.

Rowan turned with the particular rigid quality of someone who had organised their body around a position they were not going to abandon. But his eyes had the particular betraying quality of something that had heard the voices in the specific register where grief lived and had been reached there. "You cannot know that." His conviction had the particular fraying quality of something that was still structurally sound and was developing visible wear. "These sounds, whatever they are, they are deception made flesh. We must not falter."

The words had the specific weight of a truth that was also a plea, the particular quality of something said to others and also to the self.

The silence that followed was not the absence of sound but the particular quality of a weight that had been applied to all available surfaces simultaneously, pressing against skin and slipping into lungs with the specific quality of something that had taken up residence in the atmosphere. Every step had the particular quality of movement through something that had decided to resist movement, the specific heaviness of ground that had opinions about what was walking on it.

The landscape contracted around us with the specific tightening quality of a fist finding its grip, the sky darkening through the particular swallowing quality of something consuming the available light with a purpose rather than simply replacing it. The ley lines beneath cast their feverish glow with the particular quality of something that was not illuminating the dark but was itself a symptom of it.

The whispers returned. Louder. The particular inside-the-skull quality of things that had found the specific channels that bypassed the acoustic medium entirely.

Lira stumbled with the particular quality of someone whose feet had received conflicting information about where they were in relation to the available surface, the specific internal quality of something that was pulling at her in the particular register where the self was attached to the world rather than simply standing on it. The murmurs had the specific venom-and-decay quality of something that had been given permission to be specific rather than ambient.

"You are weak." The particular oily quality of the first voice. "You will fail them all." The specific cruel amusement of the second, the particular quality of something that had found the exact frequency of her doubt and was amplifying it.

Her knuckles had the specific whitening quality of nails finding palms, the particular sharp sting of something using pain as the most efficient available tool for maintaining location in the present moment. Each step forward had the specific quality of something that was also a war conducted entirely in the interior, against things that had found the particular channels where battles of this kind were won and lost.

The light ahead had the particular pale otherworldly quality of something that had been designed to look like salvation from a specific distance and was something else from a closer one. She knew it. The particular trap-quality of it was legible. And the pull toward it had the particular undeniable quality of something that had been engineered to be undeniable by something that understood exactly what she would be pulled by.

"Lira." My voice found her through the particular chaos of everything else with the specific quality of something that had been calibrated to find her in exactly this kind of noise. She turned, and what she found in my eyes had the particular quality of a burden too large for the face trying to contain it, concern in the particular register of something that was also something else that was not being named. "Are you holding on."

Her breath stilled with the specific quality of something that had been asked a direct question and was determining how to answer it honestly without giving more than the moment required. "I endure." The words came out with the particular fragile quality of something that was structurally sound and was aware of its own fragility simultaneously. "Though exhaustion lingers."

The steel in my voice had the specific quality of something that had found a softer register without losing the structural quality that made it mine. "We all bear this weight. But you are steadfast, Lira. You always have been." Not comfort applied from the outside. The particular quality of a truth stated by someone who had the specific evidence to state it.

She nodded with the particular quality of something that had received what it needed and was converting it into forward motion. "Thank you." A breath. Barely words.

We crested the jagged rise.

The land below had the particular quality of something that had been subjected to forces that had reorganised its fundamental character, the broken ley lines cutting through the earth in the specific violent patterns of something that had been disrupted at the level of its design rather than its surface. Their ghostly glow had the particular quality of light that had been changed from something that illuminated into something that expressed, a maddening combination of shifting colours that changed with the specific quality of something that was cycling through states faster than anything with stable physics should cycle. It burned the eyes with the particular quality of something that had been designed to overwhelm the visual processing system rather than to be seen.

And beyond it, rising from the particular maelstrom with the specific quality of bones that had refused to become part of the surrounding ruin, the structure. A monolith of the particular nightmare quality of something that had been assembled from materials that did not belong in any configuration that the world would have chosen for them, its jagged spires finding the churning sky with the specific defiant quality of something that had been placed there rather than grown there, that had been directed rather than occurred. The storm coiled around it with the particular drawn quality of something that had been attracted to the structure's specific presence, streaks of violet lightning finding the obsidian peaks with the particular quality of something that was not attacking but acknowledging. The air had the specific weight of burnt stone combined with the particular reek of corruption that had moved past the point of being a smell and had become a quality of the atmosphere itself, as if the world had started to spoil from the inside out and this was where it had started.

Rowan's exhale had the particular barely-there quality of something that had been compressed to its minimum by what it was looking at. "What is that." The words had the particular trembling quality of something on the edge of understanding something it did not want to understand.

Myrcanthor's voice arrived stripped of everything that was not the particular specific weight of what she was saying. "A nexus." Each syllable with the specific dread-dipped quality of something that had not been spoken lightly. "A convergence of ley lines." She did not look away from it. "If the blight has a heart." Her voice darkened with the particular finalising quality of something arriving at the word that had always been coming. "It beats there."

The words settled over us with the particular weight of something that had always been true and had now been confirmed out loud, which changed what the truth cost to carry.

Lira's gaze had the particular locked quality of something that had found what it was looking at and had lost the ability to look away from it, an unseen force with the specific quality of something wrapping around her chest from the inside rather than from the outside, tightening with the particular coiling quality of certainty rather than fear. Not the particular unknown quality of apprehension. The specific known quality of something she had been moving toward before she understood she was moving toward it. Whatever was inside that nexus was not going to simply test them.

The specific cold quality of that understanding moved through her in the particular way of things that arrived through the body rather than through the mind.

My voice had the particular gravel-and-resolve quality of something that had decided to be the sound that pulled people back from the specific edges of thought. "We are close now." Ashenfang in my grip with the particular iron quality of commitment made physical. "But caution is paramount." The specific unyielding quality of my gaze finding each of them in turn. "Whatever dwells within that place will not grant passage freely."

The particular heavy quality of the silence that followed was the specific silence of people who had heard a truth and had accepted it before they were ready, the particular dignified quality of nodding at something you could not be certain you were going to survive.

Lira's voice, with the particular quality of something barely above a breath and carrying the specific weight of stone, cut through the stillness with the particular clarity of something that had moved past the stage of deliberation into the stage of statement. "Forward we march. The path is set. The burden forbids retreat." The particular quality of those words as they found the available air and occupied it, not with volume but with the specific weight of something that had been decided rather than simply said.

The land reacted. The particular specific quality of the reaction was not metaphorical. The whispers built with the specific quality of something that had heard the declaration and had taken it as an instruction, a chorus from beyond the particular thin membrane of whatever separated this world from what was pressing against it from the other side. The air vibrated with the particular quality of an invisible presence using the air as its medium for making itself felt. The specific dread-quality of each breath. The particular low hum beneath the skin with the quality of a warning that had been woven into something below the level at which warnings were usually legible.

The steps on the particular shimmering ground produced ripples that bent light and twisted sound in the specific ways of something that had stopped being a ground and had started being a surface that was doing things with what crossed it. The specific low hum had the quality of something that was not in the air but was the air, a particular frequency that the world was producing rather than a thing in the world producing it.

They did not walk alone. The particular quality of being observed by something that was not organised the way eyes were organised, something older, patient with the specific patience of things that had always been here and would always be here and found the particular urgency of mortal presence faintly interesting. Their progress was the particular slow deliberate quality of every step being a decision rather than a continuance, the ground throbbing with the specific quality of something that had never been simply ground and was no longer performing that particular fiction.

The nexus ahead had the particular quality of something that had been waiting for them specifically, its jagged spires with the specific broken-fang quality of something that had been grown from the particular geology of ruin rather than built, the storm above it finding the specific obsidian peaks with lightning that had the particular quality of strikes that were acknowledgements rather than attacks.

From the swirling mist, a figure emerged.

He did not move the way people moved who were uncertain about their reception. He moved with the particular calm-confidence quality of someone who had watched the rise and fall of specific things that I could not have named and had assessed the particular moment of their falling with the specific cool quality of someone taking notes. He had looked into the abyss, and the particular quality of what he carried in his bearing was the quality of someone who had found the abyss less alarming than expected.

The silver of his hair had the particular quality of something that had not aged but had been changed by proximity to forces that changed the things in their proximity, flowing over robes with the specific dark-as-starless-night quality of something that absorbed rather than reflected. The runes on the fabric pulsed with the particular gentle-whispering quality of things saying things to the air that the air was capable of hearing. The smell of old parchment and burnt incense moved with him with the particular quality of someone whose specific atmosphere was part of them rather than a product of their environment, mixing with the charged ozone of the storm in the particular way of things that had been combined before and knew how to exist together.

His face had the particular map-quality of something that had been made by experience rather than time, every line the specific etching of knowledge rather than the general erosion of years, the particular furrows of someone who had been in the presence of truths that had required the face to reorganise itself around them. His eyes were the specific glacial-silver quality of something that had been looking at the heart of magic for long enough to have developed a different relationship with temperature and with certainty.

Something moved through me that was not fear in the ordinary register. A shudder with the particular quality of something that had recognised a category of power that it had no prepared response for. Not brute force. Not elemental might. The particular quality of authority that had no tether, power that had decoupled itself from the ordinary constraints that made power legible. The specific dangerous quality of knowledge that had gone where it should not have gone and had not been destroyed by the going but had been changed. The particular kind of knowing that ruined the soul before it touched the body.

Myrcanthor moved. The particular slow-shifting quality of her massive body finding a new orientation, scales with the specific scraping quality of something navigating damaged terrain, her emerald eyes finding Kael with the particular quality of something that was not surprised and was not simply cautious. Old. Unspoken. The particular quality of two things that had been in each other's awareness for a very long time and had developed a specific relationship with that mutual awareness that could not be called friendship and could not be called hostility but was something with a precise character all its own. "You still draw breath, elder." The particular crackling-embers quality of her voice.

Kael's lips found the particular configuration that was not a smile and not a smirk, carrying the specific quality of amusement combined with an emptiness that had the particular cold quality of something that had been in the presence of so many things that amusement had become its relationship with them all. "And you still burn, beast." The words had the particular quality of something not needing malice because the weight that they carried was already sufficient. A history not spoken, but felt in the specific quality of the space between the words.

Ashenfang found the particular iron quality of my grip, every nerve with the specific alive quality of something that had identified a presence it did not have a category for and was maintaining readiness while the categorisation proceeded. "You know him." The particular steady quality of my voice masking the specific electric quality of what was underneath it.

Myrcanthor did not redirect her eyes. "Kael was once a seeker of truth." The particular grief-shadowed edge on her words. "A scholar before he was a sorcerer. A man who learned too much." The pause had the particular quality of something she had said before in different forms and had never found the right ending for. "And yet remained unsatisfied."

Kael produced a sound with the particular quality of laughter that had been stripped of everything that made laughter warm, silk dragged over the specific texture of bone. Not amusement in any register I would have recognised as amusement in another context. The particular quality of knowing wearing the clothes of amusement. "You wound me, Myrcanthor." The specific whispered-beneath-the-storm quality of his voice, with the particular silk-mockery quality of something that had practiced its delivery. "Do you deem curiosity a crime?"

Her eyes had the particular darkening quality of something in which fires were being contained. The specific wing-shift of something managing a force that it had decided not to express at its full capacity. "It is," she said, with the particular guttural quality of something that had arrived at this conclusion through specific experience rather than principle, "when the price exacted is too steep."

The silence had the particular quality of something that had been filled with the specific weight of all the things that would require too long to say and that both parties already knew. Kael's silver gaze found me. The amusement was gone with the particular completeness of something that had never been structural but had been performing a function and had finished performing it. What remained had the specific impassive quality of something that was doing its assessment in the space between the surface of the eyes and whatever lived behind them, a particular abyss of thought and intent that admitted no reading.

"And you," he said. The words had the specific light quality of ash falling and the particular sinking quality of iron finding the bottom of deep water simultaneously, arriving in my chest with the specific weight of things that had always been true and were being confirmed rather than introduced. "You have awakened forces beyond your comprehension."

The wind moved through the particular sharp peaks of the nexus with the specific quality of something that had been given a channel and was using it to produce a sound that had the particular warning quality of something that had been trying to communicate for ages and had been ignored.

Lira's fingers found the particular instinctive quality of something moving toward her daggers before the deliberative system had weighed in. The pulse in her veins had the specific urgent quality of something that had decided on an action. But Rowan's glance found her with the particular sharp-still quality of not yet, and her hands found their specific position at her sides rather than at the hilts.

I produced the particular slow controlled exhale of someone who was managing what was in their chest through the specific mechanism of managing what their lungs did. Kael had not arrived. The particular specific quality of that understanding settling through me. He had been here. He had been waiting for this exact configuration of people at this exact moment. The particular weight of being the thing that something had been waiting for.

As the wind's particular mournful quality faded through the peaks, a specific understanding moved through the gathered company with the quality of something that was arriving rather than being reached. Kael's presence had the particular quality of an announcement. Not of himself, but of a reckoning whose timing had just been confirmed. The particular heartbeat-matching quality of fate asserting its particular momentum. Each of us carrying the specific private quality of our own calculation about what we were prepared to give.

We shared the particular look of people who had arrived at the same conclusion through different specific routes and were acknowledging the convergence before descending into what waited below.

Myrcanthor, from the stillness of her particular rebirth, looked at us with the specific quality of something that had been through the thing we were about to go through and had knowledge of it that was not transferable through language. Talon, with the particular war-carved quality of a body that had been through too many specific things to present a smooth surface. Lira, with the specific flame-and-shadow quality of someone who had been forged by defiance rather than prophecy, who had undergone the particular quality of transformation that left something specific behind and produced something specific in its place.

They had given more than blood. The particular quality of what they had given had the specific character of something taken from the places where the self was most essentially itself, the particular hollowing-open quality of sacrifice at the level below the physical. And the particular quality of the magic they had woken in the doing of it would mark them in the specific ways that things marked you when they had found your particular frequency and learned to use it.

Myrcanthor understood something they had not yet arrived at. The particular slow rhythmic quality of the thrum she felt through the interwoven fates of the three of them was not simply the bond of people who had survived the same things. It was the specific quality of an oath that ran deeper than any word they had spoken, forged in the particular process of what they had done for each other and what it had cost.

She regarded Talon in the particular way of something that had looked at him and had seen the specific layers underneath the presented surface, the particular harbinger-quality of a man who had become the specific kind of necessary that the world produced when things had gotten bad enough to require him.

And Lira. The particular endless-question quality of her. The enigma that would continue to be asked because its answer kept producing new questions. They had saved her. The particular cost of that saving was the specific quality of something still being calculated, and the calculation would not be complete in any timeframe that could be considered soon.

The fire they had lit together had the particular quality of something that was always both things simultaneously. The specific warmth of it and the particular capacity for devastation in it existed in the same flame, and they were not separable.

In the particular depths of Myrcanthor, something mourned. The specific quality of the innocence that had been lost had the particular weight of something that was not simply lost but had been necessary to lose, had been the price of the specific things that had been preserved. A cost too steep for any to bear was what made it the particular cost that only the ones who had no other option could pay.

CHAPTER FIFTEEN- THE NEXUS UNVEILED

THE DESCENT HAD THE PARTICULAR QUALITY OF SOME-thing that was not simply downward but inward.

Each step on the spiralling stairway produced the specific echo of stone that had been waiting for exactly these footfalls, the walls pulsing with the luminescent glow of glyphs whose script had been carved into the rock at a time when the people who carved it understood what they were carving and did not do it lightly. The air thickened with each turn in the particular way of something that had been accumulating rather than simply being present, pressing into the lungs with a deep arcane quality that found the specific places where the self was most essentially the self and applied a light, testing pressure.

My boots struck the primordial stone floor with the particular purposeful quality of someone who had decided their pace before they began and was not going to be persuaded to change it. Ashenfang pulsed with the specific green quality of something that had identified the particular frequency of what was in the walls and was both reading it and responding to it, its glow the particular beacon-quality of something that had been made to be present in exactly this kind of dark. "Remain vigilant." My voice broke the oppressive hush with the particular quality of something that had decided to be a sound in a space that preferred silence. "Whatever lurks in this abyss, we confront it united."

Behind me, Lira's fingers had the particular white-knuckle quality of something that had been gripping the dagger's pommel since before she was consciously aware of gripping it. The pressure in her chest was the particular quality of something that had been present since the nexus first made contact and had been building with each step downward, a living thing with the specific quality of the ley lines' pulse operating at a frequency just below the ordinary heartbeat, threading through her veins with the particular quality of something that was becoming indistinguishable from her own blood.

Rowan's voice had the particular thin quality of something that had been compressed by what it was in the presence of. "This place." The whisper barely reached the walls. "It's unnatural." The glow of his Warhammer was the specific weak quality of light that was trying to function in conditions that were working against the basic mechanics of light.

"It's sentient." Kael moved with the particular unnerving fluidity of someone who had been in spaces like this before and had developed a different relationship with their physics, his garments whispering against the carved rock with the specific quality of something that knew how to navigate by methods that did not include ordinary caution. "Here, the mystical currents coalesce. Their energies fettered and corrupted." The particular weight he gave those words had the quality of something that had assessed the situation accurately and was providing the assessment without softening it.

Myrcanthor's growl had the particular quality of something that used sound as a structural element, rumbling through the passage with the specific quality of something so large that the walls accommodated it rather than the other way around. She moved through the narrow space with the particular surprising agility of something that had been massive for long enough to have learned how to be massive in confined spaces, her wings folded, her emerald eyes finding the specific darkest shadows and reading them with the particular intense quality of something that expected to find what was in them. "The air is saturated with primordial magic." The rasp of her voice had the particular quality of something that had been through enough to have genuine reverence for what it was sensing. "A force far more sinister."

The staircase ended.

Not in a wall, not in another passage, but in the particular quality of a space that had simply been too large to be confined by the ordinary logic of arriving at things. The vast chasm opened around us with the specific quality of something that had been held back by the staircase and was now no longer held back, a heart of raw-force power that pulsed with the chaotic quality of something that had been in distress for a very long time and had organised its distress into a rhythm. The maze of sharp black formations rose with the particular quality of needles rather than formations, their dark surfaces veined with the specific sickly green of ley line energy that had been changed from what ley line energy was supposed to be, radiating into the chasm with the particular chaotic quality of something that had always been precise and had been made imprecise by something that found precision inconvenient.

A gasp from Lira. The particular involuntary quality of a body that has received sensory information before the conscious mind has finished preparing to receive it. The thing that found her chest was more than the visual impact of what she was looking at, more than the specific particular quality of power registering on the body's threat-detection systems. The ley lines were doing something specific to her that they were not doing to the rest of us. Reaching. The particular quality of something that had been trying to communicate through available channels and had found a channel that could receive.

"The nexus's core." Kael's voice had the particular hushed quality of someone who had been trying to get here for long enough that being here had a specific character of its own. His silver gaze was on the churning maelstrom at the cavern's centre with the particular locked quality of something that was not going to look away from it. "The ley lines' energy, here, is defiled. Contorted into an abomination of its former self."

The thunderous throb of the chasm had the particular quality of something that was both external and internal, the specific quality of a sound that found the resonant frequency of the chest and used it. Lira struggled with the particular quality of someone who was trying to maintain their cognitive functions while standing in the presence of something that was operating on the specific frequency where cognition and instinct were not distinct. The nexus heart beat with the particular living quality of something that was very much alive and was expressing that aliveness in every available medium simultaneously.

"Our next move." My voice had the particular hawk-keen quality of someone who had assessed the available options and needed to know which one we were taking. My hand had the particular vice-quality of Ashenfang's grip in conditions that warranted it. The jaw-line I was maintaining carried the particular specific quality of something holding a position it needed to hold.

Kael's eyes moved to Lira with the particular quality of something that had arrived at a calculation before the variables had been fully presented. "Equilibrium hinges on her." No preamble. The particular chilling simplicity of something that was a decree.

Lira went still. "Why me." The particular fragile quality of those two words carrying the specific weight of someone who had been hoping the answer was someone else.

"The ley lines have selected you." Kael closed the specific distance between them with the particular measured quality of someone approaching something that required both presence and care. His eyes had the particular polished-moonlight quality of something that had been looking at the specific truth of things for long enough to have developed a direct relationship with it. "Their essence now pulses within you. A connection far deeper than you comprehend." The particular stillness of those words in the space after them.

The despair that found Lira had the particular cold quality of something arriving in the specific place where resolve lived and testing the structural integrity of what it found there. "I lack the skill." The particular choked quality of the words. "I'm utterly lost without guidance." The particular quality of fear escalating with each breath in a body that was already operating at the limit of what fear was compatible with continued function.

"Ignorance is your ally." Kael's murmur had the particular quality of something choosing to stand close enough that the words could be specific rather than general. "The ley lines will illuminate your path. Have faith in their guidance. And in your inherent strength."

My hand found her shoulder with the particular firm-gentle quality of something that understood both what the gesture needed to be and what it needed to refrain from being. My eyes found hers with the particular quality of something that had been watching her long enough to know what she needed to see confirmed in another person's gaze. "You are capable, Lira. Regardless of the outcome, we stand beside you. Unyielding."

The lump in her throat was visible. She managed the particular resolute quality of a nod from someone who has received what they needed and has made the specific decision to convert it into forward motion rather than allowing it to become what it might otherwise become. Inside her, the particular quality of a primal scream that had been escalating since she first felt the ley lines reach for her found its specific location in the architecture of her chest and stayed there, contained.

We moved toward the nexus core with the particular deliberate quality of steps that had understood the destination and had chosen it anyway. Each step produced the specific quality of the earth shuddering beneath us with the particular protest-quality of ground that had been making its prefer-ence known since we entered and had not been listened to.

The air had the particular thick-buzzing quality of something that had been charged beyond what charge was meant to be, the broken ley lines pulsing with the specific erratic quality of corrupted arteries, their light the particular quality of something that had lost its rhythm and was cycling through states with the specific chaotic quality of something that had lost its governing principle. The focus required for the particular ordinary management of walking was borrowed from reserves that had other uses.

Then a guttural tremor. The particular sudden intensification-quality of the ley lines' energy surging beyond its already-exceeded threshold, and the darkness that gathered around the bright pathways had the specific quality of something that had been waiting for exactly this level of excitation to make itself visible. The shadowy shapes took the particular monstrous form of things that had been something else before the corruption found them and had been changed in the specific ways that corruption changed things that it had spent enough time with.

Myrcanthor's wings unfurled with the particular quality of something that had identified a threat and was expressing that identification physically. The emerald flames in her throat had the particular ferocious quality of something that had been building and had been given the specific signal to release. "We are not unobserved."

The menacing figures moved with the particular fluid purposeful quality of things that had no uncertainty about their objective and were executing it through every available path simultaneously, their forms shifting with the specific disturbingly-alive quality of something that was not committed to a single physical configuration.

"Defiled sentinels." Kael's voice had the particular low-unwavering quality of something that had identified what it was looking at and was not surprised to find it here. "Twisted by the corruption. They will deny us access to the ley lines' heart."

Ashenfang blazed with the specific quality of something that had received the information it needed and was responding to it with everything available. "We forge our own path." The declaration had the particular quality of something that was also a statement about the specific character of what was about to happen.

The shadows erupted. The particular maelstrom-quality of inky claws and teeth and the specific deafening-shriek quality of assault on every available sensory channel simultaneously, the air itself crackling with the particular malevolent quality of energy that had been organised into something that was not simply aggressive but specifically designed to overwhelm. The taste of copper or its echo found the back of my tongue in the particular way of something that had arrived before the damage that would produce it.

I swung. Ashenfang moved with the particular deadly-precise quality of something that had been doing this long enough to have simplified the motion to its essential components. Each severed form had the particular horrible quality of something that reassembled before the motion was complete, the specific regenerative quality of things that had been given a different relationship with dissolution than ordinary flesh, their glowing eyes carrying the particular predatory quality of something that had not experienced the specific quality of a serious challenge.

Rowan hurled bolts with the particular grim-determination quality of someone who had decided that stopping was not an option and was acting on that decision through the specific medium of every available force. The intense energy broke apart under the sustained assault with the particular shattering quality of glass, each fragment with the particular desperate quality of something using every available resource and finding each resource insufficient. His breath came in the specific ragged pulls of someone whose body had made its assessment and was operating against its own recommendation.

Myrcanthor's fire had the particular molten-jade quality of something that had been building for the specific duration of everything that had preceded this moment and was releasing at full capacity, engulfing a dozen shadows in the particular blazing quality of something that was genuinely committed to destruction. The shadows went out and returned with the specific horrible inevitability of something that had a different relationship with being destroyed than the things that were destroying them. The sulphur and the specific cold certainty of their return settled into the available air together.

"They're everywhere." Rowan's voice had the particular raw quality of something that had been through enough to have earned the specific terror in it. "What do we do."

I did not answer with words. The particular quality of what passed between my eyes and Rowan's carried the specific content of an exchange that had no adequate language, the particular silent resolution of two people who had been in enough situations without exits to have developed a vocabulary for this specific quality of commitment. My voice was the particular guttural-sharp quality of something that had made a decision about priorities and was communicating it through the most direct available channel. "Protect Lira. She's not just the key." The particular quality of the next words arriving from a place I had not consciously prepared. "She is the gate."

At the nexus's edge, Lira knelt.

Her hands had the particular trembling quality of something that had arrived at the specific point of an action it could not take back and was in the particular suspended moment before the irreversible. The pull in her chest had the specific excruciating quality of something that had been building since the nexus first reached for her and had found, at this particular proximity, the particular full expression of its intention. It was not only the nexus's power. It was the specific quality of the turmoil she had been carrying since the crypt, the particular rawness of every decision made at too high a cost, finding its reflection in the specific mirror of the ley lines' distress.

She had taken an oath. The particular sacred quality of the vow to protect the ley lines, to never manipulate their power for the specific gain of the person holding them. She was standing at the particular precipice of everything she had stood for, the specific edge of becoming the very thing she had organised her life around not becoming. The doubt found the particular places where resolve was thinnest and applied the specific whispering quality of its most accurate truths. She was not like Daegrith. The particular quality of that statement as she held it against what she was about to do.

"Trust the ley lines." Her voice was the particular fragile-breath quality of something that was more a plea than a command, directed at herself through the medium of the available air. "Let them guide you." The hollow quality of the words in her own ears. The particular lie-taste of them on her tongue. The specific quality of a justification she was constructing for something she was going to do regardless of whether the justification held.

The moment her fingers brushed the nexus, the energy found her with the particular quality of something that had been waiting for exactly this contact for a very long time and had a great deal to communicate through it. It was not the particular quality of lightning or fire or anything that had a natural analogue. The particular violation-quality of it was in its intimacy, the specific way it had found the channels of her and was using them as if it had always had access, a desecration of the particular purity of the thing it was moving through.

Her mind had the particular cacophony-quality of too much arriving through a channel designed for less, the specific blinding quality of a light that was not visual, the particular agonising quality of guilt finding its resonant frequency. Her father's face, for the specific duration of a breath, silenced the interior screaming. The guilt returned with the particular relentless quality of something that had been temporarily displaced and was resuming.

Then the voice. Vast. Primordial. Finding her through the specific channels that the nexus had opened and the specific channels that her inheritance had left available and the particular combination of those two things that had always made her the particular specific person that this moment had been waiting for. "You dare to challenge me." The boom of it with the particular deep-mocking quality of something that had been challenged before and had watched all of those challenges reach the same specific conclusion.

"You will not succeed." A cold certainty had the particular quality of not coming from the voice but of the voice confirming something that had always been there, the specific quality of her deepest fears finding their external expression. The whirlwind she found herself in had the particular quality of something that had known her specific architecture and had been assembled from the particular materials that her architecture was most susceptible to. The power surged with the particular whispering quality of shortcuts and forbidden paths, each promise carrying the specific cost-quality of something that was asking for the exact thing she had always refused to give, the particular thing that was most essentially herself.

She trembled. Her hand hovering over the nexus had the particular quality of something that had arrived at its decision and was expressing that decision through the specific physical form of the trembling quality of someone who has made peace with a choice they hate. A shuddering breath. The particular silent acceptance of what was about to follow.

Her eyes found the voice's unseen presence with the particular defiance-quality of something that had run out of alternatives to honesty. "Watch me." The words had the particular ash-taste quality of bravado that was also entirely sincere, the specific thin veneer of something that was both a performance and a truth simultaneously. The fear coiled in her stomach had the particular specific quality of something that had found its home there and was not leaving, but it had been there long enough to have been incorporated into her structure rather than simply resting on the surface of it. The power in her hand had the particular alien quality of something that felt like a violation of the specific thing she had been, threatening to take her over through the particular channels it had found.

The battle raged with the particular fierce quality of something that had been building since before we entered the nexus and had found its full expression in the specific available space of the chasm. The corrupted guardians moved with the particular unnaturally-fluid quality of things that had been given movement without being given the ordinary constraints that movement required, their forms with the particular dark-shifting quality of something that had not committed to solidity as a permanent condition. They absorbed Ashenfang's specific light and Kael's shields with the particular mocking quality of things that had always been absorbing exactly this and had incorporated the absorption into their fundamental character.

Lira felt herself changing. The mystical force moved through the particular channels that the nexus had opened with the specific intoxicating quality of something that had been designed to be intoxicating to the specific person it was moving through, the particular seductive-whispered quality of an offer that understood exactly what it was offering. She saw the particular fleeting quality of visions, the specific shape of what she could become, a darkness with the particular twisted quality of the guardians themselves, a being fuelled by the specific destruction she was trying to prevent.

Rowan's cries for help had the particular barely-audible quality of something reaching her through the specific chaotic medium of the battle's noise, and the sickening certainty arrived in her with the particular quality of something she had been hoping not to know. The choice had the particular clawing quality of something that had found the specific place where her two most fundamental commitments were in direct opposition. The full force of the nexus, the particular quality of something that seemed ready to consume everything including her allies, or the particular failure of letting the darkness take what she had vowed to protect.

The whispers had the particular urging quality of something that had decided which direction it wanted her to go and was applying the specific consistent pressure of things that had infinite patience and a preferred outcome.

And Lira knew, in the particular devastating clarity of someone arriving at an honest assessment, that she was going to choose the path she had been most hoping she would not.

My blade tore through another guardian with the particular quality of something that had been doing this long enough to have it in the muscles rather than the mind, Ashenfang with the specific viper-strike quality of something that had identified its target and was executing the strike with the particular economy of long practice. The stench of scorched shadow had the particular quality of something that was not flesh and was also not nothing, the specific absence of blood replaced by the particular phosphorescent quality of dying eyes.

The particular sickening slurp of the reformation. The specific guttural hiss of it scraping across my teeth. Sweat at my temple in the particular cold quality of something that had been building for the specific duration of this impossible engagement. Blood with the particular metallic quality of something that had found the back of my throat through the specific channels that strain and exertion used.

"They won't die." Rowan's voice was the particular raw-terror quality of someone who had been holding themselves together and had found the seam. His Warhammer with the particular pale energy of something that was giving everything and finding everything insufficient, the shimmer of the frost-quality crackling under the particular relentless pressure of things that had a different relationship with dying.

The particular cold-clammy quality of despair finding my heart. How do we win. The specific question clawing through my throat.

Kael's voice had the particular chilling quality of something that was calm in a context that demonstrated why calm was wrong, his silvery staff with the particular terrifying-grace quality of something in the hands of someone who understood it at the specific level below technique. He staggered a guardian with the particular venerable-force quality of a strike that had been preceded by the specific accumulation of considerable expertise. "The corruption." The particular burning quality of his eyes with knowledge and the specific weary-resignation quality of something that had been carrying this knowledge for longer than was comfortable. "It's the ley lines themselves. Their lifeblood. Until we sever the source, they are invincible." The word with the particular chilling finality of something that was accurate.

"Repel them!" My roar had the particular commanding quality of something that had identified the specific priority and was communicating it through every available channel. "Lira is our sole hope for victory. Her life is paramount!"

In the heart of the cavern, Lira remained before the nexus.

The force throbbed with the particular dark-awareness quality of something that had consciousness and was using that consciousness in a specific direction. Its bursts of light had the particular fierce quality of something that was not simply producing light but was expressing itself through the medium of light with the full force of what it was. The pull had the particular quality of something that had found her specific channels and was using all of them simultaneously, demanding her attention and her focus and the particular thing that had always been most essentially hers.

The whispers had become the particular chorus quality of many voices organised around a single purpose, the specific siren-song quality of magic she had been wanting to resist while simultaneously discovering how specific the wanting had always been, how close beneath the surface the other thing had always lived. Her vow, made in the particular specific quality of a childhood that had given her this as her definition of herself, had the particular heavy-shackle quality of something that had stopped being a guide and had become a constraint in the face of what she was looking at.

The whispers had the particular quality of echoing something that had been inside her, a hunger for untamed power that she had been calling fear of it for long enough to have almost believed the misidentification. She reached with the particular trembling quality of something that was expressing the internal battle through the only available physical medium. Her fingers found the nexus edge.

The world exploded.

The flood that moved through her had the particular intense quality of something that had been waiting for exactly this contact and had a great deal accumulated. The forbidden-pleasure and sharp-gnawing-pain quality of it arriving simultaneously through every available channel. She gasped with the particular quality of something that was also an arch, an involuntary full-body response to something that was too large for the body to process without full structural participation. The nexus's power with the particular living quality of something that had been alive long before she was alive and was using her as a medium for expressing things that had been in it longer than she had been.

She saw the ley lines as they had been. The particular beautiful-vibrant quality of something in its natural state, life-giving in the specific way of things that had always been there and had always made everything else possible. Then the corrupted vision with the particular darkness quality of something that was more than an external threat. The particular reflection-quality of it finding the specific darkness that had been inside her, the particular resentment she had buried under the specific weight of the vow, the particular bitterness toward a world that had given her hardship as the primary material from which to construct herself.

The looming darkness was not only outside her. It was her own self-doubt wearing the specific form that it wore when it had been given sufficient power to make itself visible.

The particular deep-resonant quality of a voice in her mind. The specific familiar quality of her own inner critic having been given form and force and a specific external address. "You dare to defy me." With the particular twisted-invitation quality of something that wanted her to feel the specific kinship it was offering. "The ley lines are mine." The particular unsettling quality of her longing for that claim, the specific truth it contained about the particular relationship between her and the ley lines that she had been calling something safer.

The choice with the particular looming quality of something that had been approaching since before she descended the stairs. Fight or surrender. Not a physical battle. The particular war-within-soul quality of something being conducted in the specific place where principles and the allure of their opposite found their shared address.

"You're mistaken." Her voice with the particular quivering-determination quality of something that was genuine despite the quivering. "The ley lines are the land's. Not yours to claim." The words with the particular feeble quality of something that was true and was finding the specific difficulty of making truth feel adequate in the presence of what she was facing.

The chilling shard of doubt with the particular piercing quality of something that had found the specific place that was most susceptible. The particular terror-seed quality of what if she was wrong, what if she was the fool, what if the darkness was right about everything.

The darkness's laughter had the particular deep-rumbling quality of something that was using her bones as its resonating instrument. "You think you can stop me?" The particular chilling reflection-quality of her own doubts wearing the specific voice of something larger. "You are nothing but a fleeting spark. Fragile and weak. You will burn out like all who came before you." Not simply a threat. The particular quality of her own darkest assessment of herself finding its external confirmation.

The nexus flared. The particular violent quality of something that had been building and had found its release threshold, the specific surge of chaotic energy rippling through the cavern with the particular quality of a loss of containment rather than a directed attack. Lira's connection shattered with the particular quality of something that had been intact and was no longer intact, and she stumbled back with the particular gasping quality of someone who has just been separated from something that was using their channels and is discovering what that separation feels like.

The air crackled with the particular residual quality of power that had discharged and was still present in the atmosphere as evidence of its own recent existence. The ground with the particular scorched quality of something that had been in contact with too much and showed it. But the worst damage had the particular internal quality of something that could only be located by the person carrying it. She could feel the ley lines' power draining with the particular quality of the earth itself using her as the channel through which it communicated its specific distress.

In that particular moment of vulnerability, the notion arrived. She could tap into the darkness. The particular terrible-compromise quality of it, the specific betrayal of everything she had been building herself around since the day she understood what her father was and what she was determined not to be. But the alternative was the particular quality of utter destruction. The weight of that choice had the particular crushing quality of something that exceeded what any single body should be asked to carry.

The taste of defeat combined with the particular terrifying-allure quality of forbidden power. She gasped not only for the specific ordinary reason but for the particular quality of something lost that could not be exactly named.

In the particular chaos of the battle, my roar had the particular concern-thick quality of something that had identified the specific thing it needed most to confirm. I paused in the specific interval between strikes. "Lira. Are you all right."

She struggled to her feet with the particular trembling quality of something that had been through what she had been through and was continuing anyway. "I saw it." The particular gasping quality of the words. "The blight pulses with malevolent life. It doesn't just warp the ley lines. It subjugates them." The particular quality of something arriving at the specific accurate description of what it had experienced. "It's an entity. Overwhelmingly powerful."

Myrcanthor's anger had the particular eruptive quality of something that had been building and had found its specific expression, her wings with the particular rapid quality of something that was using every available channel to express what it was, the emerald fire with the particular fierce quality of something that had found its target. The inferno consumed the shadowy guardians in the particular blazing quality of something genuinely committed to their dissolution. They reformed with the particular relentless quality of things that had a different relationship with dissolution than the things consuming them.

Lira's voice had the particular dread-thick quality of something that had confirmed its worst assessment. "It's intrinsically linked to Daegrith. Yes, he perverted the ley lines. But he's just a puppet." The particular specific quality of what followed. "Something far grander, far more sinister, manipulates him."

A deep resonant throb vibrated through us before we had fully metabolised her words. The chaotic glow of the ley lines flared with the particular sharp quality of something that had received a signal, casting the specific flickering shadows of the crystal formations around us in the particular quality of light that was not behaving like light.

From the heart of the nexus, a figure materialised.

A ripple first. The particular ethereal distortion quality of something that existed between one state and another and was in the specific process of choosing. Then the coalescence with the particular quality of something taking the form that it had chosen, a humanoid apparition with the particular diaphanous quality of something that was present without being solid, glowing with the soft golden quality of something that had been in contact with the ley lines' original nature for a very long time. Its features were the particular vague quality of something whose identity existed at a level below the visual, but the serenity it radiated had a specific quality that was not peace so much as the particular peace that exists on the other side of every possible loss.

"What is that." Rowan's voice with the particular awed-apprehension quality of something that had found the specific register that existed between those two states.

"A vestige of the ley lines' protectors." Kael's voice had the particular hushed quality of something that had arrived at a moment it had been oriented toward for a very long time. His silver eyes never left the apparition. "A ghostly echo of those who once safeguarded this balance. It has endured. Tethered to the nexus."

The spectral figure moved with the particular languid-deliberate quality of something that existed in a different relationship with time than everything else in the chamber. Its voice arrived not through the air but through the particular internal channel that the ley lines used when they had something specific to say. "Heirs of the ley lines, you bear their legacy and their energy. You must purify the encroaching blight before it consumes all existence."

Lira moved forward with the particular quality of something that had been pulled rather than chosen, though the distinction between those two things in her case had always been less clear than she would have preferred. "How." The particular demanding quality of her voice, trembling and still firm, the specific quality of someone who had arrived at the question that everything had been leading to. "How can I stop this cataclysm."

The ethereal figure extended its hand and the shaft of light that found Lira had the particular quality of something that had been aimed at her specifically, connecting with her through the specific channels that had been available since the ley lines first reached for her. She cried out with the particular quality of something receiving a wave of energy that was both exhilarating and overwhelming, both foreign and deeply known, pushing back the specific creeping darkness within her through the particular medium of being the thing that that darkness was the opposite of.

"Channel their brilliance." The entity's tone had the particular softening quality of something that had arrived at the specific part of the message that mattered most. "But heed this. Such power extracts a heavy toll. Sacrifice is the price of dominion. Will you pay it."

Her heart with the particular thundering quality of something that had been put to a question that it already knew the answer to and was in the specific process of confirming the knowing by continuing to beat. The particular spinning quality of her mind finding its way through the specific devastation she had seen, the twisted ley lines, the particular fallen quality of her companions, the particular shape of the only available path.

Her resolve with the particular hardening quality of something that had found its bottom and was pushing up from it. "I accept." Her voice with the particular unwavering quality of something that had been decided before the words arrived.

The being's glow erupted with the particular blinding quality of something that had been holding its full expression in reserve and was now releasing it completely, wrapping Lira in the specific light quality of something that had been waiting for exactly this acceptance. The depraved sentinels froze with the particular wavering quality of forms that had encountered something they were not prepared to encounter, their spectral quality flickering in the particular quality of something that did not know whether to run or to defy. The nexus responded with the particular dramatic-shifting quality of something that had been in one state and had received permission to be a different state.

From the heart of the nexus, darkness stirred again. The particular sinister quality of the chuckle that arrived through the available air.

Lira's form shone with the particular golden quality of something that had found the specific frequency of its own nature and was expressing it at full volume, the warm rays flooding the cavern with the particular quality of light that had been absent from this space for a very long time and was finding the specific places that had been waiting for it. The corrupted guardians halted with the particular paralysed quality of something caught between two forces and temporarily unable to execute either response. The particular flickering of their dark forms with the specific wild quality of something that had been certain and was suddenly uncertain.

In that particular brief interval, something that was not quite hope but was the specific precursor to hope found the available space in us.

Talon's grip on Ashenfang had the particular slightly-loosening quality of something that had been at maximum and had found one notch of release. Rowan's Warhammer descended from its raised position with the particular cautious quality of something that was permitting itself to acknowledge a possibility.

The clearing erupted.

I found myself on my back with the particular quality of someone who did not remember the transition from upright to horizontal, the charred earth beneath my fingers with the specific sharp smell of burnt soil and raw magic stinging the particular channels that smell used to communicate. Pain moved through my muscles with the particular quality of something that had been acute and was now settling into the specific register of damage that would be accounted for later. One thought with the particular consuming quality of something that had occupied every available space. Lira.

I pushed myself upright with the particular heaving quality of a body that had been asked to do more than it had remaining and was doing it anyway. My gaze locked on her figure at the devastation's heart.

She was gone. In her place stood the particular grotesque quality of something that wore her form but had lost the specific essential quality of what had made it hers. Her body with the particular motionless quality of something suspended, held by the particular quality of an unseen force that had found the specific points of her and was holding them. Golden flames pulsed through her veins with the particular quality of something alive and changed, the particular strange-energy quality of something that was hers and was also something else's. Her head tilted with the particular slight quality of something that was responding to stimuli I could not identify. Her eyes, which had always carried the specific gold-fierce-quality of her particular fire, had the particular dimmed quality of something that was present and was not herself, twin cold-fire quality of something that was burning but was burning wrong.

Daegrith emerged. The particular dark-omen quality of something that had been summoned by the specific conditions that this moment had created, his presence with the particular heavy-certainty quality of something that had been waiting for exactly this configuration. Behind her, the particular influential quality of a figure whose dark cloak rippled with the specific quality of air that had decided to yield to him rather than simply accommodate him. The ley line entities at his feet with the particular flickering quality of things that had been given a different set of instructions than their original ones.

My jaw had the particular clenching quality of something that had found its worst dread standing in the available space and was making a specific assessment of it. He had taken her.

His voice moved through the space with the particular soft-smoke-darkness quality of something that had practiced its specific delivery. "Your intervention was a grave error, Lord of Hougun."

My knuckles had the particular whitening quality of Ashenfang's hilt finding its maximum grip. My pulse with the particular frantic-drumbeat quality of something that had found the specific information it most dreaded and was trying to function regardless. "Release her."

Daegrith's breath had the particular chilling quality of something that found mirth in exactly this context. "Why relinquish what is rightfully mine."

A guttural roar charged through the space with the particular quality of something that had found its purpose in the specific medium of pure furious motion. Myrcanthor surged forward with the particular living-tempest quality of something that had decided to be a force of nature rather than a creature subject to the forces of nature, the Emerald Flame with the particular bowing quality of something that had organised itself around a specific target, golden eyes burning with the particular cursed-wrath quality of something that had been given every possible reason to be everything it was capable of being.

"You dare disturb the cosmic order." The boom of her voice shaking the particular roots of the woodland with the specific quality of sound that used stone as its secondary medium. "You were cast into the abyss for a reason, Daegrith. You cannot possess what was never yours."

His gaze found hers with the particular cold-unblinking quality of something that had been looking at things like her for long enough to have made its assessment. His expression had the particular stillness-carved-from-cruelty quality of something that had no relationship with the specific category of things that produced fear in it. "I do not disrupt the balance, creature." Voice with the particular smooth-ice quality of something that had been honed. "I simply restore it."

My patience with the particular snapping quality of something that had reached its specific structural limit. Ashenfang blazed to life with the particular green-fire quality of something that had identified its target and was expressing that identification through every available channel. I struck with the particular hard-fast quality of someone who had made a decision at the level below deliberation and was executing it.

Empty air.

Then a whisper. The particular breath-behind-me quality of something that had moved with the specific speed of something that did not have the ordinary relationship with spatial transition.

"Inefficient." The particular scalpel-of-ice quality of the voice. The agony arrived as the particular invisible-force quality of something that found my torso through channels that bypassed the ordinary physics of impact, lifting me from the ground with the specific quality of something that was making a point rather than simply inflicting damage. The tree's trunk with the particular impact-explosion quality of a collision that my body had not been consulted about, wood shattering with the specific quality of material that had been subjected to more than it was designed to accommodate. Bones cracking with the specific acoustic quality of something structural failing. Blood with the particular warm-fast quality of something finding its way out through the specific channels that damage opened.

Daegrith stood with the particular monument-quality of something that had achieved its precise intended effect without expending more than the minimum required. And Lira drifted toward me.

The particular specific quality of her approach was the quality of a revenant, the specific quality of movement that had been stripped of the ordinary hesitations and redirections that made movement identifiably hers, deliberate without being alive with decision. She stopped inches from me, her voice with the particular hollow-echo quality of something that was using her vocal apparatus but was not entirely housed in her body. "Do you see now, Talon? She was never meant for you."

Rowan surged with the particular raw-brutal quality of something that had run out of the specific resources required for strategy. His Warhammer singing through the available air with the particular deadly-precision quality of something aimed at the specific point that would end what needed to end. Daegrith dissolved with the particular smoke-between-stars quality of something that had never been as present as it appeared.

Rowan cursed with the particular bitter-snarl quality of someone who had been denied the specific thing they were committed to doing. He turned to Lira instead, his approach with the particular quality of someone who had identified the next available target. She did not flinch. Her hand rose with the particular glowing quality of silver fire that was not her fire, unleashing the blast with the particular quality of something that had been directed rather than chosen, hurling Rowan backward with the specific quality of an impact that was overwhelming. He hit the ground with the particular shattered-doll quality of a body that had received more than it was designed to receive, the particular coughing-blood quality of someone whose internal architecture had been rearranged by what had just happened to it.

"She's not fighting him." Kael's voice had the particular sharp-glass quality of something that had completed its assessment and was delivering it without softening. "He's devoured her completely."

The dread that curdled in my gut had the particular specific quality of something that was refusing the information it was receiving. No. I had seen Lira. Had watched her claw her way back from the specific abyss she had been dragged into. But now, looking at her, I found nothing in her eyes that was the specific thing I had always found there. No defiance. No fire. The particular specific quality of the absence of herself.

She stepped toward me with the particular drifting quality of something that had been given a direction and was following it without the ordinary engagement with the terrain between them, her sun-kissed skin with the particular darkened quality of something that had been changed by what it was hosting, the specific shadow-twisted quality of her features. Silver markings coiled across her arms and throat with the particular alive-binding quality of chains that had found a way to be biological.

My heart with the particular cracking quality of something structural discovering its own fragility.

"Lira." The particular rough-broken quality of my voice. A plea and a prayer occupying the same specific syllables. She paused. The particular head-tilt quality of something that had registered a frequency that it was attempting to locate. As if hearing from across a specific infinite distance.

A flicker.

The particular breath-of-gold quality of something that appeared behind the silver, in the place where her specific fire had always lived. The particular barely-there quality of something that was the smallest possible version of itself and was still there.

I gasped with the particular quality of something that had been waiting for exactly that specific thing and had received it. A spark. Faint. Undeniable. The particular quality of Lira enduring in the specific place where Lira had always endured, in the architecture of herself that was specifically too well-built to be entirely displaced by what had been done to it. That fragile ember with the particular igniting quality of something that found the specific fuel in me that had been waiting for exactly this.

I moved forward with the particular quality of something that had made a decision at the specific level where pain was not a relevant variable, blood blooming beneath the particular jagged ruin of my ribs with the specific warm quality of something that had found an exit and was using it. One hand outstretched. My voice with the particular raw-desperate quality of something that had run out of everything except the specific truth. "Lira! Hear me! You are not his thrall!"

Her lips parted. Daegrith's voice with the particular soft-venomous quality of something that had always known it would reach me through exactly this channel. "She is no longer her own."

"Wrong!" The word with the particular thunderbolt quality of something that had been compressed beyond its capacity and had found the specific direction of its release. "Her soul burns brighter than your shadows ever could!"

And Daegrith, for the particular first time, faltered. The specific barely-there tremor of something that had been ironclad and had encountered the specific thing capable of finding the seam in it. I saw it. Felt it. And in that particular moment the truth with the specific quality of something that had always been true and was now confirmed. If she truly belonged to him, utterly and irreversibly, why did her eyes still carry the specific defiance-quality of something that refused to be entirely what it was being forced to be.

Silver light erupted from Kael's palms with the particular wild-brilliant quality of something that had found its specific moment and was committing to it completely. "I can sever the bond!" The particular urgency-and-hope quality of his voice. "But I need time!"

"Myrcanthor!" The particular sharp-commanding quality of my voice finding the specific direction it needed to find.

The great dragon understood through the particular wordless quality of something that had been paying attention to the specific dynamics of this entire situation and needed no translation. One titanic beat of her wings with the particular quality of something that had decided to be the specific force that the moment required, heat rippling behind her with the particular quality of something that had been given a direction and was executing it at full capacity. Her roar with the particular war-cry quality of something from another age, a sound that predated the specific categories by which we organised other sounds, hurling herself at Daegrith with the particular emerald-fire quality of something that had been building since long before this specific moment.

Daegrith lifted one hand. The inferno met it and veered with the particular parting quality of water around an established obstacle. The flames splitting around him with the specific quality of something that had encountered a principle it could not burn through. But the opening was made.

Kael struck. The particular palm-to-earth quality of hands that had been waiting for exactly this specific interval, runes erupting with the particular radiant-furious quality of something that had been ready and was releasing everything it had been holding. Golden light spider-webbing across the ground with the particular racing quality of something that had identified its path and was executing it with perfect efficiency, the specific lattice of power encircling Lira with the particular pulsing quality of something that had been made for exactly this purpose. The magic with the particular twisted-air quality of something that was rearranging the available forces.

The net caught.

Lira screamed. The particular tearing quality of it through the world, not the specific sound of fear or resistance, something that had the particular quality of something being separated from something else that had believed itself fully integrated, her body convulsing with the particular seized quality of something that was the site of a contest being conducted at a level below the physical. Her hands clenching. Her limbs with the particular twisted quality of something that was being subjected to forces from two directions simultaneously. And then something broke.

The particular gold-pulse quality of something that was entirely hers bursting from her core. It met the silver chains with the particular quality of two things that could not coexist in the same space and were being forced to determine which one had the greater claim. The chains cracked.

I moved. Instinct and the specific particular quality of everything I had not yet named finding its way into forward motion simultaneously. I lunged through the storm with the particular quality of someone who had decided that distance was not a real variable in this specific equation. Her trembling hands found mine with the particular catching quality of something that had been falling and had been caught.

"Lira!" The thundering quality of my voice finding everything it had. "Look at me! You are mine, you are not his!"

Our eyes locked.

In that specific single heartbeat, the particular quality of everything shattering. Not just the silver bindings with the particular splintering quality of something that had been structural and was no longer structural. The ethereal shackles falling away with the particular quality of frost breaking beneath the specific application of something warmer and more fundamental than what had frozen it. Her eyes igniting with the particular gold-fierce quality of something that had been herself and was herself again, entirely and specifically and only hers.

Daegrith screamed. The particular sky-splitting quality of something that had lost the specific thing it had claimed, the rage and fury and loss with the particular combined quality of something that had believed in its own claim and had just been shown the specific nature of its error. The particular fabric-of-the-world trembling quality of it, the specific unmade-harmony quality of a sound that could crack the specific structures that harmony required. And as it rose, the particular breathless quality of the world teetering on the specific edge of the thing that would have followed.

The storm had passed. But its aftermath had the particular lingering quality of something that was not finished simply because it had changed state.

My hands with the particular shaking quality of something that was not responding to fear or fatigue but to the specific weight of what had almost happened, the particular crushing quality of understanding how close I had been to a specific absence that I did not have a name for that would have been adequate. Lira. The particular resonant quality of her name in my chest, not simply a name but the particular quality of something that had been going to be gone and was not gone, carrying the particular quality of a vow I had not spoken and a war I had been conducting without acknowledging it.

The silver marks still on her skin with the particular lingering quality of something that had been present and was not entirely absent. Her eyes finding mine with the particular gold-flickering quality of something that had been through what it had been through and was still the specific thing it had always been, through ash and through the particular available darkness of everything that had tried to make her into something else.

He tasted blood. The particular quality of his own and of something that had been through what this had been. The air vibrating with the particular aftershock quality of magic that had concluded and was still present as evidence of its own recent existence.

The silence that followed was the particular kind that came after screaming, the specific silence of something that had broken and the particular quality of everything that now had to exist in the space that the breaking had made.

How many times had he reached for her across the specific geography of what they had survived together. How many times had he found himself unable to hold her before the specific abyss took another piece of what they were trying to protect. He thought he had known the particular quality of grief before. But the specific hollow of this was colder. The particular specific experience of watching her body move while her soul was locked behind the particular frozen quality of someone else's glass, holding her hand and finding no warmth in the specific place where warmth had always been.

That had been his undoing.

No sword had the particular quality of something that could cut through what had coiled around her. No blade could undo the particular quality of what he had nearly permitted to happen. He had called her back with fire. He had roared across the particular void that had been opening between them. But a part of him, the part that had been in the specific place where honesty lived and had been paying attention, understood the particular truth of it.

He had not saved her.

She had clawed her way back. Alone. Through the particular quality of chains he could barely understand, through the specific architecture of herself that had been built from exactly the kind of material that resisted exactly the kind of dissolution that had been attempted. He was her saviour in name only. The particular quality of that truth with the specific taste of ash.

Now, as her breath steadied with the particular quality of something returning to its own rhythm and the afterglow of her liberation shimmered on her skin with the particular specific quality of something that had just been through what she had been through and was still luminous with it, he felt the particular weight of her pain finding the specific place in him where the things he could not fix lived. Not guilt.

Something worse. The particular quality of helpless reverence. The specific quality of rage without a target. She was here. The particular quality of the relief of that. But the particular quality of the question that was asking itself through his entire body. At what cost.

He turned his gaze away from the others. From the particular rune-glow of Kael's work. From the particular silent-approval quality of Rowan's bearing. From all of it.

Instead, he looked at the particular shadow stretching before him in the specific available light.

For the first time, the shadow with the particular quality of something that was simply his own, that belonged to him, that he had made a specific peace with. It did not have the particular frightening quality it had always carried.

It was the particular thought that followed it that carried that quality instead.

Her stepping into that shadow. The particular specific quality of that image with all of its weight. Her standing in it and not returning.

That was the particular thing that had the specific quality of something he was not going to put words to, because the words would make it more real than the particular quality of the dark he was currently managing to contain it within.

CHAPTER SIXTEEN – THE FIRE WITHIN THE STORM

LIRA COLD WAS SPECIFIC. NOT THE COLD OF AIR OR STONE or the cold of high altitude. Lira's cold moved through my hands and into the bones of my forearms with the particular quality of something that had found a channel and intended to use it, seeping into me in the specific direction of her failing rather than mine. Every moment I held her had the particular quality of something measured against a threshold I could not identify and was approaching from the wrong side. The weight of her diminishing was not the weight of her body, which I could have managed, but the weight of what was leaving it, the specific quality of something going out.

Her skin had the particular pale quality of something that had stopped being lit from the inside and was now simply surface. Each breath she drew had the particular shallow quality of something that was performing breath rather than living it. I tightened my grip with the specific instinct of something that understood that grip was not the mechanism and did not have a better one. "Lira." My voice had the particular desperate quality of something that had abandoned composure as a strategy. "Stay with me. By the gods, I beg you, don't leave me." The words tore from a place I had not previously located in myself.

She did not answer.

Myrcanthor descended close enough that I felt the specific displacement of air from her wings, the particular warm force of something that had scales rather than feathers and produced weather when it moved. Her golden eyes had the particular blazing quality of fury combined with something that was the dragon equivalent of grief, a depth that came from centuries of watching things that should not end. She lowered her massive head and the ground responded with the particular deep-trembling quality of something that had been asked to support a force it had not been designed to support. "Her essence fades, yet she clings to life." The command-quality of her voice had the particular quality of something that had made its decision before it spoke. "We must act immediately."

Rowan had the particular grim-focus quality of a man who had removed everything that was not relevant to the next sixty seconds and was operating on what remained. He wiped the red mark from his forehead with the specific efficiency of someone clearing a surface for use. The easy-going quality that usually lived in his bearing was gone with the particular completeness of something that had been put away rather than lost. "Indeed, we face a dire predicament." His fists with the particular clenched quality of weapons that had not been deployed yet. He gestured to the surrounding devastation with the particular quality of someone who had assessed it and was communicating the assessment's conclusion without softening it. "For we are decidedly not alone."

Kael, with the particular low-furious quality of someone who had been working and had found something wrong with the working, muttered through the dimming remnants of his magical circle. "He's reconstituting his forces." The frustration in his voice had the particular quality of someone who had anticipated this specific development and had been hoping to be wrong.

I moved with the particular instinctive quality of a body that had been in enough situations to have developed responses faster than deliberation, barely avoiding the specific distortion in the air that had announced itself the way a blade announced itself in the dark, which was after it was already moving. A deep groan moved through the battlefield with the particular quality of something that used the earth as a resonating instrument, shaking the ground with the specific quality of something expressing itself rather than simply occurring. The sky above had the particular twisted quality of something that had been subjected to a force that clouds and atmosphere were not designed to accommodate, storm clouds finding the specific vortex quality of something that had been organised rather than formed.

The horde came back.

Daegrith's twisted army rose from the depths with the particular quality of something that had been assembled from materials that should have had a different purpose, their forms with the specific flickering quality of things that occupied two states simultaneously, their vacant eyes with the particular locked quality of something that had been given a specific instruction and was executing it to the exclusion of everything else. They were not

here to hunt. The particular specific quality of their purpose had changed.
They were here to claim her.

My jaw had the particular clenching quality of something that had made a
decision that was not going to change regardless of what the situation continued to present. "Not while I draw breath." The particular raw-defiance
quality of those words arriving from the specific place below where words
were usually formed.

"Exactly," Kael said, his voice with the particular strained quality of
someone who was maintaining function under conditions that were actively degrading the available resources. "That is their true objective." His
hands with the particular silver-sorcery quality of something that had
already found its direction.

Rowan spun his dagger with the particular cutting-air quality of something making a declaration through the available physics. "Let's make them
earn it." The particular sharp quality of his voice with the specific quality
of broken glass.

Myrcanthor's roar had the particular quality of something that had been
building since the moment she saw Lira's pallor and was releasing through
the only available channel, shaking the specific earth beneath us with the
full force of something that had never needed to make itself loud because
its size was sufficient for most purposes and had decided that this was not
most purposes. Her enormous wings spread with the particular blocking
quality of something that had decided to be the sky above the battlefield.
Her colossal claws moved through the ley beasts and spirits with the particular brutal efficiency of something that was not fighting them but pro-

cessing them, their spectral forms vanishing with the particular dust-quality of something that had been organised and had been disorganised.

Then she lowered her head to me with the particular specific quality of something that had already decided what happened next and was communicating the decision. "Mount my back, Lord of Hougun. Time is running out."

I shifted Lira with the particular precise quality of someone who understood that the way I held her mattered to what she was holding onto and was not going to compromise that for the efficiency of my own movement. The vault onto Myrcanthor's back had the particular quality of motion stripped to its essential components, every unnecessary element removed by the specific urgency of the remaining element. Her emerald scales had the particular radiating warmth of something alive at a scale that produced its own climate, the raw power beneath them pulsing with the particular quality of something that was not simply strength but a fundamental force expressing itself through the nearest available biological medium.

Rowan moved with the particular practised quality of someone who had been doing difficult things in difficult conditions long enough to have removed the performance of difficulty from his movements. Kael paused with the particular weighing quality of someone running a calculation they had not finished, then joined us, his fingers moving with the quiet purpose of someone building something that needed to hold.

Myrcanthor rose. The particular slicing quality of her colossal green form finding its element, the landscape below dissolving into the particular blurred nothing of something that was no longer the relevant scale, her wings with the particular thunderous sonic quality of things that displaced significant quantities of air with the same specific casualness as a person moving through a doorway.

The cold of altitude found me with the particular biting quality of something that was immediate and specific and was the wrong thing to be focusing on. The wind howled with the particular quality of something that had found a frequency and was committing to it. And Lira, unconscious in my arms, had the particular shallow-uneven quality of breath that had not improved since we left the ground.

I brushed a strand of dark hair from her face with the particular quality of a gesture that was doing more than it was doing, which was everything I had available for this specific moment. "Lira." My voice barely found the wind. "Fight." The gold that pulsed weakly in her veins had the particular faint quality of a fire that was deciding whether to continue, a spark that had not gone out but had not committed to going forward.

I turned to Kael with the particular quality of someone who had run out of everything except the specific question. "Can you save her." The words had the particular heavy quality of history between people who had not spoken it.

His silver eyes had the particular clouded quality of something that had received the question and was not going to give the answer that was wanted. His jaw with the particular tight quality of someone who had decided on the specific form of honesty required. "Not here. Not while we're vulnerable."

My throat had the particular catching quality of something that had expected a different answer and was reorganising around the one received. "Then where."

Rowan's voice arrived with the particular hushed quality of something that understood the weight of what it was about to say and had decided to say it without decoration. "Hougun Manor."

The wave of revulsion that moved through me had the particular quality of something that had found the specific nerve it was looking for and had applied direct pressure. "No." The particular quality of a word that was also a wall. "We will not take her there. Not yet."

Rowan's response had the particular absence quality of everything that usually inhabited his voice that was not the specific truth required for this moment. "You have no alternative." Not cruel. The particular quality of something that had assessed the available territory and was reporting the findings with the specific accuracy of someone who understood that softening this particular truth would make it worse.

"If Kael needs a sanctuary to work," Rowan continued, the particular cold matter-of-fact quality of someone who had moved past the argument and was already at its conclusion, "Hougun is our only refuge."

My fists had the particular whitening quality of frustration finding its physical address. I understood. The particular specific quality of understanding something that you understand and cannot act on the understanding because the alternative is worse was the quality of what moved through me as I held Lira's cold weight and thought about what Hougun had been and what it contained. The memories of what had lurked within those walls pressed against the specific places where memories of that character were kept, with the particular threatening quality of things that had not finished.

Myrcanthor's voice found me through the wind with the particular quality of something that was not interested in the argument that was happening. "Your decision demands immediate action, Lord Talon. The tempest is not behind us; it lies ahead."

I turned toward the horizon and the particular quality of what I saw there was the quality of something that should not be a sky. The particular suffocating-blanket quality of darkness that had swallowed the stars with the specific quality of intent rather than simply presence, a void with the particular quality of something that had been organised, that had direction. Daegrith was not pursuing. He was waiting. The particular quality of the difference between those two things settled through me with the specific weight of something that I was going to have to navigate through rather than around.

I pressed my hand to Lira's cooling skin with the particular quality of something confirming what it already knew. The particular specific depth of what I was about to commit her to was not something I was going to pretend was not what it was. But the specific quality of the alternative had the particular quality of something that was not a choice.

"To Hougun." My voice with the particular steady quality of something that had found the specific character of its own weight and was no longer fighting it.

Myrcanthor's wings found the storm with the particular precision-cutting quality of something that had been doing this since before the language existed for what it was doing, her massive emerald form with the particular clean quality of something in its own element despite the element having been made wrong by what Daegrith's presence was doing to it. His dark presence hung with the particular suffocating quality of something that had decided to be the air rather than simply be in the air, coiled around the sky with the particular ever-watchful quality of something that was not in a hurry because hurrying would suggest that the outcome was uncertain.

I held Lira with the particular quality of something that was not letting go regardless of what the next development required. Her form with the particular slipping quality of something that was becoming less present with each passing second in the specific way of something that was not simply unconscious but was in the particular process of a contest whose outcome had not been decided. Her breath with the particular distant-echo quality of something that was performing its function with the minimum available resources and was aware of the minimum.

Not yet. The particular specific quality of those two words as they moved through the interior of me where I kept the things I was not going to say aloud.

"We're nearing our destination!" The words came out with the particular quality of a voice that was performing certainty for the specific purpose of producing it in the people around me, though the trembling quality that found the edges of the sentence was the honest version.

Above the storm's fury, Kael's silver magic had the particular wild-flaring quality of something that was operating at the limit of what could be sustained in the current conditions, his hands with the particular blurred quality of someone who had dedicated all available processing to a single complex task and was discovering that the task was expanding faster than the available processing. His usually steady hands with the particular trembling quality of something that had always been the specific anchor in this kind of chaos discovering that this kind of chaos had found a new scale.

Rowan gripped Myrcanthor's scales with the particular grim-determination quality of something that had been in difficult situations long enough to have made its peace with difficulty, his eyes on the swirling void ahead with the particular specific quality of someone who had assessed the available information and was choosing not to share his conclusion. "Really?" The particular ring-of-truth quality of his voice. "Because I see no haven, no sanctuary in this infernal expanse."

The cacophony had the particular fading quality of something that was being left behind, the screaming gale and the fiery glyphs and the clash of steel becoming the specific muted quality of things that were receding into the distance as Hougun Manor's stones materialised beneath Myrcanthor's descent.

The cold stone of Hougun's courtyard with the particular unforgiving quality of something that had been there a very long time and had opinions about what was brought to it. I sank to my knees with the particular quality of a body that had been asked to do more than it had and was now expressing the accounting of that debt, Lira's still form against my chest with the particular specific quality of weight that had stopped being body-weight and had become something else, the particular cold that had moved from her skin into mine with the particular quality of something that was no longer simply a temperature.

Her silence with the particular depth quality of something that was not simply the absence of sound but the presence of a specific absence.

"Kael!" The particular raw-broken quality of his name tearing from me with the specific quality of something that was no longer performing composure because composure had found its limit. The fury and despair and the particular primal anguish of something that had come very close to naming what it was in danger of losing. "Mend her. Instantly!"

Kael moved with the particular no-hesitation quality of someone who had been waiting for exactly this instruction and had already prepared its execution. His hands blazed with the particular incandescent quality of silver light that had been organised into specific purpose, the ethereal runes moving around him with the particular predatory quality of something that had been given a target. His silver eyes with the particular burning-concentration quality of something that had narrowed its entire existence to a specific point. The torrent of incantations with the particular celestial-hammer quality of words that had been given force by someone who understood what force meant.

The spell struck her chest with the particular violent-impact quality of something that had been given everything available to give, rippling through her form with the specific quality of energy that had found channels and was using all of them, her body convulsing with the particular unnatural quality of someone at the site of a significant amount of power being applied with the specific purpose of contradiction. The energy tore through her with the particular desperate quality of something that was trying to reignite what had been going out, to find the specific mechanism of her and convince it to continue.

She remained still. The particular unyielding quality of something that had not yet decided.

Kael's brow with the particular drawn quality of exhaustion that was also something else, the specific strain of someone who had been giving everything and was discovering that everything was not enough yet. The sweat at his temples with the particular quality of something that had been produced by genuine effort. His hands with the particular trembling quality of something that was continuing past its own limits through the specific application of will to the gap between capacity and necessity. "Respond." His voice with the particular tight-low quality of something that had been stripped to its minimum. "Return."

Rowan's jaw with the particular clenched quality of something that had organised itself around a specific function and was executing that function in the only available way, which was silence and the particular fixed quality of his gaze on Lira, the particular absence quality of the levity that usually lived in him making the specific shape of what it had been replaced with legible.

My fingers found the particular digging quality of something that was trying to communicate through the medium of physical contact with the specific message that the contact was not going to be released. No. The particular specific quality of that word moving through the interior of me where I kept what I was refusing. My breath with the particular ragged quality of something that was not managing its own rhythm. My forehead finding hers with the particular quality of something that was doing everything available to it in the only register where everything was everything.

The particular subtle quality of the scent on her skin, embers and glacial ice, the specific combination that had always been hers, present even now with the particular quality of something that was holding on. "Lira." The particular breaking quality of my voice around her name. "This isn't permissible."

The silence with the particular suffocating quality of something that had weight rather than simply the absence of weight.

Then the tremor. Her body with the particular violent quality of something that had received a signal it had not been expecting, the guttural gasp tearing from her with the specific involuntary quality of a body asserting its own continuation against whatever had been working against it, her eyes snapping open with the particular wide-wild quality of something that had come from very far away very quickly and had arrived in a place that was still too much to immediately process.

She shook with the particular convulsive quality of something whose entire system had been subjected to more than its ordinary threshold and was still expressing that subjection.

Kael recoiled with the particular quality of someone whose hands had been at the centre of a significant force and had been released from that centre suddenly, gasping with the particular quality of something that had given what it had and was now accounting for what that cost. His body with the particular exhaustion-quality of something that had been at the specific limit of itself.

I held her with the particular specific quality of someone who had found the thing they had been holding space for, my fingers with the particular quality of something tangled in her hair, my breath with the particular frantic quality of something that had stopped managing itself and was simply responding, my forehead at her temple with the quality of something that had arrived where it needed to be.

She was alive.

Rowan's laugh had the particular sharp quality of something that was the wrong shape for the relief it was expressing, incredulous and without any of the warmth that laughter usually carried, his hand sweeping across his face with the particular disbelief quality of someone who had been doing the specific calculation of what losing her would have meant and had arrived at a number that he was not going to say out loud. "By the heavens, woman, you nearly induced cardiac arrest in us all."

Lira's fingers found my cloak with the particular weak quality of something that was doing its best with what it had, her breathing with the particular uneven quality of something that had been through what it had been through and was continuing anyway. She swallowed with the particular painful quality of someone whose body had been doing something other than its ordinary function and was resuming. "I..." The particular exhale quality of words being formed at the edge of available capacity. "I sensed his presence."

The particular taut quality of my entire body reorganising around those three words. Kael's eyes snapping to her with the particular dark-searching quality of something that had moved from concern to assessment with the specific speed of someone whose assessment was the mechanism of concern. "Daegrith?" The particular falling quality of the name from his lips, sharp and specific.

Lira's nod had the particular slow-agonising quality of something that was doing this at the limit of what physical movement was possible without cost. "He tried to drag me into the abyss." The particular cracking quality of her voice finding the specific place where the words dissolved into the tremors that were still moving through her. "I was nearly..." The words with the particular broken quality of something that had arrived at the edge of what could be said and had found the edge insufficient.

My knuckles with the particular whitening quality of something that had found the specific mechanism by which fury and disbelief occupied the same body. I had almost watched her annihilation. The particular specific weight of that understanding settling through me with the quality of something that would not be put down. The thought of losing her with the particular unbearable quality of something that I was identifying in real time as the specific thing that exceeded what I had previously understood to be my threshold.

Before any of the words I had not found could find me, chaos erupted.

The cataclysmic quality of a roar that was also a violent storm of fire and darkness tearing through the specific stillness that Lira's return had produced. The ground beneath Hougun Manor shuddering with the particular explosive quality of something that had been applied to the stones from below rather than above, the dust with the particular swirling quality of something that had been solid and had been made not solid at speed.

Rowan's expletive had the particular cracking quality of something that was both genuine and compressed, carrying the weight of a man who had a specific limit on how many consecutive significant events he was prepared to process without comment. "Damn it all. Must every moment be punctuated by utter devastation?"

Kael was already standing with the particular quality of someone whose body had reached a decision before the deliberative mind had been consulted, his arms extended with the particular shimmering quality of arcane power finding its shape around the courtyard, the protective quality of it pressing against the night's oncoming specific wrongness.

I rose with the particular quality of something that was supporting Lira while simultaneously organising everything else available to me for what was coming, the tactical calculations moving through me with the specific speed of a mind that had been through enough situations like this to have the pattern but was finding that this particular instance had specific qualities that exceeded the pattern.

Myrcanthor with the particular towering quality of something that had been still and had found a reason to not be still, her golden eyes with the particular lethal-slit quality of something that had identified a threat and was now in the specific process of expressing its relationship with that threat through every available channel. Her tail with the particular thrashing quality of something that was communicating the full force of what she was through the nearest available medium. The tempest above with the particular mirroring quality of something that had taken its character from what was causing it, the swirling darkness closing with the particular quality of something that had been organised rather than formed.

A surge of malevolent energy with the particular cataclysmic quality of something that had been compressed and had found its release point shattered the gates of Hougun Manor. The protective enchantments with the particular buckling quality of things that had been subjected to something that exceeded their design parameters. From the breach, Daegrith's legions erupted with the particular unholy-tide quality of something that had been waiting on the other side of the specific barrier between its existence and the space it wanted to occupy.

My breath with the particular catching quality of something that had received visual information that exceeded the categories it had been using. This was no longer the particular fabrication quality of arcane energy assembled into threat. This was the particular organised quality of something that had always been this and had been waiting for the specific moment to express it fully.

A legion of wraiths. Hundreds. The particular flickering quality of forms that had been given bodies that were not committed to existing as bodies, their skeletal forms with the specific oily-iridescent quality of something that had learned to occupy the space between states of matter and had found it useful. The air with the particular death-thick quality of a miasma that had been produced by this specific quantity of this specific kind of presence. Their red eyes with the particular burning quality of something that had found its purpose and was executing it, the particular predatory quality of something that had been given the specific address of what it wanted and was moving toward it without the ordinary hesitations of living things.

Among them, the cursed knights. The particular hollow quality of things that had been warriors and had had the warrior removed and had been given something else to fill the specific space. Their armour with the particular blackened quality of something that had been subjected to corrupt sorcery long enough to have absorbed it into its fundamental character, unholy energy crackling with the particular storm quality of something that produced despair as a byproduct of existing. The ground with the particular recoiling quality of something that had found contact with their footfalls intolerable.

At the forefront, not a man. The particular void quality of something that had never been a man but was occupying the space where men stood as a specific choice. Daegrith with the particular shifting quality of a form that was assembled from the specific materials of darkness and impossible angles, his presence with the particular primordial-dread quality of something that pressed on the soul from the outside in the particular way that weight pressed on the body, not through any single point of contact but as a general condition of the available space.

His voice arrived not as sound but as the particular physical-weight quality of something that had found the lungs and the space behind the eyes and the specific underskin and was using all of them simultaneously. "Talon." The particular sharp-poisoned quality of my name in his register. "I warned you. You should have offered her. Given her to me. While you still had the chance."

My chest had the particular tightening quality of something that had found its specific target and was applying everything available to it. The dread that moved through me was the particular cold-simmering quality of knowing that what was standing in front of me was not something that the categories I had been using to navigate threats were adequate for. This was not a battle with the particular quality of things that battles were.

This was a reckoning.

My knuckles with the particular cracking quality of something that had been closed too tight for too long and was finding its limit. The rage with the particular white-hot quality of something that had found the specific temperature above which burning and brightness became the same thing. The metallic taste of blood in my mouth with the particular quality of something that had arrived before the wound that would account for it. "Over my dead body." The particular roar quality of those words, defiance hurled into the specific advancing dark with everything available to hurl.

Daegrith's face with the particular grotesque quality of something that had learned to use the architecture of human expression without having any of the content that the architecture was designed to express. The flicker in the abyss of his crimson gaze with the particular cold-indifference quality of something that had watched long enough to have stopped finding anything surprising. "That," the particular silken quality of his voice with the sting of something that had always known the specific location of what it was aimed at, "can be arranged." The flick of his wrist with the particular soaked quality of something that had force in it that the gesture itself was only the surface expression of.

The world detonated.

The particular cacophony quality of screams and shattering steel and the specific shrieking mass of the horde surging from the shadows with the particular chittering quality of something that had been assembled from the specific residue of things that had been something else. Their cries with the particular violent quality of something that was not sound but was using the acoustic medium to deliver force directly to thought and nerve. The stench with the particular wet-earth quality of something that had been in contact with decay long enough to have become indistinguishable from it.

Myrcanthor answered with the particular quality of everything she was. Her emerald eyes with the particular blazing quality of something born in fire and recognising the specific thing it had been made to oppose. The roar with the particular endured quality of something that was felt in the bones before it was heard, seismic in the specific way of something that used the available substrate of the world rather than simply the available air. She unleashed the particular molten-jade quality of fire that had been building since before the first gate broke, flooding the field with the particular liquid quality of fury given a medium.

The abominations did not burn with the particular quality of things that had been set on fire. They shifted. Twisted. The flames moved across their grotesque forms with the particular lover's-breath quality of something that was not being resisted, and what remained behind was the particular seared-flesh quality of something that had been heated but not destroyed, the particular mockery quality of damage that had been inflicted without consequence.

I met the first abomination with the particular head-on quality of something that had decided against the specific strategy of caution. The clash with the particular bone-breaking quality of steel against chitinous armour that had always been harder than steel was designed to address. Leyline energy with the particular blue-white quality of fire that had been given a specific direction moving through my blade, screaming its particular defiance into the specific quality of the unholy dark. The creature with the particular barely-flinching quality of something whose design parameters included being struck by exactly what I was striking it with.

Its blade with the particular whistling quality of something that had found the specific gap near my ear, the particular long-forgotten-dead reek of it moving past me with the specific quality of something that had been decomposing since before I was born and had never stopped.

I drove Ashenfang deep into its flank with the particular quality of something that had committed to the strike completely and was following through the specific quality of the unnatural flesh yielding. The sickening quality of it tearing away. The thing with the particular not-falling quality of something that had been damaged and had found that damage interesting rather than debilitating. The particular twitching quality of it registering the impact. The particular grinning quality of something that had no mechanism for the expression it was producing but was producing it anyway.

Behind me, Rowan had the particular blur-of-motion quality of something that had become what it needed to become and was no longer performing the transition. His Warhammer with the particular hand-of-vengeance quality of something that had been made for exactly this specific category of work moving through the available space with the particular wet-thwack quality of metal on meat that was a specific sound distinct from everything else on a battlefield. Limbs with the particular shattering quality of things that had been subjected to the specific force he was capable of applying. The wounds with the particular closing quality of something that had been given a different relationship with damage than living things were given. Muscles reknitting with the particular quality of something that had been told they were supposed to exist and was acting on that instruction.

"They're indestructible." The particular growl-through-clenched-teeth quality of Rowan's voice, the particular savage-calm quality of someone who had assessed the available information and had continued anyway. The particular bitter-snarl quality of his profanity arriving with the specific acknowledgement quality of a man who had been here long enough to have developed a specific relationship with impossible situations. He did not yield. The particular quality of there being no room for fear when the available space was fully occupied by fury and the specific understanding that bleeding for every inch was the only available metric.

Kael's voice with the particular guttural-relentless quality of something that was doing what it did at the specific level where doing it became its entire existence, each word with the particular war-drum quality of something that had been given force by long practice. The scent of ozone and silver with the particular searing quality of something that was producing itself at a rate the available air was finding difficult to accommodate. The runes burning into being with the particular brand quality of something that had been made for exactly this level of application, the explosive wards with the particular thunderclap quality of something that had been compressed and was releasing at full force, the battlefield with the particular flashing quality of something that was happening at a level above the ordinary visual register.

Pressed against the carved stone, Lira had the particular statue-of-fury quality of something that was holding everything in check through the specific application of will to the gap between what she had and what she was about to do. Her breath with the particular sharp-trembling quality of something that had been through what it had been through and was continuing to function. Her eyes with the particular dying-star quality of something that was burning with the specific brightness of something that does not have long.

And then she broke. Not with sound. With the particular silent-seismic quality of something that had been held and was releasing, the stone beneath her with the particular cracking quality of something that had received the specific force of what she had been containing. Her hands with the particular trembling quality of something that was not fear but power that had been coiled past the specific point where coiling was a tenable position.

The revelation quality of what came from her was not light and not magic in any register that had a name. Golden force with the particular eruption quality of something that had been in her since longer than she had been able to name it, bursting from her veins with the particular divine-destructive quality of something that was the specific voice of a universe refusing the specific thing that was trying to unmake it. It did not arc. It did not reach. It erupted. The particular surge quality of something that was wrath and was also salvation and could not be separated into those two components because in her they had always occupied the same address.

The battlefield paused. For the particular specific duration of something that had never happened before.

A supernova quality of raw untamed force igniting the specific ranks of the enemy with the particular fury-of-collapsing-star quality of something that had been building since before the nexus, since before the Sylphs' accusations, since before her father made her the specific person that his work had made her. The beasts and spirits with the particular annihilation quality of something that was not being killed but was being removed from the specific category of things that had ever existed. Their cries with the particular smothered quality of something that had encountered a force that was not interested in the sound they were capable of making.

The particular acrid-sharp quality of death thick in the air. Talon, with the particular weight-of-years quality of something that had been in enough battles to have the battle in the muscles, felt his own blood with the particular metallic quality of something that had arrived without his specific permission. But the pain with the particular distant-secondary quality of something that was not the relevant variable, because Daegrith moved.

And the sky broke.

The particular jagged-maw quality of incandescent chaos tearing above us without the ordinary transition of a sky becoming something else, simply the specific quality of something that had always been this finding the moment to be fully itself. The heavens with the particular howling quality of something that had been subjected to a force they had not been designed to accommodate. The air with the particular twisting quality of something that was not simply moving but was being reorganised at the level of its fundamental physics. A chasm with the particular screaming-darkness quality of something that was doing both of those things simultaneously, the particular bleeding-wound quality of something that had always been torn and was now allowing itself to be seen.

The particular collapse-of-Cumbrian-Mountains quality of what moved through the air. As if Scafell Pike itself had decided to arrive through a different medium than geology.

And from that infernal breach, he came. Not descended. The particular unfolded quality of something that had found the specific seams in the available space and had moved through them rather than between them. Not a man. The particular singularity quality of something that had been wearing flesh as a specific strategic choice and was no longer making the minimum effort to conceal the specific nature of what it was. Reality with the particular buckling quality of something that had found his footsteps intolerable.

His eyes with the particular twin-abyss quality of silver that had been burning with the specific detached intelligence of something that had watched too much and had arrived at amusement as its default relationship with everything it continued to watch. "Persistent fools." Not sound. The particular presence quality of something that had been given the same architecture as a voice without any of the biological mechanism that produced voices, pressing into my lungs and behind my eyes and under my skin with the particular syllable quality of something that was using my body as a resonating instrument. Each word with the particular prelude-to-oblivion quality of something that had always known where this was going.

I did not flinch. My body had the particular trembling quality of will coiled past the specific point where the body's opinion was relevant, the roar of war with the particular thundering quality of something that was still there and was not the relevant thing. My focus with the particular absolute quality of something that had made its decision at the level below where decisions were made and was expressing it through the only available medium.

A flash of green fire. Ashenfang with the particular screaming quality of ley-forged steel that had identified its target and was expressing everything available in that identification. My lunge with the particular fury-made-flesh quality of something that was not strategy but was the specific physical expression of everything I had decided to be in this specific moment. The arc of the blade with the particular incandescent quality of something that was also a last hope and was not pretending to be anything else.

Empty air.

Daegrith's form with the particular mocking-solidity quality of something that had never committed to existing in the specific location I was striking. In the particular stolen-heartbeat quality of a moment that had been removed from the ordinary sequence, he was behind me. His skeletal hand with the particular grave-cold quality of something that had never been warm, finding my spine with the specific quality of something that had always known exactly where to reach, the particular star-collapse quality of the weight it applied through every channel that weight could find.

Bone cracked with the particular quality of something structural discovering its specific limit.

"Such pathetic eagerness." The particular glacial-whisper quality of something that was enjoying its own precision. Then the agony. Not the particular burning quality of ordinary pain, not the specific quality of damage that could be located and assessed. The particular obliteration quality of something that was not simply hurting me but was conducting a specific process on me, a slow exquisite dismantling that moved through me with the particular quality of a descent into something that was darker than the available definition of dark.

His grip with the particular spiritual-erosion quality of something that was using the channels that the self used to hold itself together and was applying force through those channels specifically. Life. Memory. Essence. With the particular siphon quality of something that had always been designed for exactly this specific application. The particular bone-deep quality of something that had found the specific register below temperature and was operating there.

My teeth with the particular cracking quality of something clenching against the specific force of what was happening, my limbs with the particular convulsing quality of something that was fighting against a pressure that was not physical and that physical resistance could not address. I could not breathe. I could not scream. The particular erasing quality of what was happening to me.

No. The particular howling quality of that word through the interior of me, a primal refusal in the specific register where refusals became structural.

And then light. The particular blinding-golden quality of something that was not incandescent but was the specific character of a particular person expressing everything they had left through the only available channel.

"GET YOUR FILTHY HANDS OFF HIM!"

The particular razor-sharp quality of Lira's voice through the chaos, the particular fire-and-love quality of something that had found the specific frequency that could cut through every other frequency present. The ley fire with the particular hurricane quality of something that had been divine and was now furious, the particular golden quality of flames finding

Daegrith with the specific quality of something that had always been his opposite expressing itself at full force.

The particular casting-shadows quality of the golden flames tearing through his spectral form.

I fell. The particular crumpling quality of a body that had been held by something and had been released, the particular ragged-sob quality of breath clawing back into lungs that had been denied it, blood with the particular specific quality of something that had found the inside of my mouth through channels I had not given permission for. Every breath with the particular gasping quality of something that was fighting its own continuation. But I was free. The particular specific quality of that word as it arrived through the body rather than the mind.

Daegrith staggered. The particular warping quality of his form encountering something that had found the specific frequency where his coherence was not guaranteed, shimmering with the particular destabilised quality of something that had been struck where the striking was actually effective. Slowly, he turned.

His gaze found Lira with the particular freezing quality of something that had identified the specific thing that had just changed the nature of the encounter. His lips with the particular not-human quality of a smile that had been assembled from the wrong materials, too sharp and too wide for the architecture it was using. "Ah." The particular serpent quality of his voice. "Awakening, are we? Just in time for the main course."

Lira with the particular standing-firm quality of someone who had made a decision and was living in it, hands with the particular blazing quality of ley fire that was still there. But I saw it. The particular tremble quality of her fingers doing something I had never seen them do. The particular faltering quality of her breath's rise. The golden fire with the particular fading quality of something that was giving what it had and had less of it than it was giving.

Daegrith saw it. The particular widening quality of his smile finding the specific information he had been waiting for.

Then darkness moved. The particular blur quality of something that had never been committed to existing in sequence, a nightmare with the particular given-motion quality of something that had always been what it was about to do.

Daegrith struck.

The particular deceptively-soft quality of the sound. The particular vacuum quality of the air imploding at the specific point of impact, the particular crushing-unrelenting quality of something that had found its specific vector and was committing to it completely. The particular god's-wrath quality of the force that found Rowan, the particular bone-cracking quality of something that had been applied to a body at a scale the body was not designed for. He flew with the particular shattered-iron quality of something that had always been solid encountering the specific mechanism of its own unsettling, the jagged edge of the crumbling wall with the particular receiving quality of something that had been given more than it was asking for. The courtyard with the particular shuddering quality of something that had registered the impact.

"ROWAN!" The particular tearing quality of Lira's scream through the chaos. The particular too-raw quality of it to be anything except what it was, the specific quality of something that had exceeded the capacity of the person producing it and was expressing that excess through the only available channel. The particular too-pained quality of it to be reduced to a simple sound.

It carved through Daegrith's existing calculation and found the specific location in it where something useful to him lived. He relished it with the particular quality of something that had been given exactly the specific weapon it had been looking for.

Kael's response with the particular instant quality of someone who had been waiting for the specific moment when he was needed most and was not going to be the reason it was missed, silver runes with the particular flaring quality of something that had been given its specific direction. But Daegrith with the particular not-even-blinking quality of something that had found what it was looking for and was not going to be distracted from it. His attention with the particular fixed quality of predator to prey, the particular specific quality of the direction of his focus finding its specific address.

His voice with the particular slithering quality of something that had learned how to enter through the specific opening that a person's deepest fear represented. "You belong to me." The particular velvet-dipped-in-venom quality of it, crawling into her ears with the particular frostbite quality of something that was not temperature but had found the specific channel that temperature used and was operating there. His gaze with the particular soul-deep quality of something that was not simply looking but was doing something specific to the thing it was looking at.

The earth ruptured.

The particular exploded quality of something that had not cracked or split but had been subjected to a force that exceeded the available vocabulary for geological events, a gaping maw with the particular incandescent-silver quality of something that had found its edges and was expressing them at maximum intensity. The air with the particular scarring quality of light so fierce it had acquired physical properties, their retinas with the particular burning quality of something that had received more than the visual system was designed to process. The world with the particular blurring quality of something that had lost its reliable relationship with its own dimensions.

The sulphur arrived first. Then the soil. Then the particular reek quality of something that was older than both of them combined, the particular choking quality of something that had been present before the categories that would have described it had been developed. Something that had found the specific channels of their lungs and was using them as a medium for the particular wrong quality of its own ancient character, a presence with the particular feral quality of something that had been born before names and had found the particular expression of its specific wrongness through the one thing that even the oldest things shared with the youngest.

The breath of something that had feasted on death. A presence that had been wrong in its making before the world had the language for wrongness.

CHAPTER SEVENTEEN – THE FIGHT FOR HOUGUN MANOR

Y GRIP ON LIRA'S ARM HAD THE PARTICULAR BONE-white quality of something that had passed through the stage of conscious decision and had become structural, my knuckles against her blood-slicked skin carrying the weight of a man who had run out of the category of things that mattered except this specific one. The taste of metal in my mouth had the particular quality of something that had been there long enough to stop being registered as new information, though whose blood it was had become the specific kind of detail that was no longer relevant. The terror moving through my throat had the particular raw quality of something that had bypassed every mechanism I had built for managing it and was simply present.

We were not just losing. The particular devouring quality of what was happening around us had the specific character of something that was not interested in the ordinary concept of defeat, something that consumed rather than simply overcame.

Above the chaos, Daegrith stood still.

The particular coiled-viper quality of his stillness was the most frightening thing on the battlefield, more frightening than any of the things that were moving and screaming, because the stillness had the specific quality of something that was not required to participate in the destruction it had set in motion. His smirk with the particular quality of something that found the world's tearing apart a specific kind of confirmation. His silence with the particular blade quality of something that was sharper than any noise he could have produced.

Kael's face had the particular contorted quality of someone who had been running the specific calculation of what his remaining resources could accomplish and was discovering the answer. His hands with the particular once-graceful-now-erratic quality of something that had always been precise and was discovering the limits of precision, magic sputtering from his fingers with the particular quality of something that had been thinned by the specific sustained demand being placed on it. "He's not just ripping it apart." The particular fraying-string quality of his voice. "He's unravelling it. We're fighting a god with sticks."

My eyes found him with the particular burning-ember quality of something that had decided on its specific response to that information before the information had finished arriving. "Then we'll use those sticks." My voice with the particular gravel quality of something that had moved past the specific stage where fear was a relevant variable. "To carve our names into his corpse."

A scream of wind took whatever Kael found to say.

The sky split with the particular quality of something that had been waiting for the specific moment of maximum significance to make itself visible. The cyclone of raw magic with the particular howling quality of something that had been given a direction and was executing it through everything in the available path, the particular flesh-from-bone quality of what it did to the battlefield, the particular screams-from-lungs quality of what it did to everything that had breath to scream.

Through the tempest, a sound arrived that was not heard but felt. The particular distinction of those two things being the specific difference between something that used the ears and something that used everything underneath the ears.

A roar. The particular wrath quality of something that had been forged from the specific materials of storms and centuries and the particular fury of something that had watched too many things be destroyed and had run out of patience for watching. The particular torn-asunder quality of the heavens by emerald fire, and from the inferno and the ash, Myrcanthor descended.

Her ascent had the particular birth-of-vengeance quality of something that had been present before and was returning as something that had been changed by what had been done to it. Smoke with the particular curling quality of something leaving a surface that had been through fire and was continuing to release what the fire had left behind. Her colossal wings with the particular thundering quality of mountains deciding to fall but directing that falling with intention, each beat the particular storm quality of something that used the available atmosphere as its medium for expressing what it was. The earth with the particular trembling quality of something that was acknowledging something larger than itself. The particular earthquake-given-form quality of her landing, the shockwave rolling outward with the specific toppling quality of something that had found every available unstable thing and was expressing its opinion of instability.

Her tail with the particular vast-brutal quality of something alive with coiled fury that had found its specific expression, lashing across the field with the particular living-scythe quality of something that was not simply moving but choosing what to move through. The particular aftermath quality of the silence that followed was not simply the absence of sound but the specific presence of something that had been comprehensively addressed.

Her gaze found him.

Twin suns of molten gold with the particular burning quality of something that had been alive long enough to have extinguished a specific number of things and had found the thing before them and had added it to the list. They fixed on Daegrith with the particular predator-who-has-tasted-prey quality of something that was not going to forget and was not going to stop.

"You." Her voice with the particular smoke-and-sulphur quality of something that was using sound as a secondary medium for a communication that was primarily conducted through the specific pressure of her presence against every available surface. "How dare you defile. My. Domain." Each syllable with the particular thunder quality of something that was landing rather than simply sounding, the ozone-rich air with the specific scent of scorched earth, her breath with the particular blistering-heat quality of something that had been produced by the specific combination of fury and the biological mechanism of something that breathed fire.

Daegrith laughed. The particular slithering quality of the sound, part hiss and part whisper and part scream with the particular muffled-behind-silk quality of something that had been given an elegant surface to travel through. The reek of it with the particular unnatural-sweetness quality of something that was cloying, the particular perfume-spiked-with-blood quality of something that had no honest relationship with what it was pretending to be.

"Ah." The particular arms-spreading quality of someone performing a welcome they did not feel, the particular puppeteer-finger quality of his hands finding invisible strings. "Here comes the pet lizard. Did someone leave the Manor door open again?"

He stood unburned amid the ash and ruin with the particular obscene-calm quality of something that had made the ash and was not interested in acknowledging the irony of standing in it. His voice with the particular velvet-draped quality of poison that had decided not to hurry. "I'd begun to fear you'd missed the festivities."

Myrcanthor's scales with the particular blazing quality of something that had allowed the ley fire in them to reach its full expression, each plate with the particular inferno quality of something that had its own combustion independent of any external source. Her colossal form with the particular burning-spectre quality of something that was both physical and elemental simultaneously. The air with the particular hissing quality of something in the presence of something that had decided the air's ordinary properties were insufficient. The particular lightning-dancing quality of the storm she had gathered in her chest, her massive wings with the particular specific weight of something that was expressing its full scale.

"This is your final reckoning, sorcerer." Her voice with the particular rolling quality of thunder that had been given a specific target and was finding it. "Retreat. Or face oblivion." The particular fire-and-stone quality of something that had been shaped by an amount of time that had no useful comparison in mortal experience.

Daegrith's smile had the particular cold-cruel quality of something that had been produced without any of the warmth that smiles required for their structural integrity. His eyes with the particular pale-dead quality of something that had always been on the wrong side of the specific line between light and what was not light. "Oh, Myrcanthor." The particular savouring quality of her name on his tongue, each syllable with the specific delicate-poison quality of something that was tasting rather than simply saying. "Surely you know by now. I never leave empty-handed."

The sky tore.

Not a storm. The particular tearing quality of reality itself finding a specific seam and following it, a jagged rift with the particular glimpse quality of something revealing what was behind the surface of the world and the particular immensity quality of what was there, unshaped and untamed, not wind and not light and not time but the specific unravelling of the available substrate of reason.

The pressure flooded my bones with the particular quality of something that had found the specific register below physical sensation and was operating there, an unnatural gravity with the particular sideways quality of something pulling through my soul rather than toward a centre. The earth beneath me with the particular moaning quality of something that had been asked to maintain its integrity in conditions that were degrading the available integrity, veins of black and emerald light with the specific cracking quality of something that had been structural and was developing its own opinion about that. Power with the particular tidal-wave quality of something that had always been vast and had found the specific moment of its full expression.

Then detonation. The particular not-fire-alone quality of something that was using every available medium simultaneously, the particular shriek quality of rending metal and the particular roar quality of Myrcanthor and the particular scalding quality of sulphur-thick air finding the lungs through every available channel.

Emerald fire with the particular flame-serpent quality of something that had been given a direction and was committing to it completely, sweeping the battlefield with the particular blazing quality of something that was doing what it had been specifically made to do.

The sky burned. The particular wake quality of Myrcanthor's descent expressing itself in every available direction, arcane energy with the particular howling quality of something that had been released from the specific constraints of the body that contained it and was now free to be what it had always been. Her wings with the particular dark-eclipse quality of something that had decided to be a specific category of event rather than simply a physical phenomenon. Her descent with the particular judgment-incarnate quality of something that was not simply a dragon but was the specific expression of what dragons were the physical form of. Her obsidian scales with the particular flickering quality of emerald fire that had been invited in rather than applied from outside, the heat with the particular intensity of something that had been produced at the specific intersection of ley lines and wrath and time. Her eyes with the particular molten-gold quality of something that had been burning since before the word for burning was available.

Daegrith did not flinch.

The flames consumed him with the particular swallowing quality of something that had found its target and was applying everything available to it. His black cloak with the particular reducing-to-cinders quality of something that had been fabric and had been converted by the specific application of heat at scale. His silver hair with the particular burning-crown quality of something that had found itself in the presence of something it could not maintain its ordinary character around.

I held my breath with the particular quality of a man who had identified what he needed this to be.

The flames recoiled. Not with the particular retreat quality of something that had been overpowered. With the particular violent-rejection quality of something that had encountered a principle it could not burn through, a furious explosive backlash hurling molten rock and spectral remnants back into the storm with the particular explosive quality of something that had been applied and had been returned.

And in the hollow heart of that maelstrom. He stood. Unburned. Unscathed. The particular worse-than-unchanged quality of something that had been subjected to everything available and had found it insufficient.

My breath with the particular catching quality of something that had expected a different outcome and was reorganising around what the outcome actually was. The dread settling with the particular heavy-stone quality of something that had found the specific location in my stomach where the worst things settled and had made its home there.

Daegrith with the particular moonlight-and-nightmare quality of something that had been carved from the specific materials that light and darkness produced when they were combined in the wrong ratio. His silhouette with the particular ash-streaked-light quality of something that was using the available atmosphere as a backdrop for its own specific presence. His raised hand with the particular shrouded-in-darkness quality of something that had swallowed the available light and colour as a specific choice rather than a consequence. Then he clenched his fist.

Reality fractured. Not as metaphor. The particular quality of that distinction was the specific difference between something that was true and something that was simply descriptive of how something felt. The air with the particular imploded quality of something that had been organised around available physics and had encountered something that those physics were insufficient to accommodate. The sky with the particular shrieking quality of something that had been through too much and was communicating that through the only available register. The ground with the particular twisting quality of something that had always been solid and was discovering the specific conditions under which solid was not a guarantee.

Myrcanthor's roar had the particular seismic quality of fury and anguish combined into something that was too large for either category alone, swallowed by the particular black-tide quality of something that had decided to occupy the available acoustic space with itself. Her emerald flames with the particular twisted-dimmed quality of something that had been performing its function and had encountered a force that had decided to invert that function, their brilliance with the particular devoured quality of something that had been given to an abyss that had been waiting for exactly that specific thing.

Her scales with the particular losing-their-shine quality of something that had always been luminous and was discovering the specific conditions under which luminance could be taken rather than simply dimmed. Her massive body with the particular shuddering quality of something that had been subjected to an unseen force that was finding the specific structural elements that made her what she was and was applying pressure to each of them in sequence.

My knees found the ground with the particular quality of something that had not decided to kneel but had encountered a force that had made the decision for it. The warmth of the battle with the particular gone quality of something that had been present and had been removed rather than simply subsided. A bone-deep cold with the particular flooding quality of something that had found every available channel and was using them all simultaneously.

Daegrith's voice with the particular slithering quality of something that had been given the specific combination of low and amused and venomous and was using all three simultaneously. "Pathetic."

My grip on Ashenfang with the particular whitening quality of something that had found its maximum and was staying there. My limbs with the particular dragging quality of something that was supposed to be moving through air and had found itself moving through something with the specific resistance of material that had decided not to cooperate with the ordinary mechanics of motion. "Did you truly believe your pitiful flames could touch me?" The particular whispered quality of his words landing with the particular thundering quality of something that had been given far more force than the acoustic medium should have permitted.

His gaze found Myrcanthor. Still. Suspended. Writhing inside something that was not visible.

Then oblivion arrived. The particular not-as-a-shadow quality of something that chose absence as its medium, a wave of pure nothingness with the particular erupted quality of something that had been in his hand and was now everywhere that Myrcanthor was. The concept of existence with the particular fractured quality of something that had always been assumed to be guaranteed finding itself treated as optional. It struck her with the particular dying-star quality of something that had been given a scale beyond what scale was designed to accommodate.

Her scream had the particular elemental quality of something that was not a cry of pain but was the specific expression of a force that had always been more than its biological container discovering what the container sounded like at the moment of its failure. Silenced mid-breath by the particular crunch quality of something structural giving way. Her enormous form with the particular comet quality of something that had been in the sky and was now in a different relationship with gravity, flame and broken flesh finding the skeletal remains of Hougun Manor with the particular crashing quality of something that had been a titan and was discovering the specific architecture of impact.

The earth shook. Trees split. Stones shattered. The particular too-long quality of the heartbeat that followed with the particular mourning quality of a world that had contained something and was adjusting to its specific absence.

The impact with the particular shattering quality of something that moved through me first as physical force and then as something that the physical force was only the surface expression of, a resonance with the particular fault-line quality of something splitting inside the chest rather than outside it, the particular screaming quality of carved stone fracturing. Dust with the particular choking quality of something that had been solid and had been converted.

The taste of despair with the particular rust quality of something that had settled on the tongue and was refusing to lift. Bile with the particular rising quality of something that had identified something intolerable and was responding through the available biological channels. My heart with the particular caged-bird quality of something that had identified a fate it could not escape.

A whisper. Fractured. Raw. "No."

I turned. Desperate. The particular quality of my golden eyes finding Lira not as a tactical assessment but as the specific thing that the turning was actually about. She was frozen with the particular still quality of someone who had been receiving information faster than it could be processed, her body with the particular sculpted-from-fear quality of something that had not yet determined what it was going to do with what it was understanding. The battlefield's miasma with the particular burning-flesh quality of something that was everywhere and was not the relevant information. Her hands with the particular trembling quality of something that was slick with ley light, gold flickering with the particular weak-pulse quality of something that was deciding whether to continue.

My grip found her arm with the particular urgent quality of something that had identified the next necessary thing. "We have to move. Now."

She blinked. The particular recession quality of shock finding a specific place to go as something colder and harder found the space it had been occupying. She exhaled. The particular quality of flames that had been waiting for permission finding it, not dying but igniting in the specific way of something that had always been there and had been given a direction. "Not again." Her voice with the particular drawn-in-the-dark quality of a blade that had found its purpose. Her knuckles with the particular cracking quality of something that had found its grip.

Golden fire with the particular surging quality of something that had been conserved and was no longer conserving.

I saw it in her eyes. The particular fury quality of a soul that had been through fire and had brought scars back instead of surrender and had decided what to do with those scars. Not a victim. The particular storm-given-flesh quality of something that had found its specific form.

We nodded. The particular no-words-needed quality of something that had been said through every available channel except the acoustic one. A vow in the specific medium of blood and ruin and the particular fire between us.

The heavens split with the particular bone-of-the-sky quality of something that was using the available geology as its resonating instrument as we charged. The world's screaming had the particular not-men-not-gods quality of something that was existence itself finding its voice in the specific conditions of what was being done to it. The ground with the particular convulsing quality of something that was not responding to the battle but to the particular unbearable pressure of raw untamed magic finding the world's seams and following them. Air with the particular thickening quality of something that had become more than its ordinary self, each breath with the particular burning quality of something that had been changed by what it was in the presence of.

The dark magic with the particular falling-ash quality of something that had always been in the air and was now making itself visible, seeping into the cracks of bone and the specific soul of the land with the particular quality of something that had found the available channels and was using them all.

The Ley Lines with the particular writhing-sentient quality of something that had never been simply dormant and was now expressing everything it had been holding, screaming with the particular alive quality of something that had found a specific moment of maximum expression and was using it. Their energy with the particular wild-rage quality of something forgotten and wounded discovering simultaneously that it was being remembered and that memory alone was not sufficient.

At the centre of it, Daegrith. No longer a man. The particular wound quality of something that had become the specific expression of everything it had done to the available world, a rupture that had taken shape. His body with the particular flickering quality of something that had been committed to one form and was discovering that commitment was no longer required, his limbs with the particular shadow-stitched quality of something that had found itself in the presence of the specific force that was going to resolve the question of what it actually was. His silver eyes with the particular gleaming quality of something that had always been hunger but had been calling itself other things.

He stood still. The world around him with the particular quivering quality of something that had found his proximity intolerable and was expressing that through the available physical medium.

Magic with the particular lashing quality of something that had been given a direction by the specific force that was building in the space around us. Tendrils of blackened sorcery with the particular writhing quality of something that had found the available sky and was expressing its claim on it, pulsing with the particular heartbeat quality of something that did not belong to this world in the specific sense that this world's heartbeat was not the frequency they were using.

And still, Talon and Lira advanced.

From the shattered remains of Hougun Manor, Myrcanthor emerged.

The particular quality of what she was in that moment was not what she had been before. The particular Storm-Forged quality of something that had been broken and had found the specific process of reformation more clarifying than the original formation, her colossal form with the particular ablaze quality of ley-fire that had been invited rather than simply present, each emerald scale with the particular sunlit-forge quality of something that had always been made of this and was finally expressing it at full capacity. She descended with the particular judgment quality of something that had decided what the available situation required and was being it.

Her wings with the particular darkening quality of something that had decided to be a specific kind of phenomenon. Her fire with the particular ceaseless-torrent quality of something that was not performing but expressing, an arcane tempest with the particular meant-to-erase quality of something that had identified the specific thing it had always been the opposite of and was opposing it with everything. "The earth will not remember you kindly." The particular deep-as-the-ocean quality of her voice, the particular unyielding quality of something that had been shaped by exactly the amount of time and pressure that producing that quality required. "Leave now. Or be buried with your defiance."

Daegrith's smile with the particular cold quality of something that had found a specific way to produce the physical arrangement of a smile without any of the content that smiles were designed to contain. His eyes with the particular gleaming quality of something that had never reflected warmth, only the specific quality of ruin. "Myrcanthor." The particular slow-deliberate quality of each syllable, the particular bitter-satisfaction quality of something that had been waiting for the specific chance to say exactly this. "I could've sworn I buried you in ash and time. And yet. Here you are. Crawling back from the grave. A relic too proud to stay dead."

Then, Daegrith raised a single hand.

The world did not slow. Did not reel. The particular quality of what it did was stop. The particular held-breath quality of the sky. The particular folding quality of time finding itself in a configuration it had not been in before.

And Myrcanthor, forged in the breath of ley lines and wrath, froze mid-flight.

Her colossal form with the particular burning-emerald quality of everything she was, locked in the available air with the particular carved-from-fire quality of something that had been mid-expression and had been interrupted at the exact moment of its full extension. The power that had shaped mountains with the particular caged quality of something that was in a specific container it had never encountered before and did not have the vocabulary for.

Then the screaming. The particular not-human quality of it, the particular age-old quality of something that was neither cry nor roar but the specific expression of a force that had always been more than its container discovering what the container sounded like at the specific moment of the container's failure. A sound that had never been made before and would not need to be made again.

Myrcanthor thrashed with the particular frozen-agony quality of something whose will was entirely present and whose body was not responding to it, her wings with the particular spasming quality of something that was trying to execute commands it was not being permitted to execute. Her form with the particular convulsive quality of something that was conducting a contest within itself between what it was and what was being done to it, great shudders of emerald fire with the particular tearing quality of something that had been part of her and was being separated.

Her scales with the particular cracking quality of something that had always been the specific expression of what she was and was now being unmade at the level of that expression, shards with the particular fallen-stars quality of something that had been bright and had been converted.

The ley magic within her with the particular shattering quality of something that had been eternal and had encountered the specific force capable of addressing eternity. Not dying. The particular being-erased quality of something that was being removed from the available record of things that had existed. Her essence with the particular strand-by-strand quality of something being disassembled by hands that understood exactly what they were taking apart.

The ley lines with the particular strangling quality of something that had always been her lifeblood and had found a different instruction set.

Myrcanthor screamed. The particular not-a-roar quality of something that had been a titan and was discovering what a titan sounded like at the specific moment of being rewritten. It split the available world with the particular quality of something that had found a frequency at the specific intersection of all the frequencies that had ever mattered and was using it once. Her last quivering shudder with the particular quality of something that had always been a truth and was finding itself undone.

Then she fell. Not with the particular descending quality of a dragon choosing its trajectory. Not with the particular slain quality of something that had been defeated. With the particular truth-undone quality of something that had been a fundamental principle and had found the specific force capable of addressing fundamental principles.

"No!" The particular raw-and-primal quality of that word tearing from me without the consultation of anything except the specific place where it had been waiting to be used. The grief and rage and terror with the particular unbearable-mixture quality of something that was too large for any single register. My breath with the particular ragged-desperate quality of something that was fighting its own mechanics. My heart with the particular slamming quality of something that had found an intolerable rhythm and was unable to find a different one.

I had never seen her like this.

Myrcanthor falling with the particular dying-sun quality of something that had always been the specific anchor and was now expressing its own contingency, her once-mighty wings with the particular torn-and-useless quality of things that had been the specific mechanism of her and had been addressed at the level of the mechanism. The particular inescapable quality of gravity finding something that had always been above it and having something to say about that at last. Her fall with the particular cataclysm quality of something that had always been too large to fail and was failing.

The flickering remnants of her ley-fire with the particular desperate quality of something that was doing the last thing available to it, dimming with the particular titan-being-devoured quality of something that was less than it had been in the specific ways that mattered.

The world with the particular slowing quality of something that was making me witness every specific second of what was happening. The battlefield with the particular stretching quality of time finding the specific moment that would cost the most to observe and extending it. The sky with the particular weeping quality of something that was expressing what it was in the presence of. The ground with the particular shuddering quality of something that had been carrying something for a very long time and was being asked to carry the specific weight of that thing's absence.

Her fall with the particular exhaustion quality of a rattle that had been carrying centuries. Not surrender. The particular weariness quality of something that had been doing its specific work for longer than the available language for time could describe and had found the moment when the specific work was done.

She collapsed into the ruins of Hougun Manor with the particular mountain quality of something that had always been the specific scale of mountains and was now sharing that scale with the available architecture. The impact with the particular shattering quality of stone and earth receiving something too large for the ordinary reception of impacts. The shockwave with the particular rippling quality of something that had been produced by the specific encounter of enormous mass with available ground.

The flames along her form with the particular faltering quality of something that had always been the specific expression of what she was and was no longer being maintained by what she was.

For the first time in millennia, Myrcanthor was still.

Lira floated amidst the wreckage with the particular suspended quality of something that the earth had found a different relationship with, the golden fire with the particular extension quality of something that had moved beyond its original container and had found its actual scale. It had seeped into the battlefield and the air and the shattered bones of the land with the particular everywhere quality of something that had been given permission to be what it had always actually been.

The ley lines reacted to her breath with the particular contorting quality of something that had always been the specific power of the world and had found the specific person that the world's power was oriented toward. Bowing. Twisting. Kneeling to something that had always been there but had finally taken the specific form that required that response.

She was not changing. The particular quality of what was happening to her was the specific quality of evolution, the particular revealing of something that had been present and had been finding its specific form and had found it.

Her golden eyes with the particular radiant-void quality of something that had been defiance and rage and sorrow and had found the specific temperature at which those three things became something that had no single name. Twin suns with the particular fury quality of something both ancient and newborn.

She had been human once.

The particular quality of my uncertainty about whether she still was had the specific weight of something true that I did not know what to do with.

Daegrith staggered. The particular unfamiliar quality of that motion for a body that had not produced it in the specific collection of centuries it had been accumulating. His crimson eyes with the particular flickering quality of something that had always been certain and was encountering the specific first experience of its opposite. Fear. The particular impossible quality of it in something that had never been given a reason for it until this specific moment.

Lira stepped forward. Gold and wild and trembling, the ley lines with the particular coiling quality of something that had found its specific instruction and was following it through the available medium of the earth beneath her feet. Her voice with the particular splintered quality of something that was fragile and was carrying the weight of everything that had made it fragile and was not breaking.

"Why."

The battlefield with the particular paused quality of something that had been in motion and had found the specific moment that required it not to be. The air with the particular leaning quality of something that had been given a reason to pay attention.

"Why did you make me." She did not blink. The particular piercing quality of her gaze finding the specific thing it was looking for beneath the surface of everything Daegrith had assembled to be looked at instead. "Why did you build me into a puppet you could control. And then curse me when I didn't obey."

Her gaze with the particular penetrating quality of something that had been given access to the specific layer below the warlock's shell, below the centuries of accumulated power, to wherever the remnant of a man had been keeping itself.

"I never had a mother." The particular quiet quality of a statement that was true and had been waiting its entire existence to be said to the specific person who was responsible for it. "No lullabies. No warmth. Just cold hands. Just experiments. Just you demanding I become your legacy before I even knew what it meant to live."

The ley magic screaming around her with the particular twisting quality of something that was being given a specific direction by what she was expressing, the available light with the particular ribbon quality of something that had been organised into something other than its ordinary configuration.

"You called it purpose." The particular declaration quality of something that was naming a thing that had been called something else for the specific duration of her life. "I called it a cage." She stepped forward. The ground split beneath her heel with the particular recoiling quality of something that had been used as a medium for too much wrongness and was expressing its specific opinion. "You shaped me into a weapon. Spoke to me in riddles and commands. Taught me that love meant obedience. That power was affection. And silence meant approval." The particular wavering quality of her voice was not weakness but the specific weight of the truth she was carrying finding its full expression. "You made me believe the pain was the price of being wanted."

She stood. The particular strength quality of something that had carried this for the specific duration of its entire existence and was not going to fall under it now.

"And then." The particular sharp-inhale quality of something that had found the specific word that cut from the inside. "Jax."

Her eyes with the particular searching quality of something that needed to find a specific thing in the available space and was discovering it was not there. "Where is he." Her gaze finding the ruined sky and the edges of the battlefield and the bleeding corners of the available reality. "Was he ever real." The particular hollow quality of the single laugh that found her. "Was he a story you whispered into my dreams to keep me loyal. A ghost you planted to make me feel less alone."

Her voice with the particular dagger-across-the-throat-of-memory quality of something that had identified the specific target and was striking it. "I loved him. And now I don't even know if he existed." Her hands with the particular clenching quality of something that had found the specific location of everything it needed to express, the ley fire with the particular dying-stars quality of something that was the physical expression of her specific grief.

"I was never a daughter." The particular bitter quality of something that had been promised a category and had not been given it. "I was a theory. A spell. A solution to your own fear of irrelevance. You made me in your image and cursed me for not staying small." She took another step. "I wasn't born. I was assembled. Carved from magic and lies and left to wander a world that never asked for me." The particular burning quality of tears finding her golden eyes. "Everything I tried to hold onto turned to smoke. Everyone I've ever reached for vanished. Jax. The others. Even my own self."

"You left me in a maze and called it a destiny. You left me to rot under the weight of choices I never made." The particular faltering quality of her voice finding the specific edge of what could be said without breaking.

"And when I started to become more than what you designed." The particular quality of the pause around what came next. "You tried to unmake me."

Her eyes finding his with the particular fierce-heartbroken-infinite quality of something that had been looking for this specific confrontation for the entire duration of its existence.

Daegrith did not speak at first.

The sky with the particular cracked quality of something that had been waiting for the specific atmospheric expression of what was happening. The battlefield with the particular burning quality of golden light that had been given a direction. The ley lines with the particular wild-serpent quality of something that had found its specific freedom through the particular person who had always been its channel.

He fell to his knees. The particular not-from-pain quality of that movement, not from defeat but from the specific gravity of recognition finding the weight it had always been. His hand trembling as it reached toward her with the particular not-as-a-warlock quality of something that had removed all the specific things it had been and was doing the thing underneath all of them. Not a tyrant grasping. A father reaching for a specific child who was already on the other side of the place fathers could reach.

"Lira." The particular breaking quality of her name across his tongue, the particular forgotten-hymn quality of something that had once known how to be said with care and was discovering that it still knew.

She was a silhouette of flame with the particular gold-wreathed quality of something that had found the specific edge of divinity and was standing at it. She did not look back.

Daegrith with the particular soft quality of something that had found the specific moment when the performance was over and what was underneath it was visible. "You were always more than I deserved." The particular raw-and-small quality of his voice finding its way out of everything he had built to prevent exactly this quality from finding its way out. "You were my flaw. My greatest error." The particular specific addition of something that was the truest thing he had said in the specific accumulated centuries of his existence. "And my only miracle."

His body with the particular quiet-collapse quality of something that had been held together by the specific material of lies for too long and had finally encountered the specific force that dissolved that material. He closed his eyes. "You weren't my legacy." The particular tremor quality of something that was the specific physical expression of a truth finding its way out through the only available channel. "You were my redemption. And I ruined it."

The particular burning quality of tears finding their way down his ash-marked cheeks, long denied and now present with the specific quality of things that arrive at the specific moment they are no longer being stopped. The soft bitter quality of his single laugh echoing the particular regret of something that had always known this specific moment was the true accounting and had been spending everything available to avoid it.

"I wanted to rewrite the world." The particular quality of the full weight of what that had cost finding its expression in the specific smallness of what was left of him. "And all I did was destroy the one thing that made it

worth saving." He looked up. One last time. With the particular final quality of something that had arrived at its specific ending and was looking at
what it was ending toward.

Lira with the particular walking-away quality of something that had
already been the specific place he was looking at for longer than he had
been willing to acknowledge. "I'm glad it's you." The particular note of respect in his voice with the specific quality of something that had been
earned rather than performed.

"I loved you once." Her voice with the particular carrying quality of something that was true and was going to be true regardless of what it cost. "But
you only loved the shape of me you could control." Her hand with the particular raising quality of something that was expressing its specific freedom
through the only available gesture.

The ley lines with the particular roaring quality of something that had found
its specific direction, golden cracks with the particular racing quality of
something that had always been veins of fury and was finally flowing. "You
should have made a daughter. Not a weapon." The particular quality of the
pause before the last three words, the specific weight given to the specific distance between what he had been and what he was going to be.

"You are nothing."

The world screamed. The sky fractured. And Lira became the storm she
had been told she was never meant to survive.

Daegrith's scream with the particular not-human quality of something
that had always been beyond the available categories and was finding its

specific expression in the specific moment of its dissolution, a harsh break in the available reality that was not simply sound but the particular quality of a presence that had been in the world for too long and was being removed from it at the level of its presence. Not agony alone. Not rage alone. The particular everything-at-once quality of something that had mistaken itself for a permanence and was discovering in real time the specific nature of its error.

His form with the particular convulsive quality of something that was conducting the process of its own undoing, the particular shattering-stained-glass quality of something that had been a specific shape and was being converted from that shape into something that did not have a shape. What remained of his flesh with the particular rippling quality of something that was conducting a specific transformation at the level of its fundamental character, edges folding inward with the particular unspooling quality of something that had been a thread pulled from the heart of a dying tapestry.

The darkness with the particular coiling-inward quality of something that had always been his specific instrument and had found a different instruction set, devouring him from the inside with the particular wounded-beast quality of something that had been given its specific direction and was following it. His bones with the particular not-snap quality of something that was not breaking but imploding, the particular grotesque-angles quality of his limbs finding configurations that the original design had never included. His eyes with the particular bulging quality of something that was no longer a window into a will but the specific shattered-glass quality of something that had lost the thing it was a window for.

His magic with the particular wild-feral quality of something that had

been given the specific experience of what happened when it stopped responding to the hand that had always controlled it and started responding
to the thing that had always been its actual master. The particular tearing
quality of him being torn apart by the very force he had spent everything
to accumulate.

And then his soul broke. Not with the particular fading quality of something slipping into its natural conclusion. With the particular brutal-rend-
ing quality of something being separated from the available world by force,
a violent merciless exorcism with the particular prey-from-jaws quality of
something that was not being given the specific kindness of an ending. His
scream not only from his throat but from the particular vibrating quality
of the air around him that had always been his medium and was now the
specific thing expressing his specific conclusion.

Then he was gone.

No body. No ashes. The particular no-whisper quality of an absence so
complete that even the specific category of lingering had been addressed.
Daegrith, the particular architect-of-nightmares quality of something that
had haunted the specific bones of the available world for centuries, was less
than the particular quality of dust.

The silence that descended was the particular not-peace quality of a world
that had survived what it should not have and was adjusting to the specific
weight of the survival.

Lira, radiant and eternal, with the particular quality of something that had
turned its gaze upon what remained. The war with the particular quality

of something that was over. But the particular beginning quality of what she had become was only just revealing its specific extent.

And then a tremor moved through her. The particular sudden-violent quality of something that had been waiting for exactly the specific moment when the force that had been sustaining it was withdrawn. The golden fire with the particular flickering quality of something that had been given everything it had and was discovering what everything looked like from the inside when it was empty. The air around her with the particular dying-ember quality of something that had been at full force and was finding the threshold of its own capacity.

She stood motionless with the particular unfocused quality of something that had given its full attention to a specific task and was discovering that the attention had been the last available resource. The battle had the particular taking-more-than-just-strength quality of something that had found the specific places where she kept what was most essentially hers and had addressed them directly.

Lira's knees buckled.

The world tilted with the particular quality of something expressing itself through the available visual channel, her vision with the particular swimming quality of something that had been receiving too much and was discovering the specific limit of what it could sustain. The rush of energy that had flowed through her with the particular quality of something that had always been the specific expression of what she was had found its particular cold-emptiness quality, the specific withdrawal of something that had been present and was now absent in the particular way of things that had been used completely.

She barely registered the particular distant-echo quality of my voice finding her name.

Then everything collapsed. The golden glow with the particular shattering quality of something that had been more than human and was returning to the specific threshold of what human could hold, fading with the particular dying-ember quality of something that had been the specific fullness of itself and was now what remained after the fullness.

The earth with the particular unyielding quality of something that had always been there and was there now, the particular cold quality of stone and dust receiving her. The taste of blood with the particular sharp metallic quality of something that had found her mouth through the specific channels that finality used.

The last thing she heard before the darkness with the particular quality of something that had been building since the battle began and had found its specific moment to arrive.

"Lira."

The particular desperate quality of my cry. And then nothing.

CHAPTER EIGHTEEN - THE CHAMBER OF SPIRITS

THE BATTLEFIELD HAD NOT YET LEARNED HOW TO breathe again. I felt it in the particular quality of the air, which had the specific weight of something that had been asked to carry too much and had not yet found a way to redistribute the load. The scent of ruin did not dissipate with the battle's ending but had settled into a permanent condition of the available atmosphere, burnt earth and charred stone and the specific metallic quality of blood that had soaked deep enough into the soil to have begun its particular process of becoming part of it. The silence that followed was not peace. It had the specific oppressive quality of something that was pressing from every available direction simultaneously, squeezing against the bones of the world with the particular quality of unanswered prayers and severed fates and a history that had been rewritten in a language none of us had been taught to read.

The war was over. Its echoes had the particular lingering quality of things that had happened and did not know how to stop having happened.

Ley energy had burned into the soil with the particular molten-ruin quality of something that had passed through and left the specific evidence of its passing in the structure of the ground itself, the heat still present in the air above those veins with the particular residual quality of something that had been at maximum and was slowly discovering what it was without the maximum. Hougun Manor was no longer a manor in any category I had been trained to apply to manors. Its walls had the particular fractured-ribs quality of something that had been proud and structural and had been converted into the specific shape of something that had been subjected to more than its design parameters allowed. The stones with the particular corpse quality of things that had been unyielding and had found the specific force capable of yielding them.

Smoke with the particular dark-thick quality of something that had been produced by the specific combustion of things that should not have burned, twisting upward with the particular ghostly quality of something that was using the available air as a medium for a communication I could not parse. Ash with the particular soft quality of something falling on the bodies scattered across the field, whispering as it landed with the particular quality of something that was covering rather than obscuring, acknowledging the specific presence of the lost and the forgotten and the nameless.

And at the heart of it, I knelt.

The ruins and the shifting ash and the moaning wind through the remains of what had been Hougun Manor were the particular distant-hum quality of things that existed in the periphery of the only relevant information. My breathing with the particular frantic quality of something that had been through everything the preceding hours had contained and was still working through the accounting of it.

The ache in my bones was the specific quality of something that had been noted and set aside. The blood running down my arms from the wounds in my skin with the particular slow quality of something that had found its channels and was using them, the bruises spreading beneath my broken armour with the particular ink-under-skin quality of something that had been applied from the outside and was now expressing itself from the inside. None of it the relevant information.

Lira.

Her golden fire with the particular dimmed quality of something that had been a raging tempest and had found the specific point of its own exhaustion, a dying star with the particular trembling quality of something at the edge of a boundary it had not previously encountered. She had collapsed when Daegrith fell, the particular snapped-strings quality of something that had been held together by a force and had discovered that force's absence in the specific instant of its departure.

The power that had moved through her had been too much for the body that had been asked to be its channel. And yet she was not what she had been before any of this had begun, was she. The particular raw ley energy still pulsing beneath her skin had the specific caged-storm quality of something that was not simply lingering but was present with the particular quality of something that had found a home rather than simply a temporary address.

It coiled inside her with the particular beast-at-the-boundary quality of something that was deciding between staying contained and consuming what contained it. She was warm. Too warm. Not the particular living warmth of a body maintaining its own temperature. Something different, feverish and pulsing with the particular quality of heat that had been produced by an interior process that was not the ordinary interior process, fire expressed through skin rather than flame. And her breathing with the particular wrong quality of something that was too shallow and too slow, each breath with the particular borrowed quality of something standing at the threshold of a boundary that separated two kinds of existence.

My breath shuddered with the particular quality of something that was trying to maintain its rhythm and finding the rhythm insufficient to the moment. I wrapped my arms around her with the particular tight quality of something that understood intellectually that grip was not the mechanism and was using it anyway because it was the only available mechanism. My fingers against the back of her neck with the particular quality of something feeling the thrum of magic beneath her skin, a heartbeat that was no longer entirely hers.

Come back to me. The words did not find my lips. They screamed through my blood and my bones with the particular quality of a prayer that had no adequate delivery mechanism and was using every available channel simultaneously.

She had to come back. The particular quality of that necessity had the specific weight of something that knew what the alternative was and had refused to organise itself around it.

Behind me, boots on broken stone with the particular slow-heavy quality of something that had moved past the specific limits of flesh and will and was continuing through sheer structural refusal to stop. The sound with the particular hollow quality of something that had been marching and had arrived at the specific location where marching no longer applied.

Rowan and Kael emerged from the smoke with the particular silhouette quality of things that had been cut from ruin, moving with the particular ghost quality of men who had entered a battle as one category of person and had exited it as something rawer, something that had been stripped by the specific friction of everything they had been through until what remained was the particular blood-and-bone quality of survival distilled to its essential components.

Rowan with the particular rough-breathless quality of a laugh that had been produced by a man who had decided that if he did not find something in the available situation to use as the raw material for humour, the available situation would simply win. His lips with the particular barely-formed quality of a smirk that was tugging at the bruises on his face and the split in his bottom lip, the pain of it visible in the particular quality of the expression around the expression. "Well." His voice with the particular wrecked quality of something that had been used at maximum volume for the specific duration of a very significant battle. He dragged a hand through his sweat-matted hair. "I'd say we won, but we look like absolute shit, so I'm not sure we can celebrate just yet."

Kael exhaled beside him with the particular slow-deliberate quality of something that had identified the simple act of filling the lungs as requiring effort and was applying effort to it. The weight of something unspoken with the particular clinging quality of ash in the available air. His eyes with the particular dull-exhausted quality of something that had been through what they had been through combined with the particular sharp quality of a rage that was worse than the exhaustion and that the exhaustion had not been able to touch. His gaze finding Lira with the particular tension quality of something that was carrying a specific problem and was deciding how to present it.

Lira in my arms with the particular too-fragile quality of something that had the specific stillness of something that was not simply resting. Her skin with the particular unnatural quality of a golden glow that had the specific wrong beauty of something that did not belong to a mortal body. His jaw with the particular tightening quality of something that had identified the specific problem and was conducting its calculation.

"The ley lines should have released her." His voice with the particular low-measured quality of something that had chosen its register carefully, the particular sharp-unease quality of something said carefully by a person who understood the specific implications of what they were saying. As if saying it aloud might summon the particular greater terror of the thing it implied.

The ley energy with the particular shimmering quality of something that was still pulsing beneath her skin, a force that had the specific lingering quality of something that had found the place it intended to stay.

It should not have lingered. It should not have stayed. And yet it did.

The world shuddered. A deep aching tremor with the particular quality of something that had its origin in the bones of the available earth rather than in the surface events that had been conducted above them, a low resonant groan of stone bearing the specific weight of its own failure. The battlefield with the particular dust-spiral quality of something that had been disturbed by a force below and was expressing that disturbance through the available medium of everything that had been loosened by everything that had preceded this moment.

Then a sound. Not the sharp crack of fracturing rock. Not the brittle snap of breaking timber. A growl. The particular low-endless quality of something that had been asleep in the specific depth of something vast and had woken, rumbling through the wreckage with the particular venerable quality of something that had predated everything above it and was not interested in the specific context of the current moment. Not rage. The particular silence-older-than-stars quality of something that had been waiting and had found its moment.

Then the ruins moved.

The wreckage of Hougun Manor with the particular pushing quality of something enormous finding its way through, she rose from the ruin with the particular monolith quality of something being extracted from what had buried it. Myrcanthor. The particular tight quality of my chest finding a name for what I had been assuming was a conclusion.

She pulled herself free with the particular beast-of-legend quality of something that had been forged in fire and carved from time and had been brought to the ground and had found the specific thing that ground did not accomplish. She had fallen. She had not died. Stone with the particular cascading quality of rivers of debris finding their way down her tattered wings and the massive spires of her limbs. The earth with the particular groaning quality of something accommodating the specific weight of her existence.

But she was changed.

Her once-radiant scales with the particular dulled quality of something that had been polished like cut gemstones and had been buried under soot and ash thick enough to change what they were. Streaks of deep crimson with the particular dark-as-oil quality of something that had been produced by wounds that had never before touched her immortal flesh, gashes with the particular canyon quality of something that had been opened by a hand that should not have been capable of opening them. Her vast wings with the particular sagging quality of things that had been the specific mechanism of her flight and had been addressed at the level of the mechanism, the delicate membranes with the particular torn quality of war banners that had been through the specific category of weather they had not been designed for. One dragged behind her. The particular ruined quality of it with the particular shattered-bone and hanging-flesh quality of something that should have ended what it had not ended.

And yet she breathed.

Her golden eyes with the particular dimmed-yet-fierce quality of something that had lost intensity without losing direction, scanning the battlefield with the particular taking-in quality of something that was cataloguing everything that had transpired and was adding it to the specific accumulated weight of everything that had always been in those eyes. She saw the ruin. The dead. The fractured sky. The particular absence of everything that had been standing.

Then her gaze found me. Found Lira.

The particular slowness of her inhalation had the quality of something that had always used breath as a specific medium for consideration and was considering everything available. When she spoke, her voice with the particular gravelly quality of something that had been fractured by pain and was continuing regardless through the specific mechanism of an unbreakable will. "She exists." Not a statement. The particular true quality of something that was naming a fact at the specific level where facts were true independent of whether anyone was there to observe them.

My breath with the particular stalling quality of something that had received information that required a moment before it could be processed into language. I looked down at Lira, at the glow that was still pulsing beneath her skin with the particular alive quality of something that had not diminished with Daegrith's fall but had settled with the particular quality of something that had found its specific residence. The ley energy with the particular should-have-unravelled quality of something that should have bled back into the world and had made a different decision.

"What does that mean." My voice with the particular hoarse quality of something that had been used at a volume the preceding hours required and was now being asked for something more specific.

Myrcanthor exhaled with the particular rolling quality of something that moved through the available air and scattered what was light enough to be scattered. Her vast chest with the particular rise-and-fall quality of something expressing the weight of centuries through the available mechanics of respiration. "The ley lines have chosen her." Her voice with the particular slow-grinding quality of mountains expressing themselves through the available acoustic medium. The words with the particular rumbling quality of something that was using the available earth as a secondary channel, moving through the broken stones and the ruins with the particular whisper quality of something that had found the specific channels and was using them. "She is not what she was before."

Kael with the particular rigid quality of a body that had received information it was not prepared to organise itself around. The shadows in his eyes with the particular silent-war quality of something that had always been certain and was finding uncertainty for the first time in the specific catalogue of its experience. He had spent the particular accumulated duration of his life pursuing knowledge, bending the available mysteries to the specific architecture of his will. And yet this was the particular beyond-him quality of something that had exceeded the available categories.

"That's impossible." The particular raw quality of his voice, the particular ragged quality of breath finding its way around the specific weight of denial . His step forward with the particular reaching quality of someone looking for an anchor the available space was not providing. "No mortal can—"

"She is no longer mortal." Myrcanthor's words with the particular cutting quality of something that had passed through the specific medium of the smoke-laden air and had found everything on the other side of it. No room for doubt. No space for argument. The particular old-and-immutable quality of truth being spoken into the specific bones of the available world. "She is more than mortal breath."

I tightened my arms around Lira with the particular desperate quality of something that had identified the specific thing it was not going to do, which was let go. My fingers pressing against her hot skin with the particular quality of something that was trying to confirm its continued presence through the available physical medium. She was still warm. Too warm. Her pulse with the particular thrumming-erratic quality of something that was no longer entirely operating on its own authority.

She's still Lira.

The thought with the particular fragile quality of something that was true and was finding the specific difficulty of remaining true against the specific force of everything it was being held against, wavering at the particular thin-thread edge of something that had been pulled too far. He had felt it when she collapsed. The ley lines wrapping around her with the particular claiming quality of something that had found what it had been looking for and was settling around it, not simply passing through but staying. The air around her with the particular humming quality of something that was no longer borrowed and no longer external.

That terrified him with the specific quality of something that had no adequate response in the available vocabulary.

Behind him, the world moved. Rowan and Kael with the particular ghost quality of men who had returned from the specific place that battle took people and had brought the weight of having been there back with them. Rowan with the particular uncharacteristic-silence quality of something that had found the specific limits of what the usually-effortless smirk could cover, the blood-stained hand dragging through his messy sweaty hair with the particular shaking quality of something that had been holding things for the specific duration of a war that had taken too much. When he spoke, with the particular rough-frayed quality of a voice that had been through too many registers in the preceding hours. "Alright." The syllables with the particular scraping quality of something finding its way through the available silence. "Let's assume our girl here just rewrote the laws of reality. What the hell do we do now."

The question with the particular heavy-fog quality of something that had substance in the available air, unanswered and unanswerable, the acrid tang of scorched stone with the particular clinging quality of something that had decided on the available lungs as a permanent address. The copper bite of blood on the tongue with the particular lasting quality of something that had been there and was not finished being there.

Kael's usual certainty with the particular wavering quality of something that had encountered a situation it had not prepared for. His eyes locking onto Lira with the particular noticing quality of something that was seeing the strange shimmer of golden fire twisting beneath her skin, the ley lines with the particular living-possessive quality of something that had made a specific claim. A breath. Deliberate. The particular steadiness of his voice finding what it needed to say. "We take her inside."

I frowned with the particular confusion quality of tiredness encountering something that did not parse. My gaze toward the manor with the particular or-what-remains-of-it quality of something that was being honest about the available structure. Hougun, once a fortress and a legacy, with the particular fractured-bones quality of something that had been reduced to the specific remains of what it had been, its ribs jutting toward the heavens in the particular broken quality of something that had been proud and had been comprehensively addressed. "Inside." The particular rough quality of my voice finding the specific word that was also a question.

"Not the manor." Kael's voice with the particular urgent-cutting quality of something that had already moved past the confusion and was in the specific location of its conclusion. His eyes finding the ground with the particular reflecting quality of something that was looking at what was below rather than what was around. The ground still shaking in the particular slow-steady-pulse quality of something that was not the aftermath of the battle but something else entirely. Older. Waiting. "Below."

The particular twisting quality of my stomach finding the specific response to that word.

Hougun Manor had always been a place with what was below it. A sanctum sealed beneath centuries of silence and stone and the specific weight of lost power, buried and locked and whispered about only in the particular nightmares of those who still carried the memory of it. A place whose purpose had been spoken only in specific hushed registers between people who had specific reasons for knowing. It had been sealed. And now it stirred.

The battle had the particular fracturing quality of something that had sent its specific force deep enough into the slumbering bones below to have reached whatever was waiting in those bones and to have reached it sufficiently to produce a response. A hunger had begun to wake. Not with rage. Not with screaming. The particular watching quality of something that had been waiting with the specific patience of something that had no reason to hurry.

The air with the particular thrum quality of something that was in the ground and was moving through the available stone into the available feet, a whisper in the dust and the specific material of the ruins. The ley energy with the particular lifeblood quality of something that was still flowing across the battlefield like the specific bleeding of a wound that had found its channel and was using it. And at the centre of this, the particular claim quality of something that had already decided on Lira.

Before anyone spoke, the ruins moved with the particular not-stone-shifting quality of something that was deeper than the available surface, primal in the specific way of something that had its origin in the bones of the available earth rather than in any of the events that had been conducted above them.

A deep echoing crack with the particular tearing-open quality of something that had been closed and was finding its specific moment to be otherwise.

The ground with the particular gave-way quality of something that had been over what was below it and had been asked to reveal what was below it and had complied, the air rushing past with the particular death-rattle quality of something that had been held in an enclosed space for a very long time and was being released through the first available opening.

A stairwell before us, spiralling downward with the particular carved-into-depth quality of something that had not been made by the specific hands that had built what was above it. It had been there before the first stones of Hougun Manor had been placed. The particular whispers-and-shadows quality of something that had been waiting through the specific accumulated duration of everything that had been above it. It breathed with the particular slow-deliberate quality of something that had been asleep and had been woken by the specific events of the preceding hours.

The air from within with the particular thick-charged quality of something that was conscious of the specific people standing at its entrance, coiling around us with the particular unseen-fingers quality of something that was learning through contact rather than through observation, slipping beneath armour and finding the particular chill quality of something that went into the soul rather than simply the skin. The taste of it with the particular metallic-electric quality of blood on the tongue and sky before a storm, the specific combination of those two things that had no name.

Along the walls, runes with the particular stirring quality of something that had been dormant and had found the specific signal that called it out of dormancy. Not feeble embers but the particular pulsing quality of something that was alive and was expressing that aliveness through the specific medium of the available stone, their light with the particular sentient quality of something that was not simply glowing but was waiting, knowing, watching. They throbbed in the particular sync quality of something that had found a heartbeat and was matching it. And then, with the particular recognition quality of something that had been waiting for a specific thing and had found it, they turned their attention to Lira.

As I stepped forward with her, the symbols with the particular revering quality of something that had been looking for a long time and had recognised what it found. A chain of golden fire with the particular spreading-veins quality of something that had found its channels and was using them, crawling across the cavern walls with the particular molten-metal quality of something that was expressing its specific response to a specific presence. The walls with the particular carved-from-existence quality of something that had always been more than the available materials.

The runes did not simply acknowledge her. They bowed.

A ripple through the walls and air with the particular shuddering quality of something that had moved through every available medium simultaneously, into the bones of the people standing in the space. The particular standing-before-a-god quality of something that had a name that had been erased. A heartbeat following that was not ours. Slow. Deliberate. Rumbling beneath our feet with the particular deep-thrum quality of something that had found its specific moment to be heard. Not stone or earth shifting. The particular breathing quality of something that had been waiting and had drawn its first breath in the specific duration of centuries.

I took a breath with the particular sharp quality of something that had received too much sensory information simultaneously and was trying to process it in real time. I tightened my grip on Lira with the particular quality of something that was not going to release what it was holding regardless of what the available circumstances suggested. "We go." My voice with the particular unwavering quality of something that had made its specific decision.

The descent with the particular growing quality of something that pressed against our skin with the specific quality of unseen hands, becoming more insistent with each step rather than less. The deeper we went, the more the walls breathed with the particular slow-rhythmic quality of something that had been sleeping for the specific duration of everything above it and was in the process of returning to its full presence. The steps with the particular worn quality of time combined with the particular warm quality of something that had been in contact with something that had always been alive in this specific place.

Each breath with the particular wet-earth quality of lost magic in the air, the particular copper quality of something on the tongue that had the specific character of an unspoken prophecy.

Lira with the particular still quality of something that the runes on the walls blazed for, their luminescence with the particular intensifying quality of something that was increasing in proportion to her proximity, the glyphs with the particular throbbing quality of something that had found the specific heartbeat it had always been calibrated toward.

At the end of the path, it awaited.

A vast cavern with the particular carved-by-time quality of something that had been shaped by the specific forces of ritual and the particular nameless power that had no adequate description in the available language. The walls rising high with the particular engulfing quality of something that had been made for the specific purpose of containing something that required significant containment. And there, at its heart, it breathed. Molten gold. Alive. Writhing. The particular not-mere-existence quality of something that was a hunger, a living entity with the particular slow-predatory quality of something that had been patient for a very long time and had found the specific arrival it had been waiting for. The particular not-motionless quality of something that moved the way a beast moved before its strike, the particular watching-waiting quality of something that had made its decision and was waiting for the physics of the moment to catch up.

The ley lines did not recoil from Lira. They accepted her with the particular wraith-like quality of something that had found what it had been reaching for, wrapping around her with the particular caressing quality of something that was not simply touching but communicating through every available channel of contact, whispering with the particular skin-carving quality of something that was leaving specific truths in the available tissue.

The glow beneath her skin with the particular flickering quality of something that was doing what dying embers did, except that the specific quality of what was flickering was not diminishment but the particular too-vast-to-be-held quality of something that had found the specific moment of its full expression and was beginning to use it.

The Well of Eternity breathed. The air with the particular heat-that-doesn't-sear quality of something that had found the available space between the ordinary categories of sensation and was operating there, combined with the particular cold-that-doesn't-freeze quality of something that was working through channels below temperature and above it simultaneously. The particular seeping quality of something that was going into the bones and the soul and the specific core of existence, deeper than the available flesh.

The chamber with the particular observing quality of something that had been waiting and had found the specific moment of its purpose. The particular golden abyss with the particular slow-ripple quality of something that was responding not to sound but to a pulse that had its origin in the specific frequency of Lira's presence.

Talon lowered her with the particular trembling quality of his fingers discovering what the final act of surrender felt like. She felt with the particular impossible-light quality of something that had become less tethered to the specific physics that gave objects their weight, unreal in the particular quality of something that was partially no longer subject to the ordinary rules of what was real. The particular if-he-let-go quality of the fear moving through him, the specific void that waited on the other side of releasing his hold.

The molten gold with the particular churning quality of something that was sentient and was expressing that sentience through the available medium of its own motion, seething with the particular alive quality of something that had found the specific thing it had always been calling toward. It reached for her with the particular rippling quality of waves of liquid fire that had the specific hunger-older-than-gods quality of something that had been waiting through the particular accumulated duration of everything that had preceded this moment.

The moment her body touched the surface, the world convulsed.

A shockwave with the particular bursting quality of something that had been compressed and was releasing through every available direction simultaneously, cracking the chamber walls with the particular spider-web quality of fractures that had found the specific veins of the stone and were following them, Rowan and Kael with the particular hurled-backwards quality of bodies that had been in the presence of a force that had not been directed at them and had still been more than they could maintain their footing against. The air with the particular tearing quality of something that had been subjected to an energy that was too large for the medium it was moving through.

Lira's transformation with the particular symphony quality of something that was using every available frequency simultaneously, not simply a change but the particular becoming quality of something that was rewriting the available material of what she had been into something that would not break. The ley lines did not simply enter her. They unravelled her humanity with the particular deliberate quality of something that was making room for the specific thing that was going to fill the space, stitching her back with the particular ancient-strength quality of something that was not her original material and was stronger for being different from it. Golden veins with the particular wildfire quality of something spreading through the available network of her, pulsing with the particular lightning-in-flesh quality of something that had found its specific channel.

Her mouth opened and what came from it was not a cry. It was a song. The particular creation quality of something that had its origin before the available categories for creation had been developed, the particular destruction quality of something that used the same frequency as creation, the particular older-than-stars quality of something that belonged to the first heartbeat of the specific universe that had produced everything that was available to be produced.

Her eyes snapped open.

Not her eyes. Twin suns with the particular not-merely-orbs quality of something that was expressing at the specific level below what eyes were designed to express, the particular searing quality of something that had found the channels that burned through soul rather than through skin. Molten gold with the particular churning quality of something that had the specific heart-of-a-dying-star quality that I had been feeling against my palm since she collapsed and was now visible at the level of her eyes.

She had been human once.

I was not certain she still was. The particular quality of that uncertainty with the specific weight of something true that had no adequate response in the available vocabulary.

And yet when she looked at me, she smiled. The particular not-human quality of it, the particular eerie-unearthly quality of something that was breathtaking in the specific way that dawn was breathtaking over a battle-field still soaked in blood, the particular hush-of-the-sea-before-storm quality of something that was the precursor to something overwhelming but was itself a moment of specific stillness. Lira was not Lira anymore.

And yet. Some part of her remained. In that impossibly small, impossibly familiar smile. The particular quality of something that had survived everything the transformation had done to everything else, present in the specific frequency that only I had the particular accumulated experience of recognising.

Talon felt it. He saw it in that smile.

"You summoned me." The words with the particular soft quality of something that had been given a register for the specific benefit of the person hearing them, but beneath the softness, the particular thousand-voices quality of something that had found its full expression, layered and reson-ant and eternal. They moved through the stone and the chamber and the specific bones of everyone present. They became the available world.

His breath with the particular caught quality of something that had found its threshold. His lips with the particular parting quality of something that was searching for words it had not located yet.

The silence with the particular thick-sacred quality of something that had been produced by what had just been said finding its specific place in the available space.

Then Rowan with the particular long-low-whistle quality of something that was using the available acoustic space to express what his vocabulary had not yet caught up to, a bloodied hand dragging across his face with the particular blinking quality of someone adjusting to a level of brightness that had not been present in the preceding minutes. "Well." The particular muttered quality of something that was doing its specific best with the available situation. "That's new."

Kael with the particular frozen quality of something that had identified what it was in the presence of and was still in the process of completing the identification. His exhale with the particular sharp quality of something that had been held and was being released through the specific effort of accepting what had just been confirmed. "The ley lines didn't reject her." The particular quiet quality of his voice with the specific thread of something that was not simply awe but the particular fear quality of something that had spent a life mastering what it thought was the available territory and had found a portion of it that its mastery did not address. "They—" He stopped. Whatever came after that with the particular depth quality of something that exceeded what his voice currently had the structural integrity to convey.

Then a shadow moved. Not of flesh. Not of ruin. The particular will quality of something that had been watching from its own specific vantage point, a vast essence with the particular watched-empires quality of something that had been present for the specific accumulated duration of everything that had preceded this and had added this to the catalogue.

Myrcanthor.

She did not bow. She did not flinch. The particular enduring quality of something that had been through the specific category of things she had been through and was continuing through the available mechanism of will alone. Her massive body with the particular twisted-scarred quality of something that had been magnificent and had been subjected to a force that had addressed the magnificence, each step a testament to something that was not strength in the ordinary register but was the specific thing that persisted after strength had found its limit.

Blood with the particular thick-dark quality of something that had been produced by the specific wounds in her flesh and was moving with the particular sluggish quality of something that had always been dark and had been made darker by the specific conditions of her recent experience, carving the particular slow quality of rivers through the shattered stone. Each breath with the particular grinding-earth quality of something that was using the available lungs against the specific evidence that they had been better maintained before the battle, a sound like the particular final-exhale quality of something very large that had been through too much. And yet she spoke.

"No." It was not a whisper. Not a growl. The particular decisive quality of something that had made its determination before anyone in the available space had formed a question, final and immutable in the specific way of something that was naming a truth rather than asserting a position. The word with the particular heavy quality of something that made the chamber with the particular shuddering quality of something that had received a force it had not been expecting, dust spiralling from the cavern ceiling in the particular lazy quality of something that had been disturbed at the level of its foundation.

The ley lines with the particular flickering quality of something that had found the specific thing that warranted a pause, a breath, a moment of the particular reverence quality that the available golden vortex expressed through the specific medium of its own motion.

Her golden eyes with the particular burning quality of something that had always burned with truth rather than fire, looking at Lira with the particular quality of something that had understood before any of us had reached understanding.

The particular swallowing quality of my throat finding the specific weight of the moment pressing against it. Myrcanthor's voice with the particular raw-authoritative quality of something that had found the specific resonance that moved through stone and silence and soul and was using all of them. Rising again with the particular vibration quality of something that was not simply heard.

"Fate accepted her." Not claimed. Not taken. Not bound. The particular accepted quality of those specific words. She had not been seized by the ley lines or consumed by what was below Hougun or converted into something it needed. The particular difference between those things and what had happened was the specific distinction between force and recognition, between capture and welcome.

The words with the particular settling quality of something that was true in the way that the specific large truths settled, not with the particular impact quality of something landing but with the particular distributed weight quality of something that had always been present and was finally being named.

The ley lines had not merely chosen Lira. They had yielded to her. And the particular quality of the distinction between those two things, specific and enormous, moved through the available air and the available stone and the particular bones of everyone present who had enough of the specific capacity to feel it.

CHAPTER NINETEEN - THE ACCESSION

THE CHAMBER WAS BREAKING AT A LEVEL BELOW THE stone. The walls were cracking, yes, and centuries of dust were finding their way down through the available air in the particular cascading quality of something that had been held in place by structural integrity and was discovering that integrity was now in question. But what was breaking had the particular quality of something that was not simply the available architecture. The very fabric of the specific law that had governed everything in this chamber since it was first sealed was tearing apart at the level below its surface, and I felt it through my boots and through my hands and through the specific channels that had always connected me to Hougun's deep foundations, moving through me with the particular quality of something expressing its own dissolution.

The air with the particular thickening quality of something that had accumulated a weight too vast for ordinary atmospheric conditions, pressing in from every available direction with the specific quality of something that was filling the lungs the way a drowning tide filled lungs, creating the particular pressure behind the eyes of something that was applying force through every available channel simultaneously. The runes on the stone with the particular wild quality of something that had been dormant and had received a signal, pulsing with desperate intensity between emerald and golden hues with the particular flickering quality of two forces that had found the same medium and were conducting their contest through it. The clash between them with the particular raw-relentless quality of something that had no interest in harmony, the very structure of the manor groaning with the particular splintering quality of something that had been enduring the weight of magic older than its own construction and had found the specific point at which that endurance was no longer adequate.

And Lira screamed.

Not with the particular pain quality of something being hurt. The particular transformation quality of something that had found a sound that existed in the specific register between what the body was and what it was becoming, a scream of defiance finding its way to the surface through the only available channel. She hovered with the particular suspended quality of something that had been removed from its ordinary relationship with gravity, her spine with the particular arching quality of something that had been pulled taut between two forces that were both using her as their medium.

Her limbs with the particular trembling quality of something that had been pushed to the specific edge of what limbs were designed to accommodate, her hands with the particular spread quality of something reaching, her fingers with the particular curling quality of something grasping for a point beyond the available space. Her mouth open with the particular silent quality of something that had gone past the specific acoustic register of suffering and into the particular register of fury finding its own voice.

Golden veins with the particular burst quality of something that had been contained and was no longer being contained, spreading across her skin with the particular writhing quality of something that was using her as its specific medium, slithering beneath the flesh with the particular hungry-endless quality of something that had found its channel and was using it completely.

They were not binding her. The particular claiming quality of what they were doing had a different character. The ley lines did not steal. They absorbed. The particular assimilating quality of something that had decided on Lira and was in the process of executing that decision at the level below what either of us could address.

She was being rewritten. The particular ceasing-to-be quality of what she had been making room for the particular becoming quality of what she was going to be.

A sound from the ground. The particular rough-raw quality of something that had been compressed past its own limit and was finding its exit point through my throat. "No." My hands with the particular white-knuckle quality of something that had formed into fists before I had consciously directed them there, the blood draining from my knuckles in the particular way of something that had found its maximum and was staying there. Every nerve in my body with the particular screaming quality of something that had identified an action and was demanding it. The particular throw-himself-into-the-storm quality of an impulse I had to fight rather than simply not act on.

I couldn't. Not from fear. From the particular specific understanding that brute force was not the mechanism that the current situation responded to.

I had fought gods. I had watched them bleed. I had faced the particular nightmares that moved through both flesh and mind, had carved through monsters and through the specific category of madness that produced monsters. But this was not an enemy I could strike down.

The ley lines were rewriting her. The particular burning-away quality of what she had been at the edges of her name, making room for the particular vastness of what was being installed in its place. The golden cords with the particular tightening quality of something that had found its specific tension and was maintaining it, shaping her with the particular clay-in-a-sculptor's-hands quality of something that had decided on a form and was executing the form. She was not being killed. She was being reborn. The particular distinction between those two things had the specific weight of everything.

Talon's breath with the particular caught quality of something that had found a threshold. A tremor running through him followed by the particular stillness of something that had identified the specific nature of the available battle. This was not a battlefield for swords. Not a war conducted in blood. This was the particular will-and-soul quality of something that existed in the register where the ordinary weapons had no purchase.

If she surrendered to the current that was moving through her, if she lost the specific thread of herself in the particular force of what was rewriting her, she would not die. Something the particular erased quality of something that had been present and had been comprehensively addressed would be what remained.

A tremor moved through the shattered chamber with the particular eternal-raw quality of something that had its origin below the available geology. The air with the particular charged quality of a will that surpassed the ordinary categories of magic and power, the particular vast-unyielding quality of a presence finding its specific expression through the available atmosphere.

I turned just as Myrcanthor stirred.

The great dragon pulling herself along with the particular quality of something that had been through what she had been through and was continuing through the specific mechanism of will applied to the gap between what the body could currently do and what it was going to do regardless. Her vast body with the particular emerald-and-gold quality of something that had always been that and was still that beneath the particular soot-and-ash quality of everything that had been done to it. Her breath with the particular shaky-rasp quality of something that was using the available lungs against significant resistance, the shaking reverberating through the bones of the earth beneath her with the specific quality of something that had always been large enough to use the available geology as its resonating instrument.

Blood with the particular thick-molten-iron quality of something that had been produced by wounds that had been carved deep into her hide, pooling in the particular dark-river quality of something that had found the available channels in the broken stone. Each movement with the particular fresh-rivulet quality of something producing new evidence of its own cost, the torn edges of her wings with the particular staining quality of something leaving inky testament to the specific sacrifice that had brought us to this chamber. And still she moved. Still she watched.

Her golden eyes with the particular dimmed-but-unbroken quality of something that had always burned and was burning now at a lower level and was still burning, finding their way through the particular swirling-maelstrom quality of the arcane fury that was twisting around Lira. And she saw. Not the battle. Not the ruin. Myrcanthor saw the particular truth quality of something that had been watching long enough to see past the available surface.

She was wounded. Her emerald scales with the particular dulled quality of something that had been polished and had been covered. Her wings with the particular tatters quality of war banners that had been through what war banners were not designed to be through. Each breath with the particular slow-laboured quality of something that was performing the function through effort rather than through ordinary biological automaticity. But she was still herself. And when she spoke, it was with the particular unshaken quality of something that had been formed from law older than the available time.

"Call the manor, Talon." The words with the particular thunder quality of something that was using the available acoustic medium as only the surface expression of something that was also moving through the stone and through the air and through the particular bones of everyone present simultaneously. The particular filled quality of the air with magic vibrating through the specific chambers of me that had always been connected to what was below Hougun's foundations.

My breath with the particular catching quality of something that had been hit with a specific memory at the wrong moment. The emerald gemstone in my chest plate, dormant for the specific duration of everything that had followed its last use, stirred. A pulse. Faint at first. The particular waking-from-slumber quality of something that had been asleep and had found its specific signal. Then stronger. Then the particular quality of something that had always been waiting and had been waiting for exactly this.

It knew. It remembered.

"I—" My voice with the particular hoarse quality of something that had found the words and found them insufficient to the weight of what they were carrying. The particular barely-above-a-whisper quality of a breath torn from lips that were trying to say something about why this was the specific wrong course of action.

"You wielded it before." Myrcanthor's voice with the particular tired-rough quality of something that had been carrying too much for too long and was continuing to carry it through the specific mechanism of something that had no alternative. But the particular storm-approaching quality was still there beneath the exhaustion. "When your enemies stood before you. When death whispered your name. You called the power of this place." The pause with the particular weight quality of something that was about to say the specific thing that was also the only available thing. "And now, you must call it again."

The gem pulsed with the particular answering quality of something that had been confirmed in what it already knew. The manor had been waiting. And the power buried in me with the particular depth quality of something that had always been there and had been waiting for the specific moment of its necessity.

My chest ignited.

The particular wildfire quality of searing heat coiling beneath my ribs, unfurling with the particular violent recognition quality of something that remembered what it had been used for and was finding the familiar channel. The last time I had called upon Hougun Manor's heart it had not been a whisper or a plea. It had been a command. A force that did not yield and did not bargain and did not know the word for negotiation.

It had annihilated what stood before it with the particular swift-merciless quality of something that had been made for exactly that specific purpose, shattered legions, torn through the available dark with the particular executioner-blade quality of something that had never hesitated. It had made me a weapon of a specific kind. But this was different. The particular not-battlefield quality of what I was standing in, the particular not-bodies-and-steel quality of what I was about to call on everything I was against.

Not a battle. A war for her soul.

Lira gasped with the particular sharp quality of something that had received a new development, her back arching with the particular painful quality of something being pulled against the limits of its own structure. Her fingers with the particular curling quality of something reaching for anything that was not the golden chains around her. The ley lines with the particular hissing quality of something that had found a disturbance in its work and was expressing an opinion about it. Each thread with the particular tightening quality of something that had not received the instruction to release and was following its last instruction with the specific relentless quality of something that did not have the mechanism for hesitation.

Not like this. The particular gritting quality of my teeth around those three words, each one with the specific quality of something that was also a commitment.

My body with the particular snapping quality of something that had found its specific alignment, no hesitation, no room for the particular second-guessing quality of something that was still conducting its own cost assessment. My bloodied palm pressing to the emerald gem embedded in my chest plate with the particular quality of something that had found the specific contact it needed.

The stone answered.

A low guttural hum with the particular vibrating quality of something that was using the available metal and bone as its resonating instruments, deep and resonant, reverberating through the specific channels that connected me to the place I governed. Hougun Manor heard me. And for the first time since its fall, in the particular specific quality of something that had been asleep at the level below the available surface, it awakened.

Rowan with the particular staggering quality of something that had been standing and had found a reason to redistribute its weight, a sharp breath with the particular quality of something receiving a significant piece of information through every available sensory channel simultaneously. His fingers with the particular gripping quality of something that had identified its anchor and was using it. "Oh." The particular whispered quality of his voice. "Hell."

Kael's response with the particular different quality of something that had found the specific way the available situation looked different to someone who had spent a life in proximity to exactly this category of force. The particular stillness of him, his eyes with the particular narrowing quality of something that had recognised what it was in the presence of. The air with the particular twisting quality of something that had found a new instruction set, warping around me with the particular quality of something that had been given a direction. "He's calling it." The particular low quality of his voice, the particular reverent quality of something that was also the particular fear quality of something that understood what calling it meant.

My fingers with the particular digging quality of something that had found the gem and was not releasing it. The pressure behind my ribs with the particular building quality of something that had been accumulating since I pressed my palm to the stone and was finding the specific point at which it could no longer be contained, a crushing weight, a burning force, a scream with the particular clawing quality of something that had been compressed and was demanding its exit point.

I called upon the power of Hougun Manor. Everything it was. Everything that had been built into its foundations before I was born and everything that had been added to those foundations in the specific duration of my governance of it.

It answered.

A violent cataclysmic crack with the particular quality of something that had found the specific fracture point in the available world and had used it, exploding through the chamber with the particular fractured-foundation quality of something that was not simply a sound but was the specific expression of the world reorganising itself around a new force. Emerald light with the particular signature quality of what Hougun Manor had always been when it was being fully itself, erupting through the ruin with the particular searing quality of something that had decided it was done not being seen, a storm of raw unchecked force with the particular devouring quality of something that had been given a direction and was executing it through every available medium.

It did not creep. It did not whisper. It roared. And it was alive in the particular specific quality of something that had never been simply power but had always been also will.

The runes with the particular awakening quality of something that had been carved by hands now dust and sealed by wills long since faded finding their specific moment of return. Not gold. Emerald. Not simply force but the particular living-breathing quality of something that existed in the register beyond comprehension, beyond the available categories of time, beyond anything that the ordinary framework of the world had been designed to contain.

And Lira at the centre of it all was both its prisoner and its key.

My pulse with the particular thundering quality of something that had found its frequency and was using it, my hands with the particular trembling quality of something that was connected to a force that was larger than the available architecture of my body and was moving through that body regardless. The ley lines with the particular screaming quality of something that had found resistance where it had expected to find none, their voices with the particular rising quality of a fury that was also something beneath fury, something that had the particular quality of something that had been present in the available world since before I was born encountering something that had also been present since before I was born and discovering that the two had different intentions.

And beneath the contest, the particular buried quality of something that had always been there, present in the earth itself, in the specific bones of Hougun's foundation.

"NO!" My voice with the particular desperate quality of something that had decided to be a sound in the specific register where decisions were made rather than simply announced. "Not like this!"

The emerald fire with the particular flaring quality of something that had received the specific instruction it had been waiting for, a blaze with the particular brilliant quality of something that had always been this and was finally being permitted to be this, coiling and wrapping around the ley lines with the particular each-tendril quality of something that had found a specific thread and was addressing it. The particular clash quality of the golden energy finding the emerald and the emerald finding the golden, two forces that had always been the specific opposites of each other discovering the chamber they had both been called to.

The ground with the particular groaning quality of something that was beneath the specific collision of two things that were each larger than the ground was designed to accommodate. The air with the particular crackling quality of something that had been given more energy than the available atmosphere was designed to carry and was expressing that excess through every available discharge.

Then, with the particular profound quality of a stillness that was not the absence of the forces but their specific moment of held breath, everything stopped.

And in that stillness, I felt the shift.

The golden chains with the particular faltering quality of something that had been unyielding and had encountered the specific force capable of yielding it, writhing with the particular serpent quality of something that was trying to maintain its hold and was discovering that the mechanism of its hold had been addressed. They were no match for Hougun Manor. The emerald fire with the particular runic quality of something that had been dormant for too long and had finally found its specific purpose, fighting to reclaim what had always been its own in the particular contest quality of something that had identified its specific opponent.

Lira's body with the particular shuddering quality of something that was the site of a significant transfer, a convulsion moving through her as the ley lines with the particular buckling quality of something that had been subjected to more than its design parameters allowed. Her eyes with the particular gleaming quality of something that had found a new fire, untouchable in the specific register of something that had moved past pain and terror and into the particular territory where something older lived.

Her breath with the particular ragged quality of something that was finding its rhythm against significant resistance, each one with the particular distant-drum quality of something that had found its beat.

Talon's grip with the particular tightening quality of something that had decided this was the specific contact it was not releasing, his pulse with the particular echoing quality of something that had found its way into the available ears of everything present. "Come back to me." The particular whispered quality of a prayer that was also a command, delivered in the register where both of those things were the same thing.

And then with the particular final-deafening quality of something that had been building toward exactly this moment since before the descent, the chains shattered.

The golden light with the particular fracturing quality of something that had been a force and was becoming a thousand tiny specifics that vanished into the available air with the particular quality of something that had been converted from one state to another. The ley lines with the particular one-last-piercing quality of something that was expressing its final position, an agonised wail with the particular reverberating quality of something that was using every available resonating surface before the particular abrupt-silencing quality of something that had lost the specific mechanism of its expression.

Lira collapsed into my arms.

The particular still quality of her was different now, the particular no-longer-bound quality of something that had been held by the chains and was no longer held. The storm of power that had been conducting its specific contest through her had found its conclusion, leaving the particular faint-pulse quality of magic beneath her skin that had the specific character of something ancient making its accommodation with the available biological container rather than the particular consuming quality of something that had been trying to overwrite the container entirely.

My breath with the particular ragged quality of something that had been through what the preceding minutes had contained, my heart with the particular hammering quality of something that had been in a state of maximum output and was being asked to continue in the specific silence of the aftermath. The particular crushing quality of what had just transpired settling through me, the enormous weight of the power that had been unleashed and the particular heavy quality of what now rested in the space between my arms.

The ley lines with the particular defeated quality of something that had found their specific limit.

At what cost. The particular clenching quality of my heart around that question.

Time with the particular stretching quality of something that had been given too much weight and was finding its way through it slowly, each moment with the particular dragging quality of something that was taking longer than moments were designed to take. My arms with the particular shooting quality of something that had identified what they needed to do before the deliberative systems had been consulted. I would not let her fall. Not after everything. Not after all of it.

She hit the ground with the particular soft-thud quality of something that had been beyond what I could catch in time, her body with the particular crumpling quality of something that had been a vessel strained past its specific limit and was expressing that straining through the only available mechanism of finally giving what it had been holding.

The golden fire with the particular weak-flickering quality of something that had been fierce and had found the specific edge of what fierce looked like from the other side, exhausted by the particular quality of a battle that had moved through it rather than around it.

Kneeling beside her with the particular quality of a body that had arrived at the only available position, my hands with the particular trembling quality of something reaching for something it was afraid to confirm. Her breath with the particular shallow quality of something that was performing its function with the minimum available resources, too slow in the specific way of something that had been through too much and was still negotiating the aftermath. Her skin with the particular warm quality of something that was still present, still there, but with the particular distant quality of something that was at the edge of the specific territory where present still applied.

"Lira." The particular cracked quality of her name in my mouth, the raw plea of it finding the available air with the particular quality of a final desperate call that had used up everything I had left to give it.

The world around us with the particular held-breath quality of something that had been through what it had been through and was waiting for the specific next development.

The power that had moved through her had not simply left. It had been torn away, with the particular hollow-remnants quality of something that was leaving evidence of the specific shape of what had been through the specific medium of what was left behind. I cradled her head with the particular gentle quality of someone who had understood that the particular aching quality of the specific losses they had sustained in the available hours was still present and was not going to become lighter for being carried carefully, but was going to be carried carefully regardless.

"Please." My voice with the particular barely-a-breath quality of something that had found the specific threshold below which volume was no longer the relevant variable. "Don't leave me."

For a long moment, only silence. The particular quality of the available world respecting the specific weight of what had just been asked.

Then, slowly, her eyes with the particular fluttering quality of something that had found its way back from wherever it had been, her golden gaze with the particular dim-but-still-sharp quality of something that had been through what it had been through and had not surrendered the specific fire that had always been the particular most essentially her thing about her. Her lips with the particular parting quality of something that had identified the next available thing it needed to do.

"I'm still here." The particular struggle quality of each word, the particular weight of something that had been through what she had been through and was choosing to produce words rather than silence. But also a promise. The particular specific quality of something that was an answer to the specific question that had been asked in the specific register where that question lived.

The particular shuddering quality of my breath finding its relief. She was not gone. Not yet. Everything had changed, everything between them was going to carry the weight of what had just transpired, but she was still the specific person whose particular fire had always been the thing that was most recognisably hers.

That was enough. The particular specific weight of those three words in the available interior of me, where things that mattered found their specific address.

My chest with the particular heaving quality of something that had found the specific intersection of relief and the particular lingering fear of something that had been very close to a different outcome and was still close enough to that outcome to feel its specific gravity. I held Lira with the particular quality of something that had been released from the chains that had held it and was discovering what it felt like to breathe in the specific absence of those chains.

The golden fire with the particular soft-radiating quality of something that had found the particular warmth of dawn rather than the particular scorching quality of the storm it had been moments before. Her eyes with the particular molten-gold flickering quality of something that was still finding its specific register in the aftermath of everything they had been through.

Her gaze finding his. The particular soft-smile quality of something that had discovered it still had access to that specific expression. And something inside him with the particular breaking quality of something soft and gentle that had nothing of the preceding hours in it, the particular profound understanding quality of something that had arrived at the specific knowledge of what came next and had decided that next was going to be something that was walked together.

Rowan with the particular long-drawn-out quality of an exhale that had been waiting to be released since some specific point before the chains shattered, his voice with the particular cracked quality of something that was using humour as the specific available mechanism for expressing something that had no other adequate expression. "That was horrifically, mind-shatteringly terrifying, actually." His hand through his dishevelled hair with the particular quality of something that was doing something ordinary in the specific aftermath of something that had been the opposite of ordinary. "Honestly, I think I lost a few years off my life just watching that."

Kael with the particular motionless quality of someone who had been through what he had been through and had found the specific position of stillness, his eyes with the particular disbelief-and-reverence quality of something locked onto Lira, his words with the particular slow quality of someone who was finding language for something that was resisting it. "The ley lines didn't reject her." The words with the particular hanging quality of something that had been said and had left a specific space in the available air.

The silence with the particular heavy quality of something thick with the specific understanding of a new reality settling through everyone present.

Myrcanthor, with the particular shifting quality of something that had been present throughout and had been conducting its own specific process of the available events. Her massive form with the particular bloodied-and-broken quality of what she was now combined with the particular powerful quality of what she had always been, the particular glimmer quality of her golden eyes having seen what they had seen and having added it to everything they had always held.

"They accepted her." The particular soft quality of her voice having found a register below the particular storm-thunder quality of her ordinary authority, the particular prophecy quality of something that was not simply naming a fact but was naming a fact at the specific level where facts became the available future. The words with the particular ages-weight quality of something that had the depth of knowledge too vast for any single moment of mortal time to contain.

And as she spoke, a ripple of energy with the particular surging quality of something that had found its specific channel, a vibration with the particular bones-of-the-earth quality of something that was using the available geology rather than simply the available air. The particular trembling quality of the available atmosphere responding to the specific fact of what had just been named.

The particular tightening quality of my throat finding its response. She was no longer simply Lira. What the ley lines had done in this chamber had not been a claiming and had not been a consuming. The particular embracing quality of what they had done had the specific character of something that had recognised her at the level below the available categories and had found in that recognition the specific thing that made recognition yield.

She was not bound by her father's obsession. The particular long-held quality of what that obsession had cost her, the specific weight of everything she had been carrying since before she understood what she was carrying, was no longer the defining architecture of her available future.

For the first time in her life, Lira was free in the specific sense that freedom meant something when it was the particular absence of a specific constraint rather than simply the absence of enemies. Free to choose. Free to be. Free to define herself in a world that had tried to use her as the specific medium for every purpose except her own.

And Talon, holding her in the particular quality of arms that had found what they had been holding space for, understood that whatever came next in the particular available path ahead of them, they were going to walk it in the specific way that the available evidence suggested they had always been going to walk it.

Together.

Lira with the particular nestling quality of something that had found its specific location and was accepting the available warmth of it, her breath with the particular quality of something that had been through its specific ordeal and was finding what breathing felt like in the aftermath of that ordeal. Her golden fire with the particular flickering quality of something that was warm now in the specific way that was hers rather than the particular storm quality of something that had been imposed from the outside.

She was not simply surviving. The particular specific quality of the distinction between surviving and living had the weight of everything they had been through to arrive at it.

And as he looked down at her, he held the particular knowledge that whatever the specific path ahead contained, they were going to walk it. Together. In the particular quality of two people who had found each other through every available mechanism that the preceding events had provided for the specific purpose of either breaking them apart or confirming what held.

It had confirmed.

CHAPTER TWENTY - ECHOES OF TOMORROW

THE STILLNESS THAT FILLED THE NIGHT HAD WEIGHT. Not the particular empty quality of a space where nothing was present, but the specific quality of something that had been through enormous events and was in the particular process of finding out what it was in the aftermath of them, an ageless hush that pressed against the skin with the particular quality of something that had been watching and was still watching. The air with the particular pulse quality of untold things, echoes of the power that had moved through this place still present in the specific ways that very large forces left their residue in the available architecture.

The wind did not howl. It moved through the trees with the particular whispering quality of something that had decided on a different register, stirring the leaves in the particular soft quality of something that had witnessed what had happened and was expressing its specific response through the available medium of its own motion. Above, the sky with the particular vast quality of something that had always been indifferent and was tonight something less than indifferent, pricked with stars that had the particular distant quality of things that were not close and were still watching, their light flickering across the newly reborn Hougun Manor with the particular quality of something finding a specific changed surface and adjusting to the change.

The walls had rebuilt themselves.

That was the specific quality of what had happened, and it was the particular uncanny quality of that fact that I had been standing with for the time it had taken me to find my way to the watchtower and settle my hands on the timeworn stone. Stone by stone and whisper by whisper, the ley lines had left their mark on the structure in the specific way of something that had decided Hougun Manor was going to continue existing and had taken the available action to ensure it. The courtyard below me with the particular gleaming quality of something that had been carved and was now moonlit and pristine in the specific way of something that had never been damaged at all, waiting with the particular quality of something that had been reset to an earlier state, a state before most of what I remembered had happened.

Torches along the stone corridors with the particular dancing quality of flames in cool night air, golden embers with the particular crackling quality of something that was also a sound, the particular long-shadow quality of the light they cast across the stones, twisting with the particular restless quality of something that was alive in the specific way that fire was alive, filling the once-empty spaces with the particular new quality of something that had arrived where absence had been.

The air with the particular scent quality of damp earth and magic combined, the particular lingering quality of burnt wood that had the specific character of something that was refusing to be forgotten in the particular way that pasts sometimes refused. The ground beneath the manor not simply soil but the particular memory quality of something that had absorbed what had happened and was holding it in the specific way that Cumbrian ground held everything that had been given to it.

Hougun Manor had not simply been rebuilt. The particular awakened quality of what it was now was different from what it had been before any of this had started, different in the specific ways that things were different when the process of their becoming had involved the particular scale of forces that had moved through this place.

I gripped the timeworn stone of the watchtower with the particular quality of hands that had been doing too much for too long and were finding the specific ordinary texture of old stone and its particular steadiness a different kind of anchor than a sword grip. After the particular accumulated weight of everything the months had contained, Hougun had risen again. Not as a monument to the specific losses it had absorbed, but as something that was continuing to be what it was in the particular way of things that had been tested and had not stopped.

A subtle shift in the air before she spoke. The particular quality of a presence finding its specific approach before it announced itself, something I had been aware of long enough to have developed the ability to feel in the specific available atmospheric information.

Lira moved with the particular fluid quality of someone who had found a different relationship with the available space around her since the chamber below, her cloak with the particular trailing quality of something caught by the wind in the specific way of something that was part of her rather than simply fabric. The moonlight finding her eyes with the particular quality of something making them shimmer, the particular molten-gold quality of the glow in them carrying the specific character of something that was more than reflection. A remnant. The echo of the power that was still present beneath the skin in the particular way of something that had been integrated rather than simply hosted. She had survived. She was not only what she had been.

The night with the particular held-breath quality of something that had found the specific moment where words would be the wrong kind of intrusion.

We stood in the particular quality of a silence that had specific content rather than simply being the absence of speech. The transformation had changed both of us in the particular ways that the specific scale of what we had been through changed the people who had been through it, stripping away the particular accumulated layers of who we had been becoming to reveal something rawer that was now in the process of learning its own shape.

The particular truth of what had been crossed. The particular specific quality of the world beneath our feet being solid and also not being what it had been. Nothing could be what it had been. And yet some things had the particular enduring quality of things that persisted through the specific process of everything changing around them.

This particular vigil beneath the particular specific stars. The weight of the particular destiny that had moved through us. The night with the particular folding quality of something that had found two people who belonged in it.

Finally, my voice with the particular rough-edged quality of something that had found its register in the specific aftermath of everything that had preceded this moment. "Your silence is profound." A murmur. Steady. Not a question and not an observation but the particular quality of something in between.

A breath from Lira, barely above a whisper, with the particular stolen quality of something that the wind had taken the edges of. "Lost in thought." Her voice with the particular quiet quality of something that was also a maze she was moving through rather than simply a sentence.

I watched her. The particular tracing quality of my gaze finding her figure in the specific half-silver half-shadow that the moonlight and the darkness were producing together, the wind with the particular wrapping quality of something that had found the specific person who was now more than what the wind was accustomed to moving around. "Your thoughts." Steady. Measured. Not demanding but open.

She turned and rested her forearms on the cold timeworn stone of the ledge with the particular quality of someone who had found the specific position that allowed their eyes to move across everything that was visible and wanted to use that position. Her gaze with the particular drifting quality of something that was covering ground, the manor walls and the vast misty woodlands below and the rivers with the particular silver-vein quality of something that moved through valleys in the way of something that had always known its direction. The jagged peaks in the distance with the particular rising quality of something that had been there before anything else and was still there, their tops with the particular swallowed quality of something that the night had taken.

"The totality of it." Her voice with the particular quiet quality of something carrying a weight that the available wind could not scatter. "The war. The ley lines. The fractures in magic." The next name with the particular weight quality of something that was also a wound in the available air. "Daegrith." A breath. "The future. Uncertain as it stands."

The name with the particular stirring quality of something finding the specific place in me where it still had purchase, the subtle shift in my frame that was not something I had directed but that my body had conducted without consultation, my jaw with the particular tightening quality of something that had received a signal. The phantom of the battle flickering with the particular quality of something that had been very real and was not finished being real simply because it was technically over. I said nothing. The particular patient quality of something that had always been patient with her specifically.

Lira's fingers with the particular tracing quality of something that was moving across the stone beneath them with the restless quality of something that needed to be doing something specific with its hands, as though she was trying to leave the particular imprint quality of the past in the available rock. "Victory was won." No triumph in the tone. The particular flat quality of a statement that was accurate and was also insufficient to what it was describing. "And yet, I do not feel an ending."

She turned to me. Her golden gaze with the particular searching quality of something that was looking for something specific and was not certain the specific thing it was looking for was there to be found. "Do you feel it?"

The particular uncertainty of her voice with the quality of something that had been through too much to pretend at a certainty it did not have. "This cessation. This conclusion."

I let the silence stretch between us with the particular quality of something that was giving the question the space that the question deserved. The wind through the watchtower with the particular spectral quality of something that had been moving through old stones for long enough to have opinions about what it found there. The manor below us with the particular reborn quality of something that had been through ruin and was continuing, and yet the air was not still. The particular unfinished quality of something that was present as a shadow, an unspoken tension woven into the available fabric.

"No." My voice with the particular low quality of something that had found its honest register. I exhaled, watching the night with the particular stretch quality of something that was vast and restless simultaneously, the black sky with the particular thick quality of stars too alive, too present, as if the sky had found a specific reason to pay close attention. "It does not feel like an ending."

Lira with the particular slight quality of her head tilting, the movement slow and deliberate with the specific quality of something that had been arrived at rather than simply produced. The smile with the particular ghosting quality of something that was not amusement but a quieter recognition, the particular deeper quality of certainty that did not need to announce itself. Something that recognised something.

I drew a breath with the particular steadying quality of something that was managing the specific unease that had found its way into the available space between my ribs, my gaze returning to the heavens. The stars with the particular burning quality of something that was too bright tonight, too alive, as if the sky itself had registered the particular shift that had occurred beneath its particular endless expanse. "Daegrith's hold over the ley lines is broken." The words with the particular edged quality of thought and calculation finding their expression, the particular specific quality of something that had been assessed and was being reported. "But their essence lingers. Magic remains volatile. The currents are restless, still shifting, still unbalanced."

My fingers with the particular brushing quality of something finding the cold stone ledge and the particular pulse of the manor beneath it, the time-honoured heart of this place with the particular awake quality of something that had found its way back to itself. "And the dominion he craved." My voice with the particular darkening quality of something that had found the specific shadow in the available assessment. "Others will come for it. That hunger does not die with him."

Lira with the particular inclining quality of her head, her golden gaze with the particular flickering quality of something that was not fear but the specific quality of knowing, the particular not-surprised quality of someone who had been inside too much of the available truth to be surprised by any of its specific implications. "Such is the immutable order of things," she said, her voice with the particular carrying quality of something that was also moving through the wind, soft and knowing and with the particular edge quality of inevitability that had been there long enough to become its own kind of certainty. "The rise and fall of power, the ebb and flow of magic. It is the way of the world. Wouldn't you agree."

A gust through the old stones with the particular sharp quality of something that was also refreshing in the specific way of cool air carrying the particular scent of pine and damp earth. The storm with the particular passed quality of something that had moved through and left its particular presence in the available atmosphere, a thick tension with the quality of something that had been very large and was still leaving evidence of its specific scale.

My gaze with the particular cold quality of tempered steel finding her. I did not speak immediately. Did not break the particular tension that had the specific quality of something coiled between us, something that had been present since before this conversation and had the particular quality of something that needed to be addressed rather than waited out.

"Do you intend to leave."

The particular direct quality of those words. The specific weight of what they were asking. Not the war. Not the ley lines. The particular specific question underneath all the available questions that had been accumulating since the chamber below.

Silence. The particular deliberate quality of it, the specific weight of something that was not hesitation but was holding something that had many components and was finding their arrangement. Then Lira's head with the particular slow quality of a shake that was also a specific kind of answer.

"Not yet," she murmured. "Not presently." The particular stretching quality of the pause that followed, thin with the particular quality of something that was pregnant with the specific words it had not yet released. And then, with the particular softer quality of something that had found the register below the one she had been using, more fragile, a confession rather than a statement. "But the day will come, I suspect. There are still questions that haunt me."

My expression with the particular not-shifting quality of something that had already known this and was in the particular process of confirming what it had always known. She had been bound by chains of many specific kinds, forged not only by Daegrith and not only by the ley lines but by a fate she had not chosen, a future that had been assigned rather than arrived at. She sought more than survival in the particular way of someone who understood that survival had never been the actual destination. She sought understanding. She sought freedom. And I, who had spent the particular accumulated duration of everything we had been through fighting for her specific right to make that choice, was not going to stand in the way of it.

Not when I understood what it meant to her to have the choice.

But for now, she remained. The particular quality of that remaining, its specific character in the particular context of everything she had just confirmed, with the particular weight of something that was enough precisely because of what it was not guaranteed to become.

A deep resonant tremor with the particular quality of something that had its origin in the soul of the available earth rather than in any living throat, the particular enduring quality of something that had been here before any of the current events and was still here after them.

From the shadowed recesses of the tower, Myrcanthor emerged.

Her colossal form with the particular scarred quality of something that had been through what she had been through and was continuing through the particular deliberate grace quality of something that had found its specific way of moving in the aftermath of significant damage, her emerald scales with the particular dulled quality of something that was still emerald beneath the particular coating quality of everything the battle had left on them. Her wings with the particular folded quality of something that had found a different relationship with their own scale, their battle-torn edges with the particular testament quality of something that had been subjected to the specific forces that had been applied to them. Her gaze, those primordial golden eyes, with the particular burning quality of something that had been accumulating wisdom for the specific duration of the time it had existed and was expressing that accumulation through the available medium of its attention.

"A shared unease stirs in both of you." Her voice with the particular rumbling quality of something that was using the available stone as a secondary resonating instrument, the particular warning quality of something that had identified a specific thing and was naming it. "You sense a force beyond the now. A shadow on the horizon. Unseen but not unfelt."

My features with the particular sharp quality of something that had been cut from the specific materials of suspicion and a deeper ache that I had not been speaking. "You feel it too."

Myrcanthor's gaze with the particular drifting quality of something that had found the specific direction it needed to look, past the manor walls and toward the particular brooding quality of the Cumbrian peaks beyond, where the world with the particular folding quality of something that had decided to become more complicated in that specific direction. Scafell

Pike with the particular looming quality of something that had been there before everything available and was still there after everything available, watching with the specific solemn quality of something that had watched everything.

The sky above it with the particular wrong quality of something that had been assessed and had been found insufficient to the expected standard. The stars with the particular faded quality of something that had been hidden beneath the available shroud of something unseen, a force that was in the particular patient waiting quality of something that had always been comfortable with waiting.

"The echoes of great sorcery don't just fade," Myrcanthor murmured. Her voice with the particular low quality of something that was choosing its register carefully, but with the particular weight quality of something that had specific knowledge and was finding the specific shape in which to deliver it. "They wait." The particular slow-deliberate quality of the pause. "Silent. Patient. Biding their time for the next soul foolish enough to claim them."

Lira with the particular unmoving quality of something that had found its specific position and intended to hold it, her posture with the particular rigid quality of something that was also a testament to determination, the particular shadow quality of defiance finding its way across her features, a quiet storm with the particular gathering quality of something that had found a new reason to organise itself. "Then we shall be ready."

The deep rolling quality of a chuckle through Myrcanthor's chest, a sound with the particular knowing quality of something that had been present for enough iterations of this specific kind of human declaration to have developed a specific relationship with it. The particular mythical quality of it, vast and patient. "Such conviction, young one."

Lira's lips with the particular curving quality of something that was not quite a smile but had the specific character of one, touched with the particular wicked precision quality of something that had earned its specific confidence through the specific accumulation of having survived what she had survived. "Always."

I exhaled with the particular quality of something that had found a response to the available exchange that was not a word, my head with the particular shaking quality of something that was acknowledging something it was not going to argue with, the corner of my mouth with the particular revealing quality of something that had not been directed to move but had moved regardless, sharp and particular in the specific way of something that understood what it was in the presence of.

The three of us with the particular standing quality of something that had found its specific arrangement, the warrior and the survivor and the queen of the sky, each of us carrying the specific weight of what we had been through in the particular ways that weight was carried by the specific people we were.

From our particular vantage point, across the expanse beyond Hougun's walls, the world with the particular still quality of something that was beneath a particular calm that had the specific character of something deceptive. The stars and the rivers and the endless night, all of it with the particular untouched quality of something that had not been addressed by the specific events that had addressed everything that was visible from this tower.

But we knew. The particular specific quality of that knowing with the weight of everything the preceding events had taught us about what peace was and what peace was not. Peace had the particular not-meant-to-last quality of something that was a condition rather than a conclusion.

Beyond the distant horizon, where the sky with the particular darkening quality of something that was not simply the available absence of light, a silence waited in the wind. The particular stirring quality of something that was beginning to find the specific shape it was going to take.

Another story with the particular starting quality of something that had always been there and was finding its specific moment.

And when its time arrived, the particular waiting quality of the three of us with the specific character of something that had learned exactly what it was and exactly what it was capable of and had decided to be here rather than anywhere else.

We would be ready.

Acknowledgements

This book was never something I planned to write. It emerged from a reluctant spark and soon demanded to be told. The Emerald Guardians: Hougun Manor began as a hesitant idea that grew into a sleepless journey of doubt, stress, and moments when I genuinely wanted to walk away. Yet through stubbornness and determination, I brought it to life. Today, I stand proud of what it has become.

To my partner, Talon Briers. This book is part of our shared adventure, much like Hougun Manor itself is a cherished landmark in Cumbria. Giving you a Lord's title in its pages was more than a playful gesture. It was a tribute to the fantastical worlds you love, worlds woven from words, dreams, and boundless imagination. Your passion for fantasy, from Fourth Wing to the realms of Sarah J. Maas, filled our home with magic long before these pages took shape. Thank you for understanding my need to escape into stories, for enduring every late night and every moment of frustration by my side, and for reminding me that even the most reluctant beginnings can lead somewhere extraordinary.

To my family and friends. Your patience, encouragement, and willingness to listen carried me through my moments of rambling obsession and relentless pursuit of getting it right. I am deeply grateful for every word of kindness that helped me find my way through.

The true hero of my life is my father, Bernard Greenaway. Though he left this world in 2013, his presence still shapes who I am. He raised me with an old-school discipline that forged in me a resilience I did not always recognise until I needed it. He never stopped believing in me, not during my stumbles, not in my moments of self-doubt, not even when I had stopped believing in myself. His confidence was the anchor that kept me from drifting. A quiet, persistent reminder to keep moving forward when everything in me wanted to stop.

Dad, thank you for never giving up on me. Every step I take and every battle I survive is my tribute to the man you were. I hope you are watching. I hope you are proud. And I hope you know that your belief in me still carries me through.

My mother, Susan Greenaway, is my unwavering rock. A reality check wrapped in humour, even when that humour is wildly inappropriate and perfectly timed. She has a gift for turning the darkest moments into laughter, and she has needed that gift more than anyone should. She raised me with tough love, not because it was easy, but because she knew the world could be unkind and she wanted me ready for it. She taught me that when life knocks you down, you do not simply get up. You stand taller. You come back fiercer. Through every setback and every victory, her love has been the constant I could always count on. I carry that foundation with me wherever I go. I love you, Mum, with everything I have.

And to the story itself. You refused to let me go, even when I tried. You pushed me until I had no choice but to prove I was stronger than my own doubts.

To my beta readers. You were the guiding light on a journey that was often anything but steady. Your insights sharpened what was dull, your honesty strengthened what was weak, and your enthusiasm reminded me why I was doing this in the first place. This novel carries your fingerprints as much as mine. Thank you for the time you gave, the feedback you offered, and the faith you showed in a story still finding its shape.

And here we are.

Thank you.

ABOUT THE AUTHOR

The Emerald Guardians: Hougun Manor is Josiah's debut novel, and one he never intended to write. What began as a reluctant challenge, forged through sleepless nights and a constant battle with self-doubt, became a vivid world built from imagination, determination, and sheer refusal to quit. It is a story of magic, destiny, and defiance, themes that feel personal because they are.

The novel was born from love. Josiah's partner inspired the heart of the narrative, embodied in the character of Lord Talon of Hougun Manor, a figure shaped by their shared devotion to legend, myth, and the grand tradition of fantasy storytelling. That inspiration runs deeper than fiction. Hougun Manor is a real place, a landmark in Cumbria with which Josiah holds a profound personal connection, and his partner now carries the noble title of Lord of Hougun Manor in its honour. Here, fantasy and reality do not simply meet. They become inseparable.

Beyond the page, Josiah's life has been defined by purpose and resilience. As a probation officer in Hornchurch, Essex, and later in procurement for Havering Council, he dedicated himself to the rehabilitation and reintegration of ex-offenders, work rooted in the belief that people are capable of change. Those real-world experiences with redemption and second chances run through The Emerald Guardians like a current, reminding us that even the most unlikely paths can lead somewhere extraordinary.

This novel stands as proof that perseverance matters, that some stories demand to be told even when their creator hesitates, and that the act of finishing something difficult is its own form of transformation. More than anything, it is a tribute to Talon Briers, Josiah's greatest inspiration and the living legend at the heart of it all.

To everyone who has purchased, read, or supported this work: thank you. Your willingness to step into the worlds I create means more than I know how to say. I am humbled by your curiosity and your trust. Every page you turn and every thought you share fuels my desire to keep writing and keep growing. This journey would not be the same without you, and I am grateful beyond measure for the community we are building together.

Thank you for joining me on this adventure.

THE EMERALD GUARDIANS - SOUNDTRACK

The Emerald Guardians Soundtrack is available on all media streaming sites.